In My Hands

Sathya Achia

Ravens & Roses Publishing

Book Cover Design by Emily's World of Design

Ravens & Roses Publishing LLC

ISBN: 978-1-7372998-6-8

DISCLAIMER

The novel and the characters in this book are entirely fictional based on South Asian folklore. Any resemblance to actual persons living or dead is entirely coincidental.

For my parents who have always believed in me and my grandparents who filled my head and heart with story inspiration

In my hand there are lines,
A map to the past, present, and future, that is all
mine.
If you read them, you will see
Death and destruction belong to me...

CHAPTER ONE

MONSTERS AMONG US

ortune Falls, Virginia
Forget being normal, I'm cursed. I blame it on Appa because he could see the *rakshasi*, too. The supernatural blood-thirsty humanoid demon is only supposed to exist in the folklore of my Indian ancestors from the other side of the world.

My last memory of Appa is not pretty.

Eleven years ago Appa's terrifying shouts had ripped me from a deep sleep. I toddled wearily down the dark hallway to our kitchen where he exchanged loud explicit words with what appeared to be his reflection in the bay window of our cozy home nestled in the cove of a dead-end street.

"This is the end," he roared, pitching a wooden bowl of apples and overripe bananas across the room. "This is your end!" He spun around wildly, grabbed the bench from the kitchenette, and hurled it through the window shattering the glass.

Life as we knew it came to an end in that instant. I was five years old. I should've forgotten or repressed all the gory details that followed, but as I said, I'm cursed. My mind once again travels back to the memory.

I stood frozen, squinting at something in the backyard through the mammoth-sized crater in the wall. A shooting pain spread like wildfire through my tiny, scarred hands, and a burst of jasmine fragrance filled the air. The scars—a souvenir from smashing through a glass table as a toddler—were about to rip open. A hurricane of mesmerizing colors appeared in my line of sight, hovering in the air between Appa and me, like a ghostly watercolor portrait with no borders. I blinked and rubbed my eyes, trying to gain focus when the swarm of colors collapsed into the kitchen tile beneath us. The stench of rot and decay filled the air, making it hard to breathe. A dark inky black mist swirled up around us, and a solid figure slowly materialized. I could finally see what caused my father's alarm. There it was in all its astonishing glory—a beast straight from the worst of nightmares.

Jagged horns protruded from its skull like a ghastly royal crown, grey-leathery skin drooped from its bones as if it hadn't eaten in years, and a powerful scorpion-like tail flailed menacingly in every direction. My knees folded, and I crumpled to the floor, but my eyes remained fixed on the monster. I was scared, but curious all at once. I couldn't look away. Something in its eyes seemed familiar as it slinked toward me, tilting its head, curiously. It gnashed its razor-sharp teeth just inches from my face, flicked its long, snake-like tongue in and out, and made its bloodlust known.

"Appa," I cried. My father swiftly scooped me off the floor and the beast frantically scurried backward feeling threatened by him. I looked up in awe as the pale-white gemstone-shaped disc he wore on a leather string around his neck glowed in the darkness. The disc whirred away from his chest, moving in the direction of the beast. Appa pushed the pendant down and held it firmly against his heart as he watched me observing the monster.

"Selavu? Chandraka?" He placed a strong hand over me, creating a protective barrier between us and the creature. I buried my cheek into his palm and held his hand tightly.

"Ravi!" Amma shrieked, barreling into the kitchen with my older sister, Leena, at her side. My mother dropped to the floor and cradled my sister against her chest. "Stop this madness. There's nothing there!"

But she was wrong. The creature was there. Appa could see it, and I could too. My father was now looking at me with wonder. "You see it, Moon Child? You can see the rakshasi?" An almost mad grin spread across his face as if at that moment, a striking revelation had filled his mind. "I always knew it would be you!"

Appa took a running leap and launched himself at the monster. My mother and sister shrieked unable to see or understand he was fighting for our lives. I was the only one who could see what was happening. The rakshasi clubbed him with its giant tail, sending him spiraling out the shattered window, and into the night. It darted toward Appa like a raging bull and clawed at him violently. A cloud of black dust swirled around them, becoming thicker and thicker with every passing moment. Appa cried out in anguish as he crashed to the ground.

In the next instant, Appa and the creature vanished.

This is the fantastical movie reel playing through my head every hour of every day.

My name is Chandra Subamma Chengappa, and unlike any average sixteen-year-old, I can see the rakshasi. When I was younger, Appa had filled my head with folktales about how rakshasis could shapeshift, blend in, and emulate any human. He said a rakshasi could infect a person's thoughts, compel them to do the unimaginable, and drive them to madness. Ultimately, a rakshasi could wreak havoc on everything in its path.

So, how did I get so lucky? All I know is that just like Appa, I have keen intuition and something he had referred to as selavu—the ability to feel vibrations and read energies. Every living breathing entity radiates an invisible cosmic force field that comes from the center of their heart—the very essence of their being.

Unfortunately, my ability only works to see the selavu of individuals filled with ill intent like the average bully, charlatan, or thief or those filled with extraordinary darkness like the rakshasi. The selavu of the rakshasi emits an explosive haunting murky darkness, one I'll never forget. I have not talked to anyone about that night or what I saw. Amma and Leena carried on from the moment we lost Appa as if their memories of that night were wiped clean.

Life would be better, albeit nauseating if I could only see the good in others. Thanks to my brand of selavu, I steer clear of most people, fearful I might come across something not quite human, leading a rather lonely existence. Besides, who'd want to be friends with the girl who sees monsters?

I'm late again for dance practice and there's no doubt in my mind Amma will have a fitting lecture about how good Indian daughters are punctual and perfect. She'll more than likely ask me for the millionth time today if I did my AP math homework (*the answer is No because I failed that class but haven't told her, yet*). I pick up the pace and hustle down Main Street when a sudden cool breeze whips around me. I stop in my tracks as a strange sensation—one that I haven't had since the night my father disappeared—creeps through me. It starts with a sharp shooting pain that cuts through my scarred hands and travels up my forearms into my chest. A suffocating sweet aroma of jasmine hijacks my senses.

I wait for the moment to pass, but I know better. An unrelenting feeling from somewhere deep down in my bones tells me that everything is about to change.

I know without a doubt that *it's* already here watching, waiting, and walking among us. It's waiting for the perfect moment to strike, casting shadows on my mind, pushing me to the outer edges of reality. It's come to finish what it started all those years ago.

It's come to finish *me*.

CHAPTER TWO

AWAKENING

T he air inside Amma's yoga studio is warm and
inviting. I push aside the unsettling feeling I
had moments ago and hop to it. My dance bag slams
to the floor with a boom as I hurriedly strip off my
motorcycle jacket and untie the laces of my thick-soled
lace-up ankle boots. I wiggle my toes free from the wool
socks that have been keeping the wads of thick cotton
bandages soaked with aloe vera in place. My bloodied
and blistered feet scream out in agony before I gingerly
apply pressure and rewrap them with fresh bandages.
Jipsi jānapada nritya is no walk in the park. It's a form
of Indian folk dance Amma has been teaching me since

I could walk. Reaching into my open bag, I yank out my anklets—five rows of brass bells, each slightly larger than a quarter—and tightly fasten the leather straps.

I move my stiff body through a sun salutation. Planting my feet, I lengthen my neck upwards and swan dive down until my fingertips touch my toes. Breathe in, breathe out. Placing my hands, palms down, firmly on the floor I jump my feet back where I hold my body in plank position, push upward, arching my back and craning my neck. I shove myself away from the floor, sticking my tailbone toward the ceiling.

I'm on my tenth repetition when Amma enters the room without a word, nods at me formally, and steps up to her teakwood meditation altar. She raises a mallet and strikes a large brass gong and releases a breathy "*Ohm.*" This is her ritual to purify the air and make for a solid dance practice.

My eyes wander from the candles to her other precious relics upon the altar that she has forbidden me to touch. Appa's old wooden *tabla*, an elegant elephant carved from sandalwood with its trunk reaching skyward, a pale pink blossoming lotus that floats in a shallow vase, and the large bronze statue of the heavenly Warrior Goddess Durga riding upon a tiger's back. Goddess Durga's ten outstretched arms unfold around her like serpents, with a celestial weapon in each hand. She stands upon the body of a fallen buffalo-headed rakshasa with the body of a man, symbolic of her pursuit of ridding the world of evil and protecting the innocent.

But my eyes fixate on the tabla. The tiny hand drum is made from hollowed-out wood laced with hoops, thongs, and wooden dowels along its sides. That tabla was Appa's prized possession. Soon after he disappeared, Amma took it from the house and brought it here, placed it among her museum-worthy artifacts.

There it is again—a sharp shooting pain launches through my palms into the tips of each of my fingers, and up past my forearms. The dizzying scent of jasmine fills the air. My eyes nervously flit across the room and I see an inky black smog for a millisecond before it dissipates.

It's nothing! Get a grip, Chandra.

Today's the day I do things right. The day I dance my way into Amma's heart. The day she finally *sees me* for more than the defiant thorn-in-her-side child she knows me to be. I close my eyes and breathe deeply, willing the pain out of my body.

Once steady, I rise and take my spot on the giant peeling "X" marked with electrical tape on the honey-colored hardwood floors. The butterflies in my stomach flutter frantically, begging to be set free. I shut my eyes and listen for my cue.

The tribal drumbeat booms through the speakers overhead, reaching down deep inside me where it pairs with the rhythm of my heart. The wave of music rapidly rises and falls through intricate patterns and changing time signatures that coincide with my breath.

This is when I feel most alive.

I tap my bare feet on the surface of the floor and the bells on my anklets chime in unison.

The music whisks me into a parallel universe where I imagine I'm under the light of the new moon. I lift my chin and nod at the sliver of the crescent moon smiling down upon me as I weave between the towering blades of jungle grass with the silence and stealth of a tigress tracking her prey. My heartbeat quickens, steady and strong, as I spy upon the beast in the shallows of the great winding river. In this life, I am the mighty warrior. I stomp my feet over and over upon the earth until my wrath can be felt deep down into its core, challenging the enemy. There's power in my pounding footsteps ... *Taa Ki Ta... Taa Ki Ta... Taa Ki Ta...* I grasp the small conch shell hanging from the twine around my neck and raise it to my mouth. I push a long single breath through its cavity and listen as the air bounces effortlessly around its hard curved intricate surfaces. The sound resonates as the war cry of my people. The echo is heard far and wide through the jungle declaring the beginning of a battle. At this sound, the humanoid beast whips around to face me—its flaming red eyes ripe with hate. Before it has

a chance to react, I strike hard and fast with the staff
of the sacred *Golden Trishula* that once belonged to
the great goddess Durga, herself. I knock the beast
from its feet and swiftly turn the weapon to reveal the
trishula's three razor-sharp prongs and impale it deep
in its heart. The beast snarls and spits thick saliva and
blood through its gaping mouth before it stumbles back
in agony and falls dead at my feet. Having delivered the
final blow, I spiral swiftly around, lift the trishula high
above my head, and...

I fall flat on my face.

My grace is gone. I lay sprawled out on the hardwood
floors of my mother's yoga studio. There's no jungle,
no beast, and I'm no warrior goddess. Landing every
pirouette, snaking my arms up through the air, and
counting the beats to my steps leaves me physically and
mentally exhausted. I toss my Golden Trishula—now a
mere broomstick from the supply closet—in frustration
and attempt to catch my breath.

"Chandraka, all it takes is one wrong move. You
missed the last beat again." My mother throws her
hands up into the air, equally frustrated. She shakes her
head so hard that her thick black hair swept up into a
tight bun comes loose. The long tendrils of hair cascade
down around her oval face. "Every part of your being,
the movement, emotion, and eyes must tell the story of

this epic battle of light versus darkness. You have more work to do. Up! Again!"

"That final step is impossible to land," I say, the disappointment contorting my face. At one point, I'd been confident of getting it right. But here we are after living and breathing this dance for months.

Amma alights from her spot near the meditation altar onto the studio floors. She looks at the wall lined with mirrors and begins to move in sweet perfection. I follow her feet with my eyes, watching as she rapidly stomps, points, and turns on cue, perfectly in sync with the beat of the drums. She floats as if she's made of air with every movement. She leaps up and flutters down and sticks the ending like a good warrior should.

It's going to be a long night. She'll keep me here until I've perfected that final step or until the sun comes up tomorrow morning, whichever comes first.

Amma has been desperate for me to nail this Indian folk dance for my performance at the state's largest regional dance competition of the year. Sometimes she acts as if my life depends on it. I get it. She's been a single mother since my father disappeared, working nonstop to give Leena and me everything she never had. In her eyes, she sees it as my way to a scholarship for college so I can go on to be a doctor, lawyer, engineer, or whatever else is on her approved list of careers. I see it as my ticket out of this boring, wasteland town of Fortune Falls, Virginia.

"You'll only have one chance to get this right. Whatever *that* was will not earn you first place," she says, mocking my earlier performance by shaking her body haphazardly. She looks like she's being attacked by a swarm of bees. Her imitation of me is certainly alarming. "You must be number one!" She shakes her head again angrily as if she doesn't understand why I can't figure this out. I roll my eyes and pull myself up to a seated position, mindlessly flicking at the rows of brass bells bound to my ankles.

"I saw that!"

"Saw what?" I grumble.

"Stop rolling your eyes," she scolds.

"Or what? My eyes will stay this way forever?" I say with a snicker and purposely roll my eyes again. "I'm sixteen now. Too old for that nonsense. Your crazy Indian superstitions are ridiculous! For the record, we live in America." I flop my head of wild black and bright blue waves forward and let my head hang loose and stretch my arms out in front of me. I swing my head back letting my hair fall upon my golden-brown skin, smiling at my reflection when I see the blue highlights. I still think it was a good decision to dye it despite earning two weeks of being grounded, especially since I can tell it annoys Amma every time she looks at me.

"Really? Then why was it when little Pushpa Jain did that very thing ten years ago, her eyes stayed this way the rest of her life?" Amma's deep-seated beliefs in superstition are laughable and thoroughly provide a source of entertainment for Leena and me. We aren't allowed to whistle after sunset because the cobra snake would find its way to our beds apparently, all the way from India. We always get scolded for cutting our nails at night because, according to her, that act would summon the Spirits. There are a million more like that I could probably write a book about and cut a profit.

"I may be from some faraway village in India, but we have our superstitions for a reason." Amma shrugs her shoulders and glides gracefully through the set of bamboo doors from the yoga studio into her adjacent ayurvedic shop while I remain staring at my reflection in the mirrored walls. "Go put more clothing on. I can't have you dressed like *that* at the Dharma Yoga booth at Fall Fest. You're representing my business in public. Having all your flesh exposed like this is not becoming, and you will catch pneumonia." She scrunches her nose up in disgust as she looks at my black leggings and bra top. I let out a low groan. I forgot about the fall fair event and helping Amma with the booth.

"I'm wearing my bangles. Isn't that enough coverage?" I shimmy my hips and shake my arms above my head to sound the clamor of the bangles and clap my hands wildly as I walk to the counter in the shop. "Besides, I dance and teach yoga here. This is my work uniform. Seriously, the girls at school wear far less than this," I say, and push myself up off the hardwood floors and hobble on my battered swollen feet into her shop.

"Stop being so contrary, Chandraka. I don't care about the other girls," she replies sternly, handing me linen bandages and a bottle of aloe vera with its trademarked *Dharma Yoga* label from the shelf. "Fix them," she says, pointing at my feet.

Here, in this red-brick cottage with its carved-wooden sign that reads *Dharma Yoga*, is where I've spent most of my life after school. In between dance practices, I teach yoga, stock shelves, sniff-test countless fragrant candles, and sample the turmeric-ginger chai. Fortune Falls may be a sleepy town in the middle of nowhere, but Amma put it on the map with her yoga artistry and knowledge of alternative healing she brought with her from her small village in India.

Amma reaches behind the checkout counter for the thermos of hot spiced chai she'd prepared and brought from home and pours it into our matching colorful elephant mugs. I inhale deeply as the mixture of cardamom, cinnamon, and ginger fills my nostrils and immediately cradles me in its warmth. She places a silver tin plate of warm samosas in front of me. My mouth is watering as I devour my favorite fried pastry heartily stuffed with spicy potatoes and peas. The chai and samosas are her equivalent of a peace offering when she knows she's been extra hard on me during dance practice.

But the warmth of the hot chai abruptly dissipates when I spot the shadow hovering above the bamboo doors leading into the back area of the yoga studio. A large floating head with red saucer eyes stares threateningly at me. Rows of jagged teeth protrude from its wide gaping mouth. I release an awkward sound somewhere between a scream and a whimper and almost drop my mug as I push away from the counter. Amma moves from behind the counter and grabs my wrists, her voice in my ear, slowly, hypnotically cooing me back to reality.

"It will protect us," Amma says, smiling deliriously and clapping her hands together in some sort of twisted delight. I look back up at the frozen ghastly face and I realize that the thing I'm looking at is a painted mask carved from wood. "The beauty of this rakshasi is that it will deter evil spirits and cast away evil eyes. Akashleena brought it home with her when she came back from India last week."

I slap my hand to my forehead causing the rows of gold bangles to clamor with my movement and let out a monster of an exhale. "Are you kidding me? Nobody's gonna come to your yoga class with that thing as your mascot." Grabbing my chai from the counter, I take ten hasty steps in the opposite direction and breathe in the spiced chai, begging it to envelope me back into its radiant warmth. I take several seconds to collect myself before finally giving in to my curiosity. Slowly, I inch closer to the mask, until I'm standing under where it hangs on the wall, to revel in the artistry of it all. It looks realistic.

"When I was growing up in India, we hung masks like this one around the entrance of our homes," she says, a flicker of nostalgic excitement washing over her face as she remembers a world she'd left behind nearly two decades ago. "Although rakshasi and rakshasa are mostly perceived as evil in our mythology, they are sometimes good, helping the gods every now and then." She winks and continues to lecture me as the instrumental folk song of my dance plays over the studio's ceiling-mount speakers.

The chimes affixed to the front doors of the shop sing a welcoming tune, announcing the arrival of a customer. An older woman bundled in a wool wrap-jacket hobbles into the store with the support of a walking cane that towers awkwardly above her. I've only seen her a handful of times, but I remember her because of her exquisite walking stick. She clutches the cane below a large knobby handle that has the face of an elephant carved into it. Along its shaft, there are alternating rows of marching elephants with their trunks raised skyward and blooming flowers. As she's done on her past visits, she walks directly to the section of the store offering herbals and powders where she carefully selects a bottle of guggul resin powder. She shuffles over to the display in the middle of that aisle and chooses several white sage smudge sticks. I quietly move toward an open crate of lavender rosemary soaps I should have stacked two days ago, leaving Amma to wait on our customer. The woman makes her selections and slowly carries them, cradled in her free arm, to the front counter. She stares at Amma for a long moment, a strangled look of concern on her face.

"Sita, I'm sorry," the woman says in a hushed voice. "The time has come. The stars will turn on the moon and sun." It's all gibberish to me, but my mother's eyes grow wide, and her hands shake uncontrollably. It takes her far longer than it should to bag the purchased items and ring up her total amount owed.

Is Amma having a stroke?

I watch from a distance as it takes three long minutes before she hands the customer a canvas bag with the woman's purchases.

All the blood drains from Amma's face when she speaks next. "It can't be. There's still so much to learn."

Her delicate hands rise to her face and she begins shaking. She takes several long breaths to calm herself.

The old woman's gaze drops from Amma's face to the counter as if she can't bear to see the pain in her eyes. "It is to happen on the *nooru varshagala amavasye*—the hundred-year cosmic new moon—sometime in the first quarter of the new year," the stranger repeats, turning away from Amma. She uses her cane to brace herself as she limps toward the exit with her arm hooked through the canvas bag. She approaches the front of the store. I move to open the door and lend her a hand.

"Those are beautiful," she whispers in a hushed raspy voice, catching a glimpse of my outstretched palms as she strums her fingers along my gold bangles. "Your fortune is bright. Don't let anyone tell you differently." But all I see are my scars. I quickly close my hand into fists and stare blankly at her not quite sure how I should react.

"Sorry if I overstepped, sweet child. Thank you for your kindness," she says with a smile that reaches her large, tear-drop-shaped eyes. Her phrase seems out of place, but I can't help but nod in agreement. At that moment she seems strangely familiar. I smile politely and let her pass through. She moves at a tortoise pace, but with admirable strength and conviction despite the cane in her hand. I watch her until she's out of sight.

A loud crash sounds behind me when the plate with my half-eaten samosa hits the ground. I whip around to see Amma hurrying back into the yoga studio. By the time I get to the counter and swiftly try to save what's left of the samosa, Amma is already out of sight. I lift the plate and the fallen treat, blow on the samosa as if the gesture decontaminates it from all germs, and shove it in my mouth and swallow hard. I rush past the rakshasi mask, holding my breath the way my sister and I would always do when we passed the cemetery on 13th Street. When I enter the studio, Amma is approaching her meditation altar.

"Amma, are you okay?" I ask, but she doesn't seem to hear me as she sits in front of her meditation altar and gently rocks herself. My Amma, the most put-together person I've ever met, is coming undone. And I don't know why? Nor do I know what to do to help her.

Amma abruptly gets up and reaches for her phone on the shelf by the large green potted plant with broad leaves, ignoring me. She always says it reminds her of a beautiful banyan tree that grew deep in a jungle near her village. She flicks through several apps on her phone to shut down the music system, and then as if she just noticed the time on her device, she dims the studio lights and rushes back beyond the twine rope to the space between her meditation altar and where the general yoga classes take place. She steps up off the hardwood studio floor onto an area with a large area rug with repeated patterns of mesmerizing *mandalas* woven into it. The red and brown colors of the rug are soft and earthy and have always made me feel comfortable. She kneels before the teakwood altar and lights several large round white sage candles, and lowers herself into a cross-legged position.

I don't have to look at my phone to know what time it is. It's six fifty-three in the evening. I can't bother her for the next seven minutes unless I want to spend the rest of the evening statue-still in a plank position on my knuckles. She has performed the same ritual every night at the same time for the past eleven years. I've asked her about it before, but she's been vague. I suspect it's another one of her superstitions, but she takes offense. She says she takes the time to meditate on the memory of my father.

I settle myself in a corner of the studio to unofficially meditate. But I'm too worried about Amma to concentrate on anything else. Instead, I watch the flicker of the candle flames on the altar, keeping my eye on Amma and waiting for movement.

Amma sits cross-legged in front of the altar with her hands resting on her knees, her thumb connected to her pointer finger. She evokes the world around her with a resounding, "Ohmmm."

My eyes once again linger on her other precious relics upon the teakwood altar, and I recall how Amma had me closely inspect the statue of goddess Durga one day last week—the only trinket at the altar she let me touch—so that I could visualize my dance completely and understand the role of the warrior I was playing. Amma had told me how each celestial weapon that goddess Durga carries is a gift from several of the Hindu gods including Lord Shiva, Lord Vishnu, and Lord Brahma. The statue of Durga carries a disc, a trident or *trishula*, a sword, a mace, a javelin, a conch shell, a lotus flower, a large snake, a thunderbolt, and a bow and arrows. To me, goddess Durga embodies everything fierce and powerful—the way my mother wants me to dance.

My eyes move from Durga to the other relics at the altar. I think Amma just wanted a peaceful space that was all her own—this part of the studio, roped off from the rest, looks more like a display at the Museum of Natural History, than anything else.

Once again, my eyes fixate on the tabla. The agonizing sensation that I had felt earlier when I arrived at the studio moves through my hands again, and I try to stifle the pain.

A sudden strong blast of cold air blows through the open studio doors along the back wall that leads out onto a small courtyard area where Amma leads outdoor yoga sessions, extinguishing every candle. Amma releases herself from her meditative trance in a panic. She remains seated, her lips are moving rapidly as if she's having a conversation with some invisible entity. I can't hear her at first, but then her voice crescendos. "It's too soon," she cries, softly.

I rise to my feet. "Amma, are you okay?"

But she doesn't seem to hear me. She has her hands over her face again and takes several long breaths. She inhales and exhales several times and gently rocks herself where she sits.

What did that woman say to make her like this?

She rises swiftly from the altar. The worry in her heart reaches her face, appearing to have aged her in a matter of minutes. Her usually perfect posture is broken, and she now seems to be carrying the weight of a thousand elephants. She scrambles to her feet, steps down from her sacred space, and reaches for her incessantly buzzing phone still on the shelf. Amma frowns and asks me how to retrieve the message, despite moments before being able to seamlessly navigate the sound system. "I'm still getting used to this thing," she says. I flip through her new phone to a text from my sister and hand it back to her.

I stare at her hard. "Amma, what's going on? What did that woman say to you? You look like something's upset you?" I ask again, trying to get her to confide in me, but that's never been my forte or our relationship.

"It's nothing. I'm just worried about your dance. There's just so much you still must learn," she says. I know she's lying, but she still manages to make me feel bad. Her gaze moves past me to somewhere out the open studio doors. "I must go. Akashleena is back at the house. She's finally unpacked from India and brought some saris and dancer jewelry for your performance. You must stay here. Keep practicing the finale. No more falling. And don't leave the studio. Remember, the dancer is the warrior," she says, repeatedly emphasizing my need to stay in the confines of the studio protected by a rakshasi mask and white sage candles. She drifts toward the open double doors hurriedly and pulls them shut. She guides the large bolt across, locking the doors firmly in place.

Amma has shrugged me off countless times, but this has got to be the weirdest encounter yet. She steps through the studio doors back into the front shop where I hear her shuffling around the front counter to gather her pocketbook and thermos. The chimes ring with her departure as the front door swings shut behind her.

I shake my head, feeling utterly useless for not having been able to comfort Amma. I don't know what is going on with her or with that stranger, but it doesn't sound like Amma is going to tell me anytime soon. I suppose

I could give both of us some peace of mind by nailing down these dance steps. I place the empty cup of chai on the shelf and sashay out into the middle of the darkened studio to work the steps of my finale with the beast. I furiously stomp out the beat, again and again, until my left foot cramps. I stomp through the pain until it's beyond excruciating, and the bandages begin to unravel. I hit the floor in front of the step up to Amma's meditation altar to stretch it out and rewrap my foot. Grabbing my foot by the tip of the toes, I pull them toward me and stretch my calf muscle. "Come on feet, don't fail me now!"

I *need* to dance. I need this to work. Forget about school or even having a social life. I'm not great at either. I've skipped homework to make room for dance practice and this competition, and I'm not particularly adept at making friends. Not in this town anyway. After Emmy Rose McKay bestowed upon me the grand title of "Freak jungle girl" back in kindergarten, the rules of the social hierarchy had been permanently set. I'm the only Indian girl in the whole grade, something Emmy feels she needs to remind me of constantly. Even now, halfway through high school, I remain the target of countless pranks and bullying at her hands. Maybe it had been my fault for telling the entire kindergarten class about the little village my family came from in India and that the ugly, raised scars on my hands were from my chance encounter with a tiger in the jungle. Truth be told, the only tiger I've ever seen is the one in the National Zoo in D.C., and I'd never been to India.

Turning my hands over, I follow the lines meandering across my palms—not the raised keloid scars, but the actual palm lines that Appa had taught me about between his thrilling storytelling sessions. If I squint hard enough, I can see them through the scars—*the head, heart, and life* lines.

Appa, I miss you.

At that moment, as if messing up the dance steps wasn't enough, I make another wrong move. I look up at the altar, just a few feet away from my face, and gaze straight at the tabla, which seems to call out to me. I crawl from the spot I'd been stretching my cramped feet and perch myself dangerously close to Amma's meditation altar. I reach over the thick twine barricade and pull my hands away.

Don't do it! I scold myself. Amma will kill me if she knows I've touched the tabla or anything else at the altar.

But my impulsive side takes over. I reach back over and yank the tabla from the teakwood surface and pull it onto my lap. I begin to firmly slap down on it with a flat, open hand the way Appa had shown me long ago. The low dull sound of the small hand drum echoes through the empty spaces in my heart where he is eternally missed.

I rise to my feet, cradling the small drum against my left hip, and tap it squarely in the middle in quick succession with my right hand as I work out my footwork on the worn hardwood floor. I hammer out the first stanza of the beautiful Indian folk song I'll be dancing to at regionals. I pause and echo the beat of the tabla by stomping my feet on the ground hard as if I am trying to break through the floor. The bandages surprisingly stay intact. I can truly feel the music flow through me. The large brass bells on my anklets jingle in unison as my feet take control, summoning the dance gods to guide me to victory. I repeat it again, and again, laughing out loud with each completion of the steps.

Suddenly, the candles on the altar that had extinguished with the breeze earlier in the evening when Amma was present, flicker on, one by one in a great wave of light.

They illuminate the dimly lit room and I notice an inky reddish-black smog that sweeps across the room. Again, the mist disappears into nothingness. I release my hold on the tiny drum in shock. I scramble to catch it, but it falls too quickly, and I can only watch in horror as it smashes against the hardwood floors.

No, no, no!

Instantly forgetting about the candles, I drop to my knees, snatch up the tabla, and start inspecting it. To my horror, a large crack has erupted, climbing its way up the side of the wooden-based instrument. I cover the crack with my hands wishing it back together with all the goodness in me, but luck is not on my side. Instead, I stare closely at the large crack that bisects the instrument. There seems to be something glimmering inside the drum. I grab my cell phone from the dance bag I had dumped in the corner earlier, switch on the flashlight, and point it at the crack.

There's something golden inside. Baffled, I use the phone to pry the crack open just wide enough so that I can wedge my fingers inside. Using my thumb and pointer finger like a pair of tongs, I pull out a smooth, circular disc made from some sort of gemstone. I don't know how it stayed wedged between the two sides of the drum all these years. I hold it up to the light. There's a hole at its center large enough for my index finger to go through, making it look like a mini version of a vinyl record. Around the edge is a rudimentary etching of the moon, sun, and stars. I rotate it round and round in my hands, wondering.

The burning sensation ripples across my scar-ridden palms once again as the intense scent of jasmine infuses the air around me but this time the pain sinks deeper, reaching further up my arms, penetrating my shoulders, and now my chest. My muscles tense up and I shut my eyes tight.

I feel light-headed before I slip into nothingness.

"Come home, Chandra, come home!"

The soft voice is barely a whisper. I dart confused glances from a giant tree to the bank of a winding river. Above me, there's a lush green canopy with hanging vines and trees that reach the sky and beyond. I'm in a jungle. My eyes wander downstream, where the river appears to flow to oblivion.

When I turn around, standing before me is a beautiful woman with golden-brown skin that shimmers in the moonlight. Jasmine blossoms are woven into her long, wavy, jet-black hair. She's a vision.

"Come home!" she shrieks. "It's mine!" She puts her hand out to me, demanding me to hand over whatever it is she thinks is hers.

My heart is racing.

"Give it back!" Her mouth opens wide, and she pushes out a supernatural roar so powerful the echo resonates somewhere deep inside me, sending shivers up and down my spine. From the center of her chest, an inky, black mist begins to pour out, enveloping her in a strange darkness. The air around her swirls chaotically. My knees, weak with

fear, want to give in. Two red saucers appear before me, and I find myself staring up into the face of a gnarly human-like beast with many heads and arms, gnashing its razor-sharp teeth inches from my face. Its thick saliva slops from its mouth and onto my arms that now shield me from its wrath. The saliva burns my skin as the creature towers over me, clawing at the air between us as it comes even closer. I back away from it, trip over a large tree root and stumble sideways. But I'm wrong, it's not a tree root, it's the monster's scorpion-like tail. Unable to recover my balance, I tumble down the bank toward the river. Snarling, the monster jumps down after me.

When I look down, there's no water left in the riverbed. In its place is a mass of rolling scorpions. I fall in and they swarm me. Despite my attempts to shake them off, hundreds more continue to crawl upon me as the beast hovers above, relentlessly.

"Go away!" I scream throwing my hands, palm up at the shadowy figure. My hands glow an incandescent gold, illuminating the beast's savage face. I keep my palm up as the beast rages on uncontrollably, the golden light from my hands glowing brighter and brighter, blinding me.

CHAPTER THREE

RECKONING

I wrench my heavy eyelids open and attempt to bring the world in front of me into focus. It's hazy, but I'm standing in the center of the studio where the fading electrical tape marks an "X." In my outstretched hands, I'm holding the rakshasi mask and it's staring back at me through its unsettling googly eyes. I look down at my feet to avoid eye contact and I see the disc. Terrified, I release my grip and let the mask drop to the floor. A loud boom erupts as it hits the ground and I toss my bangle-clad arms up to shield my face. I peer through my hands down at my feet where the mask has splintered into hundreds of jagged pieces.

I gaze back down at the disc, scoop it up in my hands, and without thinking twice, shove it into the waistband of my leggings. With shaking legs, I scramble to the tabla and tighten the tongs around it. While the crack is barely visible, it is still there. But not too noticeable, I hope. Trembling, I return the tabla back to the teakwood altar and place it so that the crack cannot be noticed from the front. I move back and away from Amma's sacred space, still shaking.

Leena bursts through the studio doors from the shop.

"Oh, my goodness! Chandra, what happened?" Leena asks frantically. Her eyes dart from the shattered rakshasi mask to me and back again. My hands are up over my throat as I try to speak, but I can't find my voice. My nerves are frazzled as my thoughts wander and my body shakes uncontrollably.

What just happened to me?

In the vision, I saw a variation of a rakshasi I'd seen with Appa all those years ago, but this time, it was demanding I come home. Is the rakshasi in my head the way Appa had warned it could get into my mind? Was that a threat? What do I have that it could possibly want?

I shudder as sweat drips down my back. Shaking uncontrollably, I release a high-pitched scream falling to my knees.

"What happened to you?" Leena puts her hands to my head and wipes at my clammy face with a tissue she retrieves from her pocket. I begin to hyperventilate and feel like I'm about to pass out. Leena is caring, to a fault, and sometimes it becomes overbearing. I push her hands away, not wanting to be touched.

"What happened to the mask?" she asks.

I look at my sister's face unsure if I should say anything at all.

"Leena, I saw a *rakshasi*!" I whisper, my lips quivering as I run my hands through my tangled hair.

Her eyes are wide and uncertain, and she looks like she wants to say something, but just then Amma rushes into the studio. The look of terror on her usually peaceful face tells me she's heard every word of what I've just said. Her jaw drops open as she scans the inexplicable chaos in the studio—from the re-lit altar candles to the shattered mask to me.

"Did you do this?" she asks, trembling slightly as she points down at the pieces of the mask. She swallows hard, scanning the studio as if she's worried about what she may find. She closes her eyes, whispering something to herself, and she begins to calm, inhaling and exhaling.

Leena distracts herself by grabbing the broom and sweeping the debris from the rakshasi mask into the trash in the front of the shop.

"Shhhh, your mind is on overdrive. Be calm. Breathe."
Amma places her soft, delicate hands on either side of
my face and hooks me with the tranquil look in her eyes,
but I'm no calmer than I was seconds before.

"I know what I saw. I saw a reddish-black mist. I saw
a rakshasi. IT WAS THE SAME THING I SAW TAKE
APPA!" I say the words starting as a whisper and ending
in a shout. "It told me to come home. It's happening. I
see selavu. You know I do!" I shout at Amma. My heart
is racing, and my eyes shift from the broken mask to the
altar.

"Selavu is not real! If you keep talking like this, you'll
end up like your father," Amma says sternly, almost
desperately, looking directly into my eyes.

"Appa knew something about me that nobody else
did! He knew I could see selavu," I shout, placing my
hand on the small of my back where the disc rests.
A warmer-than-usual sensation from under my feet
causes my eyes to dart to the floor where I've reopened
old wounds and the bandages have come undone. The
wheels in my head begin to turn. And then it hits me.
"The folk dance! It's not *just* a dance...it's like you've
been training me for something all this time?"

"Stop!" she screams at me, and I sit back, stunned.
Clearly, I've hit a nerve because she's never raised
her voice. I'm certain losing control in this manner is

against some laws of yoga. There is nothing zen in the way Amma just shrieked at me.

"What happens now that the monster is in my head?" I ask Amma in a low, surprisingly controlled voice, so Leena can't hear. The color drains from her face and her eyes grow wide. "Tell me. That dance is more than just my ticket out of here. What does it have to do with this disc?" I plead with her, attempting to push the tears, frustration, and fear down that are bubbling to the surface as I pull out the disc and flash it in her face. Her mouth drops open at my words and she puts her hand out, reaching for the disc, but I take a huge step away from her.

"Give it back!" she yells, flailing her arms at her side and shaking uncontrollably. And before I know it, she slaps me across the face. Hard. It stings.

Has she lost her mind?

Never in all these years has she *ever* done *anything* like that. *Never*! Not with any of the other antics I've pulled—not when she thought I was doing drugs and was caught vaping under the bridge, not when the park ranger had to bring Leena and me home after I'd coaxed my sister into cliff diving into the Fortune Falls basin, and not when I defiantly broke curfew. I've challenged her to no end every step of the way and never has she raised a hand to either of us.

I stare at Amma with disbelief writ large on my face. I say nothing as I slowly lift my hand to my throbbing face. I slide the disc back into the slip pocket of my waistband. Amma stands still, also in shock, her hands folding into her heart. She rubs her face in anguish. She comes forward again, trying to hug me, but I recoil like a frightened animal. "I'm sorry," she apologizes in a soft, defeated whisper staring down at her hands.

Something ferocious comes over me at the moment and I want to hurl as much hurt at her as I can inflict. "Don't touch me," I growl. A rage I've never felt sweeps through me. Before I can think to hold my tongue, the words sputter from my mouth. "I wish the rakshasi had taken you instead of Appa. He's the only one who really knew what I am!"

Tears blossom in her eyes, but they stay there, frozen, just as she does in her stance.

I back away, still holding my face where her hand had made an impact. I reach down to my dance bag to grab my phone and jacket, as the tears begin to well in my eyes. I kneel, gingerly pull on my thick-soled black boots over my sore bloodied feet, and storm through the bamboo doors out the shop doors. I wait until I'm a good distance up the street before letting the tears slide down my cheeks and disappear into the chilly fall night.

CHAPTER FOUR

FORTUNES TELL

I speed in the direction of home—just a few blocks away from the studio—my mind races as I dissect every portion of the past twenty minutes. The glowing disc in the tabla, my vision of the rakshasi, and my mother's insane reaction. And what did that woman say to Amma?

What is wrong with me?

I hear a strange, muffled sound behind me and the shuffle of footsteps approaching. Feeling a touch paranoid, perhaps a little worried a rakshasi could be around any corner, I veer off down the alley that bisects Main Street with a few of our treasured spots—The

Thai Palace with the heavenly pad thai, and Marla's Ice Cream Emporium, that serves up larger-than-life scoops of my favorite flavor—Death by Chocolate. My stomach rumbles as I wait in a dark corner out of sight.

"Chandra?" The honey-sweet voice of my sister calls out. "Come back with me. Amma is distraught." Leena the golden child, the peacemaker, our *Miss Can't Be Wrong*.

She's home from India only for a few weeks and I don't need her worrying about me. She has enough to worry about. After all, Amma nauseatingly declares to every stranger who walks through her yoga studio doors. "My Akashleena is saving people of this world—one village at a time." And here she is, now trying to salvage the relationship between Amma and me.

"Leena," I say in a low voice, moving from the shadows, straight into her outstretched arms. I nestle my face in the crook of her neck, her long straight hair tickles my nose. Despite how annoying I find her perfection it is nice to have some comfort right now. "Do you believe me?" I pull away to look into her eyes searching for acceptance.

"I mean, that stuff you were saying is flat out crazy," she says in a matter-of-fact tone, conveniently avoiding my question as she pivots with one of her own. "How's your face, anyway?"

"It hurts, but it doesn't compare to my feet. Amma doesn't have much power behind her hand. It was shocking, but I'll be fine," I say, sliding a hand up to my cheek absent-mindedly. There are more pressing things on my mind than the rapidly fading sting of Amma's slap. "Do you remember Appa talking about selavu?" I ask, trying to explain everything to Leena. But she doesn't seem interested.

"Vaguely. Appa sort of spent more time with you. You needed that extra attention with all that kindergarten bullying," she says, a faraway look on her face, as if the topics of Appa, selavu, and rakshasi are not her cup of tea.

As we round the corner back onto Main Street, there's a buzz of activity, and passersby of all ages parade around joyously in their trendy fall flannel shirts, puffer vests, and riding boots, mindlessly posing for pictures with pumpkins and haystacks.

Storming out the back door of the yoga studio, I'd missed all this. The streets are sectioned off for the Fortune Falls Fall Fest. Vendors have set up booths in and around the Town Square where flocks of people are feasting on pumpkin muffins, candied apples, warming up with a spiced mocha latte, and shopping for over-priced designer fashion at the boutiques.

"Ugh, Fall Fest. The Dharma Yoga booth?" I mumble, rolling my eyes and wishing the ground beneath would open and swallow our town whole.

"Unfortunately, we must walk through this crowd to get home. I'll go back to the booth, don't worry," Leena says pulling her burnt orange pashmina shawl around her, clomping down the street in her knee-high stiletto-heeled boots. She always has had a flair for color and fashion. She fits right in with the crowd.

"Are you going to be, like hypothermic or something? You're probably not used to the cold weather. It must be hot as hell in the motherland?" I say as I pull my grey knit beanie down over my ears and hug my unzipped motorcycle jacket close to my body, wishing it were ten degrees warmer as we bob and weave through the crowd.

She shakes her head. "In the city, it is very hot, but actually, in the mountains, where Uma Aunty lives, the temperatures drop pretty low at night—blanket cold."

"What's it like there, anyway?" I ask, wishing I get to go sooner rather than later. I hope she can fill my head with her adventures and keep my mind off my thoughts.

"Remember how Amma used to say India is beautiful and tragic all at once? She was right. Things are so different there for the people in these remote villages," she says.

A strange faraway look creeps into her eyes as if she wants to disclose more but doesn't continue. Leena's the do-gooder who just can't help herself. Between high school graduation last May and starting a summer program at Harvard Medicine, she'd zipped halfway around the world to serve as an English teacher to three dozen orphans in a jungle village in the south of India. For fun. And for free.

"You know, there's no cell service so it sucks we can't talk more often," she adds. "But Uma Aunty is a blast and she's taught me so much about the villagers, and, well, you know, the gypsy people, like Appa..." Her voice trails off with an insinuation in her tone that makes me bristle.

"Why do you say it like that?" I cut in angrily. "*We* are like Appa, like those gypsy people. There's nothing wrong with that," I say. A slight wave of anger ripples through me.

"Well, you're more like him than I am. You've always been a bit more of a free spirit. You do your own thing. I love that about you," she says, playfully pulling at my long streaks of dyed blue hair. "I'm surprised Amma hasn't made you shave your head after you put those highlights in and the mess you'd made in the bathroom!"

My cheeks feel warm as I stare blankly at her. "I do my own thing because there's no other way for me. I don't have the friends you have. You've always fit in with everyone. I'll never be the perfection that is you. I'll just have to live with that," I say joking, but there's a truth behind my words. Leena is the perfect daughter and I'll never do anything as good as she does, as Amma has let me know many times. I stare over at my sister, feeling fortunate that I've got at least her to lean on, as friendless as I am.

I link arms with her and pull her close as we meander down the street. We duck down as we pass Amma's yoga studio booth, saunter out past the traveling 'Twirl and Hurl' and Ferris wheel, past the Haunted Fun House, making our way to a spot just up on the left. We're closer to home when Leena points at something. A lone orange canvas tent adorned with silhouettes of the sun, moon, and stars. My mind flickers back to the strange stone disc I found inside Appa's tabla, and my heartbeat quickens. The sun, moon, and stars on the tent look almost exactly like the pattern on the disc.

"Looks like the walking, talking freak show has lost her way," a sharp nasal voice calls from the darkness behind us. Someone shoves me from behind and I release my hold on Leena as I tumble forward into the rough gravel below. I flip over with a mouthful of dirt and dust. Leena bends down to help me up, but I'm embarrassed, and I push her away. I recognize the trio in front of me immediately.

Emmy and her two minions, Soni Lalindhal, and Hannah Norton are the insufferable hellions of the

Fortune Falls High School dance squad. They stand together in their red and gold dance uniforms, each one dressed as if trying to outdo the other. They must be fresh off their routines at one of the side stages at the fall fair. Emmy's auburn hair is pulled up tight on top of her head and affixed with a large gold bow. She's no doubt used a full can of hair spray to cement the look in place. Every time she blinks, it looks as though her false eyelashes are going to fall off. The twenty pounds of makeup caked on Soni's face, makes me wonder how she manages to keep it all in place under the heat of the bright show lights. Mine is usually smeared all over my face by the time I've finished a routine, but it's as if Soni's makeup has been permanently painted on. Her dark brown hair is pinned up with a gold bow. Hannah is wearing an offensively bright shade of lipstick, which in my opinion, desperately needs to be banned. Forever. It makes the permanent scowl on her freckled face appear even more sinister.

Emmy stands over me, one hand on her hip, the other holding a can of cheap beer. "Looks like we found ourselves the witch's lair!" Her eyes cut into me like daggers as she bobs her head in the direction of the tent just beyond my shoulder. When it comes to nightmares, forget the rakshasi. This right here is truly my worst nightmare.

"Emmy, we don't want any trouble," Leena begins to say sweetly as if she may break into song with a tiny chorus of animated woodland creatures coming out from the shrubbery about morals and antibullying.

Instead, I tug at her arm and put a finger to my lips, begging her to stop talking. "Not now," I say as my eyes settle on Emmy. A swarm of colors slips in and around her, and at that moment, I take in a deep breath and change the direction of my gaze. My eyes follow the path of her silhouette, starting at the top of her head and moving to the right. At first, there are sudden flashes of color. I doubt they are visible to the ordinary eye. They snap in and out of my sight, like a malfunctioning traffic light filtering through red-green-yellow. This swarm of colors moves at warp speed, spinning aggressively in one direction, before slowing to a stop and settling around Emmy. The colors dissipate like watercolor upon canvas from her heart's center to her silhouette until the outline of her body is a grungy shade of greens and browns. A person with a soul, but absolutely no heart, for she is cruel beyond comprehension. This is what I see when ill intention is near. It's also the reason I steer clear of most people. I get tired of seeing the dark side of the world.

"Selavu," I say, loudly.

"What did you just call me? Stop staring at me you, freak!" Emmy's voice escalates twenty decibels as she sees my large brown eyes upon her in the dusk. I finally snap out of it.

Thanks, selavu, you suck!

I blink and rub my hand over my forehead and mumble, "Sorry."

"Are you here to snitch on us?" A maniacal glimmer shoots through her eyes. "Is your momma still selling that weird voodoo crap in that witch shop of hers? Between your ugly hands and your witchy momma, it's no wonder that crazy poppa of yours up and left."

Soni and Hannah cackle like a pair of hyenas unable to manufacture any common sense or think for themselves. The three girls hover over me with menacing looks on their faces.

"I ran out of that witch bitch repellent," Emmy screeches, mocking me as she, Soni, and Hannah pretend to pass a spray bottle back and forth.

"Just look in a mirror. That ought to repel everything," I mumble under my breath. Leena who's watching from the sidelines lets out a sigh, shakes her head in disbelief, and covers her mouth.

"What did you say?" Emmy growls at me at first, before suddenly letting out a shriek. A chorus of long and sustained hissing erupts from behind me. "Oh my God! What in the hell is that?" Her eyes are wide as her gaze moves to something just over my head. Then the sound of a high-pitched woodwind instrument rips through the air.

Emmy steps backward as she points at the ground where several large snakes slink around me, out across the earth, and straight for them. There's an abrupt key change and a single note is sustained for what feels like several minutes as the snakes halt in their tracks. Each snake rises to a strike position, inflates its magnificent hoods, and exhales with eerie hissing. *King cobras.* I know I should stay dead calm, but for some reason, I'm not scared. I slowly rise to my feet and stand among the scaly creatures. All three girls shriek, dropping their beer cans, and race back toward the bustling crowd and lights of the fall festival.

I remain in the darkness until they are out of sight, then I turn toward the tent. The cobra snakes retract their hoods and shrink their bodies as they escort me to the entrance. Once I reach the flaps, my slithery protectors disappear like they were never there.

"Chandra, what in the world is going on? Where did the snakes come from? Where did they go?" Leena whimpers, hopping along beside me, worried she may come across another snake in the grass. She's got a tight grip on my arm and I feel her trembling. Unlike at the yoga studio, I'm the brave one now.

"I have no idea, but I have a feeling our answer is there," I say, pointing to the tent. My heart is pounding with the excitement of the moment, uncertain if I'm dreaming or not. A sign at the entrance to the tent reads, "Fortunes Tell: Find your destiny." A knot forms in the pit of my stomach, and my heart skips a beat. Without giving it another thought, I push through the flaps of the tent unannounced and Leena tumbles in right behind me. Inside, it's as if we've been transported into another place and time.

Hanging from the apex is a rustic mobile of gemstones that shimmer in candlelight. Along the panels of the tent are shelves stocked with unlabeled vials filled with murky substances and jars of herbs—like the ones found in Amma's ayurvedic shop—but seemingly so much more authentic. My eyes fixate on three mason jars. One holds a coiled snake, another has three cockroaches each the size of my hand, and a third with a dozen scorpions the size of a quarter. *The killing kind.* Amma had taught me that the smaller the scorpion, the more deadly its sting. I guess it's something I've just held on to.

"Oh geez," Leena exclaims, as she looks around with eyes as big as saucers. "These aren't real? Right?"

"In fact, they are," a young woman emerges from the dark corner of the tent, a wooden flute-like instrument in her hands. She continues, "Curated from my many travels around the sun."

The young girl, a teenager, not much older than me, gracefully approaches us, as if floating on air, her cascading, straight black mane somehow defying gravity as it blows in a non-existent breeze. The bells hanging from the belt around her svelte frame jingle rhythmically.

"How did you do that thing outside?" I ask inquisitively, my eyes searching the dimly lit tent as if trying to locate hefty visual effects equipment.

"I can command snakes...among other things," she says, coyly. Her eyes look past me as she watches my sister intently.

"Command snakes?" Leena sounds skeptical. "I doubt that's something a gypsy can do. Aren't your abilities limited to crystal balls and tarot cards?"

The fortune teller's lips suddenly turn down into a harsh scowl. "I'll cut your tongue out. That word is offensive," she spits. A hint of an Indo-British accent comes through. Her hand rests on the ornate handle of a dagger strapped to her side. She slips her flute into another loop at her opposite side.

"What word? Gypsy?" Leena repeats, confused.

"Where I'm from, we're called *Lambadi*," she says, glaring at Leena.

Red flushes Leena's cheeks. "I'm sorry. I didn't realize," Unfortunately, her attempt at an honest apology falls on deaf ears.

"Out," the girl says, staring hard at my sister. I follow her gaze as she searches in and around Leena. "Your heart isn't true. I don't trust you. Get out."

"What?" Leena stares stupefied.

I stand there beside my sister; my gaping mouth hangs open in shock. "Wait, Leena is nothing but good-hearted," I offer.

"I'm a fortune teller, aren't I? I can read her energy. I can feel her vibrations," the girl answers, then points to Leena and then to the tent flaps. "And I don't much like her. Out!"

"Let's get out of here," Leena says softly, turning to face me. She's clearly wounded by the unforgiving girl and is suddenly nervous.

"This one can stay," the girl says, pointing at me and cocking her head to the side as her eyes flutter around me. "Strangeness fascinates me, and you are stranger than most..."

My cell abruptly vibrates in my pocket. I yank it out and scan the text.

"It's Amma. She needs help at the booth. You go, I'll meet you at home. Tell her I'm fine," I say as Leena hesitantly turns and walks out.

Although this brusque girl was just rude to my sister, I feel a pull toward her. Ever since the vision and discovering that disc, questions have been running through my head, and for an inexplicable reason, I feel like this girl might be able to provide answers.

My eyes scan every corner of the tent, the candles, the dozens of vials lining the shelves. It's not hard to imagine these jars are filled with magical potions and elixirs.

I turn back to the fortune teller. "You are Lambadi?" I ask, suddenly feeling very warm in the tent. I shake my faux leather jacket off and drop it to the floor. My bangles jingle. I lightly caress the thick bands of gold bangles wrapped around my wrists, a nervous twitch I've had since I was a child, as the fortune teller watches my every move keenly. I pick at each bangle with my fingertips as if preparing to pluck a guitar string. I subconsciously count, starting at one and running up until I hit twenty-four. Twelve on one arm, twelve on the other.

"I'll do both the asking and the telling here," she says, picking up her floor-length *lehenga* as if it were made of air, exposing her bare feet, and fluttering herself into a seated position on the bamboo mat under the rudimentary crystal mobile. The tiny mirrors patched into the fabric of her outfit dance in the candlelight with her slightest movement. The lehenga is a kaleidoscope of colors and I find myself getting lost in the maze of patterns. It reminds me of the closet full of dance costumes Uma Aunty has sent from India over the years.

Underneath the rows of silver and copper bangles, I see a series of tattoos—black vines with luscious green foliage sprinkled with bursts of pale pink lotuses that wrap up and down her arms. My eyes fall upon a thick golden rope that starts at her shoulders and ends at her wrists. I squint. In the rope I can see a diamond-shaped head...it's no rope, it's a snake. The bangles clamor as she moves her hands to a small plate where the light from a *diya* illuminates a collection of colorful blooms. I look closely at the flowers—I've spent several summers meticulously drying and cataloging every type of Virginia flower for Amma, and these are not from around here. The sweet fragrance of the flowers takes me back to those summers when Amma and I spent hours placing the gently dried flowers in glass frames. That was the last time I can remember Amma tearing herself from her yoga studio and spending time with me, besides teaching me dance.

A strong husky scent of sandalwood fills the air and I'm snapped from my memories as the fortune teller swirls several sticks of incense, clearing the space around us before she sets them back in the stand. She claps her hands together and motions me to take the seat facing her on the bamboo mat on the floor. We're sitting fairly close—closer than I'd like to be to a stranger. There's a wild flicker in her eyes as she locks me with her intense gaze. Her hazel eyes appear to glow against her dark olive complexion. Her pupils are deep like never-ending black wells, and I'm spiraling into them. It feels like she's looking right through me. But when her eyes wander *around* me, it confirms any uncertainty I have about her authenticity. I know what she's doing because I'm doing the same. Her *energy* is palpable. She's reading my selavu, and I'm trying to read hers. I expect to see a swarm of dreary colors around her, something that warns me of her ill intentions. I expect her to swindle me out of hundreds of dollars or try to make me believe everything she has to say. But there's no selavu. Nothing happens. I'm not picking up anything with her.

"*Chandraka?*" she whispers, a sly smile spreading across her face. "*Adu nim'ma hesaru, sari. Idu chandrana artha.*"

She knows my name.

My eyes are wide and I'm speechless for probably the first time in my life. She's got skills. Impressive. I *think* she's speaking a mishmash of some Indian language—it sounds like my parent's native tongue. They'd speak their dialect when they didn't want Leena or me to understand the conversation. They would go on for hours about town gossip, scandals, and horrific news headlines.

"I'm Surya," she says, looking up at the gemstone mobile above. "Your name, Chandraka or Chandra, it means Moon. I hear a whisper in the air. It's saying, *Moon Child*."

There's a twinge in my heart and I let the slightest gasp pass through my lips.

Appa? I hesitate but eventually nod vigorously.

She makes a strange clicking sound with her mouth and takes a pause as her eyes dart and scan around me once again. Side to side, up and down. *What does she see*? I try to do the same. Use selavu to read her, but my efforts prove to be fruitless. Something changes in the air. I get the feeling she's unsure about me, which makes me uneasy.

"You're a novice, so you won't get a reading on my selavu. I'm not what you hunt," she whispers. I stare at her blankly. "While I can read all energies—the good and the bad among humans—your gift is to only illuminate the dark ones. You see what nobody else can see."

"Gift? You mean curse?" I say, letting out a nervous laugh. I never would have imagined being able to talk openly with anyone, let alone this stranger, about selavu.

"No, it is a gift, but it comes with a price," she responds.

She points to a ratty cardboard sign sitting directly above the mason jars with the morbid menagerie of dead and bloated things. There's something haphazardly scribbled across it, but all I can make out is the word 'dollars.' She puts her left hand out, palm up—the universal sign for 'pay me now.'

I fish out my little silk coin purse from my jacket pocket, thinking about the folktales Amma used to tell when we were little about unassuming travelers who accidentally traded their souls for fortune-telling. I unfold a wrinkled twenty-dollar bill shoved deep inside it and pull it out. Surya's eyes light up at the sight of cash and she grabs it. Clearly, she's looking for monetary payment and there will be no soul stealing tonight. She puts her palms together and says, "Namaste."

As we sit in silence, she places more diyas around us and lights them with what appears to be a wave of her hands. There are five candles of varying sizes on the floor between us—four of them form the corners of a square and one is placed at its center. She points to the apex of the tent above us where the five stones hang by twine. She stops and stares at me as if I should understand her charming ceremony, but I'm clueless. She shakes her head and mumbles under her breath. I think she says something about 'Americans.'

"Lambadis are the first traveler or nomad group that originated out from India. True in some areas we've been called 'gypsies' but the word holds poor meaning and connotation. We are so much more.

We were once revered by the great Maharajas who celebrated us as artists, musicians, fortune tellers, crafters, entertainers, and in some cases, warriors. But when the British colonized the country and there became fewer Maharaja courts, we lost our glory. We were pushed down to nothingness. Without the royal courts, we were merely homeless travelers, forced to live a life where we were the dirt of the dirt. We spread to distant lands through the Middle East to Eastern Europe," she says without looking at me. Her eyes are fixed on the five stones hanging above us.

"That seems unfair. So, there are more of you?" I ask timidly, not sure if she's going to scold me as she had done with Leena.

"There are more of *us*," she whispers, her eyes meeting mine once again. She makes a gesture with her hands that indicates she's talking about me, too.

"*Us?*" I ask.

"Your bangles were forged by our ancient Lambadi ancestors." She aggressively reaches for my hands and pulls them into her. "They can do things you'd never imagine. See the sun, moon, and stars, here? It's like the universe belongs to you." She traces the etchings on my bangles.

Wait, the images are just like the disc in Appa's tabla.

With all the crazy commotion, I had not put that together before. I nod half in shock and half just hoping she'll let go of my hands. But I have a feeling she's right. Appa had gifted them to me right around the time I started kindergarten. They were big for me back then and Amma had put them away until a couple of years ago when she wanted me to wear them for my dance performances.

The fortune teller starts to trace the meandering lines from the center of my right palm, repeatedly. It's soothing at first and combined with the sweet and woody scent of sandalwood incense and burning candles, a calmness sweeps over me.

Then she stops following my actual lines and starts to trace the thick, wide scars on my palms.

I stare into the jagged, raised scars. They're ugly and I hate them. The more Surya messes with my palms, the more they throb.

She continues to trace the lines but keeps getting distracted by the scars. "Head, heart, and life," she whispers. "These lines tell me the story of your destiny." I imagine each line to be a separate winding road, no doubt taking her to a different place. Then she lets out a gasp and violently jerks my hand closer to her face, her eyes wide and bewildered.

My eyelids start to feel heavy as if they carry the weight of the world. I wasn't tired before, but now I just want nothing more than to drift off to sleep. I try to fight it, but it doesn't feel right. I can't fight it any longer. My hands start to burn and the room around me spins as I become overwhelmed with the sweet fragrance of blossoming jasmine. I feel as if I'm sinking deep into the floor beneath the bamboo mat.

The world goes black and then a vision forms.

In the yoga studio, the lights are dimmed just the way Amma likes it, with only the flicker of candlelight to guide my way. The tiny hairs on my arms stand up and I shudder. It's eerily quiet.

"Amma?" I call out.

"Chandraka, I can't keep you safe anymore," she says, her voice hoarse as if she's been crying, or worse yet, screaming. I can barely make out her figure near the meditation altar. She looks as though she is kneeling. "It's coming for you. The darkness. And it will give you the fight of your life."

I feel a wave of anger rising and falling as a pool of tears gather in my eyes. "But I need you!"

"The disc is your weapon. You must learn to wield it. Hold it in your palm, and it will give you answers to the past, lead you in the right direction in the present, and allow you to see the future."

A sharp low whistle fills the room. The ground beneath my feet rumbles and it's followed by a strange noise that sounds like the clicking of fingertips on a desktop. I pick up a candle for light and lower it to the floor when I see something haphazardly skitter across it. I lurch back in disgust. There are hundreds of scorpions of all sizes scurrying across the hardwood floors of the studio and upon the meditation altar.

They crawl over the sandalwood elephant, the bronze statue of goddess Durga, the lotus, and the tabla, digging their stingers into each piece. The stingers must be filled with some form of acid because with each point of contact, they are able to damage the relics. I hear a low whistle again and they respond to the call as they creep away in the direction of the double doors leading to the courtyard, having completely ravaged Amma's sacred space.

"You must go home to the jungle. Find the others. Destroy the rakshasi," she says, breathlessly. She doubles over, screaming out in pain, and falls forward onto the altar.

The bright studio spotlights flicker on and shine down from above, blinding me for a matter of seconds. I rush for Amma as I scan the floor. The scorpions have disappeared.

"It got me," she says in a hushed voice as I reach her side and scoop her into my arms, holding her close. "Chandraka, my journey ends here," she *whispers. "Know that I always saw you. I never said it enough..." Her eyes roll back into her head.*

"Amma, wake up, wake up!" I weep as my body shakes with unrelenting sorrow.

But she doesn't wake and my heart sinks.

When my eyes open, I'm still in the fortune teller's tent, my breathing is ragged, and my heart is exploding through my chest as the vision crosses from somewhere inside my head into my reality. Panic sets in. I know Amma is in danger. I can feel it deep inside me and know it's true. I need to warn her, but I'm suddenly overcome with pain.

My hands are burning as if they're on fire. I clap them closed, trying to stifle the throbbing pain. My jaw drops open, but nothing comes out. I fall forward clenching the disc against my heart and making a fist with the other pounding on the bamboo mat on the tent floor. I feel the disc fall from my waistband pocket onto the floor next to me.

Surya does not bat an eye at my distress, her intense, kohl-lined eyes focus on the disc. She glides to the side of the tent, grabs a bottle of tiny green leaves from her well-stocked shelves, shakes it, then pinches several of them between her pointer finger and thumb and dusts them off into a black mortar and pestle. I watch through bleary eyes as she takes the handle of the blunt, clubbed-shaped pestle in her hand and moves it around crushing and grinding the leaves into a fine paste. She returns to the bamboo mat and kneels beside me. Anchored to the tassel enclosure of Surya's lehenga is a small, glass vial containing a thick, deep red liquid. With just the tips of her fingers, she unties and releases it with ease from the tassel and pours it over the paste, mixing it some more. She works swiftly, finally combining everything into a coconut husk bowl. She crouches over where I lay, reaches her arms around me, and forces me back to a sitting position. "Drink it all," she commands, the look in her eyes somewhere between concern and a threat, as she holds the rudimentary bowl to my lips.

It's vile but she tilts my head back to force every drop down my throat. The terrible pain slowly fades away. My shaken nerves begin to grip reality and my fingers tingle, but my mind is focused on one thing—the visions.

"How did you get inside my head?" I ask. She doesn't answer immediately, instead, she silently runs her fingers over my tender palms. I rub my face against my bare shoulders attempting to blot the ceaseless tears that pour down my cheeks and sloppily drip all over my hands. But it makes no difference to Surya, who continues her seemingly unhealthy fascination with my hands.

"I didn't do anything. You did," she says looking directly into my eyes. "That's all you. Another Lambadi gift. Seeing the enemy and knowing the future always comes with a price."

"My mother is in danger. I must warn her!" I try to stand, but my legs are tingling, and I plop back to the mat.

"She's not your mother," Surya says in a serious tone, keeping her eyes on the disc next to me. "She's your watcher, your guardian, whatever you want to call it. It's been her duty to keep you safe. But your mother, she is not."

I shake my head, denying what she's telling me. My hands are aching from a place somewhere deep inside and I want to close them into fists. I drop the disc into my lap and Surya grabs my hands once again and moves her index finger against my palms. Her touch feels like a dagger against my scars. I want to tell her to stop, but I've lost my words. Whatever she has fed me is causing paralysis. I can't form words or move my mouth very well. I'm a hostage in my own head.

She holds my hands in hers, palms up, closes her hazel eyes and when she flashes them open there's nothing but glowing white almond-shaped spaces. I look at her face in horror. Thick black lines creep up my arms from the center of my palms without any pain. I panic but I can't move. The lines squiggle up under the bangles, twist and turn up past my forearms, and wind up around my biceps, paralleling the black vines on Surya's arms. Her head wobbles as if she's drawing lines across my body with her eyes. Then her hazel eyes return, once again glowing against her deep olive skin. She's looking directly at me with a scowl on her face as if betrayed by something she thought she knew.

"You're not what the Elders described," she says, harshly. "You can't be the Ārisalpatta! You're just a weak, meek girl-child. A misfit who lets lesser people push her around. I came to find the mighty tiger-hearted warrior our people were promised!"

All I can do is listen, confused because I still can't move or speak. She continues with what has now become an interrogation. It feels like she's come from another time or place in the way she talks and in the manner of her dialects.

"Give me the map to the Golden Trishula!" she remarks, cocking her head to the side, pointing at the disc in my lap. I start to wonder what kind of backwoods school she must've attended to be harboring such a fixation on 'Elders' and the belief in the Golden Trishula.

"Golden Trishula...is folklorrrre," I slur, forcing the words out as her potion slowly begins to wear off. The wheels begin to turn inside my head, drawing a link between Surya's inquest for a map and the folk dance Amma has been teaching me—the one where the warrior fights the rakshasi and kills it with the Golden Trishula. The one I'm supposed to perform at regionals in a few months.

"Hand me the disc," she says, clicking her tongue against the top of her mouth again. I pull my hands from her and hesitantly pass her the disc. She inspects the disc, turning it over and over in her hands. "This is no map? It's just a Lambadi tribal medallion," she says unamused, as she tugs at a long chain on her neck with a ruby red amulet. Annoyed, she tosses the disc back at me and I shove it into the zippered pocket of my thick-soled boots."

"The map has to be here. I can feel it!" she says with certainty. "The time is coming when the stars will turn on the moon and sun. Only the Ārisalpatta—*the chosen one*—can set the balance right," she says.

The stars will turn on the moon and sun.

That's what the older woman with the cane had said to Amma earlier today—the words that sent her into her downward spiral.

"Only the Ārisalpatta can see the selavu of the —the evil one," she says. "The Dusta will come. It has lived a thousand lives. It is one part sorceress and one rakshasi. It conjures rakshasi at whim to do its bidding. It wants that map, and it won't stop until it has the trishula!" She's starting to freak me out.

"Well, I don't want to be the Ārisalpatta! And I have no idea about a map and have never heard of a Dusta." I feel defeated as I let the words escape from my mouth. "What's so special about the trishula?" I ask.

"The trishula commands the power of past, present, and future," she says, reaching for my hands again. "It can also strike down the Dusta and any evil it's created including the rakshasi." As she peers into my hands again, she squints and contorts her face, filtering through a million different expressions in the blink of an eye. There's wonder...disgust...and now fear.

"Sāvu mattu vināśa. Sāvu mattu vināśa," she mutters the words over and over. She chokes, becoming more hysterical with each iteration.

I look over my shoulder at the tent entrance, wondering if a quick escape is an option. I turn back in a panic, but the fortune teller's eyes are shut tight again.

A strange melody slides from her lips into my ears. Again, I can't understand a word, but her tone is dark and foreboding. It's haunting and I can only assume it's filled with half-truths and bitter lies about who I am or worse *what* I am.

My hands, my strange ugly scar-ridden hands continue to completely captivate Surya. She slowly tightens her grip on them, as if she wants to make them her own. Above us, the small, colorful gemstones—amber, red, green, sapphire—hanging from the apex of the tent begin to sway violently as they crash into a larger pale white- yellow one that looks like the stone disc from Appa's tabla. The clamoring sound they make as they smack against each other is unnerving, as is Surya's tone.

"*Kodaguru*? You're the last of the Kodaguru tribe?" She repeatedly questions, as if talking to someone that's not in the room with us.

Then her eyes open and meet mine and I get the sense that she is suddenly threatened by me maybe even afraid. She swiftly lifts my palms up towards the gemstones as if deciding on a whim to test whatever suspicion she may have floating through her head. In an instant, all of them stop frozen in time and space, except for the pale-yellow stone. Her mouth hangs open in shock, as does mine.

"*Sāvu mattu vināśa! Sāvu mattu vināśa!*" she moans again looking back at my hands.

Our eyes collectively remain fixed on the single gem swinging like a pendulum from side to side above us. The pale-yellow stone with golden shimmer lights up the tent like a full-moon night.

"Sāvu mattu vināśa!" she says, looking at me expecting me to heed her warning.

I remain clueless. She looks from my hands to my face. "Death and destruction!" The words erupt from her lips in a roar. She drops my hands and covers her face. Her lips are moving, but the words stay at a whisper and don't reach my ears.

I didn't know it at the time, but with those two words, she has sealed my fate. In my hands, she saw the end.

CHAPTER FIVE

THE RED SCORPION

Death and destruction are the fortune teller's final words to me, and I want no part of any of that. I snap out of the trance-like state with a singular goal. I must warn Amma. I look over at Surya who appears shaken. She grips her heart-shaped face, but her gaze remains fixated on the pale-yellow stone that continues to move above us. As the fog in my head lifts, I snatch my jacket from the bamboo mat and crawl across the floor before hopping up into a deep lunge. This is my chance. Surya is distracted when I rise to my feet, using my hands to push off the floor. The blood is pumping rapidly through my veins as I dart for the canvas flap of the tent, making a mad dash out.

Outside the tent, the skies have turned upon the earth as the wind howls and dark clouds loom above, threatening to unleash a potent storm.

I must warn Amma. Even if she doesn't believe me.

No, don't think like that. She will believe me.

I dart in the direction of the Dharma Yoga booth that Leena and I had passed on our way to the fortune teller's tent. As I push through a congested crowd trying to seek shelter from the sudden rain, I frantically reach into my jacket pocket for my phone and pull up Amma's contact profile. I pause briefly and touch the sweet face smiling back at me from the tiny phone screen. The profile picture is one of Amma and me taken during a yoga retreat she hosted in the Appalachian foothills just a couple of months ago.

She'd asked me to help at one of her workshops, adjusting postures and helping the students achieve a deeper stretch. She'd been so proud of me for once, even impressed with how I reached 'expert yogini' status in such a short time. My thumb hits the green phone button and I dial her number.

"Come on, pick up, pick up!" Patience is not my strength. I glance again at the phone and notice several missed calls from Leena, but no messages. I try calling Leena, but it goes straight to voicemail. I redial Amma again. As I approach the Dharma Yoga booth, I see a sign that reads, "Back in 10 minutes."

"Agh!" I change my course and sprint toward the studio where I hope Amma will be.

She must be at the studio.

I feel sick as I remember the cruel words I'd spat at her, my mother—my *Watcher*, as Surya had called her, and the surety in Surya's voice as she said Amma was not my mother. Surya must be wrong. Amma is my mother.

How could I have said those things to her?

My stomach churns. The remnants of the chai and samosas we'd shared just hours ago lurch up into my throat. I manage to push it back down as I zip up the street.

The sky spontaneously opens and blinding rain washes down on the tiny town. Between the rain and my fliting thoughts, I feel trapped in a blur, a horrendous nightmare. I trot through the downpour, shivering and soaked to the bone. My body heaves from the energy I've been exerting, and my feet are killing me, but I keep moving through the ten city blocks until I reach the shop entrance. The scene is a sharp contrast to the warm, inviting studio where we've spent countless hours. The windows of the cheery cottage-like facade shrouded by overgrown ivy are lit with angry flashing lights from the surrounding emergency vehicles. My level of panic reaches a new high as I scan the somber scene.

Onlookers have gathered—mostly familiar faces like old Mrs. Esposito who owns the deli a few doors down, Mr. Roper from the hardware store, and several clerks from the grocery store up on the other corner. Mrs. Esposito is leaning against her husband sobbing in his arms. They are all Amma's dear friends, and the concern is genuine and from a place of love. Everyone in this town adores Amma. They cast their eyes, heavy with sadness, away from me as they see me approach. I try desperately to ignore the obvious looks of despair on their faces and keep my eyes on the front doors of the studio.

The downpour subsides to a trickle. A glimmer of light reflecting from a familiar mirror-work skirt draws my attention to a point several feet away near the corner, leading to the back entrance of the yoga studio. It's Surya. She's pacing, trying to find a way through the crowd. I don't know how she beat me here. The dark kohl lining her eyes smears down her cheeks as if she's been crying. She appears distraught and keeps glancing over her shoulder, expecting the arrival of someone...or something.

My palms start burning once again and I clench them into fists, as a strange vibration erupts from the zippered pocket of my boot where I had placed the disc. I reach down and remove the disc. In my hands, it continues to jitter. I feel useless, holding this thing Amma had called a 'weapon' in my vision because I have no idea what I'm supposed to do with it.

I look back up to where a drenched Surya stands, and I see something. At first, it's a wave of black smog that appears out of the atmosphere near Surya and then it inches closer and circles around her in a funnel cloud. This time the smog is more than just the inky black color I remembered. I see a reddish-black mist, creep and crawl upwards, swirling rhythmically around her. But it doesn't seem to bother her. It seems she doesn't see it at all. Surya stops in her tracks and wraps her arms around herself. That's when I notice her shivering as the cool wind blows. The lurking shadow transforms into the most horrific beast, towering high over her at more than ten feet tall. It doesn't look the same as the creature I saw that night my father disappeared or the beast I saw in my vision in Surya's tent, but it has a scorpion's tail, now curled wickedly around Surya. The creature—the rakshasi—silently wraps her in a cloak of darkness.

There is no sound. There is no struggle. Both the creature and the young fortune teller disappear into nothingness, just as Appa had done eleven years earlier.

Before I can react, the disc stops moving in my hand and the ache in my palms dissipates. I look up and they are both gone. I stand for a moment, as confusion sweeps through me before the flashing lights remind me where I am.

I turn my attention to the front door of the studio and push past the two deputies who flank either side of the entrance. I immediately recognize them from the advanced Ashtanga Fire Breath yoga class I teach on Wednesdays. Their faces are somber, and they don't do anything to stop me. Once inside, my heart immediately drops into my stomach at the sight of the Fortune Falls Sheriff standing at the bamboo doors to the studio, his face ashen, as he speaks to a woman wrapped in a burnt orange shawl.

Leena.

"Chandra, I'm so sorry," Sheriff Murray says, turning to me and reaching out a hand to touch my shoulder. I stare up at him confused and move toward my sister.

"Where have you been? I called you! It's been hours. They called me on my way to the house. I just..." But her voice is lost in the air to my anxiety, and I stop listening to her. I reach across and wrap my arms around my big sister, pushing past her without hearing another word. I stare devastated past the yellow caution tape that blocks my entry into the dimly lit studio where Amma is lying face-up, her arms loose by her side on the sprawling red and brown area rug near her meditation altar. The tabla, elephant, and statue of goddess Durga have been knocked off the altar and scattered all over the floor. The vase holding the pink lotus that looks like the ones adorning Surya's tattooed arms is smashed. Crumpled lotus petals are strewn on the ground where they are rapidly decaying in a wildly unnatural way. They are black and charred as if they had caught fire.

Amma lays in savasana—corpse pose. We'd always joked about how it was our favorite pose, how we could lay that way for hours upon hours and just let the outside world fade away. "Savasana is peace. Savasana is our ultimate goal in this life," she'd said while we stared up at the full moon on that last night of our yoga workshop just months ago.

Her long black hair is loose and tumbles around her. She looks serene as if she is asleep. At this moment, she appears much younger than her actual age. She's majestic, like a celestial being.

I drop to my knees and shriek at the sight of her lifeless body. Leena kneels down next to me, and Sheriff Murray pulls a blanket over my shoulders. I shut my eyes and begin to rock back and forth, willing Amma to wake and rise from the spot where she lays. I open them again and gaze longingly in her direction. A warm, glow emanates from her heart's center. Selavu?

Instead of hugging the silhouette of her body, the colors swarm into a small orb and float up into the air, like a bubble being carried away by a light breeze. It moves in a zig-zag with the air current, taking flight higher and higher into the studio. It pings across the walls until it finds its way out the back doors that open out into the courtyard. Next to the altar, the courtyard was among her favorite places. This was a first. I've never seen what happens to the selavu of a dead person. I've never known anyone who has died. My heart is heavy, an ache from deep inside is trying to break through the surface. But I push it down, wanting to feel nothing.

"Chandra, she'd been having heart trouble. I think it gave out," Leena whispers into my ear, arms around me. Her tears wet my face.

"Those things I said. I broke her heart. I did this!" I wail. Large tears gush from my eyes and drop into my lap.

Did I see her death before it happened or while it happened? I don't know.

I turn my hands into fists and pound at the floor. But just like in my vision, she doesn't move and remains in her eternal savasana. I'm crushed by the realization that I'm without the only constant I've had in my life. My heart is heavy, pulling me down into a merciless trench of agony.

The paramedics roll a gurney into the studio and begin to unfold a black, zippered body bag. Something in me suddenly snaps. "Wake up. Wake up. Wake up!" I scream deliriously from behind the caution tape, feeling a tight twinge burst through my palms before a familiar burning sensation ignites.

"Chandra, Leena, I've known you girls most of your lives. I know this isn't easy at all. I'm going to walk you over there, but you can't disrupt the scene," Sheriff Murray says, his large arms holding me in an embrace.

Through sniffles, I nod in agreement. Leena grabs my hand, and we slowly walk toward the meditation altar and Amma.

As we reach Amma's side, I get the sense that there is *something* else nearby. My eyes swiftly scan the altar and from out of the corner of my eye, through the blinding tears, something small skitters across the wooden surface. I squint to see it clickety-clacking its way around the illuminated candles and scurrying along the cracked wall, fleeing cowardly into a tiny crevasse, and out of my range of sight.

I tighten my grip on Leena, not wanting to ever let her go, as my mind flickers back to the vision of the rakshasi in the jungle, its wicked tail, and the river of scorpions.

That's when I know what just scurried away into the shadows. All it took was one sting.

It was a red scorpion.

CHAPTER SIX

WELCOME TO THE JUNGLE

3 months later
Āne Village, Western Ghats South India

The heavy hand of the mustached gentleman in the drab khaki immigration uniform slams down on the counter on the other side of the filthy plexiglass barricade. I push my American passport and customs paperwork through the slot, trying not to touch the window covered in a greasy film of fingerprints. The thought of touching it makes me want to gag and I have half a mind to squirt my hand sanitizer all over it. But I refrain and focus on the immigration officer's captain-style hat sitting square on his head. I stand there, waiting and wishing he'd hurry up and admit me into the country.

Without as much as a smile, he lifts my passport to his face and closely scans it through wire-rimmed glasses. His eyes dart from me to the picture on my passport and back again. He briefly flips through several pages as he scans my documents. I hold my breath, the fear building inside me that he'd somehow find a reason to deny me entry. He blots his stamper in the blue ink tray on his right side and quickly presses it to the page with my travel visa. But he is impatient. He didn't press as firmly as he should have and now the stamp is a botched mess. Fortunately, from my perspective, it's still readable. He releases a muffled grunt before waving me through to the other side of the kiosk, where a dozen rows of banners greet me. One reads, "Welcome to Bengaluru Airport." Another banner that implores me to "Discover the wonders of India" has the image of a family with plastic smiles plastered across their faces as they traipse around the pristine, marble floors of the Taj Mahal.

I roll my eyes, waiting for the reprimand from Amma, but it doesn't come. I have a sinking feeling in my stomach and a lump begins to form in my throat. I miss her every moment of every day. I know from experience that the hollow feeling inside will never go away. Every day since Appa disappeared, I woke up with the same awful feeling, and it has gotten infinitely worse since that awful day with Amma three months ago. I couldn't step back into the studio after Amma was gone, leaving all the decisions up to Leena on what to do with the studio and the shop. I haven't danced a single step since then, either. It feels like the fire inside me died with Amma.

"Chandra!" A voice somewhere behind me snaps me from my pity party and I see Leena hobbling toward me dragging my black battered backpack along with her carry-on luggage and pocketbook. "I swear, you're going to get yourself lost!"

"Chill a bit," I mumble, grabbing my backpack from her and slinging it over my shoulder. I almost regret not keeping up with my dance practice routine, because it feels like I'm carrying the weight of the world on my back. I slump, and the backpack slides to the ground with a thud. Holding on to one strap, I drag it along the grimy airport floors, not caring how silly I may look. Exhausted, filthy, and feeling all sorts of melancholy, I'm in no mood for new beginnings.

Yet here we are.

We arrived in Bengaluru, India in the dead of night after a sixteen-hour flight during which I passed the time forcing myself to stay awake listening to loud punk rock music. I was terrified of falling asleep and having one of my strange visions. I could imagine the uproar on the plane and the headlines in the newspapers the next day: "Flight of Horror: Crazy Teen Sees Monsters in the Friendly Skies!"

I don't need to give Leena any more reason to have me committed.

In the three months that followed Amma's death, the complicated bond I've shared with my sister has fractured. She refuses to believe anything I try to tell her about the movie reel of visions featuring the rakshasi, the river, and the tree. I don't blame her. Would I believe her if the tables were reversed? Most definitely not. The visions play in my head repeatedly when I close my eyes at night. It has been unbearable at times.

I'm sure Leena is less than thrilled to be playing the role of my legal guardian. Fortunately, CPS didn't have to get involved because she's eighteen, but I'll bet she's wishing now that I could be somebody else's problem rather than hers. She called me "a defiant, sullen, brat" the other day when I'd refused to pack for this trip and threw a stack of neatly folded clothes across the room. In my eyes, she's a saint, and I'm grateful for her. But I worry because she has her life together and I can't help but feel I'm about to derail the whole thing.

"The grief counselor already explained all that to you. We've suffered a significant loss, your mind is stressed out. These are dreams, and they mean nothing," she said dismissively, preoccupied with setting our travel plans in motion. After hearing this rationale for the thousandth time, I lost my cool and stormed out of the house. I camped out in the yoga studio's courtyard gazebo until she'd sent Sheriff Murray out to find me.

To avoid any more confrontation with Leena, from that point on, I've kept my lips sealed on everything. More than the visions, I keep thinking about the words of the fortune-teller. About how I am the last Lambadi warrior of the Kodaguru tribe and that I'm this Ārisalpatta—the only one who can see rakshasi and kill the evil Dusta. About Amma being my Watcher. But most of all, I'm haunted by Amma's last words from my vision. *"You must go home to the jungle. Find the others. Destroy the rakshasi."*

All my life, I'd thought that Virginia was my home. But Amma had used her last breath to tell me differently. Her last words—'Destroy the rakshasi'—have been rattling around in the back of my head for months, but they scare me too much to think about what she meant. I wish Amma was still here. I have so many questions and zero answers.

One thing I know for sure is that the encounter with Surya was a peculiar one. She could not be a figment of my imagination because, with each passing day, the initial thick black outlines on my arms continue to spread, transforming into a vast colorful canvas. A new piece of the picture puzzle appears each day. Thick green climbing stems wind around my arms with several large trumpet-shaped crimson blooms. Interspliced with the flowers on my forearms and biceps are repeating images of a glowing full moon, radiant sun, and countless black stars. I keep my arms covered, dressing in long sleeves to keep them hidden from Leena. The last thing I need from her is a grand inquisition.

Outside the airport, even with no sun beating down upon us, the air is a suffocating blanket of heat. As we roll our two large suitcases from the airport exit to the curb, I clutch uncomfortably at the disc that sticks to my sweat-drenched body just below my breastbone, now regretting my choice of wearing a long-sleeved shirt to what feels like the hottest place on the planet. The disc now hangs from a thick chain with several strands of tiny kiwi-seed-sized beads I found among Amma's remaining possessions. She used to call the necklace her 'good luck charm' and would wear it to every one of my dance competitions. It makes me feel connected to her or as if she is still watching over me in some way.

"So, you're just going to drop me off to live with some non-relative, friend of the family in India who you expect to babysit me for the next several months?" I ask, angrily, as we play a game of tug-of-war with every passing cabbie who attempts to grab at our luggage and usher us into their taxi, certain we will choose them because they are offering us the best rates in Bengaluru. I restart the argument we've had nearly every day for the past few weeks.

"Let it go," Leena says, heaving a huge, frustrated sigh at my question. "I will take you back to the US in the fall. We have the studio and the house to go back to when we want. You may be bored here at first, but you're going to be fine."

"Fine? I'm anything but fine. I see monsters that shouldn't exist. I have visions of terrible things. Amma is dead. That's not fine!" I whisper through gritted teeth to my sister who scowls and moves away uncomfortably.

She turns on her heel, flashing an excited smile as she waves down a white Tata Motors Jeep with black trim. The body of the vehicle is boxy and has a ladder on the back door near the spare tire that leads up to the roof rack. I imagine it's the kind of vehicle you'd take to go on safari, but I haven't any idea how that would work in the middle of a bustling city like this. The driver brakes and swerves to a stop just inches from where we stand.

"Uma Aunty arranged this. Don't complain," Leena says from the side of her mouth without looking directly at me. If she had looked at me, she would've seen me rolling my eyes. Again. The driver with the white hair, bushy mustache, and sunlight for eyes, pops out of the vehicle and strides over to us from the driver's side, which I notice is on the right side of the car instead of the left. He wears a simple stiff starch-pressed white cotton button-down shirt tucked into his blue-colored *lungi*. The sarong-like garment is neatly wrapped around his waist, exposing his knobby knees and scrawny legs.

Our driver beams as he folds his hands together and puts them to his forehead with a slight bow. "Hallo, Ms. Akashleena. Good to see you again," he says, bobbing his head back and forth and simultaneously delivering a sweet goofy grin. His smile reveals the gaping black holes where he's missing teeth. He gently reaches for our luggage.

"Sagar, this is Chandra, my sister," Leena says, a genuine smile stretching across her face—a smile that I haven't seen in months. "Chandra, Sagar is from the village near Uma Aunty's estate. Amma grew up nearby."

I nod politely, mirroring his gesture by placing my hands in a prayer position at my heart's center and saying, "Namaste."

"Little Moon sister, welcome here," he says in broken English, once again smiling warmly as if he's never seen a hard day. I smile back.

He seamlessly hoists not one, but two of our suitcases up on top of his head and walks to the back of the vehicle, showing off his impeccable balancing act before tossing both items into the trunk. He comes back around and opens the back doors for us, and we slide in. Sagar revs the engine and we're off. I stare out the window, as the vehicle dodges and weaves through the bustling city. The road's arteries are clogged with a chaotic mix of traffic, people, and animals, even at this late hour. Every other driver slams down on the horn, creating a discordant symphony, enough to drive anyone insane. It's all just noise. I'm never going to get used to anything in this country. The jeep painstakingly crawls to the outer city limits. The congested streets give way to a stretch of road lined by trees, small shacks, and empty fields before we enter peaceful darkness.

Just when I start to enjoy the ride, the terrain seems to change and the jeep rolls over bumpy, pothole littered roads, vigorously jostling us around the backseat like a pair of rag dolls riding one of those old-time, wooden rollercoasters.

This goes on for more than a few hours and I see the need for the heavy-duty vehicle. Leena had warned me that the journey was going to be a slow crawl. I do my best to not fall asleep. The fear of having a vision in the proximity of this stranger scares me to no end.

"Sagar, could we roll the windows up a touch?" Leena asks, politely from the back seat.

"Air not work well," he retorts, moving his head from side to side as if to say, 'Yes' but in actuality, he's saying 'No.' The dust from the dirt road wafts in. He rolls up the back windows but insists on keeping his window down. I creep a little closer to Leena in the backseat.

"I sorry. I fall to sleep if I don't have wind on my face," he adds. "Just a little time, please?"

"Of course," Leena says, kindly. "We are thankful you could come get us. I know it's a long journey."

He shoots a toothless smile into the rearview mirror. "You are kind, Ms. Leena. I see why Aarav likes you. My grandson says he wants to go to America and study computers one day. He doesn't have a computer, but he saw one in his college-prep school. But now I need him to help me with my work and at the farm because we are having no rain lately. It is tough because Lambadis have returned for the special hundred-year harvest festival."

"If he works hard, I know he will get there," Leena says with a funny little smile crossing her face. She catches me staring at her and her cheeks turn a shade darker.

"So *that's* who you've been texting?" I whisper.

"We're just friends. He's been traveling to the city for his school and back to the farm," she says in an abnormally squeaky tone and looks out the window.

But I rewind the conversation to the actual word that tweaked my interest. "Did you say Lambadi? What's a hundred-year harvest festival?" I ask, leaning forward so Sagar can hear me over the wind blowing through the car.

Leena gives me a perturbed glance and mouths, 'No!' but I can't resist. "Our Appa used to tell us stories about Lambadi when we were little."

"Your Appa? How he know? This is our local mystery, magic people," he says. "They are full of hocus pocus," he says, taking his hands off the steering wheel for a split second, weaving his hands in the air as if casting a spell.

"He was—," I begin to explain, but Leena whacks me in the arm for not heeding her earlier warning and makes 'shut up' eyes at me. I whack her back.

"Lambadi from all over come back to our village to celebrate the hundred-year harvest festival. It is a tradition of the villagers and Lambadi people," he says, apparently not noticing the silent sisterly fight occurring in the back seat.

He politely asks to put his music on, changing the direction of the conversation.

A mad electronic rhythm booms through the jeep's shoddy speakers and a woman with a piercing voice starts to croon dramatically before she is joined by a male vocalist. Sagar's hands are waving around above him. He flicks his wrists into the air and snaps his fingers as he throws a little shoulder shrug in double-time, clearly enjoying the beats.

"South films have good music. The music makes this whole country happy. You must see some of our films!" he says, excitedly.

I scoot to the far side of the back seat discreetly and cover my ears slumping so Sagar can't see me, and peer into the darkness outside.

Another two and a half hours have passed when I'm suddenly ripped from my daze. We jolt forward as Sagar slams on the breaks bringing the vehicle to a screeching halt. It's a wonder we didn't fly through the windshield. He puts his index finger to his lips. The only light on the narrow dirt road ahead of us comes from the faint glow of the jeep's headlights. The ground beneath rumbles.

"Āne, right there!" Sagar says with slight agitation, creeping into his otherwise calm demeanor.

"Āne?" I repeat from the backseat, squinting out of the dust-covered windows into the dark.

And there it is, standing on our path, a large, tusked elephant, trunk raised above his head as if he's about to swat and squash us like a couple of ants. His stance reminds me of the elegant elephant carved from sandalwood that sat prominently at Amma's meditation altar. It appears as though the elephant is about to trumpet and sound an alarm, instead it gracefully kneels its enormous body down in front of the vehicle.

"Bahahaha!" Sagar erupts in amused laughter. "Āne is elephant. We have reached the Āne Jungle. Uma Aunty lives up there," he says as he reaches into the glove box and pulls out a flashlight. He points the flashlight in the direction of a leafy overgrown path, winding up through the lush, rolling hillside.

My eyes grow wide when I look up the path—it is clearly impossible to pass by foot. Sagar is watching my face, and says, "Jeep can't go there. Prakasa take you!" He waves up to the elephant blocking the road.

I look at Leena confused. "What? Is he serious?" She nods. "How do we drive an elephant?" I ask, letting out a nervous laugh. "Have you done this?"

"I came from a different direction before, but it is closed because of a landslide," she says.

"Prakasa," Sagar gently calls out as he wanders to the seemingly gentle giant in front of him. The elephant's trunk reaches out as if it recognizes the tiny human and wraps him in what looks like a tender embrace. "New American friends, Prakasa," he says with a chuckle. "Now, you go. You in good company. I bring the luggage by cart later," he smiles.

We mount the elephant with some effort—Sagar gets out of the car and helps hoist us up—and we seat ourselves on a rough, wool blanket atop Prakasa's back. I climb on first, before Leena settles behind me, wrapping her arms around my waist. Sagar motions us to sit still and instructs me to hold the reigns loosely. This is nothing like the elephant rides they had at the circus when we were little kids. At the circus, we'd climb up a metal step ladder to load up on the elephant's back. There are no trainers here to help us, or railings or belts to secure us in place. We're entrusting everything to the giant beneath us. The enormous elephant rises to stand and the view around us is breathtaking—the earth looks vastly expansive from our new vantage point, on top of the world. Prakasa takes a thundering step forward as we enter the jungle.

"Pinch me," I whisper, unsure if I'm in the midst of another one of my fantastical visions.

"No, pinch me! I've never come up this way before." Leena says, smiling at me as Prakasa lumbers up the narrow path framed by bamboo and leafy greenery. We hold on to the reins as instructed by Sagar. There's no steering. Prakasa seems to know exactly where to go and maintains a steady pace. As the sun climbs up over the rolling hills of the Western Ghats, the landscape stretches to oblivion.

For the first time in what feels like forever, I feel this ridiculously long journey has been worth the while, and I remember Amma's direction to me. *"Go to the jungle."*

CHAPTER SEVEN

THE MISSING

When we reach an area of flat terrain, Prakasa gently lowers his giant body to allow us to dismount. Ahead of us is a quaint, cottage-like clay house with a peaked roof, reminding me of the facade of Dharma Yoga back home. A round, jovial, sari-clad woman stands at the entrance between the home's farm-style doors, waving with fervor.

"Welcome, welcome," she says with a smile so radiant and warm, my cold, cold heart may be melting. "I am Uma. Your mother was a dear friend, almost like a sister to me. We spoke often—much more lately because Akashleena has been here with me," she says to me.

She comes toward us and throws her arms around my sister and squeezes tightly. My sister reciprocates wholeheartedly.

"Akashleena, I have missed you. You look more and more like your sweet Amma each time I see you."

Uma Aunty's eyes peek out through gold, wire-framed glasses, her thick, silver hair pulled back into a tight, matronly bun. A simple string of fresh marigolds in her hair complements the sweet floral print running through her cotton sari, which is wrapped softly around her and pinned in place just over her right shoulder with a beautiful floral-shaped golden broach. She places the palms of her hands on either side of my cheeks and squeezes, "Chandraka, your Amma used to tell me what a beautiful dancer you are." I move away to hide the heat rising in my cheeks, feeling like a fraud. Amma would be disappointed in me if she knew I stopped dancing.

"Come, come, you will stay in the room with Akashleena," she says, gliding through a heavy wood threshold and across a reddish clay tiled floor. In the entranceway, we pass a wall of masks of varying sizes, all representing one thing—rakshasi. Their snarled frozen faces have ogling eyes, gaping mouths, and razor-sharp teeth. I gulp hard, despite them being nothing compared to the real thing. And I would know.

"It's to scare intruders, not you!" Uma Aunty giggles as she whisks us to a room in the back. "The room is simple and not much like you are probably used to in America, but this is the best I have," Uma Aunty says and smiles again.

My eyes wander around the room. There's a double bed with four narrow posts that are draped with a soft, white-net material, and a desk in the far corner. On the desk, meticulously organized, are a small collection of framed photos—one of Leena, Amma, and I, from last year's regional dance competition where I won first place. I'm glowing in a gold silk sari. The only time I'm not wearing black from head to toe is when I'm on stage performing. I loved that outfit, the choreography, and everything about that day.

Amma had called that performance, "Dance of the New Moon" and she'd been so proud of me. I wonder if Leena brought it with her the first time she came to stay here. Another photo is older, of Leena and I, sitting on the front porch drinking lemonade with our arms wrapped around each other. The last photo is black and white—a young woman with a single long braid down her back wearing a plain sari kneeling by a hut with a stethoscope on the heart of a small child. I gaze at it for a long time—I'd know Amma's face no matter how old the photograph.

"Where did you find that one?" I ask.

"Uma Aunty found it. Amma was the Āne Village doctor. She took care of the children at Uma Aunty's school," Leena says.

"Wow! The resemblance is incredible. You look so much like her," I say to Leena in awe. An ache fills my heart as I glide my fingers over the young version of the woman who had dedicated so much to us.

My eyes fixate on the white netting. "This is a mosquito net," Uma Aunty explains, following my gaze. I jump at her voice. For a second, I had forgotten she was in the room. "Here in the mountains, the mosquitos are rarely a problem anymore, especially now that we are in a drought and the water level of our once mighty river Kaveri is the lowest it has been on record. But it gives the room a bit of a fairytale touch."

She reaches out and caresses my face again. The warmth of her touch radiates through me. "Really, you look so much like your father, Ravi." My gaze falls to the ground, and I don't know how to respond to that. Other than sharing his strange talent of seeing rakshasi, nobody had ever said that to me before.

"My school is closed for an extended holiday, so it will be rather quiet around here," she says, a strange sadness coming over her. "Akashleena, I wanted to call and tell you, but so much has happened and you girls have already been dealing with so much. Some of the children have gone..." her voice trails off.

"Gone?" Leena gasps.

"Missing. It is an incredibly sad thing. And the crops are slowly dying because there has been almost no rain in the months since you left. This is an unfortunate time for you to be here."

"What do you mean, missing?" Leena says, with an audible tremor in her voice.

"*Moella*, here in these remote jungle villages, we have a lot of superstition and folklore. There are temple ruins, abandoned ancestral homes, and old battle forts from centuries before," she says in a hushed voice as if the jungle can hear the stories of the old schoolteacher. "The villagers have noticed activity at an old fort rumored to have once belonged to a lunatic queen who engaged in dark magic. It could be outsiders or treasure hunters. We get a fair bit of those too."

"Treasure hunters?" I ask, with a heavy dose of skepticism in my voice. Does Uma Aunty think we're children to believe stories about buried treasure?

"Oh yes, they're real. They come to the jungle searching for a mythical weapon called the Golden Trishula. It's said to be guarded by the warrior ghosts from the extinct Kodaguru Lambadi tribe. A weapon that Goddess Durga herself is said to have used to abolish the buffalo-headed rakshasa. And, most importantly, it's said to be solid gold. *That's* the main reason we get all these crazy treasure hunters looking for it," she says, looking solemn. "I'm not sure if it's treasure hunters this time, though. The villagers have been whispering about the rise of a powerful, wicked force."

I'm listening to Uma Aunty, but my mind is stuck on what she called the treasure—the Golden Trishula. The last time I practiced my folk dance, Amma had told me how I was supposed to be emulating a warrior who hunted a ferocious beast and killed it with the Golden Trishula. Is this some story that Amma and Uma Aunty grew up with in this jungle, or is it something more?

Leena's sharp voice brings me out of my musings. "That sounds unacceptable! Isn't anyone looking for the children?"

"We are a small region, not much in way of resources of authority. Families have been searching for their lost little ones, but they have received threats in the form of the Curse of Death," Uma Aunty says.

"That sounds like old, Lambadi black magic you told me about before I'd gone home," Leena says. I can't tell if Leena is merely curious or really believes in everything Uma Aunty is saying.

"Yes, it is. Dark magic that was supposed to be long gone," Uma Aunty replies, sadly. "The Curse of Death comes in the form of an old, weathered bottle that has a thin metal scroll inside. A sharp tool is used to etch an incantation upon the scroll, then the dark spellcaster puts their lips to the bottle rim and pushes their breath inside, filling the bottle with malicious thoughts and ill intentions," she says, wringing her hands together. "Opening the bottle releases the Curse of Death into the air and the person who opens it will die within days. Something wicked is upon us indeed."

"So, to protect the living, the families who have received these curse bottles have stopped searching for their children?" I ask, trying to make sure I understand.

Uma Aunty bobs her head up and down, "Yes."

Leena and I are speechless. Frankly, I'm shocked that there could be someone else teeming with more superstition and folklore than Amma. Uma Aunty sees the looks on our faces and laughs uneasily to break the tension.

"Now, come. We mustn't dwell on these sad things. I'm sorry, you've already been through so much. I will take you girls to the village this afternoon. Now, let me leave you, my niece from the UK will be joining us later. Please wash up and come for the meal, then you can rest for a time."

Leena and I venture to the far side of the house where a rustic, semi-outdoor shower stall stands among the bamboo, above us is a low-lying canopy of large, almond-shaped leaves, and above them swirls the vibrant morning sky. I walk into the stall and turn the faucet, but not one drop of water comes out.

"Here, take this bucket and scooper," Leena says, standing over a little clay oven with a large metal pot on top. "The water comes from the well down the hill that the housekeepers bring in those copper pots, and they heat the water here to make it useable. Take this to the stall." I take the warm bucket of water that sloshes around, dripping out on my toes, and set it in the stall. I watch as Leena expertly adds kindling to a clay oven to heat more bathwater.

"I didn't realize we'd be camping this summer," I say with a half-laugh. My sweat-drenched clothing sticks to my body like a second skin. Leena doesn't seem to be bothered by the shower situation and keeps her eyes low. "You'll get used to it fast. Makes you realize how lucky we are at home."

After not sleeping for more than twenty-four hours, my overtired mind blabbers. "Sorry, I've just never seen anything like this," I say sheepishly, realizing I'm acting like a brat. "Bucket bath it is!" I shut the stall door and drop my clothes in a pile. Careful to keep my necklace on, I stand among the towering bamboo shoots that serve as a wall. I use the small cup inside the bucket to pour water down my arms, and that's when I notice something peculiar. The colors are now much deeper and more vibrant than ever before, the images appear as if they are coming off my skin at me. I notice a pair of glowing tiger eyes staring intensely up from the inside of my left forearm, surrounded by greenery.

The scent of jasmine fills my nostrils, as a burning sensation rips through my hands. This sequence of events has now become the norm for me, having now experienced a constant stream of visions since finding the disc. Realizing that I may pass out in a matter of seconds, I back up against the stall and brace myself. I slink slowly downward, clutching the disc between my hands as the world around me becomes hazy. I begin to slip away into the far corners of my mind.

I'm standing in the corner of a candle-lit room with walls made of bamboo and clay, holding a clear, orb-shaped object. I'm a mini version of myself, maybe four or five years old. I rotate the orb in my tiny hands over and over. There's a brightness emanating from it as if it encompasses all the joy and goodness in the world. It's beautiful.

A draft that flows through an open window sends shivers up and down my spine. Water dribbles down the sides of my face, and I look down to see that I'm drenched from head to toe with the water pooling at my feet. My long skirt and shirt are soaked and heavy.

In the same room with dirt walls, there's a young woman pacing by an open window. She fidgets with the red glass bangles on her wrists, counting them to make sure they are all there. Then she flicks at the decorative tassels on her midriff blouse that clasps just under her heaving chest and bites nervously at her nails. She appears unsteady and pulls her fingertips through her hair several times before she starts braiding it. She stops fiddling, putting her hands in front of her face. They're shaking uncontrollably. She resumes pacing and murmuring until something outside takes her attention away. A gentle, steady swish and lull comes from somewhere outside the hut, telling me there's a body of water nearby. The woman becomes inexplicably frantic—whatever she's thinking about gets the best of her—her hands cover her mouth to stifle her fear from escaping. Her eyes dart towards me and the window. Her lips are moving, but her words are inaudible.

She runs to the door of the hut where there's a booming male voice coming from the other side. She turns and holds her index finger to her soft, full lips and says sweetly, "Shhhh, Moon Child. Stay here and stay quiet." She goes outside pulling the straw door firmly closed behind her. Outside, the voices begin to escalate. There are several other voices, but I can't hear what is being said. The tone and volume begin to scare me. I look back down at the orb and smile. It soothes me in those moments. Then, suddenly the woman is screaming, "Nooooo! You can't take her. She is mine!" She comes running back into the hut and slams the door and throws her body up against it. There's a fire in her eyes that wasn't there before. She's different, perhaps even dangerous. The colors swirl around her. They are beautiful gold, silver, and magenta. Then her light—the energy field around her, her selavu—abruptly becomes washed in grey and brown.

"No, no, no! They've ruined me," she cries looking down at herself. Her eyes turn to me, and I instinctively hug the orb against my chest as if it's a favorite toy I have no intention of sharing. I back away from the woman, lips quivering and trembling in fear unable to understand what's happening to her. The orb is changing too. There's a swirl of mist that overcomes the space within and it begins to darken. It becomes dark grey and dismal similar to the new shades of her selavu. I look down into the orb and begin to cry. The woman notices the darkness of the orb, too, and collapses to her knees and crawls toward me. "Give it back!" she spits out. Something is taking a hold of her from within. She clenches her teeth and falls to the floor where she tosses and turns in agony. The woman crawls closer to me and directs her anguished screams at my face. I shut my eyes, back away, and grip the orb tightly to my heart. I'm bawling, my entire tiny body is heaving with every drop that slips from my eyes. The woman's screams turn into booming howls that pound into my core. With one hand on the orb, the other hand flies up to my ears to stop the sound from hammering into my head. The sound echoes through my body, into my heart, and into my core. The horrific noise continues to pound.

I fall to the floor and the darkened orb rolls out of reach. The woman sees this and dives for the orb just as I raise my hands, palms out. The orb rolls back in my direction pulled by an invisible force. I crouch down quickly and lay my hands open on the ground to let the orb roll up into my palms. Holding it close, I lightly blow on it. In my hands, it shatters into a million little pieces. I yowl in pain as the shards pierce deep into my small hands and watch, astonished, as each piece of the orb dissolves into oblivion. The woman is coming at me, now completely wrapped in a cloak of inky, black fog. There's a powerful fury in her bloodshot eyes and she comes at me, her mouth wide open expecting to devour me whole.

CHAPTER EIGHT

THE JUNGLE SPEAKS

My eyes pop open. I'm back in the bath stall, gasping and shaking. A million thoughts whirl hysterically around my mind. That child *was* me—I am certain of it.

Was this a memory of a forgotten past?

Excruciating pain soars from my fingertips through my forearms and biceps. My hands feel as if they've been crushed from the inside out. I flex, and then gingerly open and close them attempting to rehabilitate myself and gain regular feeling back in my hands.

How can there be glass shards from the orb in my hands?

"Chandra! Chandra!" A voice in the distance rings ceaselessly in my ears when I wearily heave my eyes open. My bare rump is smacked on the stone floor, my back against the bamboo walls. As I gain focus, I see the debris of splintered bamboo shoots. My eyes move to the empty spot in the wall where the shower door once hung. Leena is hovering over my crumpled body carrying a bundle of folded towels. She drapes a rough orange towel over me and crouches down by my side. Her mouth hangs open as she stares at me horrified, eyes fixated on the images that cover my arms. She reaches out to them, but I flinch, not wanting to be touched.

"Don't! I'm fine," I mumble. "Just incredibly exhausted." The lie slips through my lips easily, as I have no intention of alarming my sister, but it may be too late because she grabs a second towel and applies pressure to the images on my arms. My head is pounding like never before and I flop it into her arms.

"Where did these come from?" She stares bewildered at my arms. "When did you get tattoos?"

I've had a response prepared for this question for months. I knew this question would come at some point. "I got it done a week or so after we had the memorial service for Amma," I say, hoping she'll accept it and move on.

"Learn to lie better, Chandra. Those look exactly like the tattoos of the Lambadi mystics." She points at the blooming crimson flowers on my arms. "Those flowers grow wild in *this* jungle. As if you've ever seen anything like it back home? And what is that around your neck? Amma's necklace? What is that circle thing hanging down?"

I shrug, covering up my bare chest that's been out on display. "Yeah, I found it with her things. Her good luck necklace."

Uma Aunty appears in the doorway, and I grab the other towels from Leena and swing them around my shoulders and body to avoid any more questions about the fortune teller's artwork on my arms.

"Oh, *moella*! Did you hit your head?" she asks with genuine motherly concern. "Come, you must need food and rest. You American girls are far too thin. Akashleena, lift her from there." Uma Aunty walks in, pushes her arms under my armpit and Leena mirrors her action. They hoist me to my feet and guide me back to our room.

"Seriously, I'm fine, Aunty," I say. "Really, I just get these headaches from time to time. I think you're right; I need to eat."

She looks worried, but nonetheless, nods her head. "I took the liberty of pulling a few of my niece's outfits. You should wear something for the festivities. Lambadi festivals are colorful, magical events, full of life and music! I will take you to the heart of Āne Village later,"

Uma Aunty says, motioning toward the bed with her outstretched hand where she has generously laid out several outfits. It's like our own private showroom with outfits of every color of the rainbow. Reds, oranges, yellows, blues, greens, purples, and pinks. "Let's eat! Dress up and come."

After the vision I had, I am in no mood to go to any festival, but how can I disappoint this poor lady? Perhaps it'll be a good distraction for us all. Leena calls dibs on the hot pink cotton *salwar* tunic top with intricate mirror work across the chest. The mirrors line up in a V-shaped pattern along a plunging neckline. Neat and simple. It suits her perfectly. She wiggles into the matching pantaloon bottoms and grabs a sheer pink *dupatta*, a long, sheer scarf, to drape over her shoulder. She looks like a delicious pink gumdrop.

My eyes immediately fall on a beautiful electric blue *lehenga choli*. The mid-riff blouse matches the fading, blue highlights of my wavy hair. I tug at them and think of Amma. Oh, how she hated them. But that thought makes me miss her more. My eyes move to the intricate pattern of gold thread on the lehenga that spirals into gorgeous flowers and stretches from my waistline down to the hem. The border of the hem is lined with marching elephants and concentric mandalas. The intricate gold thread continues along the cuffed short sleeves of my blouse. The back is completely cut out and comes with long strings that I tie together at the nape of my neck. At the end of each string are thick, bell-shaped tassels of gold thread. I grab the matching dupatta to cover my arms and hopefully distract from the tattooed images. I hardly recognize my reflection staring back at me from the mirror.

Not bad. I clean up okay!

While it's certainly a departure from my usual all-black wardrobe, motorcycle jacket, and big boots, I can't say I mind it at all. I can breathe and move, and I'm just delighted it fits. I realize that I have no dress shoes, and I refuse to wear flip-flops walking in a dusty jungle village, so I put my big, chunky boots back on under the floor-length lehenga. Since I've stopped dancing, my sore wounded feet slip into them much easier without the heavy aloe vera soaked bandages. I tuck the disc inside my blouse and strum my gold bangles.

I reach for my backpack and spill the contents onto the bed. My laptop, e-reader, a couple of extra t-shirts and tanks, and my trusted black kohl eyeliner. I take to my reflection and line my eyes. Still looking into the mirror, I realize I need a *bindi* to finish the look, but I don't have any, so I make up my own design. As I look at the spot between my dark brown, doe-shaped eyes, I skillfully use the kohl liner to draw a simple line and five tiny dots—one at the top where the line starts, and stagger two more dots on either side of the line. I put my hand down and glance at my reflection.

It'll work.

Leena works on unpacking her suitcase and placing items in the large, teak armoire. I wander out of the room and down the hall where I pass a larger door adjacent to our room on the left and a sitting area out to the right. Seconds later, I am hit with the warm smell of cumin and coriander. Uma Aunty has cooked something mouth-watering. I use the back of my hand to wipe at the drool escaping my mouth. I'm noticeably salivating and not even the slightest bit embarrassed. Despite the outpouring of love and casseroles from the entire town after Amma died, we haven't had a real meal in months—not that I've had an appetite for food.

I slide onto the bench at the dining table quietly and peer into the large stainless steel pots set out on the table. It's *idli sambar*—rice balls and lentil curry—Amma's favorite south Indian breakfast. I hover over the giant pot of sambar, giving myself a full steam facial, when Uma Aunty nudges me with a ladle, breaking me from my food daydream.

"Rani!" Uma Aunty says, excitedly. "The villagers will mistake you for a long-lost Indian queen." I hover nose-first over the massive pots of food in front of me, inhaling the aroma. "Maybe you just *look* like a queen! Your American table manners are questionable. I love that you've brought your appetite," she says, laughing. Her round belly jiggles under the sheer, featherlight sari, and her soft, brown eyes smile back at me. She hands me a starched-white cloth napkin embroidered with tiny, pink hydrangeas, and dutifully loads my plate with *dosa, potato masala,* and *idli sambar.*

"Chandraka, eat while hot. Don't be shy." She gestures with her hands, pinching her thumb, index, and middle finger together and moving it to her mouth.

A fleck of light catches the side of the large steel pot and I'm distracted like a cat chasing the red dot of a laser pointer. My hands start to burn and a strange sound hums in my ears. The distinct fragrance of jasmine fills my nostrils, and my head falls forward into my hands and onto the table. I desperately think "*not again*" before I slip away completely.

Darkness surrounds me—there's earth above and below as if I'm in an underground tunnel. Water is leaking steadily from above and child-like whispers coax me deeper into the passageway. As I walk, the whispers turn into cries full of dismay and longing. In the path ahead is a small girl in a torn lehenga that looks to be two sizes too large because the hem drags in the mud beneath her bare feet. She's wearing a t-shirt and her hair is in two braids that frame her face. Her eyes are wide saucers, begging me to come closer. She extends her arms out for me, longing to be held, but instead of moving toward me, she turns on her heel and charges in the opposite direction. I run after her, but I can't seem to catch up to her.

"Let me help you!" I stop running and call out to her.

She hunches her shoulders and tiptoes hesitantly two steps toward me. She stops and shakes her head and puts a finger to her mouth and whispers, "You woke her. She won't let me leave. My work here is not done."

The girl runs deeper into the tunnel, turning back to tell me. "Hide! She wants the Moonstone."

"Who?" I ask.

"The queen."

"What queen?"

"The rakshasi queen."

"How do I find her?"

"In the village circle." She turns and runs away.

Something yanks me violently by the back of my blouse and I'm sent hurling backward in the opposite direction through the air like a puppet on a string. Before I know it, the child has disappeared deep into the tunnel.

My hands turn into fists, and I wake hammering on Uma Aunty's wooden farm table. Leena is wrapped around me, shushing me in a low, sweet tone. My face is flat against her chest, and I can feel sharp points of the mirror-work patches on her salwar dig into my cheeks. Uma Aunty hands her a soaked washcloth, gesturing to place it on my head, then stands motionless, and continues to stare at me, horrified.

"She's okay, Uma Aunty. This happens. She gets awfully bad headaches," Leena says as she tries to brush off my strange episode.

I grab Leena's arm, pull her close and moan, "I have to find the little girl!"

"Who? What are you even talking about? I don't think you're going anywhere," she whispers, looking me straight in the eyes with a concerned frown.

"Head pains? No, no. Those are more than pains," Uma Aunty interrupts and nods at me. "Not too long ago, this was happening to my oldest niece. Monsters came in Nala's dreams. It drove her mad."

Well, that's comforting.

Turning to face Leena, my heart is still racing. "Some rakshasis are good, right?" I deliriously ask, fairly certain of the unfortunate answer.

"Amma used to say that, but I don't think she was right," Leena says, slowly. I know she's wary of indulging my new obsession with rakshasi. "People classify them as legendary creatures, sometimes demigods, but anything with fangs protruding from its mouth with claws capable of tearing human flesh apart is bad news in my book. You need some aspirin or something. Stay put!" She rushes from the kitchen back down the hall.

"They are mostly monsters," Uma Aunty interrupts pursing her lips together and shaking a finger at me. I didn't realize she had heard my question to Leena. "Mostly rakshasis or rakshasas are nuisances. Occasionally they helped the gods—but they exist to give balance to the light and dark of the universe." I look up at her, somewhat reassured by what I'm hearing because it makes me feel a lot less crazy.

As I'm about to launch into a full-detailed discussion about rakshasis we're interrupted by the rumble of rolling wheels along the clay path. Leena returns to the kitchen, and we lean out the dining room window to see Sagar staggering and breathless, as he pushes his large heavy wooden handcart. He emerges from a different path than the one we came on with Prakasa. Leena had told me that Sagar does all of Uma Aunty's grocery shopping for her in Virajpet, the nearest 'big' town. The cart is piled high with burlap rice bags and vegetables, and although he's huffing and puffing from the uphill climb, Sagar is still smiling. I'm beginning to think nothing can make this man frown. Leena runs out to greet him. I hustle along, right on her heels.

"Sagar, your feet! Where are the shoes I brought for you?" Leena rushes back to the front stoop to grab a tiny copper pot, presumably filled with rainwater. She bends down to help him clean his blistered, dust-caked bare feet.

"No, okay Sagar is," he says still smiling. "Aarav has the shoes. He needed them more."

"I've brought another pair for him," Leena mutters, half blushing. Confirmed. Leena has fallen head over heels for Sagar's grandson, Aarav the cow herder, who lives on the hillside.

I peek into the cart and spy a few suitcases, a few large stalks of plantains, coconuts, and several burlap bags. Then a movement in the corner of my eye makes me tear my gaze away from the ripe, succulent vegetables.

Rounding the bend of the expansive green courtyard is a slender, older teenage girl cloaked in an Indiana Jones-esq, desert-chic khaki ensemble. She looks like she's ready to hit the fashion runways of Milan, but also do some off-road adventuring. She pushes at the side of her black, cat-eye framed glasses that are sliding down her nose. Her hair is pulled back into a high, tight ponytail, making her angular face look more harsh and severe.

"My guest of honor!" Uma Aunty gushes as she waddles through the double doors and down the steps to the main gate. "Come, come, my Varsha." Uma Aunty doesn't waste a moment before she engulfs the woman in a hearty embrace. She squeezes tight, and Varsha's body automatically stiffens as if she's unfamiliar with a simple human touch. In her aunt's embrace, she bends backward unnaturally and looks as though she may break in half.

"Hello Aunty," she says flatly, with a hint of a British accent. She barely smiles as she gives Uma Aunty a quick peck on the forehead, before taking a step back to crouch down and touch Uma Aunty's feet three times, each time returning to touch her heart and then back again.

"Bless you, child. This is our custom—showing respect between the younger generations and the older ones," Uma Aunty narrates for our benefit. "Varsha is my adopted niece. Varsha, these are Akashleena and Chandraka," Uma Aunty says, brimming with sweetness. "Varsha is on her way to becoming a prolific historian in the United Kingdom. She is studying abroad at just seventeen years old in a special program for gifted students. A young success! I am immensely proud of you, *moella*."

Varsha folds her hands together, clearly to avoid human contact, and forces out, "Namaste."

"Aunty, one day I'll be a professor. I have a very long way to go yet!" She promptly reminds the older woman before quickly changing the subject. "You look well. I'm sorry to hear about the school and the children," she says, glancing around nervously as if searching for something she's lost. "It's been too long. You need to retire and come away from this place."

Uma Aunty scrunches her flat nose and stares past her niece. She blinks furiously, forcing herself to keep her sunny disposition. "We all miss your sister. I'm simply happy you're here at all. Now I have people to cook for."

I mouth "*Sister?*" at Leena but she just shrugs, apparently she is in the dark as I am.

Varsha snaps her head in our direction and inspects us from head to toe. "I suddenly feel underdressed, but glad *my* clothes fit each of you," she says without expression.

We shift uncomfortably, unclear if she's giving us a compliment or if she's being passive-aggressive that her aunt has handed over her fancy wardrobe.

"That one was my sister's... she never wore it," she says eyeing me from head to toe. "It fits you like a glove." Then, as if realizing that her social graces barometer is shot, she snaps out of her odd robotic inspection of us and says, "Sorry, it is fine. I don't have time in London for frills and thrills if you will. I've been studying ancient civilizations of this region, particularly—the Bommandava, the original settlers of this area, and the Lambadi, a nomadic people of magic and myth. The university where I'm doing my program will have a group excavating one of the old temple ruins. I'm trying to put my dear aunty's mind at ease. The missing children part is just some sort of coincidence and has nothing to do with my studies," she finishes sternly, trying to convince herself as much as the rest of us.

"Lambadi? Can you tell me about them?" I ask.

Varsha gives me the tiniest of smiles as she launches into a description of the Lambadi. I can tell she loves her work of studying people, probably even more than she enjoys actual people. "They have a rich history in this area. They're said to have a secret temple somewhere in these jungles. Centuries ago, they worshipped these five sacred gemstones, representing the five Lambadi clans. The stones remained in the temple until maybe a few thousand years ago, when the Lambadi became more nomadic and began traveling through the Middle East and up into eastern Europe, Romania, and beyond. Today, many of the core clans have begun to settle back in and around this area. It could have something to do with the hundred-year harvest festival—a sort of homecoming and reunion for them. They now keep the gemstones in each of their villages for worship."

"There's an evil in the jungle taking the gemstones from those villages, killing the crops, and draining our precious River Kaveri," Uma Aunty interrupts suddenly.

"Aunty, that's all legend," Varsha says dismissively, waving her hand. "Yes, the sacred gemstones are missing, but the land is not cursed—it's over-cultivation of crops and not giving the land a break. As for the great River Kaveri, well, she's been over-used and abused. The people are paying the price." Varsha turns back toward me and Leena. "The villagers, the Bommandava, worship Kaveri as well, and it's not flowing as it once did. These people are on the brink of losing everything."

Wow, she seems to have all the answers.

"These people?" Uma Aunty barks at her niece, uncharacteristically angry. "YOU are a part of these people. I may be a silly, old Bommandava villager who has never seen anything beyond those hills," she says pointing off into the horizon. "But this is my home, and this is your home too. You don't want to bring a curse upon you. What would your ancestors say?" Uma Aunty is glaring at Varsha with shame in her eyes.

"Aunty, I've been away for too long, forgive me. But my interest in studying the area comes from all of that and I will do it justice." Varsha's voice is calm, almost unemotional compared to Uma Aunty's.

"Varsha, you can't take things from here and put them in a museum and take that money—it's not right. I know that's what you're doing here," Uma Aunty says, a heavy sadness in her voice.

Varsha discharges daggers at Uma Aunty with her eyes. "I know what I'm doing and how to respect the sacred ruins. So, what if I take a little something with me? After all, this place took the one and only thing that meant something to me—my sister!" she says, looking utterly perturbed.

I shoot an uncomfortable glance at Leena, but she looks away, trying to avoid making eye contact with me.

Uma Aunty's crafty hospitality gene takes control. "You must be hungry, *moella*," she says, awkwardly, attempting to end the hostile conversation. "Indian food in the UK cannot compare to the authentic stuff right here. Come, come, wash your hands and eat," she returns to the cottage.

Varsha shakes her head in frustration but follows her aunt. As Leena and I bring up the rear, Sagar emerges, once again struggling to push his heavy wooden cart closer to the house.

"Ch-Chandraka," Sagar stutters. I turn to look at him. His trademark smile is gone, and his white, bushy eyebrows are in a furrowed V-shape as he hobbles toward me. "It's coming. The end! The end is here!" He stammers again, wide-eyed, and desperate.

I rush to his side. His words hit me hard because they were Appa's words back on that night he broke the kitchen windows—the night I first witnessed the rakshasi.

Sagar is still muttering, delivering a warning that I don't understand. A sudden breeze whips through the surrounding fruit trees and greenery, as reddish-black smog swarms around us. My mouth drops open but before I say a word, Sagar roars, "The end!" And falls with a sickening thud.

CHAPTER NINE

THE CURSE OF DEATH

My eyes follow the smog into the jungle, and then out of sight. Although it no longer hovers nearby, my nerves are shot. I shake my head and stare at Leena dumbfounded, trying not to bring attention to myself. We quickly drop to our knees and attempt to wake Sagar. He's breathing, thank the gods. He wakes suddenly, swatting wildly at the air above him, as if he can see something we can't.

He's got to be confused or delirious from the heat.

"Water. Do you need water?" Leena places her cupped hands to her face and makes fish lips in a poor attempt to slurp imaginary water from her hands with the hope he may understand.

He ignores her, as if he doesn't even hear her, and instead drags himself to the cart, propping against the large front wheel. His eyes dart from one end of Uma Aunty's property to the other, as if he fears being spied upon. I follow his quick glances up into the jungle canopy and down into the dense green vegetation and flowering blooms of every color growing up and over the concrete fencing of the estate.

"Has someone followed you?" I ask, craning my neck to figure out what he is looking at.

He puts a finger to his mouth and cups his ears to say, "Shhhh, the jungle listens."

Perspiration drips out of every pore of the poor man's body. My stomach turns in knots filling with worry. He needs to relax or he's going to give himself a heart attack. His ragged breathing and heaving chest, make it look as if his heart may launch skyward at any moment. The creases in his face, worn from years of work in the rice paddy fields, pool with sweat. He lifts the bottom of his sweat-stained shirt and wipes his face.

He accepts the copper water vessel Leena had brought him and takes a sip before he harshly grabs my arm and pulls me closer. He looks me in the eye and grunts, "Go from here!"

He releases his hold on me and cups his palms, pushing them to the sky as if I'm a bird he's setting free. He winces and his hands move to his head, his eyes shut tight, and his jaw tightens. Sagar yelps, and rolls to his back, writhing in pain. In the very next instant, he moves back to a sitting pose and uses one of the cart's giant wheels to hoist himself up, as if nothing happened.

He reaches onto his cart and grabs a dilapidated, rectangular cardboard box held shut with twine and shoves it into my hands. He pulls my other hand to meet it and secures my grip around the package as if his life depends on it.

"Something in the jungle wants you," he says, this time looking straight into my eyes. "Go from here," he insists, looking serious and shooing at me like I'm an annoyance—a mosquito buzzing in his ear. He is paranoid and afraid. I miss the sweet, old man we'd met less than twenty-four hours ago.

He takes the handles of the cart and pushes on toward the side of the house to unload the groceries for Uma Aunty when she appears from the house.

"Sagar, what's going on?" Uma Aunty asks with genuine concern, holding a small stainless-steel cup. "We saw you collapse. Please sit with us, take rest, have some chai." Varsha remains watching near the side door.

I pull Leena with me to the cover of a low-laying mango tree with branches that hang downward, heavy, and full of fruit, to shelter us from the hot sun while we eavesdrop. At first, all we can hear is gibberish as Sagar speaks in a hushed, anxious tone. He's returned to his native tongue, and he continues to scan the jungle, his eyes wild. Sagar releases his hold on the cart of food and supplies and clasps his hands together in a prayer position. The name *"Nala"* is the only word I understand as he begins to cry.

Varsha turns pale, and Uma Aunty steps forward, calmly. "Sagar, come have some food," she says as if this is her mantra. Feeding people is her business.

"I not come back!" He looks to Varsha, tears pooling in his eyes. "Children are missing, the river has little water, there's no crop in the fields." He pauses to wipe his tear-stained face. "You want treasure. The gemstones are gifts from this land, and they belong to the Lambadi people who believe in the magic. Don't take from here." He reaches to unload a crate of coconuts and plantains gently placing the rest of the items and Varsha's luggage on the side of the house.

"I'm not taking their gemstones, but I'm interested in the temple," Varsha says, a sadness creeping into her voice. "I'll leave soon."

"Take nothing from here." He turns away from her and silently unpacks the cart before cautiously hobbling away on wounded feet down the rudimentary path from which he came.

Back under the mango tree, my eyes fall on the mystery parcel in my hands. A thick packing twine wraps around the box, multiple times, making it impossible for me to untie it and peek inside. Leena watches when I attempt to pull at the twine with my bare hands, wanting it to dissolve into nothingness with my touch, but I quickly realize I need to reconsider my approach and hurry into the house. Leena follows close behind. I stride past the horrific wall of rakshasi and rakshasa masks through a sitting area with an exposed wood sofa and colorful embroidered square cushions. My stomach growls as I walk past the dining table with the spread of South Indian delights. I stop in a small, dark room with a stone sink across from a clay oven similar to the one near the shower stall. The oven looks like a large earthen pot turned upside down and plastered with clay. Just beneath it, Uma Aunty has set the kindling and coal to make the fire. At the surface of the oven is a gaping hole where the heat of the flames dance as they lick the bottom of a pot of curried stew sending it into a steady, bubbling boil. My stomach grumbles again as the decadent aroma of cumin, coriander, and rasam spices fill my nostrils, reminding me of my hunger. On the side of the red stone kitchen sink, sitting by itself in the drying rack, is a butcher's knife.

"Do you think Sagar is okay?" I ask Leena who is mere steps behind me. I know there's a particularly good chance that a rakshasi is involved, having seen the reddish-black smog hovering along the perimeter of the property. But I know she won't believe me.

"I don't know. Something really spooked him," Leena says watching me grab the butcher's knife and as I start to cut through the twine. "That's extreme," she says, turning and moving back into the dining room to fix herself a plate of food.

"I don't really see another option," I reply, looking around.

I slice through the rest of the twine quickly and dig through mounds of shredded Indian newspaper. A musty smell fills the air as I dig deep down into the box where I find a weathered, greenish-colored glass bottle with a long, elegant neck that weighs heavy in my hands. Curious, and with complete disregard for Uma Aunty's spooky stories about Lambadi black magic, I decide to find out what's inside. I pop the cork and clear liquid gushes up through the bottle's neck and spills out all over my hands. I yelp in pain and watch as red, angry blisters erupt all over my hands, burning them immediately. I lose my grip on the bottle and it rolls from my hands and shatters on the floor revealing a long, narrow, cylindrical metal object scroll. The strange, hammered metal is as thin as a sheet of paper.

Reddish-black smog swirls in the air around me, and I feel the unwelcome presence. The blackness begins to fill the room. Despite the pain, I drop to the floor and keep an eye on the strange smog as I reach for the metal scroll and unravel it.

A killer message in a bottle.

With a sinking feeling, I think back to the Lambadi curse-in-a-bottle Uma Aunty talked about earlier. Etched onto the metal are considerably basic drawings. I recognize the rudimentary images of the sun, moon, and stars as seen on my bangles and the disc.

The disc on the end of Amma's old necklace begins to vibrate with increasing gusto from beneath my blouse, just as it had done back home when I'd seen the rakshasi disappear with the fortune teller. I turn away from the entrance to avoid Leena's gaze.

I fish out the disc and hold it between my blistered hands as the vibration becomes stronger. I let it rest on my right hand and watch it slide around, exploring the movement, using my fingers to gently apply pressure to different points on the disc. I watch in wonderment as it moves around my hand. As I peer through the disc, I can see past my scars and home in on what appears to be scattered letters scrolled across my hands. I squint and notice dozens of strange uneven black lines, some squiggly, others dotted, some solid, and dozens of tiny arrows. That's when it strikes me.

This is a map. There's a map in the palms of my hands! Is this the map Surya, the fortune teller, was after?

Leena rushes back into the kitchen. Blood drains from her face when she sees me on the floor with the shattered glass and the strange metal sheet. "Is that what I think it is?" The dark smog envelopes Leena.

"Can you feel anything around you?" I ask, writhing in pain as I keep my eyes on my sister.

She shakes her head. "No. Nothing." Her eyes grow wide in shock at the disc moving by itself in my hands. The disc is shaking uncontrollably but stays within my hands. The dark smog darts upward, high above Leena, before it escapes through the open kitchen window. I wonder if the smog was intimidated by the disc. "Oh, my God—your bangles!" Leena points at my wrists.

I hold my wrists up to see my bangles pulsating around my forearms, exactly like the disc that continues to move in my hand. Each bangle connects to the neighboring one. We watch, not believing what we're seeing, as they come together, magically tightening and binding to each other. The gold shifts as if it's turned from solid to some sort of gelatin-liquid substance. The patterns of the sun, moon, and stars become smaller until there are hundreds covering the surface of the gold. The patterns sink deeper into the metal, becoming more and more pronounced. The gold surface becomes hot, burning my skin. They begin to harden until the bangles are no longer individual bands upon my wrists, but a set of glowing golden cuffs. I stare at them in awe, looking at them from every angle. They make me feel strong, maybe even powerful. My palms begin throbbing. The pain shoots down deep into my hands and up my arms into the core of my chest. I double over in excruciating pain and drop down to my knees.

"Chandra, your eyes...they're glowing," Leena kneels on the floor with me. The look of fear in her eyes says she wants to hold me but is terrified to put her hands on me. I put my palm up, signaling her to stay back.

Tears pour down my face and a sharp shooting pain in the center of my forehead overwhelms me. My throat constricts and I gasp for air. Fragrant jasmine fills the air and patches of white light emerge and then disappear before I'm pulled into the now familiar darkness.

I wade into a frigid river until I'm waist-deep, wanting to stop, but can't because I'm being compelled by something beyond my control. The golden cuffs on my wrists and disc hanging in the center of my chest shimmer under a moon-lit night. My body feels unnaturally heavy, like I'm wearing a suit of gold and carry the weight of a million tons. In my right hand, is a tightly clutched burlap pouch. It's sealed, its mysterious contents heavy in my hands. In my left hand is a collection of broad, green, almond-shaped leaves. I draw circles upon the water with the leaves and chant: "Rais, kāvēri dēvate. Rais, kāvēri dēvate. Rais, kāvēri dēvate..."

My chanting starts softly at first, becoming louder and more forceful as I repeat each word. The circles become more vigorous. Darkness descends upon the river and the water rushes around me with an irrepressible energy. My heart is pounding in my chest, building anticipation within me. I am steadfast—I feel strong, unafraid. At first, the pouch glows a brilliant blue, as if I've trapped the sky within. I throw the sealed pouch into the water and watch as it swirls around and sinks.

The sky above me, grey and cold, opens as if on command—as if I commanded it— releasing an astonishing amount of rain. As the unrelenting shower pours down, an icy chill sweeps over the earth and creeps into my veins. Havoc erupts around me as the earth shakes violently beneath—leaves and branches from the jungle canopy crash down, littering the river water and the jungle floor. The wind tosses tree limbs across one bank to the other, becoming so powerful at times it uproots several large trees. The trees crash, but the turmoil surrounding me doesn't break my concentration.

I struggle to see beyond my hands, in the blinding downpour, but I continue to chant, my voice strong and my words deliberate. "I call upon you, Goddess of the River, I call upon you to…" Before I can finish the incantation, I sense something in front of me and my words are lost to the chaos. I squint in hopes that the image will appear more clearly.

A faceless, ghostly figure rises before me in the middle of the river. As it floats toward me, all I see is unforgiving darkness. I stand, gripped with anticipation.

And then it speaks. "I have waited an eternity," a husky voice roars. "Now child, you will come with me." An icy hand slips around my throat and tightens its grip. My breathing becomes labored, and the world around me begins to disappear.

My eyes open wide. I want to scream and run—anything—but I can't. "Help!" I try to yell, but it's barely a whisper.

A hand slips into mine, and I realize there's no storm, no river, no ghosts. Leena is hovering above me, her eyes huge on her delicate face, telling me this episode was horrific to watch. She rolls me over to my side, props me forward in a seated position, and rubs my back, trying to soothe my tortured existence.

"What did you see?" Her voice is barely louder than my own. I look at her, searching her face. "You believe me now?"

"Yes. Chandra, oh my gosh, yes. Your eyes, they were white and glowing. I don't know what is going on...but I believe you. What did you *see*?" She asks again insistently, still gripping my hand tightly.

My head pounds, my throat is dry, and I can't swallow. I'm exhausted from these visions. "It had no face..." I tremble, my voice hoarse. "It was the end. I saw the end."

CHAPTER TEN

LEGEND

"I have to find the river," I whisper, releasing a throaty cough.

My fingers pluck at the round beads of the necklace and anxiously move until they hover just above my rapidly rising chest. I wrap my hand around the disc, which serves as the anchor that binds me to reality, soothing my nerves and calming my inner child. I close my eyes and rock myself back and forth.

"Chandra, come back to the present," Leena's voice breaks through my trance-like state. I focus on my sister's concerned face, soft and calming, pulling me back to the here and now. Her mouth is stiff, she doesn't smile. The cheer I am accustomed to seeing in her face is gone and is instead replaced with worry. I reach out for her and hold her hands on my face and squeeze. I want her to forget whatever she just saw.

"What does that mean—the end is coming?" Leena asks. "The bottle you broke, is it the Curse of Death? Maybe we need to take those off you?" She reaches for the cuffs on my wrists, but I pull away.

I look down at my hands, fully expecting to see the blisters from the acidic liquid that exploded when I popped the cork, but there is nothing. As if the combination of the cuffs and the disc protected me from the cursed bottle.

"No. I can't explain it, but these cuffs...they're protection. The liquid in the bottle burned me, but those wounds are gone now. And this disc helped, too!" As I think back to those moments, I recall a surge of instant power as I'd watched the bangles transform. On the other hand, maybe this insightful boost is the result of each new vision like the pieces of a puzzle coming together and moving me closer to the clarity I need to understand what's happening to me.

"How can I help you?" Tears slide down Leena's face. "I'm so sorry I didn't listen to you before, when we were at home after we'd lost Amma. I didn't want to believe in any of Amma's weird superstition stuff!" She pulls me in and holds me close.

"Leena, it means a lot, but this could be extremely dangerous." I bury my face into her neck. Deep down, I am thankful that she wants to help me, but I'm not sure I want to drag her into all of this. "I need to figure this out—magic bangles, missing kids, the Curse of Death, seeing rakshasi..."

"You mean we. I'll help you. You won't be alone anymore," Leena says.

I take a deep breath, followed by a second, and then a third. "I think we need to start at the village. Earlier I had a vision of a little girl. She told me I could find the rakshasi in the village circle." Leena nods slowly.

"You go back to the room and rest for a bit. I'll clean this up and see when Uma Aunty can take us to the village," she whispers. I nod in agreement, and she pulls me in once again, wrapping her arms around me tightly.

I gently extend an arm out and put my hands against either side of the narrow hallway as I amble back toward our room. Daylight spills into the hallway up ahead, shining through from the ornate doors of the room adjacent to ours.

Without thinking twice about where I am, I enter. Varsha's plain black suitcase that Sagar had unloaded from his cart sits on a small wooden stool along the wall in the corner. As I pass by, I see dozens of zipper-locked plastic bags with rolled clothes and labels on them. She must love to be in control. I bet she still wears the "Day-of-the-Week" underwear as I did in kindergarten. My eyes wander around the room where there are two full-sized beds, each with large posts and the mosquito nets draped gracefully from up high. On the far wall is a series of open, wooden shelves, stacked with boxes, trinkets, old picture frames, hundreds of National Geographic magazines, and a ton of books—encyclopedias and textbooks from the beginning of time that is now probably only found in libraries. This must've been Varsha's playground and how she'd nurtured her love of learning.

I drag my pointer finger along the never-ending line of books when a picture frame lying face down atop a large scrapbook catches my eye. I lift the wooden frame and wipe away the thick layer of dust to find two young girls staring back at me. The tall, lean girl with a thick, black braid that hangs down along her shoulder to one side has her arm wrapped protectively around the little one, who's wearing black-rimmed glasses and a high-on-her-head ponytail. This must be Varsha and her older sister, Nala—or as Uma Aunty had said earlier, "the one who dreamed of monsters." As I place the frame where I found it, my hands brush the thick, leather-bound cover of an album beneath it. Curiously, I pull it down and open it up to find a cluster of unfixed black and white images on weathered photo stock and yellowing pages written in cursive.

"The Tale of Three Sisters," a voice calls out from behind me, startling me, and I clumsily let the heavy book slip from my hands and watch as it falls to the floor. I whirl around to find Varsha on my heels, her eyes on the ground staring down at the mess I've made.

"I'm really sorry," I say, feeling my cheeks burn. "I didn't mean to go through your things."

"Aye, I do think it's rather intentional. You Americans tend to be a snoopy sort." She doesn't make eye contact and drops to her knees to reorganize the cluttered chaos. "Maybe you should mind your own business?"

"Listen, I'm sorry." The words fall out of my mouth like word vomit. I'm not one to admit to being wrong, but in this instance, I blatantly invaded her privacy. "Really, I think I'm just fascinated with all that stuff you were saying about your work and the Lambadi. See, it's my roots, too. My father was Lambadi, but I know nothing about it all."

"And you thought you'd learn through osmosis by coming into my personal space?" She retorts angrily, but she is quiet for a moment before her expression softens. "I get it. I am Lambadi, too, raised by Uma Aunty. She took my sister Nala and me in after our parents were killed in a landslide when we were younger. We had been coming to her school. I'm part of the *Vidvānsa* tribe of scholars and Nala was part of the *Mēkar* tribe of craftspeople, but she could fight like a Kodaguru warrior! She was fearless. That's why she thought she could go up against the rakshasi, but she was blind to the monster. It got in her head in a bad way," she says sadly, trembling as she speaks. It's obvious that the loss of Nala is still fresh in her mind. "She was my age when she died seven years ago."

"Wow, that's so young. I'm so sorry." I say quietly. A long pause fills the air, and the silence makes me uncomfortable. Finally, I ask, "What do you know about the Kodaguru tribe other than that they are extinct?"

"I'm afraid not a whole lot. I do know there is a temple with a chamber dedicated to the fallen warriors, but most knowledge about the Kodaguru tribe itself is shrouded in mystery. Likely because it had to be that way to protect their secrets of how they can vanquish evil."

I look to the ground, disappointed, wishing she had more that I could go on to understand what it means to be a Kodaguru warrior, especially if what the fortune teller said is true—that I'm the last of my kind. My eyes fall to the photo I've been holding in my hands.

"The Tale of Three Sisters—are these the three sisters?" I ask, holding up one of the black and white photos. In it, three little girls, with long, dark hair tied into two braids on either side of their round faces stand together, each one has an arm linked with the other, bright smiles on each of their sweet little faces. "They look so happy." Each one is wearing a black beaded necklace with a gemstone affixed to it, reminding me of the gemstones that hung from the apex of the fortune teller's tent.

"Yeah. They were Lambadi," she pulls the image gently from my hand. "One of the shopkeepers in the village had given me a forgotten box of books for a project I'd been working on, and I found the photo stuck under the flap. I asked around and the story seemed to grow and grow. These three sisters were supposed to grow up to be powerful Lambadi women. One was prophesied to be the most powerful high priestess, the *Unnath Purohitharu,* in all Lambadi history. Another a healer or *Vaidya*; and one a scholar, or *Vidvānsa*. But that wasn't in the stars for any of them. One of them died and the other two fell apart, or so the story goes."

I look back down at the photo, wondering how such a moment of happiness could go so wrong. "That's a depressing story," I mutter.

"What's even more depressing is the lore around their fallout. The older two sisters caught the younger one messing around with some dark Lambadi magic. The kind of magic that was forbidden centuries ago—," she says in a whisper.

"Do you mean like the Curse of Death?" I interrupt.

"Yes! How do you know about that?"

"Uma Aunty," I say, without mentioning that twenty minutes earlier I had broken one myself, hoping that my gold cuffs and the disc will continue to protect me from the curse.

But before I have a moment to ponder on that, Varsha is back to her history lesson. "Well, where was I? Right, the youngest girl was found doing some shady magic down by the river and the older two sisters ratted her out when they were in their late teens. A bloody shame, ya know, because the youngest, littlest thing was said to be the mightiest among 'em all. To have your own blood turn on you, I can't even begin to imagine, but that's what they did, they turned on their own flesh and blood and reported her to the Elder Council that governs the Lambadi tribes." Varsha's hands are moving at warp speed as she describes every bit in vibrant detail, no doubt embellishing heavily, and I'm going along for the ride, I just can't stop listening to the fascinating story.

"That's heart-wrenching," I say aloud, as my mind flutters to the countless hair-brained things I've done over the years and how Leena had always kept mum to Amma on everything. All that ammo she could've used against me but didn't. The thought of Leena ever turning on me or ratting me out would end me in the worst possible way. "I can't even imagine!"

"Oh, it gets worse!" Varsha launches right back in, clearly enjoying having an audience. "In Lambadi society, there were five tribes, each represented by one of five worshipped gemstones. The Elders from each tribe came together and exiled that poor babe. She was just a kid forced into the jungle to live on her own, relinquishing her Lambadi magic and sense of belonging. She was supposed to be this almighty powerhouse high priestess and, boom! Just like that, stripped of everything."

"Well, if I were her, I'd be waging the worst possible revenge on those who hurt me." I release a nervous laugh, not sure if Varsha is done or not.

"She's said to have turned one sister into a mighty tree, and she wages an eternal war with the other one and anyone who dare defends her," Varsha says. She lets out a deep exhale exhausted by her own storytelling. "I'm sorry, I get excited about this stuff."

"Wow! That's a wild story. I appreciate the crash course in Lambadi folktales!" I reply as she tucks the photo back into the album and places it up in its resting place on the shelf.

Varsha turns and notices that her shirt has come untucked. She quickly tucks the shirt back into her tight khaki pants. She flips her head forward to undo and readjusts her high, tight ponytail. A flash of excitement comes over her. "If you liked the stories, you'll love the real stuff. Let's take you to the heart of the action."

CHAPTER ELEVEN

BIZARRE BAZAAR

Leena and Varsha easily convince Uma Aunty that I'm fine enough to explore the village bazaar. She seems eager to get out of the house after the disagreement with Sagar and has it in her head that the Lambadi harvest festival is what she needs to get her mind off her missing students.

The rhythmic beating of drums rises from the expansive valley below Uma Aunty's mountain dwelling. Together, Uma Aunty, Varsha, Leena, and I, follow the dirt path flanked by rows of sprawling coffee plants, sweeping jungle grasses, and towering bamboo. We duck down under dozens of mango and orange trees ripe with fruit, and finally out toward a sprawling village of straw huts, clay buildings, and colorful canvas tents.

"Those are Lambadi tents," Uma Aunty announces, pointing toward the far outskirts of the village. "They worship the river, too. I hope they will sing to the river Kaveri and fill her basin with their magic and songs."

Varsha walks slowly as she guides Uma Aunty carefully down the path. She wraps her arm protectively over Uma Aunty's shoulder as if worried that her aunt may take a spill. "I think you will enjoy the festival!" Varsha says to me as her lips curl into a half-smile. "I haven't been to a Lambadi festival since I was a kid. I have such wonderful memories."

"As I mentioned earlier, the Lambadis are the original 'gypsies.' They migrated from north India into Europe, Romania, here in the south, and beyond. They come from the East to make money by harvesting the plantation crops—coffee, black pepper, and tea leaves. These are hot commodities in this region. Once the harvest is over, they move seaside, further West. The men work on the fishing boats, the women create beautiful handmade crafts. Like your necklace." Varsha's eyes fixate on Amma's necklace, dangling around my neck before she moves on.

"But they can be trouble with their ghost stories," she says wiggling her fingers as if she were casting a spell upon us. I swear I see a hint of a smile ripple across her lips again. I had been certain she'd turn out to be a stuffy professor-type, but I'm wrong. She's quite the engaging historian.

I glance over to Leena who seems to be strangely aloof, staring blankly down the path. I feel guilty that she had to see me in a fit, experiencing my vision, but I don't want her to worry. "You okay?" I mumble, and she nods, but I'm not fully convinced she's listening at all.

Varsha keeps the stories coming as we follow her and Uma Aunty down the hill.

"To be honest, the culture isn't completely lost. The five tribes I was telling you about have been returning to the region in large numbers, even building villages nearby. I want to find and preserve what is left of our ancestors. My sister Nala and I were born Lambadi, but we grew up outside the tribe. Uma Aunty has always had close ties with the Lambadi, and she took us in and raised us. Lambadi people live simple lives, using what Mother Nature provides. They heal everyday ailments with powerful potions and elixirs, commune with jungle beasts, and some can even predict the future."

Varsha is glowing and appears to be right in her element.

We make our way through the clusters of canvas tents and huts, becoming engulfed in a sea of people. As the drums play on, I sense a familiar pull toward the music. A sharp, penetrating melody of a wind instrument hums above the drums, reminding me of the folk music Amma played as she taught me the *Jipsi jānapada nritya*. I find myself drifting in the direction of the sound.

Leena turns and moves toward Uma Aunty, who appears noticeably damp with sweat under the late afternoon sun. "I'm going to take Chandra around and show her some of the nice places you've taken me. This will give you time with Varsha."

Leena threads her arm through mine and we meander through a mesmerizing crowd of humans, cows, and stray dogs, making our way toward one of the aisles of the outdoor market.

A man with soft, glassy eyes standing next to a woven straw basket whistles a tune through his wooden flute as three cobras rhythmically bob and wind their bodies up and out of their cozy nest. My mind flashes back to Surya the fortune teller and how she'd controlled the snakes with her flute just like this. Onlookers stand at a safe distance, nervous yet captivated by the scene before them. Leena shudders, grabs my arm, and directs me toward the next corner, where nearly a dozen little girls and boys, no more than seven or eight years old, dance, sing, and clap their hands next to a giant fruit stand. To the dismay of the vendor, they grab at the perfectly arranged oranges, mangos, guava, and plantains, and launch the fruit high into the sky and begin to juggle and perform backward flips and daring acrobatics. Their eager smiles stretch from ear to ear, knowing they've stunned the entire crowd with their energetic street performance. They continue to sing loudly as they toss the fruit from the cart back and forth.

Finally, the tall, bearded man from behind the fruit cart yells, "Little thieves! You must pay!" The children swiftly scatter in different directions into the mass of people who had stopped to watch. Clearly, they are well-versed in their act of conning the hopelessly entertained. As the fruit stand man runs off in a huff into the crowd after them, the audience members slowly realize that they've been outsmarted. A man checks his empty pocket where his wallet once was, while a woman reaches for her neck and screams that her necklace is missing. I guess they would have to take it up with the street kids if they could find them again. Although I know there is nothing in the pocket of my elaborate lehenga, I pat my legs reflexively, just in case.

We move further on down the cluttered street where a man sits cross-legged with his eyes shut in the middle of the dirt road beating a *dholak*—a barrel-shaped, two-headed drum—that lays across his legs, as a gorgeous woman dances around him. She's dressed in a sheer purple lehenga that moves with her, fluttering like a light curtain in a soft breeze. She shakes and undulates her hips in fluid motions, hypnotizing every passerby, moving about as if she's made of water. Around her waist is a coin belt that matches her backless midriff top, which chimes as she dances in a circle. She tiptoes to where the man playing the dholak sits, reaches behind him, and emerges with a long, wooden stick almost half her size. With the flick of the wrist, it fans out revealing nine more wooden arms. She continues to shake and shimmy as the man lights each wooden stick on fire and she begins twirling them like batons. The crowd inhales and exhales in awe. She twirls the fiery baton with ease, lighting up the night. Bystanders applaud.

As we pass a middle-aged woman selling bangles, she calls out to us, "Bangles, bangles for the *videshi* girl."

"Oh, please, let me." Leena turns to me pleading. "She showed me some stuff I loved last time. Promise—I'll just be a second."

But before I can say a word, Leena is sitting in front of her. The woman grabs Leena's wrists and pulls her into her, forcing magenta glass bangles over my sister's hand. Leena squirms in her grasp and lets out a wince because the bangles are a smidge small.

"Another size?" I ask gently.

The woman grunts with a frown and swats her hands into the air in my direction as if to tell me to "buzz off." She doesn't bother looking up, but I can tell she's annoyed that I'm saying anything at all. Then, as if something calls her to look up, she turns her attention to me, nostrils flaring, and I have a feeling she's going to give me the third degree. But the fight in her eyes dissipates into fear just as quickly. She looks up at me from head to toe and begins to tremble. Her eyes fixate on my golden cuffs for several moments.

"Lambadi?" She points at my wrists. "Those only for Lambadi Kodaguru warriors." Before I answer, she drops Leena's hands and grabs my arms above the cuffs, pulling me into her and hissing a phrase I don't understand. Her demeanor and body language suddenly changes. She's terrified and frantic. *"Nanna magalannu a dushtavasthuvinind thegedukollayithu—avalannu nanna haththir kke tanni,"* she cries, hysterically.

Leena's listening intently, attempting to translate. "Her daughter was taken...by that 'wicked thing.' She's telling *you* to bring her daughter back to her!"

My heart sinks causing a strong urge to throw up. I gulp down the nausea. "Sorry, I don't know how..." I say as I yank my hands away from her feeling helpless. I back away quickly, wanting the piercing sound of her wailing to go away. I don't know what else to do other than shake my head and walk away. I wonder if the tiny girl in the tattered t-shirt and lehenga I saw in my vision is the daughter she is longing to have back home.

Apparently, I'm being offensive, because she aggressively wraps her hand around my bicep and yanks me toward her. And then I see it there in her eyes—the desperation—she's not listening with her ears, but rather reacting with the broken heart of a mother who longs for her child. I lose my balance and fall into her, and I feel her grabbing at my necklace. "No!" I shout, shoving her away and jumping to my feet. I bend back over to pull at Leena to rise with me and we bolt.

We scoot down the next alley. And as I turn to figure out where we should run next, something reflective catches my eye. A small patch of glitter or shiny beads—no tiny mirrors! A woman crossing the street has a lehenga decorated with tiny mirrors, just like—

The fortune teller?

Without thinking, I drop Leena's arm and follow the woman from a safe distance, feeling compelled to do so, down a winding path between the outskirts of the bazaar and the Lambadi tents.

"Chandra, what on earth are you doing?" Leena asks, following on my heels.

"It's her—the fortune teller from home!" As I try to keep my eyes focused on her, the dust from the street stirs and wafts straight into my face. I stop to rub my eyes with the backs of my hands. A moment later, when I open them again, she's gone, quickly swallowed up by the tons of milling people and free-range livestock wandering the streets. I yank at my hair in frustration.

"I'm sure there are dozens of women around here with that same skirt," Leena offers. "Come, this way, let's go find some food."

We circle back toward the heart of the bazaar, steering clear of the bangle shop. The music draws us back toward the marketplace where there are fiery torches on posts blazing at every turn. The bazaar has become a maze filled with a menagerie of colors and aromas from all directions. It's still bustling with activity as villagers barter with shopkeepers for fruit, meat, home goods, and handmade crafts. We sidestep another dozen free-roaming sacred cows and street dogs hungrily rampaging around the dumpsters for something to eat. Overhead, a troupe of baboons swings across overhanging trees.

"This way," Leena grabs my hand, and we move through the crowd as one.

There are rows of villagers sitting cross-legged on the ground chattering with each other in tongues neither of us understands. The next aisle is full of fresh spice that stretches into oblivion. A spectacular scene of color with brown, gold, and red powders of every shade.

Then, we find ourselves in the middle of a horror show—Butcher's Row. Slabs of bloodied goat meat, mutton, and pork, hang from sharpened cleavers from the rafters, waiting to be stewed into some sort of curry. We hurry past a man with a sharp knife, raising his arm up high above his head and slamming it down upon the fresh meat. He portions out the order and drops a few chunks of meat in old newspaper and binds it with twine before handing it to the woman on the other side of the counter.

We take a sharp turn down the next aisle, panting in chorus, thirsty as can be, and stroll down a row of embroidered cotton textiles and silks. The stench of mothballs fills the air around us. Leena drops my arm and walks over to a cart where a young boy is selling coconuts. With three quick strokes of his machete, the boy slices the top of the coconut. As he hands Leena the first coconut, they begin to chat.

I stand slumped against a solid wooden post overwhelmed with the intense scent of jasmine and brace myself for the impact of another vision. But it doesn't come. I feel a warm hand on my shoulder, before a raspy voice whispers, "Moon Child, welcome home."

I turn ever so cautiously, not really wanting to see what I'm dealing with, but too struck by my own curiosity. Hunched before me is an old, toothless hag clutching the most exquisite walking stick—carved with elephants and lotus flowers—that towers several inches above her. This is *that* woman! The woman from Amma's yoga studio. The one who had sent Amma into a frenzy, the one who had said those strange things about the sun, moon, and the stars. I'm scared and confused, and my heart feels as if it's about to explode from my chest.

The woman appears more haggard and twice as old than what I remembered. Her grey hair is long, thinning, and unkempt. Her skin is deeply weathered from years under the hot Indian sun, her clothing ragged. Despite her shocking physical appearance, I find myself drawn to her. There's a light in her deep, dark eyes—the same smiling eyes I had seen briefly that day in the studio. The day everything changed.

I know you.

"Beautiful child, I'm happy you've come back to us," she says. An elated gummy smile rolls across her tiny face. "It's time for your truth. I see you have at least part of your armor now. The others need you. Soon, everyone will know, our warrior has returned." Her eyes shine brighter than before.

The drums begin to pound incessantly, and she turns away.

"Moon Child, I mustn't let the rakshasi find me," she says, a whimsical look upon her face. "Until we meet again." She hobbles no more than five steps away and pounds the earth three times with her walking stick and disappears in a blink.

The roar of rumbling motor blasts through the air, startling and ripping me from my deep thoughts on the old disappearing woman who knows me somehow. I cover my ears with my hands to block the annoying screeches of the intrusive vehicles and wait for Leena. I look over my shoulder and see her consumed with multitasking—balancing the coconuts in her arms as she looks at a table of handicrafts nearby.

The ground moves softly under my feet as the booming engines come closer. Moments later several teenagers riding dirt bikes zip through the narrow roads, nearly knocking me off my feet. The bikes with large black wheels, powder-coated, and red-rimmed, are painted in neon greens and oranges. A small emblem of what looks like an animal is painted on the bumpers. I squint hard, but I can't tell if it's a wolf or a tiger.

Annoyed villagers and shopkeepers shout explicit words as the teenagers zig-zag through the market, sending them scrambling to either side as they try to move to safety. One of the riders pops the bike on the back wheel, no doubt showing off to the rest of the group, causing the red clay dust to swirl in the air around him. The young boy at the coconut stand watches the rider in awe, then dizzily tumbles backward, landing flat on his back. Most of the riders don't seem to care they're making a scene as they corral their bikes near a tiny booth serving chai and other local delicacies. The buzz of the engines abruptly shut off and the therapeutic beat of the tribal drums returns.

I exhale deeply and continue to watch from a distance as the trick rider, who has quickly set his bike into park, races in the direction of the coconut boy.

"Ronan! Really sorry, kiddo!" The rider, who's about my age, sixteen or seventeen, speaks with a cockney British accent. He pushes his long, dark hair from his eyes with massive, gloved hands and kneels beside the boy. A reflective, oval-shaped, amber amulet resting against the trick rider's chest catches my attention. It's shimmering in the light, like a tiger's eye.

He pulls the child up off the ground and dusts him off. He takes a black bandana from the pocket of his cargo pants and wipes at the boy's clay-caked face. He checks the boy's arms and legs searching for scrapes and bruises. "You're a tough one, young warrior! Remember, I told you to stay away from the roadside when you hear the engines."

"I know, I just got excited!" Ronan beams like he's conversing with the superhero of his dreams. "I knew that buzzing sound meant you'd be here, Tarun!" The child throws his arms around the rider and squeezes hard. The young man wraps the boy in his arms.

"I've got that remote-control toy you asked for. I'll bring it tomorrow." He flashes a broad smile at the child.

The boy's smile crumbles, and a frown takes its place. He looks as if he may start to cry. "I don't care about that anymore. My sisters are missing. They're *gone*!" The boy cries. "You've got to find, them. That's why you're here, right?"

The young man's face grows serious. "Ay, I will surely do what I can," he says, taking the boy into his arms for one last embrace. "Now, it's getting dark, you should be going home soon." The boy nods in agreement, obediently.

The teenager rises, ruffles the boy's hair, and heads back to his friends feasting on pastries, plantain chips, and *jalebi* a sticky, pretzel-shaped sweet.

A frown crosses the face of the skinny man with a big, bushy, black beard standing behind the booth worried he may not be able to keep this unruly group of adolescents under control. They continue to talk loudly, laugh, and shove at each other.

Part of my dupatta drops to the ground and as I go to pick it up, my eyes are drawn to the big black, thick-soled boots like mine—they're not wearing the typical flip flops I've become accustomed to seeing here. I take another quick look. Some are wearing cargo pants, like the trick rider, and others are wearing jeans and t-shirts. They could be from anywhere. Are they the outsiders Uma Aunty was worried about? Or could they be part of the local student group helping Varsha at the temple site she is studying?

Leena comes up behind me and hip-checks me, handing me a green coconut shell that serves as my drinking cup. I sip the refreshing coconut milk through the straw, quenching my thirst. She pulls me in the opposite direction back toward the village circle.

"Where were you? You missed the excitement with the dirt bikes and all," I say as we walk along.

"Sorry, I'd bumped into one of the parents, a cobbler, whose child attends Uma Aunty's school," she says with a frown. "The son is fine, fortunately, but they were hoping I could come and visit. It might cheer him up."

"Well, if anyone could handle that, it would be you," I say, slurping the last of the coconut milk and discarding the shell in a bin nearby.

As we approach the village circle, now fully lit by the full moon of the harvest season above and the blazing torches around us, the bass drums beat in perfect unison with a strong, steady pulse. The music gradually crescendos and echoes deep within every organ and bone in my body, and I can't keep myself from following the sound.

A large group of people are dancing and moving together as one. We're engulfed by the crowd of villagers and Lambadi who have come for the hundred-year celebration. The colors are brilliant the sounds hypnotic. The Lambadi are easy to spot because of their beaded necklaces like mine with amulets affixed to the end. The varying colors of the amulets represent each of the tribes. Leena points them out—the amber tiger's eye gem is for the healers; the green jade for the scholars; sapphire for the makers; and ruby red for the mystics.

The Lambadi, young and old alike, are dancing to a folk tune, telling some sort of epic story with their bodies, swaying side to side and I'm captivated. The women sway gracefully with their arms held up above their heads, undulating in a snake-like motion. The men clap their hands, and their deep voices fill the air. I think they must be dancing for the river Kaveri as I read the lines of their movement and the joy in their bright eyes and smiling faces.

A group of teenagers passes by, rambunctiously shoving each other. One of them takes a misstep and stumbles onto me. My dupatta attaches to his jacket and rips as he and I move in opposite directions, and I'm sent crashing down into the earth.

"Jerk!" I grunt, wiping away the red clay from my face as a large hand reaches down to pull me back up. The hand is covered in red clay, just like my face. It belongs to the boy who crashed into me.

"Sorry! Miss, it's my fault," he says far too jovially for someone who just knocked an innocent girl to the ground. From my vantage point, he's at least ten feet tall and must spend a large part of his day engaged in heavy lifting because his arms are thick and his chest broad. I recognize the amber stone around his neck. He's the rider who was talking to the child in the marketplace earlier.

"Tarun! Tarun!" Voices holler loudly over the music. He turns his attention toward the voices but offers me his hand in resolution. Instead of taking it, I sit in the dirt staring stupidly into his large, open hand.

"I'm Tarun. I don't bite, promise," he says, sensing my hesitation. He wicks a bead of sweat dripping down his square jawline. I dismiss his hand and scramble to my feet on my own, trying to straighten out my lehenga in a lady-like fashion and hide my embarrassment. As I rise, the tiny string of black beads around his neck catches my eye. It's remarkably similar to the one I'm wearing. Unconsciously, I raise my hand to my neck, as my eyes follow his necklace down to the center of his muscular chest. There's an intricate etching of a tiger on the amber gemstone. It occurs to me that this must be the same design on the back of the dirt bikes. He looks from me to the medallion hanging in the middle of his chest.

"Grrrrrrr," he growls noticing my fixation on his medallion before he breaks into laughter. I look up into his face, and for a moment, our eyes lock. "It's tiger's eye—the gemstone, not an actual one," he says with a smirk.

"*Kill the watcher.*"

An intrusive voice echoes in my head. I look around, but I can't figure out where it came from. The thought echoes in my head. I shake my head and cover my ears with my hands like a small child afraid of the terrifying boom of fireworks.

I stop breathing for a split second, wondering where the eerie voice has gone. I snap out of it only to be distracted by Tarun's greyish-colored eyes that are glowing brightly against his dark brown complexion. It feels like I'm sinking into him, or his mind. He abruptly shakes my gaze, blinks fast, and looks past me.

"Tarun—c'mon, mate, you're up next," a male voice yells above the hum of the music. Leena whips her head around and her face lights up when she sees the owner of the voice.

"Aarav!" Leena calls, excitedly rushing toward the other young man, also wearing khaki cargo pants and hefty boots. She wraps her arms around him. He must've been one of the others on the dirt bikes. Around his neck is a scarf tucked down under his chin, but no Lambadi medallion.

"Hiya, Leena," he says with a big, bright grin. "I didn't get to see you today, my grandfather left without me. He wasn't well when he got to Uma Aunty's place. He said you and your sister helped him. Thanks for that."

Leena blushes and I swear her pupils just turned heart-shaped. She's hooked on this one. I elbow her arm and when she looks at me, I raise my eyebrows, suggestively. She's got a mad smile plastered across her face. Admittedly, lovesick looks good on her.

"This is my sister," Leena says, ignoring my dancing eyebrows as best she can.

Aarav puts his hands together and says in a sing-song voice, "Namaste! Welcome, little American sister!" I smile genuinely and return the gesture. "Now we've got an 'around the world' theme going on here. Tarun's a Brit so is old Professor Varsha here. Ashwin flew in from Singapore. And wild child Raya, well, I guess that one is from all over the place at this point. She's been traveling everywhere, but now she's finally come home," he bursts out laughing, unable to contain his excitement that all his friends are home. He continues, "Raya's probably been obsessively following Tarun around everywhere like a lovesick puppy, right, lover boy?" He jabs Tarun's midsection with his elbow, just like I did to Leena, but Tarun doesn't react or flinch. His abs are probably made of armor.

Aarav turns to me. "I've gotten to know Leena very well and she tells me how great the schools are in America. I hope to go there one day," he says, with a dreamy twinkle in his eyes. "Most of my friends have gone to the big cities or left the country! I can't wait for my turn. I'm going to make video games."

"He's a creative computer genius," Leena gushes. "He was offered a scholarship from MIT. He turned it down to take care of his grandfather." I guess it makes sense Leena and Aarav found each other. I'm sure they'll join forces and do perfect things together.

"Well, hacking things I'm not supposed to may not be the smartest use of my talents, but they get me a little extra cash for now," he says with a laugh that reaches his eyes and swipes his long bangs back from his face. I like this guy.

"Varsha came in with us, but I don't know where she is now," Leena says. "And where's Raya? You've told me about her, but I don't think I've met her yet?"

"Trouble with a capital T. Let's call her Tarun's old flame," Aarav laughs and dodges Tarun's incoming shove.

"Right. All ancient history, my friend. Raya's off in her own world these days. Something's up with that one," Tarun murmurs, pulling his long, dark hair back from his face, snapping the elastic from his wrist, and wrapping it up into a bun. He turns and looks directly at me. "So, does the little American sister have a name?" He asks, purposefully switching topics.

"Chandra. I'm Chandra," I answer, trying to act casual, but feeling strangely out of place. Nervous energy sets in and my cheeks flush with red heat. I'm unable to look him in the eye.

What is wrong with me? Stop flaking out!

"Aye, you're the dancing sister! Yeah, Leena's been bragging about you all the time. You're a champ, right?" Tarun asks, enthusiastically.

"T is our resident daredevil and playboy," one of the other guys in the group says, playfully punching him in the arm.

"How do you all know each other? Are you all Lambadi?" Leena asks.

"Some of us are Lambadi...and then some of us *pretend* to be Lambadi to hang with the cool kids," Tarun says, elbowing Aarav playfully. "This is our party if you will. This hundred-year harvest festival celebrates a cosmic moon that is believed to have a special sort of energy. That's what the ancestors believe anyway. It's just another excuse to feast, drink, and dance. We worship our Elders, our river, and sacrifice little American sisters," he says with a chuckle watching the shock of what he just said rise to my eyes. "Kidding, kid!"

"You're used to getting a reaction, aren't you?" I say flatly. I'm trying hard to ignore my thumping heart.

Tarun smiles at me and then looks down at my arms, which are now fully exposed since he ripped my dupatta.

"Nice artwork! I have a friend who creates similar tattoos," he says, trying to make small talk. "Did you get this done in the US?" He attempts to reach out and touch them, but I swiftly move back and hide my arms behind my back now that I can no longer hide behind the ripped dupatta. I'm sure this guy is used to every girl fawning over him, but not this one!

"Yeah, just a few months ago," I say, worried he's going to keep talking about them. I force out a big, long yawn.

"Oh, am I boring you with my questions?" He asks, and I feel a little embarrassed.

"You're not boring, I just haven't slept in like forty-eight hours," I say, following up with a genuine yawn.

"When did you last visit here? You seem familiar." He looks up to the sky trying to recall where he's seen me.

"Never. You must have me mistaken for someone else," I say, thinking suddenly about the vision of me as a child. "I grew up in the US, my parents were from somewhere here. They always hoped they'd bring us here, but they never had the chance." A slight cramp spurts under the surface of my hands. I turn them into two fists by my side. "What about you?"

"Oh, most of us were born here, a few raised abroad after we turned like ten or so.

We hold our Lambadi culture and this land close to our hearts. I've come home every six months—whenever I get a break from school. My boarding school is in London. I see Varsha often, she's like an older sister. My grandmother is still here. She's the Elder of our tribe. Think wise like a Jedi Master but beyond Yoda-wise."

I roll my eyes at him.

"Don't do that, you know your eyes will stay that way!" He lets out a genuine laugh. I shake my head at him. "Sorry, my grandmother says that to me all the time."

"Yeah, my Amma used to say that all the time, too," I say, trying to swallow the hard lump that seems to have lodged in my throat. "By the way, not every American is obsessed with Star Wars."

"Aye, at least you caught the reference. Really, I thought it was some sort of prerequisite. Aren't American children forced to watch Star Wars when they come out of the womb?" He chuckles and then looks at me. A softness settles in his eyes. "Hey, really, I'm sorry I barreled you over earlier. I'm not a bad guy."

"Said every bad guy, ever," I say, managing a smile.

"You've got to be a Scorpio—your zodiac sign? There's zero opportunity for forgiveness with you. Am I right?"

Zodiac signs? Really, who is this guy?

With his looks, accent, and horoscope knowledge, he'd be a big hit with the ladies and gents back home.

"Oh, I forgive. Just not so easily."

"Something tells me there's no truth to that," he says, turning his body toward Aarav, but his eyes linger on me, and my heartbeat quickens ever so slightly. He shakes his head. "You're a tough bird to read."

"Hey, T! You have to get going," Aarav shouts to Tarun, "hurry up, man. It's showtime."

"Bloody hell, I'm moving, Aarav," he laughs and saunters away from us toward the center of the village circle and the sound of the drums. I keep my eyes fixed on him as he walks away.

Tarun enters the village circle where the Lambadi dancers had been earlier. The musicians hammer down on the drums with greater intensity than before. Several other male dancers gather around him, posturing down in a low crouched position, some sliding on the floor. One by one, they pounce up and appear to "fight" him. The amber amulets around their necks tell me they must belong to the same Lambadi tribe as Tarun. As he moves, Tarun bends his lean, athletic body forward and lets his hands down.

They continue to move through the choreographed scene of dance fighting, which reminds me of Amma and the dances she used to teach me. The crowd watches in silence as Tarun plays his part of the 'tiger,' moving with the beat, spinning, and ducking as each "hunter" lunges toward him, attempting to be the first to slaughter the tiger. The drums fade out as a dramatic, high-pitched flute plays an eerily familiar melody above it all, and that's when I see *her*. There, in the crowd on the other side of the circle, a familiar twinkle of tiny mirrors catches the light. The fortune teller from the canvas tent at Fall Fest back home in Virginia is twisting and turning her body under the full moon as she pushes her breath through the wooden flute.

My eyes lock in on her. I know she had something to do with Amma's death and I'm going to find out at any cost.

CHAPTER TWELVE

POSSESSION

"**O**VER THERE!" I hiss, tugging at Leena's arm. "That's the fortune teller from back home! *She's* the one who *killed* Amma!" I point in the direction of the young woman rocking gently side to side with the other musicians. "She has something to do with the rakshasi!" But Leena doesn't seem to hear me. She's turned away, her face inches from Aarav's.

I continue to wave and point my arms toward the fortune teller until Aarav finally takes his eyes off Leena to notice. He looks in the direction of my outstretched arm.

"Her name is Surya? Right?" I shout so he can hear me over the loud music.

"Yes, how'd you know? We call her Raya. That's our troublemaker!" he says with a chuckle.

My jaw drops open. Just as I'm about to charge the woman and give her a piece of my mind, the music changes abruptly. Surya along with her high-pitched instrument dissolves into the background as a low, dark melody creeps in and replaces the earlier tune. Sudden stabbing pain in the left side of my head drives me to my knees. My head is instantly in my hands, and I slap my temple, trying to relieve the pressure to no avail. My nostrils once again fill with sweet jasmine, and my hands burn as if on fire. Leena stoops down next to me and rubs my back. But I knock her aside as an impulse from within takes control. I begin to hum a tune I know I've never heard before.

A piercing chill displaces the warm air, and an icy cold tremor creeps up my spine.

"Chandra, what's happening? Are you having a vision?" Leena grabs my arms to stop me from hitting my head. I shove my sister and rise, compelled by the music. I march straight for the dancers in the village circle. Leena is screaming for me to stop, but I disregard her and move farther and farther away. I'm aware of her screaming, but the sound fades away.

I glide, as if in a trance, toward the circle of dancers. I've got no control over my body.

Surya, or Raya, or whoever she is, is watching me, one hand wrapped around her flute, the other on the dagger at her waist. Our eyes meet, and she mouths the word, "STOP." I ignore the warning and enter the village circle from the opposite side.

Tarun and his friends continue to please the audience with their performance. They haven't noticed that I'm in the circle with them. He now holds up the dagger that he's claimed from the last warrior, who has now fallen at his feet. There's nobody left for him to fight.

Except me.

In a blink, I stand in front of him and snatch the dagger away.

How did I get here? How did I do that?

I'm a puppet under someone else's spell as the droning drums beat on. I clutch the ceremonial dagger against my chest as if it were my dearest possession and stomp my feet on the earth as I had done before in another folk dance Amma had taught me.

Ta ki ta ta ki. I stomp the pattern out as if I'd never stopped dancing. Tarun's eyes are on me, searching and trying to figure out why I'm behaving this way.

"Bloody hell, have you completely lost your mind?" He shouts at me over the music. "What are you doing?"

My eyes drift to the dagger, the raised etchings of the hilt dig into my scarred hands. I've never held anything like this before. A powerful surge of energy takes hold of me.

I hear it again. A low, raspy voice whispers relentlessly, "*Kill the Watcher.*" My eyes dart around to see who could possibly be speaking to me, but Tarun is the only one near me.

The voice is in my head.

"*Kill the Watcher,*" the voice commands. My lips tremble as I try to force out any words that can somehow warn Tarun, but I can't. My thoughts are clouded. I clutch the dagger tighter. Clearly, something otherworldly has taken a hold of me, and there's nothing I can do to stop it.

"What are you doing?" Tarun is furious that I'm making a mess out of the ceremonial dance fight. I shake my head violently, unable to respond as if my tongue has been cut out and my arms and legs belong to another. I can't stop myself.

Too many things happen at once. With a jolt, my arms fly up above my head, still clutching the knife. The disc hidden under my blouse begins to vibrate violently against my skin as if it wants to break free. My gold cuffs release themselves into the individual bangles they had been once before. They clatter loudly against each other, as I gulp hard and close my eyes.

What would Amma do? I ask myself. She would tell me to be convincing, to be the warrior. She would tell me to try harder. I can think for myself, again—a moment of clarity—as if I've pushed out the malicious voice commanding me to do unthinkable things. My bangles magically begin to weave themselves back together as they did when I first opened the Curse of Death. Something is trying to destroy me, but a greater force is trying to protect me. My mind flashes back to the mysterious old woman with the cane. She had looked at the cuffs and said that I had found my 'armor.' The enchanted cuffs *are* protecting me.

How do I stop this?

I take a deep breath and fill my lungs with all the air possible before dropping my mouth wide open and releasing a long, deafening howl that echoes up above the music, trying to drown whatever is compelling me.

Just when I think it's over, Tarun drops and rolls away from me before lunging to his knees and lifting himself up. He charges at me like a raging bull ready for the fight of his life.

No, no, no! Does he have a death wish?

He grabs my forearms, just above the cuffs, and I push back on him with everything in me. As I drive my body against him, the intrusive voice inside my head returns, louder than before and repeating the same phrase: "*Kill the Watcher.*"

Tarun is struggling. He can't keep his balance or keep me at bay. This is a grown young man and yet I can tell I'm stronger, more powerful than him. I thrust my elbow into the middle of his body and leverage him off his feet. He crashes to the ground, and I pounce on top of him, pinning him beneath me.

The voice within rages on.

"Kill the Watcher! Kill the Watcher! Kill the Watcher!"

Then I see it—the inky black, mist. The rakshasi must be near, compelling me to do its bidding.

No! I won't let you win!

I shut my eyes and the cuffs pinch and tighten around my wrists, encouraging me to take drastic measures. I take in another long breath and release a second, horrifying wail. The dagger, still clasped firmly in my hands, plummets into the earth just inches from Tarun's throat. Somehow, I manage to thwart his assassination by my hands.

The music stops abruptly and a hush sweeps over the crowd. I'm not sure if they think this is all part of the performance or if they are horrified by my bizarre behavior. Tarun lays frozen beneath me and gulps hard as his eyes focused on the blade of the dagger mere inches from his flesh.

A radiant warmth floods the air, displacing the cold. The gentle ring of bells breaks through the darkness.

A beautiful woman dressed in an ivory-colored lehenga embellished with gold thread and jewels enters the Village Circle atop a white stallion. The giant horse has a long white and turquoise tail of peacock feathers instead of a regular horse's mane. The woman's long, loose flowing black hair is adorned with white lilies. Gold chains are threaded through her hair and on her forehead is a jeweled *tikka*, a large, oblong, gold trinket embellished with rubies, emeralds, and sapphires. She looks like a queen...or maybe a goddess, but I see that she, too, has a green Lambadi medallion signifying that she is of the scholarly tribe. I hear murmurs from the crowd as each villager and Lambadi alike bows and whispers her name. "Elder Shalini." She must be part of the Elder council.

Then they chant, "Shalini, our peacekeeper, our high priestess!"

Shalini is flanked by a dozen women and men who wear plain, white tunics, and scant gold bling.

"To the mighty river we give thanks for the life she gives us at her fertile banks," Shalini says, raising her hands theatrically toward the sky. As she moves, she's accompanied by a choir of light, cheerful bells. Her voice, her movement, and her very presence lift the crowd's mood, and a calmness settles in.

Shalini's face is peaceful. She drifts over to me and doesn't appear to be threatened by my possessed psycho-killer, knife-wielding dance. "Rise, child. Free the boy," she says, barely making eye contact with me. I'm scared and wait for the low, raspy voice to command me to "*Kill the Watcher*," but it's no longer there. I close my eyes tight and wait a few seconds, before realizing that the only voice that remains in my head is my own.

I rise, shaking a bit as I release Tarun pinned beneath me. Shalini bows and lightly slips her hand into mine. She gently sweeps at the cuffs on my wrists, studying them as she removes the dagger from my grip. The bold shimmer of the cuffs reflects in her eyes.

"The Elders said you'd come," she whispers, standing just inches from me. I bow my head, not sure if she's royalty or heavenly.

Shalini sways elegantly as she hooks the dagger she took from me to one of the hundreds of gold chains around her waist. Now with her hands free, she moves her arms in front of her in figure eights. The delicate bells sounding from her anklets prompt several others from her peaceful entourage to join her. They form a circle around her. Through their collective spins and pirouettes, they gently push me out of the circle and toward the onlookers without laying a hand on me.

"Lunatic," a deep, voice growls behind me. I turn and smash right into Tarun's broad, heaving chest, straight into his tiger's eye medallion. He glares down at me through a curtain of dark brown hair that's come undone from the band.

"That wasn't me," I mumble as I back away from him, not really knowing how to apologize to someone I just tried to kill because I was possessed. Then it occurs to me that the rakshasi can compel and get inside the head and control others.

Is that what just happened to me?

"Something else took control of me," I blurt.

But he steps in front of me, challenging me, his eyes fixated on my necklace. "You said you're not from here?" He sneers. "Liar! What tribe are you? Show me!" he demands.

"Show you what?" I'm confused by his demand.

"Show me your gemstone!" He snarls as he reaches for my throat.

Reflexively, my hand comes up to push his away. But as our hands come together, there's a sudden surge of energy between us. I have a sneaking suspicion that no scientists would be able to understand or explain this form of energy. All I know is that I can feel energy pouring out of Tarun and into me. His eyes widen in the same instant, confirming he felt it too. Before he can say a word, I quickly release my hand from his grasp and shove my other hand into my blouse and free the medallion. I hold up the disc, ensuring the necklace is still anchored to me. He examines the carvings of the stars, sun, and moon, delicately brushing his thumb on the disc several times like he's come upon some long, lost treasure.

"Where did you get this?" His voice booms with anger. For a second, I'm speechless, and then angry with him for shouting in my face. Who does he think he is?

"I found it!" I yell back. "It belonged to my father."

"That is a Kodaguru medallion!" He bellows even louder. "That tribe doesn't exist anymore!"

"Well, obviously they exist if I have one!" I snap, his thundering anger reaching down into my chest. "Are you the *Watcher*?"

A strange look comes across his face as he threateningly lunges toward me. My arms fly up to shield myself from his attack, when a familiar tattooed arm wrapped with dozens of silver bangles comes between us, forcing him back.

"Tarun! Stop!" A woman stands between us. "I can't have you rip this poor, frail thing apart. Unfortunately, we need her."

"Raya, when did you get home?" Tarun asks with a furrowed brow.

I shove Raya's hands away from me. "Don't you touch me. I know *what* you are. I know the truth about you!" My hands turn to fists, and I let them fly, but instead of hitting her, I find myself smashing what feels like a brick wall. I let out a squeal as my wimpy left hook falls flat. I drop my wounded hands to my sides and shake them out to get the feeling back as I look up at Tarun, who is now standing between Raya and me.

A fierce gust of wind sweeps through the village circle shaking the tiny huts, blowing through the tents, and extinguishing most of the torches. The crowd becomes silent as a hooded figure draped in a heavy, gray cloak appears out of thin air and now stands before the crowd.

The air around me fills with jasmine, my palms begin to throb, and a sharp shooting pain pings through my head. But this time instead of a vision, there's something else.

A strange, black, inky mist snakes out of where the figure's heart should be, shoots up into the air, and then falls back down, cloaking its silhouette. The black energy whirls around the figure at warp speed, like a tornado.

I gasp.

I look to Raya who is standing squarely by my side. The black energy was never hers. It belongs to the thing hovering in front of us.

My eyes follow the strange mist and when it settles, I know it's not human. It's a monster like no other. This is the rakshasi.

Chapter Thirteen

Wrath

Nobody screams or moves—they just stare at the human figure in front of them. But I can see it for what it really is.

Long, bony fingers with claw-like nails rise to meet its head and push the drapey hood back. At first, it reveals several flaming red-orange horns protruding in a crown-like fashion from its skull. Dark, hollow eyes search the crowd as saliva drips from its large gaping mouth full of sharp, gnarly teeth. It turns to the side to survey the crowd and its scorpion tail beats the earth beneath it, sending a tremor that apparently only I can feel, judging from the frozen looks on everyone else's faces.

And, still, nobody moves.

Only I see it. My entire body trembles. The disc at my chest vibrates and the gold cuffs pulsate tightly around my wrists.

The rakshasi shakes its head and body in a frenzied manner at hyper speed as if seizing, purposefully. When it stops, the rakshasi exposes ten more cloned heads with horns and giant arms. Grey, leathery flesh hangs from its bones as it begins to stomp upon the earth.

"Get a grip! You're shaking." Raya glares at me like she wishes I would disappear. Then her eyes grow wide, and she pulls Tarun toward us and they each flank me, steadying my stance, holding me up in place. They shoot stunned glances at each other and Tarun waves at Leena and Aarav, motioning them to come closer.

"Can't you all see it? Right there in plain sight—the glowing horned head, hollow eyes, those teeth, all those heads? It's a rakshasi!" I whimper. But they all continue to stare blankly ahead, unalarmed.

"She's not that repulsive. She's just a woman in tattered clothes," Aarav whispers.

"We have to get these people out of here!" I say, the urgency growing in my voice.

A hush comes over the crowd as if on command. Onlookers are frozen in place, and I wonder if they're compelled as I was earlier when I tried to stab Tarun.

The rakshasi spins counterclockwise, creating a swirl of dust. When the dust settles, a woman appears. She's striking, maybe even more beautiful than Shalini but full of rage. I can see it in her dark and vengeful eyes. The long grey cloak is embellished with black metallic thread in a pattern of hundreds of scorpions. Beneath the cloak, she wears a floor-length lehenga. Her arms are adorned with tattoos of black scorpions of all shapes and sizes.

A thick, dense fog sets in, and I can vaguely make out the outline of something at her feet. My hands cover my mouth as I realize that the "something" is in fact, several *someones*. The contents of my stomach begin to lurch up into my throat. A dozen Lambadi dancers have fallen before this mysterious figure, their blood pooling at her feet.

The black dagger she clutches in a vice-grip drips blood. She looks down to witness her handiwork and then lifts her head to look at the crowd with a devilish smirk across her face. Her eyes narrow when they find Shalini.

There's no scorpion tail, no horned crown, and no leathery skin. But I know she is the rakshasi. A black mist clings to her silhouette.

"Dakini, you are not welcome here," Shalini says in a calm, steady tone like she's dealing with a small child preparing to throw a tantrum.

"You know why I'm here, sister dearest. One reason and one reason only," Dakini says in a low, raspy voice as she approaches Shalini. I quickly recognize it from my visions and as the voice that was compelling me to attack Tarun. Dakini slinks toward Shalini unafraid and with unexpected grace. With each movement, a dull, hollow knocking sound comes from the belt of skulls and bones around her waist.

"She's not here. You will never find her. Return the children you have taken," Shalini says, head high, eyes hard and fixated on the woman in front of her.

"Wrong, dear sister," Dakini tosses her head back and releases a deep, throaty cackle. "After all this time, I have found her once again," Dakini says with a sneer. "She's brought me the map. Now I just need to take what's rightfully mine." She turns to scan the crowd.

Her eyes settle on me, and her human form fades away and she's once again, at least to me, the rakshasi.

As the whirling of the disc sitting against my chest gets stronger and the gold cuffs cling tightly to me, I stop trembling and take a brave step forward. A wave of confidence rushes through me and I announce, "No, it's mine!"

"Don't be stupid—she's egging you on!" Raya shouts, grabbing my arm and pulling me back in the opposite direction. Tarun grabs my other arm and grips it tightly as if he doesn't plan to let me go anytime soon.

"We're not ready to sacrifice you just yet," he murmurs, and I can't tell if sarcastic humor is how he deals with stress or if, ultimately, that's the plan.

Dakini claps her hands twice in quick succession summoning a strange human-like creature that staggers toward the center of the circle, pulls a recorder from a tattered belt, and blows through it, sending an unnerving, high-pitched melody into the air. She stomps her bare feet on the clay beneath her, digging her heel into the ground with a quick twisting motion with each effort. The two dozen rows of black bells around her ankles ring out an eerie, discordant noise. Her stomping becomes louder and louder, and she appears to be growing in height with each thundering step, leaving a deep imprint on the earth. She raises her hands above her head and moves her wrists round and round in a circular motion as she orchestrates the symphony of turbulent clouds gathering above. Seconds later, the dozens of slaughtered Lambadi dancers rise from where they lay dead, but they've changed. They appear to be ashen and zombified exactly like the odd human-like creature playing the recorder at Dakini's command. Their once-vibrant festival attire is drained of color and they appear as a swarm of grey, each one wearing chains of skull and bone. Despite the way they lumber forward on stiff, petrified legs, arms out, reaching for the living, they move surprisingly fast. The more they move, the more their limbs loosen, and they're able to pick up speed. They join Dakini, stomping in unison until the ground is shaking uncontrollably.

This time everyone feels the earth tremble.

"Śavagala—it's the undead!" Raya says over my head to Tarun, confirming they see the zombies, but not the rakshasi.

"Take your hands off me! We need to get all these people out of here," I yell at them again.

"Fine! Get the others to go to the jungle," Raya shouts at Tarun and Aarav. Aarav grabs Leena's hand and as they dart toward the jungle, they attempt to point others in the same direction, too.

But it's too late. Chaos erupts in the marketplace as the villagers and Lambadi scatter in different directions. The clay huts crack and crumble around us and the canvas tents blow apart. People and animals are being thrown through the air and we duck and dodge, stopping to help where we can. All I can think about are Uma Aunty and Varsha. I haven't seen them for hours. I need to find them, too.

I notice Leena is alone, with Aarav nowhere in sight, as two of the undead creatures have her cornered. The usual pink of my sister's cheeks is drained of color, and she stands frozen in horror. I muster the courage I have left and shove one of the creatures and kick the other away.

"Move!" I scream at her, but it's like her soul has left her body. More of Dakini's undead hoard are fast approaching.

Aarav appears from around the corner, chucking anything he can get his hands on to ward off the creatures and protect my sister. "Leena! Come on, move!" he urges, but she still does not respond.

"Keep going," Raya yells as she pushes through the crowd with several others.

I turn around and my heart fills with a moment of relief when I see Varsha and Uma Aunty headed our way. But it's quickly replaced with panic. Varsha is struggling to herd Uma Aunty in the right direction, and they are moving at a pathetically slow pace.

"Chandra, that way," Tarun says, pointing toward the jungle as he bends down and throws Leena over his shoulders as if she weighs nothing. I stop and turn swiftly, running back toward Varsha.

"Varsha! Uma Aunty! Here!" I yell for them, frantically waving my arms back and forth instructing them to follow us. Varsha moves behind Uma Aunty and steers her our way. But aunty can't keep up. She can't move as fast as her young niece. One of the zombified Lambadi dancers jumps onto her, clawing at her violently.

The śavagala hooks onto Uma Aunty's sari with its clawed hands and begins to pull her toward it. Varsha loses her grip on her aunt. I run to Varsha's side and together we reach for Uma Aunty and hug her tight, but the zombie continues to rip at her. The creature yanks Uma Aunty with a mighty force in the opposite direction, unraveling six yards of material anchored to her petticoat. I try to release the sari from her petticoat, but I can't hang on to Uma Aunty. She shuts her eyes and screams in terror.

Dakini creates a powerful earthquake, causing pandemonium at every turn. The earth beneath our feet breaks apart, crumbling into pieces. We wage a game of tug-of-war for Uma Aunty. Varsha and I against the creature that is hungrily gnashing its razor-sharp teeth at her head. Uma Aunty manages to turn and shove Varsha who loses her balance and is sent hurtling backward onto more stable ground. But I'm still hanging on to Uma Aunty.

"Chandra, take care of my Varsha," Uma Aunty says, as a calmness abruptly washes over her. She looks me in the eye and unclasps my hold on her with her free hand. "Run!" She flies backward into the creature as it closes its giant arms around her. The earth continues to collapse beneath them, and we watch helplessly as they disappear into the dark abyss below.

"No!" Varsha shrieks, her sad sickening whimper resonating painfully inside me. "No!" Varsha staggers to the edge of the rubble, drops to her knees, and screams hysterically for her aunt. Her cries are piercing. It breaks my heart into a million pieces, and I feel sick inside. I want to cry but the tears do not come. A chill fills my core and my skin tingles as goosebumps raise on my arms. I tune out the screaming to disconnect from the horrific scene. The disc vibrating on my neck serves as a reminder that I must keep moving. I attempt to shelf my emotions and wrap my arms around Varsha, squeezing her tightly, understanding her sorrow. The sadness is unbearable. I hold on and force us both to our feet. Grabbing her arm, I pull her in the direction of the others.

But Varsha is making it difficult. The more I pull her toward the jungle, the more she fights me.

"I can't leave her," Varsha cries. Her chest is heaving as she sobs, and I'm worried she'll have no energy to move forward.

"Those *things* are gonna find us!" I yell, pointing back to the village overrun by the undead with one hand, as I clutch her wrist tightly with the other. "We have to move," I bark.

Another thundering boom from Dakini's feet sets the ground beneath us into a frenzy. Varsha nods, sobbing, and we start toward the jungle together. Foliage, trees, and other debris pound down around us, as we run towards the tree line. The earth continues to shake and the wind whips wildly. Soon, we are deep into the brush.

Up ahead, Tarun, Aarav, and Leena, who is now finally on her feet, along with about fifty or more villagers escaping the death and destruction have stopped in front of an area of dry, cracked red clay where dozens of large leafless petrified trees stand. Their jagged branches reach skyward for a reprieve from their sordid existence. A strange array of thick, thorny branches grows around the base of the mighty tree trunks.

"What on earth?" The words escape from my lips. A sudden sadness overwhelms me when I look at the petrified trees. They resemble the human form, as if hundreds of people had dropped to their knees, clasped their hands together in prayer, and begged for mercy.

"*Duhkhagala kanive*—this is the Valley of Sorrows," Varsha whispers. "This is where the evil one, Dusta, slaughtered hundreds of innocent villagers long ago. This is where Nala confronted that monster before it drove her insane." She vigorously points in the direction of Dakini.

"The fastest way is through it," Raya says. "We've got to be very careful."

"It's enchanted," Varsha says, wiping off her tears. "We can only hang onto the tough woody branches and thick vines. At all costs, avoid the thorns at the base. Don't fall because it's said that the earth is poisonous."

"Why should we believe any of this?" Leena finally forms words, grabbing my hand and holding it tight. I'm half worried she's going to turn and run the other way.

"Because your life depends on it," Tarun barks as he leaps onto the petrified tree, grabbing the twisted branches, before hopping to the next and then the next. It appears he has done this sort of thing all his life. Varsha and Raya, and many others follow his lead with careful attention as to where to place their hands.

I turn to my sister to find Aarav standing by her side, patiently coaxing her to move, but she continues to stare blankly ahead.

"Leena, we need to trust them," I say impatiently as I glance over my shoulder, knowing that Dakini's undead army is fast approaching. "I know it seems crazy but poisonous ground, is like, the least-crazy thing we've seen today. We can't turn back now. We must stay away from the rakshasi."

Leena blinks, a conflicted look on her face. Aarav takes her hands in his and puts them to his face. "I know you're scared, but we have to move," Aarav says softly as he pulls her toward the first tree. "I'm not letting you stay here." She looks into his eyes long and hard before finally nodding her head in agreement.

I attempt my first leap and hang on to the outer branches as I creep up the first tree, watching my sister who follows close behind, with Aarav bringing up the rear. As I look back to check on their progress, my eyes meet Aarav's and I mouth the words, "Thank you" as we continue forward.

We move along from branch to branch, vine to vine, stopping every so often to rest tired arms. Midway through the Valley of Sorrows, the fiery pain in my hands creeps into my chest. I look down to see the disc glowing vibrantly.

The chill in the air ushers through the message of urgency. Dakini and her zombie hoard must be closer than we thought. Moments later, we turn to see they've congregated at the edge of the jungle. From there, they leap onto the poisoned soil and begin slithering like snakes somehow gaining momentum as they drift across the cracked earth. Unfortunately, the poisoned land does nothing to deter the undead.

Dakini, who I can still see in her rakshasi form, lets out a piercing howl as she attempts to cross from the jungle onto the clay. I watch in horror as the monster's skin peels back and away from her skeleton. Her skin begins to burn, and her hands burst into flames. She claws her way back into the jungle and the injured rakshasi releases a powerful roar of defeat. She whips around, eyes crazed searching for her mark until her death gaze lands on me. The crown of horns upon her skull glows a fiery red matching the color of her eyes, making it clear how displeased she is about her predicament. The disc on my chest glows a brilliant white light.

"You!" She wails and points at me with a long crooked, clawed finger. The disc continues to act as a force field against Dakini but not her undead army. They persist, slithering toward us across the barren earth.

"Get her now!" Dakini orders her undead army.

"We're almost there, Leena, c'mon," I shout at my sister who is lagging in pace.

"Don't look back! Just look forward. Keep your eyes on me."

"Listen to Chandra!" Aarav encourages from a nearby tree, keeping his eyes on Leena.

"I can help," Raya says from her petrified tree perch nearby.

"I've got my sister," I reply with a scowl. Raya turns away and moves silently ahead with Varsha and the rest of the pack. "Grab my hand!" I shout to Leena.

"Watch out!" Aarav shouts, attempting to swing his way closer to us.

Dakini's undead army begins to swarm the base of the petrified tree Leena is hanging on. I double back, climb a larger neighboring branch, wrap my legs around its trunk for security, and reach my hand out to her.

"I can't!" She shrieks over the grotesque moans of the undead slithering their way up her creeper, grabbing at her dangling legs.

I wiggle toward her, attempting to get as close as possible, but there's still a lot of room between us. Her hands are gripped so tightly around the thorny limb that they are bleeding profusely. We are both exhausted.

"Give me your hand!" I yell. But she's too scared to let go.

The swarm has now completely enveloped the base of the petrified tree and the fear growing in Leena's eyes is unbearable. I swing my legs toward the vines hanging horizontally from my tree and angle my body as I launch myself toward the tree holding a terrified Leena. I reach for her hands, but I only catch air as she loses her grip on her branch and plummets down into the mosh pit of the crawling śavagala.

I try to scream, but the sound is stuck in my throat.

I'll come for you. Trust that, I will come for you...Leena.

I grip the thorny vines around the petrified tree, frozen and horrified as the *śavagala* latch themselves to Leena's arms, legs, and torso, carrying her off in the opposite direction and back toward the hateful beast—their rakshasi queen.

Along the perimeter of the jungle, the lush, green foliage has been destroyed— just like everything else in the demon's path. It is void of color and life.

My eyes turn to Aarav who's wedged himself between the tree branches for stability. He drops his face into his hands and begins to sob heavily, his body shaking as he lets the pain of watching the zombie hoard take Leena wash over him. Within moments, Tarun and their friends from the village are by his side, attempting to console him. But he clings to the tree, refusing to let go. Tarun presses his head to Aarav's and holds it there as he rubs his back.

"It should've been me, not her! And what about my Thatha? He is missing in all this, too!" Aarav spits into the air between sobs. "I should've been there for them both!" He pushes Tarun away. Tarun moves to give his friend space as Aarav swats at the outstretched hands of their friends, denying their help, wanting to be alone in his agony and loss.

"Aarav!" I call out, unsure if my quivering voice is loud enough to be heard. I push my tears down. He stares in my direction, blinking at me for a few moments with tears still streaming down his cheeks and I know he can hear me. I steady my voice and keep talking. "Leena would want you to keep moving. Your Thatha would want you to keep moving! You know they would! Just like you told Leena back at the jungle's edge, you have to keep moving!"

He remains still for a long moment, covering his hands over his ears, trying to block the rest of the world out. He lifts his head and looks back from where we came, and then his eyes move to the jungle on the other side. He decisively pulls his sweat-soaked shirt up and wipes vigorously at his tear-drenched face with his shirt. Finally, he begins to move toward safety with his friends.

"There's no other choice you have to come with us," Tarun says, solemnly now in a tree on the other side of me. "Let go," he says as he grabs my wrists and pulls me into him.

I look back the other way, in the direction Leena was taken, and watch in dismay as Dakini and her army of śavagaḷa march away with my sister into the darkness.

I say nothing as I secure my hold on Tarun, wrapping my legs and arms around him as he moves us toward the far side of the Valley of Sorrows. At the opposite end of the petrified forest, we dismount the tree and I unravel myself from him. Raya, Varsha, Aarav, and their friends are up ahead and keep moving through the jungle. Tarun pushes me along patiently under the cover of the foliage as we move deeper and deeper into the brush.

The glow of my disc is long gone, and we're surrounded by darkness. Fortunately, he appears to know his way.

My heart is pounding in my ears, and I'm growing weary. The girl who confronted the rakshasi has disappeared. My body begins to shake, and my confidence is shot. My lehenga catches on a vine, and I lose my footing and fly forward into the jungle grass and debris. I lay in the brush and my lips feel wet with blood.

"Let me help?" Tarun reaches out a hand to help me up.

"I don't need you!" I shout, shaking when I try to stand. But I turn too quick, and trip again, falling back into the brush once more. This time he yanks me up without waiting for my permission.

Everything I've been holding inside me bursts out. Watching Uma Aunty plunge to her death, and my sister being taken by the undead army. My chest is heavy and about to explode. Tarun tries to approach, but I shove him away.

"No!" I release a blood-curdling screech, freeing all the pent-up anger, heartache, loneliness, and pain I'm feeling inside, at this moment, and for all the moments from the beginning of my time. I snap and start pummeling my hands against a giant tree. I do not feel the pain as I shred my hands on the rough bark, ripping them open, and letting them bleed. Tarun moves between the tree and me. I start pounding on him, beating my bloodied fists at his chest. He stands silently, taking my abuse once again. I don't know how long it goes on, but I don't stop until I'm too exhausted to move another muscle.

"You may not need me, or anyone else for that matter," Tarun says, with an expressionless face, "but the thing is, our people *need you.*"

Fat tears rush down my cheeks in quick succession as I turn away from him and race forward blinded by the tears. I hear the whoosh of water moving, rapidly. I lose my footing and stumble down the uneven riverbank. Through heaving sobs, I stagger forward into waist-deep water, longing for the current to drown my sorrow.

Chapter Fourteen

The Watcher

"*H*ead. *Heart. Life, these are the lines of your destiny, Chandraka,*" *Appa said, his tender voice in my ear as he gently used his index finger to smooth over the thick scar tissue puckering up from the center of my open palms. The raised scars looked like a mountain range winding through a low valley. "Your lines are like a map—they guide you through impossible moments, like this one,*" *he said as he softly swept the tears rolling down my face with his fingers.*

"They laughed. They called me a FREAK!" I cried, recalling the looks of horror on the faces of my kindergarten classmates.

"In your hands, I see greatness. Yes, there are scars. They may never go away, but they are a part of your story. You must wear them proudly."

"I can't be proud of something so ugly," I sniffled.

"Each line tells me something special about you. Here, look. Line of Head, Line of Heart, and Line of Life," he pointed at each line. "Your head line tells me you use your brains and think fast on your feet. Your heart line stretches across your hand, which means you hold wonder and hope in your heart and always think of others," he said with a smile. "And the life line! Moon Child, I've never seen such a life line before...your life line appears to have no end. I think you'll leave a mark on the world." He took my hands in his and pressed my scarred palms against his cheeks and over his dark, brown, soulful eyes. He used my flattened hands to trace his thick eyebrows, then along his hooked nose, and finally set a thousand kisses in the middle of each hand.

The image fades away as if the transmission signal is failing.

A thunderous jolt shakes me to my core and a pair of giant grey leathery claws rips Appa and me apart. Appa becomes a fractured caricature made up of triangles and squares and appears as though I'm looking at him through a kaleidoscope. Through this strange ocular device, I see him being hurled through a damp, dismal underground tunnel before landing in a dark forest with charred trees where he becomes trapped in a maze of thorny stems and vines. He gags before pulling his shirt up over his face as the boorish stench of rotting and decayed vegetation wafts up his nostrils. Under his feet the earth is a thick sludge, making it impossible for him to move. As large globules of sludge fall from the sky, he throws punches into the air attempting to attack an invisible entity.

Black, inky mist swirls up from the sludge and I want to extend my arms through the looking glass and pull Appa out of the dire situation he's in, but it's an impossible feat. The giant, gray leathery claws of the rakshasi explode up from beneath the muck on the other side of him. It swats Appa sideways with the flick of its wrist and squashes him deep into the earth, but he manages to resurface. As he tries to pull himself out, a flicker of pink opposite him appears, something that reminds me of life and love.

Leena.

She reaches her arms up and beats at the giant rakshasi claw that has her trapped.

Suddenly, the rakshasi's wicked face appears, and it roars, "GIVE IT BACK!" The earth shakes in the strange swampland before Appa and Leena are pulled under. I shake the ocular tube I'm viewing them through, hopeful they may resurface again. But I fear their luck has run out...

"Leena!" I wake with a start, but I don't hear the words aloud. My hands fly to my throat, "Help!" I barely whisper. I reach for my face and feel my jaw open and close, but don't hear a sound. Frantically, I reach for my lips and stuff my fingers into my mouth, trying to pull the words out, but they are lost somewhere inside. I begin to cough and gag uncontrollably.

"Appa...where are you?" I say to myself. I clutch the disc, which is still around my neck, and hold it against my heart. I bolt upright and glance around frantically.

Wait, where am I?

I am sitting on some sort of makeshift cot with an itchy straw-stuffed mattress that pokes and scratches at my exposed flesh. A heavy wool grey blanket is crumpled up to one side of me. I search the dim candle-lit room to find walls made of a mixture of bamboo, straw, and caked red clay. My eyes move to the ceiling thatched together with broad palm leaves and more straw. Something tickles my nose and I try to swat my face, but my hands are each bound with a light, linen cloth. Some sort of green vine secures them in place. I sniff at a thick gel-like ointment that oozes from beneath the bandages. The ointment has an aloe vera base just like Amma would make me put on my battered dancer's feet. I stare back to scan my bandaged hands and notice red clay wedged under my nails, triggering my memory.

The rakshasi queen moved the earth.

The village crumbled.

Leena is gone...

Panic sets in as the horrors of my recent past flood into my present. I gasp for air and clutch at my pounding chest. Amma is not around to remind me to keep moving forward, and there's no Leena to wrap her arms around me and tell me it's going to be all right. I start to scream in a panic, stripping the dressings on my hands and littering the blanket and straw bedding in a frenzy across the room. On the opposite side of the small room, I see my lehenga and blouse draped over a stool, with my black boots arranged in the corner. *What?* I look down at my body, quickly scanning myself to find that I'm wearing some sort of white sleeveless, cotton tunic with long slits along either side. My bare legs are covered in cuts and bruises that must've penetrated through the clothing in the jungle.

I scamper toward the stool and grab at my outfit. But it's a cold, soggy mess in my hands, made wet from when I had fallen into the river.

"No!" I shriek.

It doesn't matter. I need to find Leena.

As I tear off the stark-white, stiff tunic and throw it carelessly to the dusty clay floor, I hear the quickened patter of heavy footsteps. A large set of arms hold on to me as I thrash about like a fish out of water.

"Let me go!" I kick and scream, "Leena. Appa." But the thrashing depletes the energy I had, and I quickly succumb to exhaustion. Feeling utterly defeated, mentally and physically, I collapse into the heavy-set arms.

"They aren't here," a familiar male voice says, calmly. I swallow hard and realize I'm clinging to Tarun. I immediately push at the arms around me, back away into the opposite corner and wipe the tears from my face. When Tarun's eyes dart away from me to the hut's ceiling, I realize I'm standing in front of him with barely anything on except for my tank top and undies, my gold cuffs, and the necklace that anchors the disc to me.

He reaches for the tunic I dumped recklessly on the ground, tosses it to me, and leaves the room.

"Where am I?" I demand, trying to sound stronger than I feel and struggling to unfold the inside-out tunic. I sweep the tunic over my head and pull it down. Every inch of my body aches and I release an agonizing howl.

"You will heal," a gentle female voice reassures from the entrance of the room. My eyes swiftly move to a narrow opening in the walls where I'm greeted by a pair of warm smiling eyes. "You are safe here."

"You?" I blurt, staring at the toothless hag with the oversized walking stick.

"I am Gowri. You can call me, Gowramma, as all the youngsters in our tribe call me," she says. "And I know you must have many questions."

I look at this stranger's calm face, fixate on her soft knowing eyes, and take in slow exaggerated breaths as Amma had taught me to do before taking the stage at the dance competitions. My breathing begins to ground me, and the panic within deflates.

But that is short-lived when Tarun returns to the room. My blood boils and my rapid, haggard breathing returns. He carries a washcloth and a small clay bowl, brimming with a golden-colored liquid that sloshes from side to side with each step. He hands it to the old woman. I narrow my eyes and glare at him wishing he'd disappear.

"Don't mind the boy," Gowramma says, noticing the scowl on my face. "He just happens to be a part of this series of unfortunate events. But I assure you, he means no harm."

"Bloody hell! *Thaye*, she's stubborn," Tarun says to his grandmother.

"No doubt, like her father. Now, grandson, please go get the lentils. She needs to eat," the old woman commands, softly. He moves across the room, gathers up the wet, torn outfit with one arm, and lifts the stool, placing it by his grandmother's feet. Without making eye contact, he exits the room once again.

"He's your grandson? You're a Lambadi Elder?" I ask, vaguely remembering the conversation I had with Tarun shortly before I'd tried to fillet him very publicly in the village circle. Gowramma nods at me and leans her cane against the wall. She ushers me back to the cot and takes her place on the stool across from me.

Pulling my ravaged hands toward her, she lays them delicately onto her lap and peels back the remaining bandages from the wound. My hands are skinned badly, and my knuckles are caked with dried crimson blood. I hadn't been able to stop pounding them against the rough bark of the jungle trees. Gowramma tenderly dips the washcloth into the bowl of golden liquid and pats it upon my hands, dissolving the blood and pus that weeps from the wounds. The cool moist feeling brings forth great relief to the burning in my hands.

"This ointment will heal and purify your wounds," she explains, looking into my eyes. "Your Amma used mixtures like this in her shop."

"I need to find Leena," I say, ignoring her preamble and getting down to business. I smell the lavender in the healing ointment, but it has no calming effect on my crummy disposition.

"We will help you find Akashleena, but you must gain your strength first," she asserts, gently. "And, yes, I am Lambadi and Elder of the *Vaidya* Tribe. We are not only healers but also mighty protectors of the jungle and the river Kaveri. I am also the Chief Priestess of the *Hiriya parisattu*, which is the Elder Council. What I say goes around here," she declares in a single breath.

I'm amazed at her confidence and spunk for a woman who has been around the sun more than a few dozen times. I stare at the heavy lines on her wrinkled face. She must be well into her eighties, but she seemed to hold the fervor and heart of someone in their twenties.

"Wait. You were the one I saw in Amma's yoga studio, but you were..." my voice trails off.

"Different. I can change my appearance when needed," she replies with a wink, following my gaze to her cane against the wall. "You recognize the *Ūrugōlu*, my enchanted walking stick. It transports me from one place to another in a flash," she says excitedly.

"Those words you said to Amma, just before she went into a fit—some babble about the stars turning upon the sun and moon and darkness prevailing?" I ask.

"And now the child has the power of eavesdropping. I did not recognize this was among your great abilities." She chuckles, wiping a tear from the corner of her eye. Her face turns serious once more. "I visited Sita often over the years. The last time was to warn her of what she already knew—that the rakshasi was growing power hungry—and it sensed that you had found the map. Sita was on borrowed time, and she knew what she had signed up for from the beginning. The phrase, *'when the stars turn upon the sun and the moon, darkness prevails'* is an ancient Lambadi prophecy, signaling the beginning of the end."

"The end?" I repeat. "I've had these visions, I'm not sure which of them I can trust."

"The dark magic of this rakshasi is full of trickery. She can compel you, get inside your head in a way most evil cannot," Gowramma says, the look in her eyes is one of caution.

"At the harvest festival, I heard the rakshasi's voice in my head. She was asking me to kill the Watcher. I think she wanted me to kill Tarun," I say looking at the old woman.

"The rakshasi has a vendetta against me," Gowramma sighs deeply. "It blames its fate on me and wants revenge. I can only assume it wanted you to kill my grandson. Tarun may grow to become a Watcher one day, but he has a long way to go yet. But he is not your Watcher," she says, unraveling the bandages.

"But Amma? She was *my Watcher*?" I exhale the words, nervous about what she may say next.

"Yes. I hand-picked Sita to be your *Mātagāti*—your Watcher. Sita was a loyal and trusted healer of the

Vaidya tribe. She was a widow who needed a new beginning. And your Appa was in the same situation. The Elder council decided to send them to that tiny town in America hoping you'd never be found." She pauses and shakes her head in dismay. "Even after the rakshasi attacked your Appa, Sita vowed to keep you safe and hidden. But we knew we couldn't hide you forever." She points at the glowing disc on my chest.

My heart dips into my stomach. "So, she really wasn't my mother?" I ask, my eyes dropping to the floor. I realize that Raya had spoken the truth when she had read my palms.

"I'm sorry. No, not exactly," Gowramma says with sad, apologetic eyes, looking at my face.

The room begins to spin around me and my heart falls into my stomach. I feel like I'm losing Amma all over again.

"But believe me when I say she loved you like you were her own flesh and blood. She was hard on you, but she needed to teach you discipline because of what you are to us."

"So, I was born in this jungle? Who is my birth mother?"

"Your birth mother was a Lambadi, but she moved on from this world the moment you were born," she explains, without making eye contact.

"So, my mother died, and you sent me to live on the other side of the world?" I ask with an accusatory tone.

"I had no choice. I knew from the moment I laid eyes on you, that you were the *Ārisalpatta*—the protector of our people and the only one who can *see* the rakshasi, our greatest threat," she replies, a dreamy twinkle in her eye as she looks at me, as if she had turned back time and entered those moments all over again. "You were so small but so sure of yourself. And bold and brave, like there was nothing that could break you down. Your Appa brought you to me. You had deep, bloody open wounds—large gashes all over you—it was as if a wild animal had clawed you and left you for dead. Your hands were the worst. He'd carried you for miles through the jungle to reach me and all he would say is that you had an accident playing by the river."

Flashes of the vision I had of the hut by the river, the screaming banshee, and the orb enter my mind as Gowramma continues to speak. I nod, looking down into my scarred hands where the golden-liquid healing ointment Gowramma applied has turned into a gel-like substance and hardened into the creases of my hand. I look at my arms and notice the golden gel has crept up into the outline of the colorful tattoos. The designs are mesmerizing.

"Your Appa, Ravi, came from the Kodaguru tribe, who were Lambadi Warriors with mystical gifts that enable them to see the enemy through selavu or sense them in other ways. He was among the very few blessed with the rare ability of selavu, the ability to *see* the monsters among mere men. His mother had the ability, but she never had to use it," she says. "And now, there's only you who can see the evil in the world. It was brave of you to try and warn the others when Dakini appeared at the festival."

"Blessed? This is a curse!" I grumble. Her eyes grow wide as she studies me, and I fill with guilt. "I would never wish the ability to see rakshasi on anyone. It's a creature you can never unsee," I say with a shudder.

"It sounds dreadful. While it may be a curse to you it is a blessing for those of us who can be saved," she says. "We've never *needed* the *Ārisalpatta* before. This is the first time in nearly one hundred years."

"I don't understand. Why now?"

"Because in a few weeks, we have a special moon rising. The Lambadi call it the *Nooru varshagala amavasye*. It's a cosmic wonder that only illuminates the sky every hundred years. Dakini, the rakshasi, wants to use it for an ancient ritual to sink our world into permanent darkness. The dark magic she uses has not been practiced for centuries. She needs the sacred gemstones from each of the five Lambadi tribes—the healers, the scholars, the warriors, the makers, the mystics. Each tribe worships a gemstone they believe brings life and blessings to their kinfolk. Dakini has already taken the gemstones of the other tribes, only the Vaidya tribe, still have their gemstone. You will see it outside at the altar where we worship."

Uma Aunty had been right when she said something wicked was afoot. Dakini is the reason for the famine, missing children, and now the sacred river running dry.

"But if the Kodaguru tribe no longer exists—with the exception of me—then where is their gemstone?" I ask.

"It's a moonstone," she says, slowly.

"It's pale-yellow and glows just like the moon?" I ask, a quiver enters my voice as my eyes flit from Gowramma and back to my scarred hands. "I had a vision of it."

"Dakini needs you for the ritual because the moonstone is embedded in your hands," Gowramma says.

"Then why does she need this?" I hold up the disc. "What does she need the map for?"

"The disc illuminates the map to the trishula, which is protected by a force so mighty, not even a rakshasi as powerful as Dakini dares to go near it. Dakini needs the power of the trishula—the three prongs represent the past, present, and future—to complete the ritual that will plunge the jungle into darkness. One can only assume that she wants control of everything."

I shake my head as I think about the folk dances Amma had been teaching me all these years, and how this last one I had been working on involved wielding a trishula! She wasn't just teaching me the dances to keep me connected to my roots, she was showing me how to do my *job. How to kill the rakshasi.* "And I'm the *Ārisalpatta*, the one that can see Dakini in rakshasi form and put her in her place?" I wave the disc in front of Gowramma's face. "This has got to be some big mistake!"

"You and your ability to see selavu of the evil that walks amongst us is no mistake of any kind. That monster cannot be stopped by any man, animal, or by any god. It can only be stopped by one woman. That *woman* is *you*!"

"You don't understand. I'm a screw-up! *This* can't be really what I'm meant to be?"

"True as that may be, Chandra, you're what *we* need," Gowramma says, bobbing her head. "You are exactly what we need."

Chapter Fifteen

Hope in Dark Places

I continue to stare at Gowramma wondering if I'm listening to the rantings of a mad woman or if she does have her wits about her.

"I've only seen a rakshasi. I've never fought one," I respond, feeling glum and hopeless. My heart begins to race, and fear sets in at the thought of it all.

"That's why I'm here! I will teach you all that you need to know," Gowramma replies.

"How? You're my weapons master and combat trainer?" I blurt in disbelief, my eyes dart from the tiny woman in front of me to her cane propped up against the wall just inches away from where we're seated.

An amused expression crosses Gowramma's face. She releases a deep, throaty laugh and says, "I understand your uncertainty. I'm old and rickety. I hobble around with a walking stick. But don't mistake the deep wrinkles of my skin, my twisted crippled hands, or the limp in my step for weakness. I'm stronger than I ever was in my youth." Her eyes shine bright as she taps the side of her head with her index finger. "My greatest and sharpest weapon is what you can't see. It's inside of me."

"I'm not sure I follow," I say, glancing down at my hands and pulling at the gold cuffs, embarrassed by my preconceived notion that the frail-looking woman seated in front of me would not be able to teach me how to wage war on a blood-thirsty, she-demon. "Are you saying my selavu is my greatest weapon? Because this good for nothing disc is doing nada for me."

"Selavu is not so much of a weapon as it is a shield. Same with those cuffs they are part of traditional Kodaguru warrior armor," Gowramma says, forcing me to think, but I can't because my head is throbbing, and my thoughts are foggy. "Learn to look deeper. Nothing is ever as it seems."

I hold the disc up just inches from my face and squint. She lets out a wild, raspy guffaw.

"Listen, child, I may look like a frail, elderly woman and the disc may seem like a useless rock, but I assure you, we are both much more!"

I stare back at her, my expression dumb.

"You are the grounding force of our people. You were created to fight for the innocent. You must fight against anything that comes in the way of their prosperity, peace, and dharma. You are our light over the dark. You are our warrior."

She rises swiftly, releasing a dagger with a hilt that is embellished with ornate carvings of elephants from a heavy, silver chain belt looped around her plain, white, cotton sari. The dagger is remarkably similar to the one I'd taken from Tarun at the harvest festival during my harrowing moments of being possessed by the rakshasi. She lunges toward me with the curved blade at my neck and I sit there hypnotized by blind trust, unwavering, instead of dodging out of the way. Gowramma tugs at my necklace and cuts the disc free. She holds the disc out in front of me, balancing it on the tips of her crooked, fingers.

"The disc is known as the chakra. It will only work in your hands. Here, take it." She passes the disc over to me and begins knotting the ends of the necklace to preserve the beading and loops it back over my head. I look at the carvings of the sun, moon, and stars, bracing with anticipation and expecting to be overwhelmed with a surge of power like the whirring and vibrations it had created when the rakshasi was nearby.

"This is a deadly weapon?" I snicker, staring down at it, wondering if it's going to explode in my hands. Nothing happens. I stare at it with great intensity. It still does nothing. "It's not doing anything. What if I can't do this? What if I fail?"

"If you fail, then we perish, all humanity is lost, and darkness prevails," Gowramma says bluntly.

"Geez, so no pressure, huh!"

The corner of Gowramma's mouth curls slightly but she chooses to ignore my sarcasm. "Ask yourself what you're fighting for and when you find the answer go set the world ablaze!" She encourages, but I am still clueless and feel defeated, nonetheless. I flop the disc beside me on the straw-stuffed mattress and nervously run my hands through my knotted hair.

"Look at me," she demands, refusing to let me wallow in uncertainty. She tugs at the string of dark green, oval-shaped beads around her neck, and my eyes fall upon the thick, solid gemstone she's now holding in her hands. A large, blooming lotus is etched into the center of the smooth reddish stone. My mind flashes to the pale pink blossoming lotus Amma had kept on her meditation altar in the yoga studio and the same ones inked on Raya's arms.

Gowramma's shriveled fingers clutch the gemstone as she points to the images circling the massive lotus. "The Ārisalpatta wields the ten weapons of goddess

Durga—the chakra, the Golden Trishula, the bow and arrow, the Sword of Knowledge, the lotus, the thunderbolt, the snake, the conch shell, the javelin, and the mace. Over the past few decades, the Lambadi tribes have worked together to collect these weapons. We now have them all in our possession, with the exception of the chakra, which you're holding, and the trishula...which you must find."

"This is nonsense! I have two hands. And you want me to wield ten weapons in them?" I ask, scoffing at the old woman. The bamboo walls of the damp hut feel like they are closing in on me. I shake my head skeptically at this so-called solution. "This is wrong. I'm not what you say I am, and I don't want this! I just want to find Leena and go back home to Virginia," I whisper, almost pleading, willing all of this to go away. Tight knots form in the pit of my empty stomach, making me nauseous.

"But you are home. And you're the only one that can help us," Gowramma implores. "There's a darkness rising, Chandra. You saw it yourself last night. We need you on our side," she says. "I can teach you, Chandra. I can teach you to find the Light. And we'll help you find your sister." She reaches for me and puts her tiny hands on mine. The warmth of her touch moves me. "With each passing day, Dakini's powers grow. She's taken three out of the five sacred Lambadi stones. These gemstones mean everything to our people."

She pulls at my hands and points at the chakra, motioning for me to grab it. I hand it to her, and she places it into my right palm. The chakra begins to glow, illuminating the magnificent miniature map in my hand.

"This here," she says, pointing to a low valley and a temple in the left upper quadrant of my scarred hand, "this is where you will find the trishula. Right along our sacred River Kaveri." I do not understand why she is able to read the map and not feel disoriented. I had believed the raised scars of my hand served as the mountain range that cuts this region into east and west. Instead, it's the river. "The location of the trishula has always been hidden. Until one of our young, Lambadi mystics had a vision about a map."

My cheeks flush warm with each quickening heartbeat. The Lambadi mystic she's talking about must be Raya.

Our tête-à-tête is interrupted when Tarun strolls into the room with another red clay bowl cupped in his hands. Gowramma leaves the chakra in my right hand and squeezes my free hand tightly before releasing them. She rises from the stool slowly. "Eat now. And heal. I'll return in the morning and then the real work begins." She reaches for her cane and heads out stopping at the doorway. "Grandson, you must take your post. I must go tend to my duties and check on the others," she says as he crouches down and lowers his head so she can reach him to place her palm on his forehead. She whispers something in his ear and gently presses her hand to his head, bestowing a blessing upon him.

Tarun nods obediently before gently placing the bowl into my hands and taking his grandmother's spot on the stool. He squats down on the seat, looking uncomfortable as his long limbs and muscular frame, spill off the stool. I wonder how long the stool can hold his weight before falling apart.

I stare into the bowl of curried lentils. I close my eyes and let the overwhelming smell of peppercorns, cumin, and coriander assault my senses, taking me back to Amma's kitchen in Virginia. Especially, the Sunday afternoon cooking sessions when she'd curry everything under the sun. It's probably the exact same recipe.

But the pair of eyes staring at me now rips me from my homesick fantasy and the worst possible thought pops into my mind. "What have you mixed into this? Some potions to make me agree to this madness?" I spew the words before I can stop them with the sole intention of provoking him.

"That'd be suicide! Besides, you're gonna need your strength if you are what Thaye says you are," he murmurs. He lowers his eyes to avoid mine and runs a hand through his long damp hair, focusing on the chakra at my side.

"You sound thrilled," I growl, turning my attention back to the curried lentils. Its fragrant aroma is thick in the air, and I feel a weight lift off my chest as I settle into its warmth.

"Nah, I anticipated that if an Ārisalpatta ever existed, it'd be one of us. Not some outsider."

"Huh!" I'm being snarky, but the truth of his words bruises me in a way I never thought possible.

"Just, don't screw up, okay? Thaye is all I have left." He bobs his head sideways toward the adjacent room where Gowramma is wobbling around stirring a pot of bubbling, gold liquid over the clay oven. It looks like the concoction she used to tend to my wounds. She chants something as she moves the ladle around the pot before leaving the hut through a thatched straw door.

"Like I have a choice! I know I must get this right. Your grandmother made it clear that there's not much room for error." My voice crescendos and I'm aware I sound like a belligerent toddler.

"Right...and now it's my job to keep you in the right direction," he says with a heavy sigh. He gathers his loose hair in an elastic band, setting it atop his head in a bun.

"You've got to be kidding me. You're my babysitter?" Grumbling, I rise and storm from the room with my warm cup-o-curry in my hand, and out into the muggy jungle air.

Tarun is hot on my tail, stomping out into the night after me. We walk several feet into the jungle before he grabs my shoulder, forcing me to whirl around and face him.

"Hey, it was you who tried to slash me open in the village circle. I'm the one who should be bloody mad here, not you," he says, angrily. I roll my eyes and hungrily take a swig of the lentils. I pull the cup away from my lips, wipe the curry dripping down my chin and let out a frustrated grunt. He has a point, but I'm not about to admit it.

"And, yes, I'm your babysitter for now, so take it down a notch, ay?" He takes a deep breath and rubs his face hard. "Look, I get your anger and uncertainty. I was just like you. I didn't believe any of the things my grandmother said. She sent me away when I was around eight years old. I went to a boarding school in the UK and came back here for holidays. I was happy there! Until a couple years ago when I started having visions of the jungle, the river, and Thaye. It all was calling me back to this place. There was this magnetic pull. It's really hard to describe, but here I am." His voice trails off as I continue to walk further away from the hut toward a beautiful large tree with long, draping branches pulled toward the ground. In the belly of the tree, in a spot where the trunk has been carved out, is a large amber gemstone.

I stop beneath a coconut tree and search our surroundings. "Where are we?" I ask, looking around at the tiny collection of clay and straw huts interspersed with canvas tents. In a fenced area, several grey large-eyed water buffalo stand together in their herd, by the feeding troughs. Just beyond them, is the wide-open jungle.

I look back toward the tree where dozens of candles flicker along the path leading up to its trunk. I move closer to get a better look. And then I see it clearly, above a wooden altar, there is an oblong amber stone about the size of a bag of sugar nestled into the cove of the giant tree. It has a large red dot on it with three horizontal markings like I've seen on the foreheads of holy men at the temples and on images of Hindu deities. It's a holy gemstone?

"This is the village of the Vaidya tribe. Thanks to the healers and a shielding spell from the Lambadi Mystics, we're hidden from Dakini. At least, for now," he says, looking down at me. "It's the only Lambadi village still standing. The remaining tribes have been driven out of the lands they had occupied, hence the overcrowding and surplus of tents here. Everyone comes here for sanctuary."

"And that amber stone represents the Vaidya tribe?" I ask, pointing toward the gemstone and staring into the amulet of the same color hanging in the middle of his chest. Fresh flower petals and fruit lay at the altar each representing a holy wish or offering made with heartfelt intent. I remember Amma doing the same as part of her daily prayer ritual. But here in the jungle, these offerings are presumably for the sacred gemstone.

"How can a rock have so much power?" I ask, unable to comprehend.

"Their hearts are open. They believe in its magic and that's all that really matters. A leap of faith," Tarun says, nodding at a young, sari-clad woman with an infant strapped to her chest using a broad band of woven fabric walking past us. Her cream-colored sari with a rainbow border is covered with dirt and the hem is in tatters. She holds a large, metal platter filled with deep, red blooms, plantains, and a coconut. I recognize the flowers because they are identical to the ones Raya tattooed on my arms. Amaryllis. The woman takes her offering to the tree, sets it down in front of the stone at the altar, and gracefully kneels in front of it. She places her hands together, collapses her body forward, and bends until she can almost kiss the ground. All the while tenderly cradling her infant.

"Food is scarce, but she's brought all the rations she was given for a week and is offering them to the Vaidya gemstone instead, praying for protection, for some sort of a miracle," Tarun says as he plays the part of narrator. I've never seen anything like it before. She has nothing but the clothes on her back and yet, gives away what she has because she believes in the power of the gemstone to protect her. I stare at the young mother awestruck. Several others arrive to pray with the woman—men and women of all ages. They set their offerings at the foot of the tree and take a seat next to the young woman. They sit cross-legged, each quietly in a meditative trance.

Their belief in something so simple is uniquely powerful. I look away and stare into my hands, feeling a touch embarrassed about my reaction and apparent ignorance of everything here. Then I begin to wonder if I should've done more at the harvest festival to protect everyone.

I shake my head, as my eyes lift from my hands and move back to the small gathering of people devoted to a rock. "I felt helpless," I confess as my inner thoughts start to pour out to Tarun. "I could see that monster, but it didn't help. And then I just let it take Leena..." my voice begins to crack.

"No! You did what you could with the knowledge you had. Knowing the rakshasi was there helped us get a lot of people to safety. Next time, we'll be more prepared," he says, moving closer and awkwardly placing his hand on my shoulder, patting it. "Hey...what is it like to see with selavu? And to see a rakshasi?" he asks like he has been thinking about it since that moment in the village circle.

"Dreadful and shocking. At first, I see a figure and bands of color. Every color of the rainbow. The colors pour out from the center—the heart. I wish the vibrant colors would stay, but if it's something with ill intent, the colors quickly change to grungy greens and browns. And if it is something evil, I see black. The color settles around the silhouette and the transformation of a monstrosity takes place," I say, describing it slowly and carefully. "Lately, I've detected a presence of a black, inky mist. Sometimes it's reddish-black in color. I've been seeing it throughout the jungle. I was only five the first time I ever saw the rakshasi in its body. It stalked and taunted me but didn't lay a claw on me. Instead, it took my father. Then I saw the rakshasi with Raya outside my mother's yoga studio the night Amma was killed," I say, forcing down the huge knot now lodged in my throat. And for the first time ever, it feels good to finally open up about what I've witnessed to someone. It is comforting to talk about the heinous things I've seen as though I'm no longer alone, living with the knowledge that something so wicked could exist. It feels good to be accepted as I am—cursed and all.

"Raya?" he says with a frown. "So that's what she's been up to."

"Yes, Raya. She had something to do with my mother's death!" I say, my voice on the verge of breaking.

"No way," he says sure of himself. "She's got a mean streak, but she would never harm an innocent like that."

"She's maniacal and unhinged!"

"What do you even know about her, us, or these people, and this jungle?" He spits, triggered by my summation of his ex-girlfriend. "You have no clue what it means to have your very existence threatened. You're nothing but an outsider looking in!" His voice stays low and controlled but swells with anger.

His words come at me like a spray of rapid-fire bullets, tearing through my sensitive psyche, and I find it hard to run for cover. Outsider. It is the second time he's called me that. The word pierces through me, gutting my core.

"It's true! I'm not one of you," I say defeated, unable to strike back at him with a witty comeback. Maybe he's right?

"Raya is a lot of things, but I swear on my life, her intentions were not sinister," he says, defending the girl I'm sure he still carries a torch for. "Raya is of the Atīndriya tribe, which makes her a Lambadi mystic. She reads selavu of regular people and can see the future. She manipulates what the jungle gives us to create potions and elixirs. She must've come stateside to deliver a message! Dakini must've followed Raya to you for the map," he says. The expression on his face slowly changes into a noticeable grin as if he's proud of himself for piecing the puzzle together.

"How do you know about the map?" I ask, surprised.

"I overheard my Thaye. Plus, Varsha had told us stories about it. That's all she's talked about since her sister, Nala got sick and died all those years ago." His voice trails off. His stance shifts into full interrogation mode as he looks into my face. "I'm right though, Raya told you something?"

I bite my lower lip in deep thought before responding. "She told me what your grandmother has now confirmed. I'm the Ārisalpatta. I'm the last of my kind from the Kodaguru tribe. Raya had a more theatric delivery though. She said my future is grim. She saw death and destruction," I mutter.

"Grim indeed," he says, shaking his head.

"And not untrue. Death and destruction have been following me around..." I say, my voice trailing.

The tranquility of the moment is ripped by a sudden shrill and agonizing wail. It is from the woman holding the infant at the gemstone altar by the tree. Her voice shakes me to my core, wounding me deep. Her pain feels like my own. She screeches words I don't understand.

"*Naksatragalu sūrya mattu candrana mēle tirugidāga, kattale mēlugai sādhisuttade.*"

The others around her attempt to soothe her, but she is inconsolable. She turns in her seat and sets her eyes upon me. She lifts a feeble finger and points toward me, but collapses, quickly. A hush sweeps through the crowd and Gowramma shuffles out of one of the canvas tents with her cane. She passes us, rushing straight for the woman.

"Tarun, what did she say? She pointed at me." I begin pacing nervously.

"A foretelling. A warning of the Elders," he says, distracted. "When the stars turn upon the sun and moon, darkness prevails."

I stand in shock in the middle of the candlelit path. A little girl with a sweet doll-like face framed with two long braids that reach her waist walks up to us and tugs at my tunic. "*Māntrika yōdha, nānu nim'ma kaphgalannu sparśisaballe?*" She looks up at me, eyeing the gold outlines of my tattooed arms and cuffs.

"She's calling you 'magical warrior,'" Tarun says with a smile, translating for me. "She is asking if it is okay with you if she touches your Kodaguru warrior cuffs?"

I blink a few times, not completely understanding what is happening before I nod and squat next to the child. She shoots me a timid smile as she gingerly runs her pointer finger along the sun, moon, and stars etched on the surface of my cuffs. I recognize her from the bazaar. She is one of the children who had danced, clapped, and juggled her way into the hearts of every person in the crowd before stealing her share of fruit. Her large brown eyes are wide, and her face is caked with red clay. Below the rim of her ripped lehenga, her bare feet stick out, bloodied, and blistered. Something in her face reminds me of the little girl from my vision—the one who had told me about the rakshasi queen—the girl I desperately wanted to help but could not.

I motion for her to sit down on the ground next to me and pull at the hem of my cotton tunic. I struggle, but eventually, I'm able to tear at the hem, leaving the bottom of my outfit jagged. I gently wrap the torn, cotton hem around her foot with the hope that it will take the pressure off the points where her foot meets the earth. It reminds me of Amma and how she used to dress my swollen dancing feet.

"*Nam'mannu ulisalu illiddāre?*" She asks gently, tracing the gold outlines of my tattoos before folding her hands together.

Tarun looks from the little girl and then to me, before he hesitantly says, "You are a goddess in her eyes. A legend. She wants to know if you are here to save us..."

I rise to my feet unsure of how I could answer that question. I scan the crowd gathered at the mighty tree sheltering the sacred gemstone and watch as Gowramma settles her people. She holds her hands over her head, and the crowd falls silent. I don't understand a word of what she speaks, but she delivers her message with a strong, steady voice. Her words seem to reach their hearts, judging from the encouraged expressions on their faces.

Whatever she is saying convinces her people, building them up, making them stronger together because they throw their arms up as one and chant with her. They promptly bow their heads before Gowramma and the sacred gemstone.

Their lives hang in the balance, and yet they believe. They are hopeful, offering what little they have left to the rock.

Their hearts are brimming with light and hope.

Any doubts I have about my abilities begin to diminish as I begin to realize that there's something more powerful at work here.

"*Nam'mannu ulisalu illiddāre?*" The little girl asks again, tugging at my bandaged hands. She drops to her knees, places her hands together in prayer, and chants silently to herself at my feet as if I were a goddess who could grant her an infinite number of blessings. Overcome by her gesture, I fold my hands together and lower to one knee in front of her.

Goddess and Legend, I am not! But this child believes in something that is greater than I can comprehend.

And, if she needs something to believe in, I guess I can be it.

"Yes," I let the whisper slip from my lips. "I will do everything I can to help you." I nod, hoping the gesture is universal and she understands what I'm trying to say. She rises and throws her arms around my neck, nearly knocking me to the ground. She holds on to me as if she has no intention of ever letting me go. My eyes fixate on the beautiful tree and the gemstone it cradles. As I hold this small child in my arms, I begin to understand the true power of the stone.

I will do whatever it takes to keep the stone and these people out of harm. I silently vow.

CHAPTER SIXTEEN

SUN VERSUS MOON

The protection spell cast by Gowramma and the Elders of the Atīndriya tribe of Lambadi mystics allows us to remain hidden in plain sight. I envision it to be like living under an invisible dome the size of a small town maybe the size of Fortune Falls back home. With each passing day, our protected jungle hideaway deep in the green becomes home to nearly one hundred Lambadi and Bommandava villagers seeking refuge from Dakini and her undead army of destroyers.

A handful of the young, strong men and women, and teens like Tarun, Aarav, and their friends, Varsha, and Raya, are tasked with leaving the confines of camp to search for anyone in trouble or without shelter in the remote mountain villages of the jungle and bring them here. They report blight and famine in many areas outside the protected village. I join them from time to time because Gowramma has me on a hearty regimen of yoga and meditation, claiming it will help with my healing. Often, it feels like being back home in Virginia with Amma. Begrudgingly, I obey her commands, but as the days pass on I want to run away, find Leena, and go home.

Although there are more bellies to fill and food is becoming scarce, Gowramma and the Lambadi Elders don't turn away anyone who comes seeking refuge and welcome them into their safe haven.

Village life is exhausting. I was prepared for all-out boredom, but there's not been any time to let my mind wander. Our days start before the sun fully launches into the sky and end only when the moon hangs high against a black, blanketed night. Each member of this new consolidated village performs their assigned duties throughout the day. Within the protected area the jungle is still prospering.

Some days, Varsha and I help forage the foliage in search of valuable healing herbs the Vaidya use to create ointments, medicines, and teas. On others, I spend hours climbing trees with Tarun along the river's bank, plucking juicy ripe guava, oranges, mango, and papaya.

Once, when I was on hunt duty with Aarav, we searched for wild boar. But when I made an uncoordinated attempt to strike my prey with a rudimentary spear I tumbled to the ground, and we lost our chance with the boar. Laying there flat on my face on the jungle floor reminded me of that last day back in the yoga studio with Amma and how I never really mastered that step. Amma. Even now, it still hurts to think about her. Or to think about dance. Word about my debacle traveled back to the village and I was quickly rotated off duty and joined the cleaning and cooking crew. I haven't been invited to go hunting since. But I did get to reap the rewards when the villagers cooked up pandi curry, a traditional spicy dish of pork belly infused in a thick masala of kachampuli, black peppercorns, coriander, cumin seeds, and bay leaves. Amma used to make it from time to time.

No one is spared, not the very old, not the feeble, not the crippled. "If you can think, you can do. We all have gifts!" Gowramma reminds us all. "Everyone has a part in making this better."

The tribes come together in remarkable ways, sharing their special skills, enabling each of us to become a jack-of-all-trades. Members of the Lambadi Mēkar tribe skillfully show us how to weave large tree leaves to create additional shelters and create pottery from the thick clay found on the floor of the riverbank. The

Vidvānsa tribe of scholars meets with the Elders on a regular basis, helping them govern this fractured group, as the Vaidya continue to serve as hospitable hosts.

Today, I'm tasked with water duty which means walking the mile and a half downhill to the river before the scorching afternoon sun reaches her peak and lugging full copper jugs back up to the village. I'm already drenched in sweat as I carefully balance two medium-sized empty copper pots atop my head. What I wouldn't do for a little bit of rain to cool me down.

"Hey, wait up!" Tarun shouts, his hands wrapped around two of the largest-sized copper pots. "I heard you're a wonder at balancing large copper on that thick head of yours, so I had to see it for myself," he chuckles to himself. I playfully shove him with my hips while maintaining a perfect balance of the empty pots and laugh back. These past few weeks, we've spent a great deal of time within each other's orbit, through daily tasks and meals. He seems to be good at just about anything he tries and he's always lending a hand, especially to the elderly of the group, gaining much praise from the Lambadi elders. The girls of the group fawn over him to no end, but somehow, he doesn't let it go to his head.

We walk toward the peaceful whoosh of the river, but instead of going to the usual spot further upstream, we stop in an area surrounded by giant trees with a curtain of lush vines that hang down from the intricate canopy above.

"So, this is how you were so good moving from tree to tree!" I say looking up into the sky as I place the pots at my feet to wipe the sweat dripping down my cheeks. "Oh my goodness, this heat is killing me," I whine.

"And your stench is killing me," he says with a laugh. Tarun drops the pots he is carrying in the grass and flashes me a boyish grin before running for the vines hanging out over the river. He leaps with ease through the air and swings back and forth on the vines, gaining momentum. After a minute, he releases his hold of the vine and hovers through the air, and somersaults into the water.

When he doesn't resurface, I begin to panic. "Tarun! Tarun!" I shout, jumping into the water. When I come to the surface, I find him standing in the shallow water doubled over laughing.

"Was the great Ārisalpatta actually worried something happened to little old me?" he laughs, wiping at his face. The light trickling down through the canopy hits his greyish-colored eyes in a way that makes them sparkle unnaturally. Standing there in that moment, he's like a beautiful, chiseled bronzed statue.

A fluttering sensation rises in my stomach and my face is hot. I look the other way, so he doesn't notice.

Stop it, Chandra! He's just your friend!

"Nah ... You're so full of it!" I laugh back, awkwardly.

"This is refreshing! Come on!" He wades past me and his hand grazes mine. My eyes follow him as he leaps out of the water in his soggy clothes and runs back for the vines. I hesitantly follow him, waddling under the weight of my wet tunic. "Okay, you're going to master this." He grabs one of the vines and pulls it toward us. He reaches around me as he positions my hands on the vine. His touch, his hands on mine makes my heartbeat quicken. I let out a nervous giggle. "Don't just rely on your arms. Hold tight but use your core like when you dance or do yoga. Swing for a bit, but release your grip just over the water," he puts his hands on my waist as he pulls me back. Then he lets go of me and I'm on my own.

I'm swinging out over the water and back to the riverbank. Back and forth, the warm breeze whips around me, and for a moment, I forget the life and death circumstances we're under. Tarun grabs his own vine and pushes away from the riverbank. And the two of us are just swinging life away and it's exhilarating.

"Now, let go!" he shouts, as he releases his hands and plummets into the water below.

We resurface at the same time, laughing together. I wipe at the dripping water and attempt to gather my heavy drenched hair.

As Tarun reaches for a strand stuck to my face, his fingertips graze my lips and linger on my cheeks and stay there, for a moment longer than either of us expects. He stares down into my face with those eyes ... and I have to quietly remind myself that we're just friends!

The loud crash of metal against metal from the direction of the pots on the riverbank breaks the tension and we divert our eyes to find Aarav, Varsha, and at least a dozen of our friends from the village milling along the riverbank.

"How's the water?" Aarav calls to us, running for the nearest vine. He swings out and drops into the water, as others follow his lead.

Within moments, Tarun and I are no longer alone. Varsha swims over to me and throws her arms around me in a surprising show of affection. She's become my 'Camp Lambadi' roommate—we now share the tight quarters of a small canvas tent—and we've become close.

Together with the others, we spend the next hour splashing around in the water and losing track of time. For once, we get to be a regular bunch of teenagers who have nothing but time on our side.

Missing from the bunch is Raya, but this is nothing new. She's made it a point to steer clear of us, choosing to spend her time with a gaggle of village gossip girls who constantly shoot scrutinizing glares at Varsha and myself for hanging out with the boys.

No big deal. I was used to it back home. Besides, judging by the dagger eyes she constantly shoots my way, I'm certain Raya has it out for me. She surely didn't appreciate me accusing her of teaming up with the rakshasi back in the village circle, but she hasn't done anything to plead her innocence either. Over the course of the past few weeks, I've been the target of a flurry of magic-infused pranks and I've got a sneaking suspicion that it could only be Raya.

The first prank started with me biting into a guava that appeared to be ripened to perfection on the outside but was overwhelmed with a black, fleshy center and worms on the inside. Then there was the 'herbal soap' I used that was made with poison ivy from the jungle floor. In less than ten minutes after use, my entire body was covered in gigantic blotchy-red hives. I had itchy marks all over my body for weeks.

But then came my breaking point.

After the fun at the river, we eventually move downstream to fill all the copper pots and return to the village with plenty of water. As Varsha and I reach our tent, I push through the door flaps and my eyes fall upon something moving along the ground in the far corner, just beneath our blankets.

"Did you see that? It went under there!" Varsha points to the blankets and moves to the side. "Stay back," I whisper and reach for the blankets sharply tugging at the corner to lure out whatever is hiding under. I throw the blanket over my shoulder and see a twelve-foot-long cobra, bobbing its hooded head as it propels its body toward us with swift, winding strokes. I blink and suddenly there are five more snakes.

Varsha's dramatic shrieks begin to draw a crowd as the old, blind snake charmer from the bazaar is led in our direction. He begins to whistle and play a melody on his wooden flute, disarming the snakes and drawing them out into the open. Onlookers bring an empty wicker basket from a nearby tent, as the snake charmer lures the snakes inside. And just like that, the creature slithered its way out the door.

There's only one person to blame for this drama.

I storm out of the tent to the makeshift cafeteria where I know Raya is serving food.

"Why can't you just leave me alone?" I yell at her, drawing eyes from every person within earshot.

"Chandra, chill out! Ha, isn't that what you Americans say?" A gratified grin spreads across her face knowing her taunts are festering and wearing me down. "You are going to cause those nasty bitter hives to explode." She snickers, continuing to stir the pot of lentils she was serving.

"The snakes in our tent. I know it was you!"

She sneers bitterly. "So, you found them? They weren't mine. They belong to old man Ramu. He played his music two nights ago and lured them in from the jungle. Besides, snakes do no harm, golden girl," she says, looking over at my arms and at her handiwork. Over the course of the week the vibrant coloration of the tattoos settled into my skin but the black outline of each shape continues to transform to gold. "Always quick to jump to conclusions, aren't you? There's nothing you won't accuse me of," Raya says, refusing to admit her crime. Her constant denial makes me lose my head. I want to wipe the smug look from her face. I want her to shut up!

My hands clench into fists. I impulsively fling my arm forward, but a solid wooden cane slaps down against the earth between us sending an echo through the small, tented dining area. Fear whips through me and I drop my hand.

"Enough!" Gowramma yells. For the first time since we met, there's no smile in her eyes. "We've worked too hard to heal you. Be grateful." She shakes her head in disbelief as she looks from my face to the hands that she has worked so hard to heal over these past several weeks.

I clutch my hands to my chest and whisper. "Sorry."

Gowramma points toward a winding path into the jungle, away from the village, and gestures for us to lead the way. Raya takes the lead and I begrudgingly join her. Gowramma quietly hobbles along the path behind us until we reach a clearing with a large boulder in the center. Evidence of Dakini's wrath can be seen in the barren leafless trees bypassing the protective barrier. Gowramma limps around as she draws a large circle several feet in diameter on the muddy floor using her walking stick. Inside the circle, she drags the cane to draw a line down the middle, cutting it in half.

"Don't cross the line," she says. On either side of the line, she draws an "X" and directs Raya and me to stand on these points. She limps back to the large bolder and leans her tiny body against it. "Do you know why you're here?" She glares at the pair of us like she is about to discipline two toddlers who do not know how to play nice.

"Are we in some sort of teenage timeout?" I grumble, scowling at Raya.

"It is," Raya says, in a tone that tells me she has been here before. She is fuming, but her eyes are fixated on Gowramma, not me. "Gowramma worries when she senses a disturbance in her ranks. You need to stop letting your anger for me consume you." She glides forward toward the line in the clay, challenging Gowramma's rules and tempting me to pass over the line. Gowramma stands firm, now looking like she is getting bored with us. A noticeable heat rises on my face.

"For obvious reasons. I don't trust you," I bark, storming toward the line in the clay, now standing just inches from Raya's exquisite face.

"You don't know me, and you refuse to even try," she growls back. Raya moves forward until we are almost nose to nose. "You're too stubborn believing what you think you saw."

"At the yoga studio, you let that thing kill my mother!" My voice escalates in tone and fire. "I saw you with rakshasi right before it whisked you away."

"I tried to stop it, but I couldn't see it," She yells. "By the time I got to Sita, it was too late. "And it didn't whisk me away! I barely escaped it with my life. I felt its presence, the air around me got bitter cold. It must've become distracted, likely sensing you and the chakra. I don't know! I couldn't see it. I acted fast, cast a transport spell, and got away from it just in time before it completely closed itself around me."

"I don't believe you," I shout, trying to keep my voice steady.

"I'm telling you the truth. Was I wrong about your fortune? Did I lead you astray? NO! I was right. I was right about everything. Gowramma confirmed all of it. You are the chosen one...the Ārisalpatta! You're the last

Kodaguru warrior. You see the rakshasi! And you don't deserve any of it." She sneers at me. "Ten days before I had the courage to come and see you in person, I did a leaf reading. I saw an American girl with a Lambadi soul and warrior's heart. I had to find you and see for myself, and that thing knew where I was going. It tricked me! I cast an incantation to throw it off my trail, but I failed," Raya says, clearly frustrated.

"You led that thing to us and now I'm motherless!"

"It killed my mother, too," Raya roars. I detect a slight quiver in her voice.

But her face quickly tightens, wiping away any sign of emotion.

My heart drops and it hurts for her because I'm not sure she ever let herself feel the pain. "I didn't know..." My words trail off and I don't know what more to say.

"There's a lot you don't know. You're overly consumed with disliking me. You should put that energy toward destroying the rakshasi. You're not what I saw in the leaf reading at the river's edge. I saw a woman so powerful in her action, but tender of heart. She rallied and led an army of nobodies and made them somebody. She changed their destinies," Raya says, her voice steady, unbreakable. "But you're damaged. Weak and pitiful. You're useless. We need someone to believe in, and it's not you."

Each word spurts from her mouth and hammers into me, splintering my heart.

"Surya, enough," Gowramma finally interjects, raising her cane and placing it between us. Placing an imaginary wall couldn't make Raya stop. I doubt it, she is relentless.

"I'm not done!" She throws the words back at Gowramma defiantly, turning her stance to face the wise woman. "She's worked for nothing and yet she has everything. How is that fair? It should have been me. I should've been the Ārisalpatta."

"You can have it if you want it so much. I never asked for any of this," I shout at Raya, but she's not listening. Her attention is intensely fixed on Gowramma.

"I've known it all along—about who my father was—that he was a Kodaguru warrior. I know the Elders wanted to keep it from me," Raya says, giving me the cold shoulder and turning to face Gowramma. "Aryana told me before she was destroyed by her own sister, Dakini!"

Gowramma's expression hardens ever so slightly, her eyes on an insolent Raya.

"I'm guessing you haven't told her yet. Is it because she's still a delicate flower who can't handle the truth?" Raya hisses at Gowramma and deliberately crosses the line, shoving me back with her chest. Raya is now standing face-to-face with me. I'm caught by surprise. A part of me thought that whoever crossed Gowramma's line would spontaneously burst into flames. But no consequence of any sort happens as Raya stands before me. She is just a hair taller than I am, and once again I'm distracted by her immaculate beauty—her flawless, golden-brown skin, and hazel eyes—just as I was the day we first met. She glares at Gowramma waiting for an answer, challenging her with everything in her.

Finally, Gowramma shakes her head softly and whispers, "No. I have not told her anything."

"Alright, golden girl let's put an end to this charade," Raya snickers, still looking at Gowramma, coaxing her to make her move.

And it works because before Raya can say another word, Gowramma steps forward, grabs my hand, and says, "This will sound complicated. I wanted to wait until you were strong again, but perhaps I've waited too long," she pauses, exhaling deeply.

Dread fills my heart as Gowramma continues. "While Akashleena, Sita's daughter, is your sister by heart, Surya is your sister by blood."

"Half-sister," Raya says with emphasis on the first word. "We have the same coward of a father. Different mothers."

Their combined words feel like a sucker punch. The world as I've known it has just exploded, and I feel as if I'm spinning out of control. My mouth goes dry and I'm not sure I've any fight left in me. I close my eyes and drop to my knees.

But the bad news keeps coming. Gowramma continues, "Just as the sun and moon are sisters who rule the sky together, peacefully—each with an important task to keep daylight and night in order—you and Surya are..."

"Sisters," I complete for her. In my shock and dismay, I'm sputtering words, trying to understand everything. It's like I've opened a chest of drawers and all the contents have been set free, capsizing from their secure confines, and haphazardly bombarding me all at once. "Sisters? Wait...It's us. Our names. Surya means the sun...and Chandra means the moon." I gasp realizing the literal translation of each of our names. "Is this some sort of cruel joke?" I cry.

A stunned look crosses Raya's face in the very same instant as she looks from me to Gowramma. "That ridiculous Lambadi prophecy...When the stars turn upon the sun and the moon, darkness will prevail."

CHAPTER SEVENTEEN

SHAKTI

"Maybe it's not a literal translation, right?" I turn panicked, looking to Gowramma for a shot of her eternal wisdom.

"Our biggest threat is Dakini the rakshasi if that is what she is now. The Elder council views her as the fallen star. She was prophesized to be one of the most powerful high priestesses before she evoked the dark Lambadi magic," Gowramma says. My mind immediately jumps to Varsha's storytelling session from the first day she arrived. "Wait, she's one of the three sisters from the Lambadi legend?" I ask.

"Yes. It was Shalini, my mother, Aryana, and Dakini," Raya brusquely cuts in. "The sisters were at odds and the older two sisters, Shalini and Aryana cornered her. Dakini went into a jealous rage and used dark magic that turned my mother into a banyan tree on the river's edge."

"Does the tree have long, drooping branches that turn down toward the earth? I've seen the tree in my visions," I offer. "So Dakini is the one in the forever war with Shalini?"

"If you believe in fairytales, which is something I've never subscribed to," Raya says flatly, as she whips around searching the perimeter of the jungle surrounding the clearing. "Where's Gowramma? Typical, she left!"

I stare down at my tattooed arms. "Why did this happen to my arms?" I ask Raya.

"It's Lambadi mystic magic. An Elder in my tribe mentored me. When I caught wind that I might have a sister, I begged her to teach me. She told me that if you were in fact my sister—my blood, your arms would bear these marks under the surface. Sure enough, when I laid my hands on you, my energy combined with your energy to reveal them."

"You've known then? All this time you've known we're related and didn't bother to mention it?"

"Yeah, I've known. It's the only reason I haven't killed you myself. You're my blood."

"So, I guess we should at least try to be civil with each other with us being sisters and all," I say, extending an olive branch.

"Like I said, I don't believe in fairytales," Raya growls in response and backs away from me. "Probably best not to fly too close to the sun, little sister, you may just get burned." The light reflects in her eyes a slight twinkle dancing about as she moves away from me and beyond the circle, making her way back to the path toward the village.

The next morning, before there's light in the sky, Gowramma hustles around gathering the young and agile, including Tarun, Aarav, and Varsha, but Raya is nowhere to be found. Gowramma means business, standing in front of us looking more like a drill sergeant with a hardened look in her eyes and a tough-as-nails attitude.

"You will mediate and be strong," she instructs the group. We all work on our sun salutations every morning before we spread out to attend to daily duties. "These practices will center each of you and make you cognizant of everything around you," Gowramma says. "Connect to each of your inner selves." She reminds us over and over to which I only respond in grunts as I try to activate my core. It's not as easy as it looks, and honestly, there is nothing peaceful about it. There is a lot of strain and visiting those tiny dark places that I would rather keep hidden. Legs crisscrossed, thumbs connected to my pointer fingers, palms to the sky. I have mastered just about every yoga pose under the sun, and just when I think I've attained perfection, Gowramma is there to remind me how much work I have ahead of me.

Nothing escapes Gowramma's scrutiny. "Try holding the postures longer. Really sink into yourself. Try harder, Chandra," she scolds, without facing me as if she's got eyes in the back of her head. "Body and mind must be healthy and strong," she says no less than one million times a day.

A few days later, Gowramma asks me to accompany her for a lesson to learn how to focus, control, and manipulate the chakra.

"Ask it and it will show you what you want to see," Gowramma says. "You must evoke the chakra with your mind and soul. Most of all, you must trust your instincts like never before. If you fail to trust yourself, you risk losing everything."

"Place the chakra over your hand as you do to read the map," Gowramma instructs. "You will throw it at an angle, across the clearing, and into that tree." She points to a sturdy teak tree among the bamboo.

"Shouldn't we start with a closer target?" I suggest, looking at the impossible one she has set to be my first.

"Tsk!" She clicks her tongue and shakes her head in disagreement. She motions to the tree with her free hand, clutching her walking stick in the other. I follow her instruction, but the chakra stays suspended in the air over my palm, before dropping into the spotty patches of the browning jungle grass below.

I try to make it fly about two dozen times all when listening to Gowramma's incessant critiquing. This would be the right time for a music montage. I attempt this same action a dozen times but make little progress.

I plop to the ground in frustration, dropping the chakra carelessly into the grass, and pound my fists on the soil, mimicking a toddler throwing a tantrum in the candy aisle of the grocery store.

"Chandra, you *must* try harder..." she urges.

"Harder? Gee, thanks for the news flash. I'm aware," I retort, my voice laced with sarcasm. I pick up the chakra and chuck it again. It plummets to the ground.

"You don't understand. This is not just a physical ability. It is a mental one. Why do you think we've focused on yoga and meditation and connecting your mind to your body and to your soul," she says. "Focus the energy on your intention and the reasons *why* you're doing any of this."

I roll my eyes.

"Don't roll your eyes, they will stay like that," she scolds, and her words remind me of Amma.

For Amma.

I rise and change my stance. Instead of the slumped shoulders, I stand tall and firm, digging my feet into the ground as if they were the deep roots of a great tree extending into the earth below. I stand still, close my eyes, and take a deep breath. Blocking out Gowramma's presence, I focus internally.

I see her face. Amma, my Watcher, who loved me unconditionally as if I were her own. The one who sacrificed everything for me, and never wavered in her will to ensure I made something of myself.

I see Leena. My rock. And while we were never too compatible, she was everything to Amma.

Then there are the people of this place, full of spirit and hope in the wake of having lost their homes, children, and loved ones.

I hear the tiny, insistent voice of the girl in the tattered lehenga from the night in the village braver than I ever was, willing me to bring an end to the rakshasi queen.

I remember Uma Aunty and her zest for life and her nurturing ways.

And then I see the dark, soulful eyes and his hook nose. I hear his laughter and his stories reverberate within me. Appa...except for my vision, I had not thought of him for a while. For a split second, I'm back with him in a happy time and a happy place and I can almost feel him here with me. For only an instant. Then he's gone and I'm left with a longing in my heart. The realization is upon me that I know I can't change the past. I cannot bring those I've lost back, but I can change what's ahead of me.

I can help Leena. I can help the little girl and the lost children. I can show them all that I do belong.

When I open my eyes and look skyward, the sun hangs joyfully at its highest point, radiating its heat down upon my body. Sweat drips down the sides of my face and the tunic clings to me like a second skin. My arms and the tattooed images glisten beneath the light and that's when I see it. The eyes on my forearms now belong to a furry face with whiskers. It belongs to a tiger.

I search for Gowramma, scanning my surroundings. I'm about to panic when I spot her beneath a large tree with scant leaves at the jungle's edge taking a snooze. She begins to stir.

"Ah, she is back. You've stood there in deep meditation for a few hours. As you can see, it is now high noon," Gowramma announces, staring at me from where she lay comfortably.

I turn my attention back to the chakra and the target Gowramma had chosen for me hours ago. "For Amma,

Leena, and Uma Aunty. For the children and the people of this land." I half-whisper and turn the chakra in my hand, raising it to my chest and placing it against my heart.

Igniting a spark within myself, my energy is transferred to the chakra. The pale-yellow smooth stone illuminates into a shimmering gold light.

I send my heart's intent into my movement as I release and hurl the chakra forward into the air. This time, the chakra cuts through the space between me and the tree, swirls as light as a leaf in the breeze, and takes flight, moving at warp speed. It spins through the air and a set of wings emerge from the chakra. I focus on the wings and realize they're not wings but razor-sharp blades. In a matter of seconds, the chakra has reached its target and embeds itself into the hardened bark of the massive tree on the other side of the clearing.

"Yes! I did it...it flew!" I let out a victory cheer and jump up and down as if I just scored the game-winning goal at the World Cup. I turn to Gowramma who rises from her resting spot, grabs her walking stick propped against the tree, and promptly launches her arms into the air. She limps toward me and releases a high-pitched hoot and raises her staff again before quickly placing it back on the ground.

She grabs my hand and with her eyes still fixated on the chakra sticking out of the tree she says, "Now for the real magic. Call it."

"Call what?" I follow her gaze from me to the chakra embedded several inches into the tree. "Nah, you're kidding! What? You want me to call it like I'm calling a puppy?" I ask with a snicker. "Here, chakra, chakra, chakra! What more can I possibly do?"

"The same thing you did before."

"No way! That thing will slice me into pieces!"

"Do it," she says firmly.

"This is crazy," I mumble and put my hand out, repeating the process I had done before. I place my palms up and go to all the safe and happy places in my mind. This time, my intent is clear in my heart from the beginning.

A strong gust of wind moves through and around me and I open my eyes to find the glowing chakra hovering above my outstretched hands. I search the sky. The sun is sinking and it's nearly dusk.

I look back at my hands to the chakra. There are no words that describe this feeling. *I did it. It took all day, but it's progress.*

"Our people believe you to be *shakti*. You are pure energy and power," Gowramma says. "You were sent away for many reasons. Exiled to another world completely. Now you have proven yourself. But remember, when wielding the chakra, you must act not out of the hatred or the pain in your heart. Your action must come from your love of the good, the want to liberate the people who depend on you, and never from vanity. It is how you mark your greatest journey. This is your soul's path to freedom."

I gulp hard. The weight of what she says slowly sinks in, impressing upon me. "That's heavy stuff, but I can do it." I look into her eyes. "I *will* do this."

"Now that you're starting to understand the power of the chakra, you must master the *yodhana sastrasthragalu*—the Warrior's Weapons," she says. The sun's rays cascading through the jungle trees reflect in her eyes. She pulls out her amulet the one depicting the lotus and the collection of weapons.

"But there are ten weapons! I don't have nearly enough hands to carry all of them," I say, noticing the look of a disapproving pout stretch upon Gowramma's tiny face. As I look down at my hands, my eyes fail to focus. At first, I feel as though a lace veil has been cast over them, creating a hazy illusion in front of me. I blink several times and each time, my vision becomes more clouded. Suddenly, I'm seeing double, triple, and quadruple sets of hands. My hands are multiplying. I must be hallucinating. I blink and blink again. "What you're saying, Gowramma is doable only if I had a few more sets of hands," I say.

"True. But that's not in the cards for you, and it's unlikely you will sprout them overnight," she calls over her shoulder as she hobbles along with her cane and walks the jungle path that leads to the village. We hear the echoes of voices from the base camp as we walk back together. I'm lost deep in thought as I try to figure out how I can make it all work. My mind filters through the stories Amma had told me about the warrior goddess Durga and her ten arms wielding the ten celestial weapons given to her by different Hindu gods. And that's when a spark of what feels like hope spreads across my heart. I smile like an idiot, beginning to hop around the idea in my head. I release an unexpected squeal that stops Gowramma in her tracks.

"Child, you mustn't scare old women like this. My poor feeble heart!" Gowramma scowls as she waits for me to stop jumping up and down in front of her.

"The weapons—all ten of them—what if I told you I can wield them all?" I ask.

"I'd say it will be nothing short of a miracle," the old woman says, looking up into my eyes, perplexed by my sudden proclamation.

"Then a miracle is what I'll deliver." I beam as we head back to the village together.

CHAPTER EIGHTEEN

A WARRIOR'S HEART

As Gowramma hobbles back toward her hut, I walk through the cluster of tents and tiny huts with excitement and hope. But once we part, I'm full of nerves, wondering if I can make the impossible, possible.

When I enter our tent, Varsha is standing in the middle of the room trying to shove her unusually large head through the opening of a white cotton tunic that looks like mine. I'm shocked she's trading in her neat and tidy couture Indiana Jane ensemble for something simpler.

"So, to what do we owe this change of wardrobe?" I ask as I flop onto a pile of crumpled blankets on the floor.

"Stench!" Her voice is muffled and lost under the tunic. "I smell like a farm animal, and I can't take it any longer. Having a bath is off the table. We must save the water for drinking. Since we were last at the river, the Elders said the levels are depleting."

I stand up, place my hands on either side of her tunic, and yank it down so she can wiggle through. Yep, it's true, the odor is enough to knock me out, but I can hardly complain because I don't smell much like a fresh flower myself, especially after spending an entire day roasting in the sun learning how to wield the chakra.

"Thanks," she says. A slight smile on her lips shows she's thankful to have something *clean* to wear. She pulls the elastic from her hair and uses splayed fingers as a brush before pulling it back up into a high ponytail. She wipes at the sweat across her forehead. "It was a long day out there. I was on kitchen duty," she says, removing her cat-eye glass frames and rubbing at the lens with her tunic to rid it of smudges. "I heard about that throw down of yours with Raya. Tsk, tsk, you naughty thing, you!"

"Really? That was days ago."

"Well, you know those village girls she's befriended. They keep your stories alive," Varsha says. "Plus, there's a rumor flying around that the pair of you are sisters, hence your matchy-matchy tattoos! Oh, and that you're secretly lusting over Tarun."

"*Half*-sisters," I emphasize the now seemingly important fact, much in the way Raya had done when Gowramma had revealed it.

"Still, that's significant, is it not?" Varsha asks. She tilts her head to the side the way my grief counselor back home did whenever she wanted me to spill all my deepest, darkest thoughts. But I keep mum, knowing that flapping my tongue will only get me into hot water.

"Look, I tried with her. She's stubborn as hell. She made it clear she has no interest in getting to know me. I do wonder what she knows about my Appa, I mean, *our* father, but I doubt she barely knows him. She called him a 'coward,' but he was anything but that when I saw him last. When the rakshasi took him, that is."

"Raya will come around," Varsha reassures me. "She's always been difficult. It's hard to crack that nut."

"And, about that bit about me lusting over Tarun. Yeah, he's no doubt a gorgeous male specimen. But I doubt he's into me. Besides, weren't Raya and him a thing?" I ask. A slight heat rises to my face, and I shrug, trying to appear unhinged. If Varsha noticed my coloring she doesn't show it. I struggle to pull my tunic up over my head and Varsha comes to my rescue and pulls it off for me. I reach for my lehenga and blouse that now functions as my 'every other day outfit' and wriggle into them.

"Well, they were together for a while. But I think Raya's essence is that of a true wanderer. She doesn't like to be tethered to anything or anyone for too long. Tarun is the opposite. Maybe that explains the chemistry between them?" Varsha says.

My heart dips with disappointment and I'm not sure that's really what I wanted to hear. I try to seamlessly shake it off. "I wish people would quit talking. Don't they understand there's a lot at stake?" I groan.

I finish redressing myself and watch Varsha fluffing the blankets in our cozy quarters. She nestles down on her side, folding her arm underneath as a pillow. Within moments she is asleep, but I doubt she will stay asleep for long. These past few weeks, we have become each other's confidants. She reveals more about her swanky student life in London, and I find it hard to believe she ever grew up here.

Every time we venture out to gather fruit or search for others in need of help, she walks along with timid measured steps, as if she is afraid the jungle may swallow her whole at any moment. I've come to learn that she is fragile from mourning and traumatized over losing her sister, Nala. Just as almost every member of our camp, Varsha, too, is haunted by her losses.

I look over at her as I push myself beneath the blankets next to her, listening to her breathing change and she begins to whimper in her sleep. She has cried in her sleep every night since the beginning. She calls out for her sister most nights, other times, I hear Uma Aunty's name repeatedly. I move closer to her as I've done these past few weeks when I hear her sobbing and place my arm around her, holding her tight.

I lay awake beside her, rubbing her back as I mull over the ideas swirling in my head.

Why did I rush and tell Gowramma I know what I'm doing?

For my plan to work, I need my newfound friends to agree to extraordinary measures. If Varsha is this fragile, how will I convince the others of what needs to be done? I need Aarav, Tarun, and possibly Raya to trust and agree to my plans. But Raya has been avoiding me since our teenage timeout with Gowramma. She made it clear she wants her distance. My concerns mount. My heart is heavy and I worry I may have overpromised on the miracle I told Gowramma I would make happen. This plan of mine is sure to backfire.

Early the next morning, after a restless night full of self-doubt and chronic worry, I ask Gowramma for permission to gather Tarun, Varsha, Aarav, and Raya before the morning meditation. I watch Gowramma from a safe distance, speaking to Raya on my behalf. Raya glares in my direction, turns to Gowramma, and shakes her head before storming off the other way. I guess this means she won't be joining us.

"Chandra, what's this about?" Varsha asks.

"Have you found Leena?" Aarav asks eagerly, a hopeful smile crossing his face.

"Well, before we can find Leena, we need to have a game plan," I say, feeling self-conscious because I've never done anything in the way of rallying the troops. I don't think I've ever led anything. Ever. "Before we do anything, *we* need to know how to use the *yodhana sastrasthragalu*." I turn to Gowramma and ask her to hold up her amber amulet, hoping nobody notices the slight shaking of my hands. She obliges.

"We only have a few weeks until the *nooru varshagala amavasye* until Dakini casts her magic and destroys the jungle. I need more time to master the chakra, and there's no way I can be an expert at every one of the warrior's weapons," I say, gently taking the amulet from Gowramma and holding it out to show the others. "While the rakshasi can only be killed by the trishula or the chakra, the śavagala can be killed by these other weapons. There are ten weapons in all and I've only got two hands! But there's all of you, and possibly, Raya, and if I divide the weapons amongst you, we may have a chance after all!"

"Have you gone completely mad?" A voice sounds from somewhere behind me. I turn to find Raya circling the group. Although she had refused to come, I had a hunch her curiosity would lure her in, and she couldn't keep away just as it had kept her motivated when we first met in her fortune teller's tent. She stops next to Tarun, crosses her arms over her chest, and stands glaring at me. She taps her feet indicating her impatience. The look in her eyes speaks volumes, almost as if saying, "Hurry up, I've got other business to attend to."

"Chandra, the only things I can manage are cows and computers, I'm not sure I can fight the undead," Aarav says, apologetically.

Varsha nervously shifts her weight from one foot to the other and busies herself by adjusting and readjusting the seam of her tunic.

Tarun, who is crouched down in the dirt twirling a twig in his hands, looks up and says, "Guys, maybe she's on to something?" He seems to be the only one even moderately interested in anything I'm saying.

Frustrated by the reactions, I march over and grab the stick from Tarun. I squat down in front of him and draw a javelin and mace upon the dirt. My quads ache, so I drop to both knees and crawl to where Aarav stands and etch my best imitation of a bow and arrow. I turn to Varsha and scribble a sword and thunderbolt in the cool clay at her feet. And finally, I get to Raya, where I hesitate, fully expecting her to give me a swift kick to the head. But she doesn't, instead, she continues to keep her sharp eyes on me. Nonetheless, I draw my funky, preschooler versions of a snake, conch shell, and a lotus. I inch myself up off the ground, dust off the red clay, and watch as each one of them stares in wonder at the rudimentary sketches. There is a long silence before anyone says a word.

"Interesting choices," Tarun says, optimistically. "Tell us more."

"I'll carry the chakra and the trishula. Once we locate it," I say, slowly.

"A sword? Me with a bloody sword? This is a joke, right?" Varsha says, swatting the air with her forearm as if it's a sword.

"How else are we going to fight the bad guys," Tarun remarks.

"I am not a killer and I have no idea how to wield something like that," Varsha says with an audible tremor of fear. "I'm not made for this!"

"It's us or them," Raya says without batting an eye. Her words startle me because I was expecting her to be the most resistant.

"What would I even do with that thing?" Varsha says, flailing her arms erratically in the air, as she once again mimics holding an invisible sword. "And a thunderbolt? Seriously!"

"Look, I felt the same way with the chakra, but I think I'm starting to understand it now. If we don't do something, this place, the people, your home, it will all disappear for good," I say, looking at each of their faces. I hope and pray I'm getting through to them.

"Why do you even care? This is really our fight. You're the outsider in all this," Raya growls.

I falter, trying to find the words but Varsha speaks on my behalf. "Raya, it's not her fault she was sent away. She was exiled by Gowramma to keep her out of harm's way. She never knew any of this existed. I can assure you she cares about this place and the people as much as the rest of us." Varsha takes a long breath before continuing. "Fine, I can try, Chandra. I will certainly try, for you. Moreover, I will try in the name of all that has been taken from me."

Aarav shakes his head in agreement. "I can be taught new tricks." He smiles hopeful, looking starkly like his grandfather, Sagar.

"Truth," Tarun chimes in. "I've seen you change. I called you an outsider before, but I see the way you help around here, the way you sit with the old, play with the young, take on duties that are beyond the scope of what you've ever done before coming here." Tarun turns and faces Raya, "It's a leap of faith, Raya. We have to give Chandra a chance."

My face flushes with warmth at Tarun's words of support and encouragement for me, but I quickly snap out of it and switch gears.

"We've all lost so much. We have to stop Dakini," I say, with fire I hadn't felt earlier. I force myself to hold my head up high, the way I've seen Gowramma do when she speaks to the tribes, believing each word has its own magical force. "We have to do this and the only way it can be done is if we work together. You have to be the extra hands I don't have," I say, exhaling sharply. I pray I've been convincing enough.

"Before I agree to this insanity, tell me why it is that I've got three weapons and Aarav only has one?" Raya asks, aggressively, almost as if she wants to pick another fight.

"Raya, you're the only mystic among us and we need your expertise. You have the skills to be creative with them. Besides, we all know you can control snakes," I say motioning to her tattooed arms where the snake and lotus interplay. "Something tells me they were meant for you."

I turn to the others and announce. "If you are all in agreement, Gowramma will show us the way. She's the weapon's master."

Gowramma hobbles over and reaches to retrieve her amber amulet. As I drop it into her weathered hands she says, "Now come, make a circle and hold hands."

She waves us in together and we each reach for the person next to us, clasping hands. She holds her palms out, closes her eyes, and to everyone's amusement, the gemstone hovers above her hand as she whispers something, and taps her *Ūrugōlu* cane upon the earth. The ground beneath us rumbles and begins to fall out from under us and soon it is not there at all, and we are swept away in a spinning, fury of bright light. When the world around us stops moving and we regain our balance, we find ourselves in a shimmery hall of white marble floors and walls. There is a gold inlay deep in the walls depicting some sort of procession of humans, elephants, tigers, and monkeys. The images appear to be walking toward the weapons that hang at the far end of the room amidst a solid, wood altar. It is breathtaking. The flames on all the lit brass lamps dance as we pass by. They're as tall as I am. We walk together, exploring the magical gold etchings on the wall as we approach the celestial weapons.

"This seems heavenly. An armory in a hidden palatial vault? I thought I'd seen it all!" Aarav says excitedly and does not wait another moment before taking the bow and arrows from the wall. "May I?"

Gowramma nods gently. "We are hidden deep in the jungle. Only the *Ūrugōlu* can bring us here. Over the past decades, as the Lambadi tribes found each weapon, I brought them here to hide away." She points her walking stick to the vault. "The Kodaguru tribe, our warriors, oversaw this vault. But they are no longer, and it has been left to the Elders."

I step up in front of my friends and take a deep breath to further explain the weapons in front of them, channeling Amma and everything she had taught me through both dance and folklore.

I keep my hand on the bow and arrow now in Aarav's possession. "The bow and arrows represent good character. I chose you to wield this because I believe you know the value of it. From what I've come to know about you, you are a good, honest, hardworking person, Aarav. I value this about you."

I turn to Tarun. "You'll carry the javelin and the mace. The javelin symbolizes the hidden power of humans to overcome all obstacles in life. The mace symbolizes devotion and surrender. Both will be needed to extinguish the evil around you."

"Raya, you oversee the snakes, the conch, and the lotus. You are a Lambadi already touched by magic and already wield a lot of power. While it may seem your conch and lotus are not in fact weapons, don't be fooled. The conch comes from the beginning of creation when the universe first became what it is today. Blow through it. This is the battle cry of protection. It can destroy all negative energies. The lotus represents the ultimate happiness yet another way to dispel negativity. And we already know how you can command the snakes."

"Varsha, you will wield the *Sword of Knowledge*, representing intellect and wisdom. The knowledge of right from wrong. Seems fitting for our resident scholar! You will strike when you know it is right. You will also carry the thunderbolt which symbolizes the firmness of spirit. It can be directed at the enemy and obliterate their wrongdoing."

"Chandra, how do you know all of this?" Tarun asks. "This sounds like it's more of Varsha's hobby!"

"I owe it to my Amma. When she taught me the folk dances, she had me study goddess Durga long and hard. She wanted me to understand the symbolism behind each weapon the warrior goddess carried," I say. My mind flashes to the statue of goddess Durga that Amma had on her meditation altar. Last summer, we sat in the gazebo in the yoga studio courtyard, filling my head with story after story about each celestial weapon. Amma knew what I would be faced with one day. She had been preparing me from the beginning.

Gowramma, noticing that I seem distracted, adds. "Chandra has the map in her hands that can only be read using the chakra. It will be used to locate the Golden Trishula,"

"But aren't you going to show us how these things work?" Varsha says awkwardly holding the golden sword and a glowing, gold-shaped thunderbolt on the verge of panicking. I'm genuinely worried she may decapitate one of us before any sort of training begins.

"You've already been training these past few weeks. Meditating and focusing your energies, wielding these warrior weapons is really all mind over matter," Gowramma says. "We'll return tomorrow. Now, back to the village for your daily duties."

We gather around Gowramma and the Ūrugōlu, and in a flash, we are whisked from the dreamy ancient Kodaguru armory, and return to the hidden village.

After dinner, Gowramma tends to the tribes and villagers and suggests that we all need to get some sleep soon because weapons training will start early. But I can't relax. It feels like the night before a dance competition and I'm unable to find a way to calm down.

"Chandra, come here. We want to know more about the map," Varsha pleads from where she sits by a small fire pit.

I join the others, wedging myself between Tarun and Varsha as I share the wonders of the chakra. Even Raya has dumped her usual gossipy company and joined us. I place the chakra over the scars on my right palm, and it illuminates the path we must transverse. Varsha reads the different quadrants and regions on the map aloud, explaining that there are many miles between the areas and it will take time to get from one point to the next. I try not to let the proximity of Tarun and the warmth of his breath on my cheek distract me as he leans into me to get a better view of the map. He casually lays an arm across my back and listens intently.

"It's going to be an epic journey," Varsha says, pointing out and pronouncing the unfamiliar names scrawled across each quadrant.

She rests against me, holding my hand in hers tightly, as she squints in the firelight. "We need to follow the region along where the mountains meet the river and cut through this swampy area called *Shadoulyand* or, Shadow Land. We must be on high alert because the area is overrun with river monsters the locals call *mosale rakshas*. They're intelligent creatures and are said to be a humanoid-crocodile mashup." She releases her grip on my hand, searching each of our curious and overwhelmed expressions.

"Clearly, you've lost your mind," Raya grumbles.

"Really? But Chandra's the one that sees the rakshasi?" Varsha gently bumps me with her elbow and laughs.

"Fair enough," I say, chuckling.

"The river monsters are likely starving and in a foul mood because the river is near dry. Anyway, you will find an ancient, abandoned temple where the river turns. The Temple of Souls, *Ātmagala dēvālaya*. Over here, in this region, was where the student group was supposed to excavate this summer."

"You knew what you were looking for when you landed up here this summer, didn't you? You're here for the trishula?" Raya asks with an air of suspicion in her tone.

"More than the trishula, there is a lot of treasure in that abandoned temples. And yes, I was going to take some of the artifacts back to the UK. I was going to show the professors I've come to know. I have this idea for an Ancient Lambadi Civilizations exhibit." She looks around at the concerned frowns and furrows on our faces. "Look, until a few weeks ago, this was in fact how I was going to be able to pay for school. True it exploited the riches of our home, but I'm with you now for the greater cause," Varsha says, earnestly.

"Whatever," Raya says in a snarky tone as if she doesn't fully believe any of what Varsha is saying.

Tarun ignores Raya's outburst. "Sounds like you and Chandra will have to navigate, be our guides. As kids, we were forbidden to go anywhere near the swamps."

Varsha nods and extinguishes the firepit flame. "It's getting late. I need to up my game and figure out how this sword-wielding stuff works. I'll need all the help I can get."

"She's right. Let's all get some shut-eye," Tarun replies agreeing with her.

As we walk back to our canvas tents, I check in with Aarav who has been putting on a brave face.

"We're going to find my sister and I'm still hopeful we'll find Sagar, too." I try to reassure the usually jovial cow herder. He is fixated on nervously cracking his knuckles.

"Chandra, thanks. But if we haven't found my grandfather yet, I don't expect we will at all. I'm not in the business of doubt, but the truth is his health was ailing. I heard about what he'd done at Uma Aunty's. His outburst, that is. Something frightened him. I hope he is away from all the pain and suffering. That's what I want for him. Now, my energy is focused on finding Leena. I am hopeful for that, but I feel I'm not equipped enough for such a task." He pauses to take a breath. "You know I'm not Lambadi. I'm a villager and have nothing to bring to the table," he says. It's hard to see his otherwise cheerful face devoid of happiness.

"You don't have to be Lambadi to save the day, Aarav. You're with us for a reason. I know you are the one who kept Leena going after Amma died. She seemed to really look forward to your correspondence. We have to work together and bring her back to us," I say. We reach the tent he shares with Tarun. He flashes me a quick smile and bids me farewell with a fist pump.

I walk across the way past a couple of huts and I'm almost at my tent when I hear hushed voices nearby. I creep around to the side to find Tarun and Raya huddled closely together. Hidden between the tents, I watch and listen.

"You need to calm down and change your mindset," Tarun whispers. "I'm glad you found Chandra, but the stuff you do isn't safe at all."

"Why? Would you miss me if something happened to me?" Raya asks, leaning into him and puckering her lips. She stands on her tippy toes, trying to reach his full, kissable mouth. Her hands slide down to the belt of his cargo pants, her face dangerously close to his square jawline.

My hands cover my eyes as if I'm watching a horror movie. I turn to leave but trip over a large rock and crash to the ground.

Oh, please don't notice.

I rise to my feet instantly and scramble around the corner to my tent. I fall through the flaps clumsily, scooching in close beside Varsha.

"Feeling lonely?" Varsha laughs.

"I just saw Raya and Tarun. Ugh, you're right. They have chemistry. Maybe a little too much."

"Jealous much," Varsha asks, half awake. "I wouldn't worry. I think that ship has sailed. I don't think he's into Raya like that anymore."

I cover my face with my hands and release a frustrated squeak. "I mean, it doesn't matter. We're on the verge of fighting this evil thing. I've got no time to be having all these feelings," I say, mostly trying to talk some sense into myself.

"So, you admit it? You have feelings for him?" Varsha's voice sounds chirpy in the darkness of the tent.

"I guess. If that's what all the stomach dips and cheek burning episodes are supposed to be?" I whisper. I can't believe I'm even having this conversation, but Varsha is the only person I have ever talked to like this way. Back home, I had just closed off myself to everything and everyone.

"Who said you can't have it all?" Varsha says. "I see the way Tarun's been looking at you and the way you look at him. At the river, at meals, at the firepit. Always together. I mean, old blind snake charmer Ramu can see the way the two of you flirt with each other. Trust me. Tarun is completely into you. Just kiss and get it over with already!" she replies with a yawn slinging her arm over me and snuggling tight.

In a few seconds, she is snoring lightly next to me, and I'm left with my tormented thoughts of kissing boys and fighting the rakshasi. What a combination.

I lay awake a while longer staring into the darkness before nodding off to sleep.

CHAPTER NINETEEN

TRAINING DAY

We wake just before dawn and the stars are still scattered in the sky. The morning air is crisp and cool, a welcome change from the sweltering heat that will bring on the day in a matter of hours. We sit in our now familiar meditation circle. Apart, yet together, our legs tucked beneath us. We inhale the cool air and exhale a warm, fiery breath, readying our minds for our separate journeys into ourselves.

When we open our eyes and rise, time and space have changed dramatically. The once dew-drenched jungle grass is bone-dry as the sun beats down relentlessly.

A short time later, we retrieve the weapons from the Kodaguru hall and return to the clearing near the village. Gowramma is in her element as she works with us on our weapons training and more. By mid-morning, she calls a break, and we separate into smaller groups. Gowramma rallies the Lambadi and villagers to participate. Although there isn't a celestial weapon for everyone, she tells them that they are needed as the war against Dakini draws near. Varsha joins with members from the other Lambadi tribes, while Aarav accompanies Raya to teach another group some of the combat strategies we have learned.

Gowramma sends Tarun and me to a second clearing nearby so that I can have an open range with the chakra and set my sights on targets further out, while Tarun can swing the mace and javelin as wildly as he wants without harming any innocent person in the process.

As we walk together, a wave of excitement flows through me, both for time with the chakra, and time with Tarun. While we're each focused on mastering our weapons, I try not to look up at Tarun for fear of becoming distracted from the task at hand. I attempt to push down any feelings Varsha and I decided I have for him. He keeps his hands firmly on the mace and javelin and his gaze alternates between me and our surroundings.

Around the perimeter, the trees have been hit hard with a disease. The leaves are brittle, brown, and wilting, and are falling fast, signaling that the Lambadi protection spell has almost run its course. It is yet another reminder of why we need to put an end to Dakini's persistent terror.

Tarun moves on a little past the clearing as he drives the mace through the air. I wander nearby, practicing and perfecting my new craft, connecting with the chakra, and controlling its energy with my hands and mind. The connection and power I feel with the chakra sets me ablaze from within. A feeling I've never known before.

I've never felt so alive.

I stretch my arms out and spin, propelling the chakra to lift upwards and watch in awe as it spins along with me. In my head, I hear music. Sweet, sweet music that makes my heart swell with joy. I quickly recognize the rhythmic beat of the tabla from the Lambadi folk song I used to dance to—the one Amma worked so hard to teach me. The essence of the pulsating drumbeat reaches down into my very soul with a hopefulness I have not felt in a long time. I begin to move my feet as if I'd never stopped dancing.

Ta ta ki ta ta. I hammer the beat through my feet into the warm red clay.

Just like that, I'm dancing the steps that had once been second nature to me. A miraculous happiness washes over me, one that I never thought I'd find again. For a few moments, I'm able to forget the pain and devastation that holds my heart hostage in a death grip. Then she appears, a faint image of Leena in my mind. Leena, who is being held captive by a monster. Leena, Amma's only daughter, and legacy. Leena who I must save, if not for myself, then to honor Amma. To honor her memory and the sacrifices she made not just for me, but for all the Lambadi people. *Our* people.

My arms snake above my head drifting high and low. I twirl wildly, freeing myself and getting lost in the movement. I glide along the perimeter of the clearing, reaching forward and touching decaying tree trunks, withered shrubs, and browning jungle grasses, before pulling away. The glowing chakra shadows my movement, dancing in unison with me, blades retracted. And that's when I see it, crimson blooms begin to appear on the bushes and trees I've just touched. I look down at the floral tattoos on my arms gifted to me by my half-sister and turn my attention back to the magnificent tree line. All around me, hundreds of red amaryllis blooms burst open, bringing the jungle to life. Life that was devoid in the area until moments ago. When I stop dancing, the blooms fade away, but they leave me with immeasurable delight. It's been a lifetime since I've felt this way.

I sense something watching me from somewhere deeper in the jungle. My heart skips a beat as a pair of gleaming eyes emerge and appear to float in the darkness of the brush before making its way into the light. It's a giant tigress—that stands close to the size of a rhinoceros. This tigress is the thing of legends. She gracefully strides toward me, her muscular body moving with contrived purpose. Her eyes remain focused on me, strange, yet familiar. She stops inches from my face and looks down at me, her large, round head high above mine.

A gust of wind blows my waves of hair wildly around me, and I hear the words. *"Keep dancing, Chandraka. I'll never stop watching you."* I stare back at the tigress dumbfounded, and without a second thought, I reach my hand up and stroke its thick black and orange striped coat. The black stripes are dizzying. My hands move through its fur coat and it's softer than I imagined it. The creature bows its giant head and pushes itself into my space with its massive muzzle. We are eye-to-eye and as I stare at her, I can only think of one person.

Amma.

I blink and the tigress is gone. Maybe I hallucinated the entire episode, but the feeling inside me tells me otherwise. If I ever believed in reincarnation, this was one of those moments. Once again, as if on command, the music is in my ears, and I remember the tigress' words.

Keep dancing. I'll never stop watching you.

I spin on the tips of my toes and come down on flat feet, pounding them into the ground. My lehenga moves with me, the light silk floating in the air as I twist, turn, and sway. I lose myself in the beat playing only in my head. Once again, the chakra moves with me.

"Cool, you twirl through time and space while I club the air like an idiot," Tarun's voice pulls me from my trance. I put my palm out and the chakra lands in my hand. My eyes pop open and I see him approaching from the opposite direction, the javelin and mace strapped to his back with a thick-textured twine. I search for the giant tigress, but she's nowhere to be found. I keep moving. The drumbeat continues to sound in my head and heart. Tarun walks toward me with an armful of guava. I fall dizzy to the ground still lost in my momentary buzz.

"I've spent my life spinning in circles. That's what you do when you don't have any friends," I say, getting back up and propelling myself into a pirouette.

"Yeah, I get that," he says. I look back in the direction of where I saw the giant tigress and shake my head, smiling. I turn around and find myself looking up into Tarun's handsome face.

"You never really have that problem, do you? You're one of those people who fits in everywhere you go? Popular, athletic, sort of smart," I say with a laugh.

"*Extremely* intelligent! Why do you think everyone follows me around in the first place? There's more to me than just my charm, brawn, and these devilish good looks," he says with a chuckle. I giggle. "Your smile is infectious! It's a pretty one," he says, his voice uncharacteristically cracking ever so slightly. His eyes soften as he looks at me. Heat rushes to my cheeks and I hope he doesn't notice. Fortunately, something else has caught his attention. His eyes grow wide as they dart around the jungle perimeter.

"Wow! Those are amaryllis my grandmother's favorite flower. How are the leaves above now green?" He asks in shock and awe. His gaze drops to my tattooed arms where he spies the flowers. A bewildered expression crosses his face before he smiles widely. "Maybe there's magic in you yet, Chandra?"

"So, you are capable of saying nice things?" I stammer, finding myself distracted by his sudden proximity. Together, we stare up at the blooming flowers in wonder.

"I know I've given you a hard time. But you're so much more than you give yourself credit for. This plan of yours to have us train with these weapons and make them our own, even though they should all be yours, is clever," he says, kneeling in the grass and letting the guavas gently roll to the ground to avoid bruising them.

He removes his drenched shirt revealing a sculpted, heavily tattooed torso. Etched into the side of his midsection is a large, black panther emerging from lush, green jungle foliage with colorful bursts of hyacinth blooming all around. The panther's eyes are wide, glowing, and something about them seems all-knowing. The beauty in the lines is like the ones on my arms, and I realize they could be the handiwork of one person.

"The panther, it's very cool. Really life-like," I mumble, moving closer to investigate.

"Yeah, Raya's artwork. I was her canvas for a moment in time," he says, reaching for a guava. He wipes it and takes a bite. "I have a few others, but those are hidden, if you will," Tarun gestures somewhere below the belt.

"Yeah, it's ok. I don't need the details," I say, turning away awkwardly and throwing my hands up over my ears. I did not need any more details about what they have or have not shown each other.

"Ha! Nah, on my legs," he laughs, trying not to spit the guava out. "You, dirty little magical bird!"

"So, are you still into each her? I saw you...," I say quickly, but then wish I could take it back and not have said anything at all.

"Ha! It was *you* we heard stumbling about in the dark." He laughs hard and now I feel as if there's a bright neon arrow pointing at me, flashing, giving me up. I'm so embarrassed I want to shrivel up and die of humiliation. "We had bets!"

My hands cover my face and I speak through them. "As a Watcher-In-Training is your sole purpose to gather as much ridiculous nonsense on others and bring it to their attention?"

"Nah, Chandra, you're just an easy target for our nonsense," he says, laughing again, eyes focused on me this time. "Seriously, though, Raya and I were a thing once upon a time, but that's the past and things are much different now. Ancient history. We've always been there for one another. She's a reckless one with a thick coat of armor. But she's full of good intent. It's just buried down in there. You'll see, in time."

"I highly doubt that, but whatever," I say, attempting to focus on the chakra again, as he devours the guava and grinds on its seeds.

"Hey, this thing is delicious. Must've grown with whatever magical dance you were doing that made those flowers and vegetation grow." He throws a softball-sized guava up in my direction.

My lack of coordination for catch chooses this moment to highlight my gross weakness as the guava whacks me in the face. Hard. My hands move to my aching cheek.

"Aw sorry," he says, scrambling to his feet. "Let me see." In seconds, his large hands are cradling my face.

"I'm fine," I say, grabbing his wrists with the intent of moving his hands from my face. But I don't. I can't let go of his hands and that same raw energy that seems to follow us everywhere we go—from the night we met, to the river, to the firepit—settles back upon us. I don't want to let go of him.

Hypnotized by the flicker of light dancing in his eyes, I move closer, and he doesn't fight me. My eyes fixate on his full mouth. "This is probably not right," I say, feeling breathless. He nods, but he's thinking the same thing because he takes me in his arms and lifts me up so we're at eye level. I wrap my legs around his waist. He doesn't say anything, but his eyes remain focused on me as he leans forward. Our lips meet and my mind goes blank. All I can feel is the intense need to breathe in his scent. I want this moment to last forever. Our lips remain locked as our tongues dance a perfectly choreographed interlude. My hands move through his thick hair, pulling and pushing while his hands move seamlessly down my back, caressing my hips and bottom.

An electrifying surge of energy zips through me. Tarun feels it too because he grips me tighter against his chest, squeezing me. His hands grab my hair. It seems like nothing will tear us apart. Except, it comes and without warning. A shooting pain travels across my temple and a deep burning begins in my palms. The intense scent of jasmine fills my nostrils, and my head starts to throb. I try to ignore the pain, but it's impossible to push aside. Moments later, my head is filled with flashes of color and choppy pictures that I don't want to understand.

The river is void of water. Inside the belly of the dry, cracked riverbed are hundreds, if not thousands, of scorpions scurrying around. The leafless banyan tree stands naked and exposed with its large branches drooping to the ground as it decays rapidly. A strange growth, an airy blue fungus, covers the roots and is willing its way upward. Dakini in her rakshasi form barrels down onto the riverbank. She holds five pouches made from betel leaf wrapped with twine. Despite them being on the opposite side of the river, the unsettling force of Dakini's destroyers, fill my ears. They are circling Leena, her arms bound behind her back, coaxing her to jump into the pit of scorpions. She makes a stunning hostage, wearing a strawberry-colored sari, dripping with gold jewels from head to toe.

"Release Leena," I yell loudly as the spinning chakra hovers above my outstretched palm. "You chose wrong," Dakini roars at me. "You betrayed me, now Leena, this jungle, and these people will pay the price."

Leena shrieks, thrashing around in the grasp of the zombies. The scorpions in the riverbed rapidly part, revealing a black hole beneath them. I frantically send the chakra to ward off the onslaught of zombies, but hundreds more appear. And then, the Ūrugōlu falls from the sky. Gowramma's Ūrugōlu. My eyes dart up to Dakini, who now has Gowramma in her clutches.

"The old hag is mine. Never again will she outsmart me," Dakini growls. "Prepare to meet your end. All of you!"

Dakini maniacally wraps her claws over Leena and Gowramma's heads and squeezes. They fall to their knees in agony. Dakini thrashes her tail upon the earth, causing the ground below her to crumble. I watch in horror as she releases her hold on Leena and Gowramma and they crash into the dark abyss below.

My heart pounds as if it may explode through my flesh. The vision abruptly ends and I'm unable to see what comes next. The more we engage with each other the more the vision reveals. Tarun's arms tighten around me, to the point where I'm having trouble breathing. I can only assume he sees what I see too as if we are channeling each other's energy outright.

A terrifying howl rips through the air, and our moment abruptly comes to an end.

We spring apart and our attention moves up into the canopy of tangled vines above us. We're unable to see how the vision ends. Searching the trees above, a troupe of howler monkeys swing aggressively among the vines, casting their ominous shadows upon us, filling the air with their eerie warning that echoes through the jungle. Utter chaos.

Red petals of the blooming amaryllis wilt apart and flutter down around us. The leaves of the neighboring palm and teak trees shrivel up and brown in color.

"We should go," Tarun mumbles. His eyes search the sky, the ground, the jungle everywhere but me. He refuses to look me in the eyes, and I feel like this was a big mistake. As the flower petals continue to land around us, their edges become black and they begin to disappear, as does my previously elated mood.

"Look. At. Me," I yell as I grab his chiseled face between my hands and pull him toward me. "You saw something, too. Didn't you?" I ask, or rather tell him, hoping he will explain more.

"Sort of," he murmurs. His furrowed brows confirm my suspicions, but he doesn't volunteer any more information. He moves away from me toward the path that leads back to the village.

"Coward!" I yell out at him. He stops in his tracks, turns, and grabs me by my wrists, pulling me into him. He kisses me hard and quick on the mouth. I don't want him to stop, but it's over in a flash. There's no chance of the vision resurfacing.

He caresses my face as he releases his hold on me and storms ahead of me through the thicket back to the village.

I'm left with a wounded ego. *He's never going to kiss me again.* I trudge up the hill at the pace of a sloth, feeling the fool.

Back at the village, the others gather under an evening sky brushed with brilliant oranges and reds. They unwind by the fire pit, there's laughter and comradery in the air. *Hope among the masses.* They are coming together in a way that was never possible before and I want to relish in this excitement, but I feel the old, cynical me reemerging. The version of me who would rather spend the time inside herself and alone.

Meanwhile, I watch Tarun hurrying off in the direction of Gowramma's hut. I walk on, feeling like a complete fool, toward my tent. I can't help but think he is telling her everything that just happened. My stomach turns and there's a lump in my throat.

Why am I such an idiot?

I see the mighty hollowed-out teak tree trunk that cradles the Vaidya tribe gemstone. The amber glows and its luminescence draws me close. I plop down in front of the altar, cross my legs under me, and gaze into the oblong gemstone with its three holy markings made from ash. A strange calmness sets in as I reflect on the extraordinary events of the day before our lips met. Rediscovering my rhythm in dance, the brief blooming amaryllis and restored jungle vegetation, and the giant tigress. The chakra was working for me in ways I never imagined.

A familiar shuffling of bare feet on the dirt pulls me from my deep thoughts. A small, wrinkled hand gently presses down on my shoulder.

"Come with me," Gowramma whispers. "Worry not about the visions."

Chapter Twenty

Innocence Lost

I rise to my feet and walk back with Gowramma. My hands reach for my flushed face when I speak. "He told you?"

"He means no harm," she says, assuring me I have nothing to be embarrassed about. "He is just trying to protect us."

As we walk along, Gowramma asks me to craft a path due west. I evoke the chakra. With its blades activated, the chakra tunnels through the decaying vegetation, creating a path we can take. Much easier than having to slash the path with a sickle or machete. Gowramma hobbles with the *Ūrugōlu*, her magical walking staff, now glowing an effervescent orange, lighting our way through the jungle. As we venture deeper into the forest, I'm eerily aware that we are no longer under the protection spell that encompasses the Vaidya tribe village. A thick dark fog settles over the contrasting green of the lush foliage. At every turn, we see troubling signs of the forest dying under Dakini's reign of darkness.

The earth is cracked and dry, shriveled leaves crunch beneath our feet with every step few signs of life. The jungle is devoid of the melodic songs of the red parrot. The silence is disturbing. With no tropical canopy above, the lion-tailed macaque has nowhere to go. The pungent stench of rot and decay of animal carcasses is unbearable. The once towering stalks of bamboo and giant trees have fallen against each other in a twisted complex where they lay decomposing. The devastation is incomprehensible.

The odor is getting to me, I slump against a thicket of fallen bamboo and dry heave, but to my dismay, nothing comes up. The sky grows darker with the night as we continue on our way. We stop at the sound of water trickling. Gowramma points to the clearing ahead of us and smiles. "This is where the river of all rivers once began," she says, staring at a small stream of water emptying into the basin below. "This was once a mighty waterfall."

On the far side of the bank, there is a giant tree full of large leathery elliptical-shaped green leaves with branches that sweep down into the river and the ground beneath it. It is the same species of tree that holds the Vaidya tribe gemstone.

"This is *the* tree? Dakini's sister, Aryana?" I ask, breathless from excitement. My eyes linger on the beauty of the flourishing tree.

"Yes, this is what's left of her. She was of the *Atīndriya* tribe. Aryana was a mystic," she said. "Stand with me. Just look at the—"

But I don't hear her. My eyes are drawn to the tree and the empty space in its trunk where I assume the Atīndriya gemstone was once nested and worshipped by the tribe.

"Dakini was let down by her sisters in the most unforgivable way. They sullied her past and robbed her of her future," Gowramma says quietly. "This was the first village to feel Dakini's wrath because it was Aryana's tribe."

"What did they do to her? Did this have to do with the dark magic she was forbidden to practice?" I ask.

But I don't hear her answer. Instead, another voice calls to me from somewhere above.

"*Chandra, come to me.*"

I step in front of the tree and gaze skyward. It's the most beautiful thing I've ever seen. Without another thought, I raise my arms, palms out, and reach for the tree.

"STOP! Don't touch that," Gowramma shouts.

But it's too late, I ignore Gowramma's warning and continue toward the tree. As I reach the massive tree trunk, an inky black mist swarms around me and up into the tree.

The tree continues to whisper to me, "*Come my sweet warrior, come home.*" It swoops its long root-like branches toward me, inviting me in for a warm embrace. A sudden flash of blinding light erupts across the horizon as I place my palms against the smooth bark of the tree trunk and lean in.

"Never let me go," I whisper wanting to forget everything that's happened. I want to let go of the rage and sadness within me. I belong here in the arms of this tree.

Gowramma's warnings are faint murmurs of a past life. There's nothing but darkness for what seems like an eternity. That's when I see *them.*

Three women stand atop a rocky perch above the waterfall's summit, their expressions grim. The water is plentiful, pouring down over the edge of the boulders and into the river's basin.

"Dakini, you can't be here," a woman with dark skin and hazel eyes says, shooing away Dakini.

"Aryana, they took her from me. Surely you know where? She's mine. She is everything," Dakini cries.

"You crossed a line! You know you did." Aryana responds. "Wasn't compelling Ravi to lay with you enough? Then you had his child? He was mine!"

"It's nothing compared to what you and Shalini have done. You turned your backs on me. You are my sisters! And now you've taken the only thing that matters to me," Dakini says glaring at her sister. Her eyes dart from her sisters to the bank.

"We don't have her, Dakini. The Elders made the decision. You must go before the council," Shalini says, arms crossed over her chest, standing her ground firmly. Aryana retreats to the other side of the bank. Dakini pushes past Shalini and hurries after Aryana.

"You've both been jealous of me since we were children. You kept me on the outside," Dakini shouts at Aryana.

"Keep your voice down," Aryana barks, but manages to stay composed as she looks around. "This tribe is everything to me, these are my people. I can't have you poison them against me."

Shalini marches straight for the two women and plants herself between Aryana and Dakini. "There's a darkness in you, Dakini. It has always been there. Ever since we saw you playing with that strange straw doll. The black magic was forbidden, yet you chose it," Shalini says in a calculated manner, manipulating the conversation. Her eyes are raging, but her tone is bored, indicating she has had the same dialogue a hundred times before.

"I found that thing," Dakini erupts. "It was never mine. I wasn't practicing anything sinister. I was a child! You were supposed to be taking care of me, showing me the way, instead, you left me there holding the Dārk myājik gombe. That strange doll with no eyes was hideous." She shudders, remembering it clearly. "I was the weak, quiet little one. The perfect scapegoat you needed. You wanted to cut me out ever since we were told about our futures."

Aryana shoots a disturbed look at Shalini and wraps her hand around her arm, "She's right, Shalini. We can't do this to her anymore. We need to help her," Aryana whispers, furiously into Shalini's face.

"And lose everything?" Shalini spits back. "Never!" She turns to Dakini, her eyes hard and body rigid. "We told you to leave this place and never come back, but you had to have that child! How did you think anyone could love a monster like you? You are pathetic, Dakini. Leave now, before I make you

go away forever!" Shalini's words bite with bitter h
atred and disgust.

"You turned me into this monster!" Dakini's soft
voice escalates into a vicious roar. "I won't let you rest
until I see her again."

Shalini stands squarely in front of Dakini
unafraid, her eyes hard and intense. She makes a
twisting motion with something in her hands and
Dakini doubles over, clutching her midsection in
pain. Dakini's legs fold beneath her and she drops to
her knees before falling forward in agony. Shalini
opens her hands to reveal a tiny straw figure before
crushing it and tearing it limb by limb.

"Maybe the Dārk myājik gombe was never yours,
but who will believe you now?" Shalini glares at her
fallen sister.

Dakini looks up and her eyes go dark.

"Give her back. Give me my daughter!"

The vision passes and I'm left with a deep
excruciating pain that penetrates my throbbing hands
up my arms and into my chest as if they are on fire.
A moment later, the sensation shifts, and it feels like
millions of tiny shards of glass are being plucked one by
one out of my hands. I wail in pain, unable to stop the
invisible force extracting the slivers from my palms.

"Hush, it won't be much longer," a raspy voice
commands. "Stay still."

My eyes flutter open for brief moments before closing again. At first, I see a human, a beautiful woman with golden-brown skin, wavy dark hair laden with fragrant jasmine blooms, and familiar wide, doe-shaped eyes. But then, her head shakes in quick, sharp motions to reveal five horns protruding from her skull and her lovely face begins to distort and melt away before my eyes. Grey, leathery skin takes its place, and a long, black tongue flickers in and out of the creature's gaping mouth, licking at my palms and retracting. Its hands are glowing red and moving rapidly. She is no longer human. She is now the wretched rakshasi.

The rakshasi uses its claws to slash at my hands along the scarred lines, opening them up. Blood pours from the gashes as the creature tears through my flesh over and over. The pain is unlike anything I've ever known. The blood loss and pain leave me dizzy and lightheaded. I fall into darkness.

CHAPTER TWENTY-ONE

TO DANCE WITH A DEMON

T he gentle lapping of water against my cheeks coaxes me awake. The sky above stretches to an infinity of tranquil blue parrying a cloudy canopy. Weightless and serene, I float on my back in the shallow river. The tree has now transformed, taking on its true form, rotting from the inside out. It is only at this moment it occurs to me that the monster compelled me yet again and I fell for its con. It shapeshifted itself into the beautiful banyan tree of the Atīndriya tribe and tricked me into believing it was a sign of hope.

The pain lingers in my hands, radiating all over my body. I would probably hurt less if I was in the boxing ring with a champion heavyweight boxer and beaten to a pulp. I scan myself but see no evidence of bruising or breaks except for my battered hands. I attempt to stand and cut my feet on the debris of the shallow riverbed. There is a thick layer of a black, tarry substance on both my palms. It is so thick that I can no longer see the lines on my hands. I remember the flurry of images when I was in and out of consciousness the rakshasi licking my palms, poking and prodding me.

I drop to my knees, whimpering incessantly, sounding more like a wounded animal than a human. My mind is racing as I try to scrape off the black substance that covers my palms. All I can think about is the map.

"Gowramma," I wail, scrambling to the riverbank, searching for her. Screaming and cursing, I crawl on all fours. "Gowramma," I shout again. But nobody answers.

I attempt to reach for the chakra in my pocket, but the pain is excruciating. I wrap my hands around it and pull it out, but it weighs a million times more than I remember. My hands are so tender I can barely hold it. My heart pounds against my chest and my erratic mind is unable to summon the power. The only sensation coursing through me is agony.

I continue to try again putting everything in me, focusing my energy to summon the magic of the chakra. To my dismay, it just remains motionless in my outstretched palm. I am unable to connect with the abilities I worked so hard to learn.

The rakshasi took everything and I'm left with nothing.

Leena, the people, the river. How can I help them now?

My eyes search the rotting tree where I made the impact. I dash to the trunk and find my handprints. I do not touch the tree for fear it may strike me again.

"You want them back?" A voice booms behind me. "Your hands...the map...your beloved Leena...and Gowramma?"

I whirl around to find Dakini in her rakshasi form hungrily staring me down. She hovers above the water revealing her ten-horned heads, hundreds of arms, and the menacing scorpion's tail. Sharp, jagged fangs protrude from her mouth and her black tongue lashes out toward me. A crystal orb floats mere inches above her cupped, claw-like hands.

I look back down at my darkened hands. "You erased the map to the Golden Trishula," I say angrily, lunging toward her. "Give it back!"

The orb radiates serene energy, casting a magnificent warm moonglow. It is quick to disarm me. My eyes remain fixed on the orb. A mist within it swirls through hundreds of images before settling on one of Leena. Her hands are bound behind her back, and she stands against a tree. She is draped in a red silk ceremonial sari, and ornate gold chains embellished with gemstones. Her hair is adorned with orange and yellow marigolds. Leena could pass for a queen if it weren't for the haunting look of terror in her eyes. One of Dakini's henchmen holding a human skull pushes Leena backward, grabbing her by her face. He squeezes her cheeks aggressively tilting her head back, and forces Leena to drink a glowing red liquid that flows from the skull. She makes a feeble attempt to spit it out, but they force her to drink more.

"Dusta's dark magic. That is her evil blood. She ordered this—your sister will slowly forget who she is. Leena now answers to a higher power."

"Stop this! Take me instead. Set her free!" I roar leaping forward from the river, punching at the air around Dakini. But it is no use. She is out of my reach and helpless I fall back into the water.

"Not in your wildest dreams, child," Dakini roars. "Now it can all be mine. I'm taking everything back."

"That orb you hold is the moonstone and that's mine!"

"Wrong again! Let me refresh your memory." The orb rotates under Dakini's control, hovering between her claws. Inside the orb, the scene shifts like a magical movie reel. The scene is no longer focused on Leena in captivity but switches to a familiar one. For a second time, I see the fidgety nervous human woman with jasmine blooms in her hair. The one who screeched and commanded the child version of me to give the orb back to her. I watch again as the orb rolls between the woman and me and as she changes before my eyes. The orb rolls back into my grasp before it shatters into a million little pieces, impaling and dissolving me into oblivion.

My eyes dart from the orb to Dakini and back down to my tar-covered hands. "YOU!" I finally connect the dots. "It was you all along?"

She motions with her claws and the orb turns again. I see another vision I had after locating the chakra, where the beast had roared at me to "*Come home*" and commanded that I "*Give it back!*"

"You again? You were the thing calling me to this place," I say loudly, trying to make sense of it all. "The last vision I had, when you trapped me here, I saw you in your human form with your sisters. The Tale of the Three Sisters—that's your story?"

"Don't call them that. They are nothing to me!" She says void of emotion, although her eyes look crazed. She motions with her hands and turns the orb several more times revealing more snippets of the past.

"They were cruel to you," I say, softly this time.

The images come back in fragments, but Dakini rotates the orb several times over, taking us even further back in time.

Dakini begins to narrate as I keep my eyes focused on the scenes in front of me. "You don't know the half of it. Shalini and Aryana always kept me on the outside, from the time we were little. They lied about me using dark magic all those years ago. The Lambadi Elders banished me. I had to live in a hut by the river, but I could not use the river waters. My sisters completely abandoned me, and I believed I was not worthy of love. Lost and alone, I made a pact with a *Dārk māntrika*—a dark sorceress, known as Dusta—the evil one. She promised me I could keep the power I was meant to have as a Lambadi High Priestess in exchange for the moonstone hidden deep in the riverbed of the mighty river Kaveri. The moonstone has the power of courage and intuition. Even more, she swore to help me get revenge on my sisters."

She pauses, her rakshasi eyes softening for a moment before she continues. "For years, I had to answer to the evil Dusta. And then I met your father, Ravi, who was betrothed to my sister, Aryana. They had a child, a little girl, Surya. I do not know how, but he learned about the vicious lies my sisters had told about me. He swore he would help me gain my place with the Lambadi once again. We fell in love and you came along. The three of us were happy for a while."

Stunned, I stand speechless with my mouth hanging open. I replay Dakini's last words from the vision repeatedly.

Give her back. Give me my daughter!

I gulp hard as the meaning of her words sinks into me. "No! It's not true. It can't be true. I am not *your daughter*." I slump onto the riverbank. "You are *not* my mother!" I scream. Blood rushes to my face and a pounding begins on my left temple. My chest is heaving. This can't be real.

"They took you from me all those years ago, and I've been punishing them ever since. You were mine, Chandraka. My Moon Child! The light in my darkest of times. You are the greatest love of my life," she roars. "They took you and I changed. My heart turned cold, my power grew vicious, and I became this monster."

My throat goes dry. I can't think straight. I don't want to believe what I'm hearing.

"Not true!" I shake my head violently in denial and move my hands to the pocket nervously clutching the chakra.

"They've poisoned you against me," she cried. "I am cursed. You are cursed. You can see me, but you can only see me this way."

My breathing becomes labored. "You're a master manipulator, just like Shalini. Aren't you? You're manipulating and compelling me to believe in these lies you are spouting." I turn my back to her, shaking my head and squeezing my eyes shut.

The sound of the rotating orb forces me to look at her again. This time, Dakini rotates it counterclockwise. We go back to the time when she had her daughter.

"You were a happy bold and beautiful child. But, Dusta reemerged, and my sisters pit Ravi against me. They told him I had not changed my ways. I had debts piled up with the devil herself and it was time for me to pay. Ravi happened to see me with Dusta on one occasion and drew his own conclusions. What he didn't know at the time was that she had threatened to take you from me. She was privy to the prophecy, and she knew you would become the Ārisalpatta. She gathered you were special. Ravi believed I was plotting against the Lambadi with Dusta, and left me, but I was pleading for your life."

"The hut by the river, is that where we lived?" I ask, recalling the moment in the hut where I stood drenched, dripping with water. "You sent me to retrieve the moonstone?"

"I couldn't enter the river; it was part of my banishment from the Lambadi community. But you were not forbidden to enter the river. It took days of you submerging yourself in the river and coming out empty-handed, but you were eager to please me and never stopped searching. You were so brave. Finally, on the fifth day, you came out with the moonstone. The problem was that the moonstone *chose* you." She shakes her head as if she was reliving those moments all over again. "Somehow, you instinctively knew you had to protect it and you knew that there was something very wrong with me. That's when you absorbed the moonstone into your hands. When I failed to provide Dusta with the moonstone, she sealed my fate with a dark curse that you, my child, would never see me as your mother again and that you would only see me as a monster until my death."

If the beast could shed a tear or show emotion, I think this would be that moment, but Dakini keeps her eyes fixed on the orb and the tiny version of me inside it. For a split second, through the orb, I see the two of us. Dakini is in her human form. We're running through the tall jungle grass together. The tiny version of me falls and scuffs both knees. I lay on the ground crying, but Dakini scoops me into her arms tenderly. She wipes the tears off my face and carries me back to the hut where she dresses my wounds. I throw my arms around her.

Dakini doesn't dwell on her pain, instead, she bitterly spins the orb again, continuing with her narrative. "The moonstone shattered, maiming you."

"Then Appa came back and found me with bloodied hands. He took me to Gowramma," I whisper, recalling Gowramma telling me about the first time she had seen me.

"And I've been looking for you ever since."

"So, now you live somewhere between the madness within you, unable to do the right thing? How could you kill those innocent people at the festival? Destroy this jungle? Take those children?" I stop my rage to catch my breath. "You killed my Amma—my Watcher! I saw the scorpion in the yoga studio."

"I did no such thing! That was not me. I promise you. Dusta killed your Watcher." She shakes her head. "But I'm guilty of the rest. That is my curse. I am evil in its truest form. I thirst for blood, power, and destruction. I took the children because I wanted the Lambadi and the villagers to feel my pain. What I felt all these years without you."

"There must be some humanity left in you. Or you would've squashed and dismembered me by now?" I attempt to challenge her.

"I could never harm you. You are my flesh and blood and I have always loved you," she says, floating in front of me. "I've spent my life hoping to see you just once more. I saw you for a few moments when I took Ravi. Moon Child, you must know that even the darkest of souls want to walk in the light of love."

Her words splinter my heart and fill it with hope in the same instant. And just like that, I realize Dakini is not compelling me this time. Maybe I'm being stupid, believing a monster. Amma's words come to my mind.

"*Although rakshasis and rakshasas are mostly perceived as evil in our mythology, they are sometimes good.*"

Dakini's far from good, but there's a minuscule glimmer of goodness in her yet. "Why do you need the trishula?" I ask. "You understand it's one of the ten weapons of the Kodaguru warrior. It is meant to be used against you. To kill you."

"I'm aware. But the trishula also gives the holder control of the past, present, and future. If I can turn back time, I can make things right again. Stop my sisters and their lies. I never would have made a pact with Dusta."

"Dakini, time travel never turns out well. You could change the course of everything!"

"Anything is better than this existence," she says.

"And the moonstone? It's one of the last Lambadi gemstones you need to seal the curse? To bring darkness to the land?"

"It was never my intention, this is Dusta's plan, not mine. But I answer to her," Dakini says with guilt in her tone.

Suddenly, the orb turns in the opposite direction and bolts away from Dakini's grasp. It floats above us, just out of reach.

A strange unfamiliar voice sounds from a distance. "Chandra, you are nothing without your band of misfits." Dakini and I look up once again at the orb where the mist swirls and settles on images of the hidden Vaidya tribe village.

Everything is ablaze, the flames are rising upward as Dakini's zombies savagely raid and pillage what was our last hope. My new-found family—Raya, Aarav, Varsha, and Tarun—run for their lives. Tarun clutches the Vaidya tribe gemstone against his chest as some strange demonic version of myself appears before him, thrashing the air and the earth with the mace.

"NO!" I continue to watch in horror, my eyes turning from Dakini back to the orb. "What are you doing? That's not me. Make it stop. Now!" I'm about to lash out and strike her, but the look on Dakini's face is one of pure confusion. We turn our attention back to the scene inside the orb.

My crazed doppelganger creates havoc and snatches the amber gemstone from Tarun and tosses it over to one of Dakini's zombie henchmen, who carries it off in the opposite direction.

"This is Chandra's fault," Tarun yells to the others as he points toward my evil double. "She's an outsider and she'll always be an outsider." He rushes forward wielding his javelin at the thing and pierces the evil version of me. In a flash, the evil me becomes nothing but dust particles floating in the air.

"What have you done? You've ruined me," I scream at Dakini, pulling out the chakra and praying that none of what we've just seen is real. I'm in a blind fury, seeing my friends, the people I've come to know, and the stolen gemstone in harm's way. I shut my eyes and focus, pushing the chakra against my heart. Miraculously, the chakra begins to vibrate and glow. It begins to spin at a warp speed in my hands as my eyes turn to Dakini.

"That wasn't me," Dakini says, preparing to defend herself against the glowing chakra. "I'm here in front of you. I can't possibly be acting as your doppelganger." Dakini turns her body, thrashing her scorpion tail upon the river, somehow creating the illusion of more water than what's there, and I watch in shock as the waves rise above my head. My bangles grip my forearms and the cuffs come together just as something blazing hot passes over my cheeks. As the largest wave settles down, Dakini releases hundreds of poison stingers from her tail. Intuitively, I raise my cuffed arms up to my face and deflect the stingers from penetrating my skin. One by one they fall at my feet.

"What is it then? Who did that?" I scream back at her. "Are you going to blame Dusta again?"

"You wield great power," Dakini declares, almost amused. She puts a hand back up and the orb returns to her, free of whatever power had been controlling it moments before. The images are now gone, and a gentle light is alive inside. It glows a tranquil, pale yellow once more.

"Dakini, you've found me, and you have the moonstone. Now you need to set the lost children free. I will retrieve the trishula," I say, trying to sound bold negotiating with a demon. "Imagine the pain you've inflicted on those families. The terrible void they are all experiencing. You can make good and change this—you can show everyone you aren't the monster they say you are."

There's a long, uncomfortable silence.

"Fine," she says abruptly, snapping her fingers. I look to the orb and witness the children being released from a dark hidden cave covered in moss. They run free into the jungle. Minutes, maybe hours have passed, but in the scenes that follow within the orb, we watch as they reunite with their families somewhere on the fringes of where the village once was. I see villagers and Lambadi at the border, the happy tears, and warm embraces of reunion.

"Now, give the moonstone back to me," I command.

"Get me the trishula."

"I will retrieve it but I make no promises to you," I throw back.

The orb spins fluidly under her control, turning and turning until the mist within it settles and an image of

Gowramma appears. Dakini's eyes glow red and move from the orb to meet mine.

"I'll hold on to Gowramma for added insurance, so you'll do what I need you to do," Dakini growls with a smirk before tossing her horned head back and releasing a deep roar. In the next instance, she disappears in an inky black fog.

Adrenaline courses through my veins and my heart feels as if it is beating for the first time. My mind is fixated on one thing and one thing only.

Getting my hands on the trishula.

Chapter Twenty-Two

The Shadow Land

I trudge through the decaying jungle debris and return to the Vaidya tribe village. The flames blaze with fury but are not as intense as the moonstone orb had shown. The huts and tents are fried to a crisp, but it seems everyone made it out. Nothing is in a recognizable shape except for the tree. On my way to Gowramma's hut, my eyes linger on the once magnificent banyan tree and its empty belly. The stone is gone. My heart drops into the pit of my stomach. I want to completely break down, but I know I've got to keep moving.

My thoughts are racing as I sift through the chunks of information from my strange encounter with Dakini.

Once Dakini hands over the Kodaguru moonstone to Dusta, they will have all the Lambadi gemstones for the ritual. But they are missing the trishula and must wait for the nooru varshagala amavasye—the cosmic moon that comes only once every hundred years. Although Dakini claims she wants the trishula for redemption, I'm not certain she can be trusted. On the other hand, Dusta needs the trishula for the ritual, to plunge the jungle into a paranormal darkness and control the only thing that could destroy her. I look upward to the sky, and it dawns on me that the nooru varshagala amavasye will be here in just a few days.

I inhale deeply. My mind flips through thousands of scenarios, processing what must come next. I need to retrieve the trishula. Locating it will be tricky without the map in my palms. I recall Varsha saying we had to go to *Shadoulyand* and the *Ātmagala dēvālaya*—Temple of Souls. I don't really know what I'm getting myself into, but I need to get the trishula before anyone or anything else.

The bright orange sun hangs in the middle of the horizon. It is already midday. I attempt to recall what the map in my hand had shown. I close my eyes to focus my energy and vaguely visualize my hand in Varsha's and her pointing out the different regions.

I need to follow the river toward the Shadoulyand.

So that's what I do. For hours, I walk along the riverbank, using the chakra to cut myself a path through fallen jungle vines and bamboo when needed. Nits are drawn to me like bees to honey, their annoying buzz filling my ears. I swat randomly into the air to move them away and wipe at the sweat dripping down my face.

My journey becomes more difficult as the terrain changes. The earth turns thick, dark, and soggy, and I know without a doubt that I'm entering *Shadoulyand*. I gather my lehenga, twist it in a knot, and pull it up past my upper thighs so it can't impede my progress through the muck of the swamp.

As I wade further into the ankle-deep mud, I hear a steady drum beat from somewhere in the distance. After another four or five steps, I find myself knee-deep in the sludge. Here, maybe because it is out of Dakini's reach, the foliage hanging above is still intact. The trees have a labyrinth of aerial roots that twist and turn at every angle. The bizarre roots resemble long limber fingers, sprouting from the center of the main trunk, supporting the trees where they grow in the mushy soil.

Several sharp needle-like pricks pierce through my skin along my arms, calves, and upper thighs. At first, I swat at the sensation, but soon the feeling changes to something taking hold and digging deeper into my skin. I look at my arms and want to hurl. Dozens of giant blood-sucking leeches attach to my skin, their hungry mouths greedily feeding upon me. Their shriveled, slimy bodies quickly transform with each gulp of my blood. I make every attempt to pull them from me, but by the time I peel one off, several more have joined the feast. I grab the chakra and shove it between the surface of my skin and the leeches. It's unexpected but they begin to sizzle and fry on contact with the stone. I do not waste another moment, getting as many leeches off me as possible. Every time the chakra touches my skin, I wince. I lose count after the twenty-five.

They've left small craters all over my body. I pass the chakra over the wounds after the leeches are gone. The chakra appears to leave traces of shimmery, gold dust behind, filling the void of the bites. It appears the chakra is controlling the blood loss by cauterizing my wounds. It reminds me of the gold healing ointment Gowramma had applied to my wrecked hands months ago when it all began. With each step, exhaustion sets in, and I grow weary. I want to curl up in a ball and sleep.

A dull growling rumble from the dark corners of the swamp snaps me back to attention. I catch a glimpse of something large and reptilian-like, angrily whipping its thick, rubbery tail. It must be more than twelve feet tall. This must be the *mosale rakshas*—the river monsters—that Varsha had warned about. It charges toward me with a wild look in its eyes as it ravenously snaps its razor-sharp teeth. I try to move, but my feet are stuck, almost like I've stepped into a pool of quick-drying cement. The mosale rakshas is now close enough for me to see it clearly. The creature has thick arms, a broad torso, and legs of a titan, but the head and tail of a crocodile. Another step and it towers over me trying to knock me over with its flattened snout. Thick green saliva oozes from its gaping mouth as it gnashes its sharp teeth at me with the intent of turning me into an afternoon snack. I bob and weave from my waist, trying to free my feet. I dodge and dive from its advances, only to find myself surrounded by several more mosale rakshas. I grab a branch to stop it from clamping its jaws on my arm, but the branch breaks off inside its mouth, preventing it from closing shut. The sheer size of the beast makes it clumsy. I decide to use this to my advantage. As the other mosale rakshas charge and dive for me, I evoke the chakra. The glowing pale yellow disc ricochets through the cove, chopping branches from the canopy above to use at my disposal. I catch the falling debris and heave thick woody branches into their mouths. But they outsmart me, releasing their next line of defense. Their gaping mouths open wide, shooting fire. The frenzy of flames burn down the branches to ash and once again, they lunge toward me—their teeth-gnashing and fire blazing. I raise my arms to shield my face and the cuffs tighten along my forearms, allowing me to deflect the scalding flames, though I can still feel the intensity of the heat. My arms reach around for the dangling vines of a nearby tree, and I hoist myself upward to move from their line of fire. I'm hanging above the mosale rakshas as they awkwardly attempt to climb the trees, but they're too heavy to reach me in the high woody nook above them.

The drum beat I heard in the distance earlier is getting louder and seemingly closer. The tempo quickens, now beating like my heart in double, possibly triple, or quadruple time. Over the clamoring beat a calm, yet forceful voice commands, "STOP!"

The mosale rakshas disperse, retreating into the swampy darkness like a pack of dogs responding to a higher master. But moments later, they are back, and they create a line along the perimeter of the small cove as if trained to do so.

"You don't belong here," a deep baritone male voice warns.

"Probably not," I whisper, staring down from my perch at a man emerging from behind a shadowy tree. He carries a small tribal wooden tabla nestled under his arm as his free hand taps the thin, drum skin. He is draped in simple saffron-colored clothing. My eyes follow his long, greying beard down to the middle of his chest. Although his beard extends somewhere close to his knees, my eyes stop at a shiny object peeking out from beneath the dozens of wooden necklaces around his neck. A shiny black gemstone. He appears to be a *sadhu*, a wise holy man. Amma had told me stories of such people who renounce worldly pleasures to devote themselves to spiritual life.

"Neither of us belongs here. Why would anyone seek enlightenment here? In this dismal place?" I ask, my eyes fixated on what looks like a Lambadi medallion hanging from his neck. I use the tree line as monkey bars and make it to the firm ground where he stands. I drop down a few feet away from him. "A *sadhu* or Lambadi—which one are you?"

"Observant, you are," he says, following my gaze to the middle of his chest. "I'm not either. Not anymore. I was exiled by my own kind long ago."

"What tribe?" I ask again, focused on getting an answer.

"I'm a tribe all my own," he replies smugly, not wanting to play my game. "I protect these temple grounds."

I stomp past the man, but the river monsters impede my path, blocking the opposite side where I assume is the temple entrance.

"You're not equipped to go in there," he says, following my line of sight toward a dark narrow passage.

I raise my palms and use every ounce of my meditative power to evoke the chakra once again. It begins to spin in my palm.

If only Gowramma could see me now.

"You must not take the trishula from this place," he says. His eyes are bright and sad all at once. "The malevolent spirits of warriors past who guard this holy weapon make this task near impossible."

"Don't worry. I'll manage."

"Moon Child, call off the chakra."

"What did you call me?" I ask with biting anger. I steadily back away, but I can feel my body tensing up and begin to shake. He said *Moon Child*...nobody calls me that. I try to keep my looming panic in check. "You're one of Dakini or Dusta's illusions, aren't you?"

He pulls at the black stone pendant hanging on twine around his neck and holds it up.

"Call off the chakra and *look* at me," he pleads.

I ignore his appeal and keep the chakra spinning as I focus on him. His eyes are looking deep into me. Our eyes meet and I sense a flicker of familiarity in his dark brown soulful eyes.

I know this man.

Reading my thoughts, the chakra instinctively settles back onto the palm of my hand, and I slump in disbelief against a crumbling, stone wall. I search the face of the man in front of me and attempt to steady myself before the word falls from my mouth.

"*Appa?*"

CHAPTER TWENTY-THREE

SHAMBHALA

"**A**ppa?" I repeat. "But how?" My lips quiver as salty tears descend my mud-streaked face. He stands motionless and unsurprised.

"You're not real!" I say as a sudden pang of fury rips through me. The feelings of hopelessness and abandonment I'd pushed down into the far regions of my heart bubble to the surface.

He's been alive all this time? Why didn't he come for me?

Old wounds open, evoking a landslide of emotion I'm unable to control.

"Breathe," he says, raising a hand and using his tone to calm me in the same manner he had controlled the river monsters. But I cannot find my breath, and despair courses through me. "I left to keep you safe," he whispers after a long pause.

"Keep me safe? What about Amma and Leena? They deserved to be safe!"

"Sita knew what she was doing," he says in a steady monotone without emotion. It confirms the nature of their relationship. An agreement made of necessity after he'd taken me with bloodied hands to Gowramma. After that point, Gowramma had appointed Sita to be my Watcher.

He has changed so much over the years. The way he speaks gives me the impression of a broken man, a stark contrast to the Appa I remembered— a man full of life and laughter. The shell in front of me is nothing like that version of him.

My tears have stopped, and my lips turn down into a frown.

"You won't understand. I had to come back to this place to follow my journey. My destiny. I had lessons to learn. My duty became preparing the tools you would one day need. I helped locate most of goddess Durga's celestial weapons. This was my path," he says slowly. His lack of emotion is starting to wear on me. "I see you found the chakra. It was once mine but was always meant for you. I sent it back to Sita—your *Amma*—for safe keeping."

I hold the disc in my hand and shove it into my pocket. "I grew up without you," I scowl as my voice crescendos. "The selavu never went away. It kept coming. I couldn't connect with anyone. I was far from normal. You were the only one who could really understand that part of me. And you weren't there! I grew up feeling like a freak. A lonely useless freak."

He deflects my emotional tirade. "That last night when that rakshasi found us, it was not after the moonstone. It had come for you."

"I know. I know that monster is Dakini and I know she's my mother." I spit the words out angrily. "And I know you loved her once. I know you have another daughter, too."

His eyes grow wide, and he strokes his long beard as if it provides him some sort of distraction to channel his nervous energy.

"You seem shocked I know so much," I say, but I don't let him respond. "My selavu allows me to see the monsters among us, but right now it is showing me a coward. You abandoned us when we needed you most. I needed you more than anything," I say, harshly ripping into him with the years of pent-up resentment I never realized I had. I hold nothing back. "Why didn't you come back to us?"

"I couldn't. I was forbidden to leave this place after Dakini brought me back here years ago. She wanted me to go before the Lambadi Elders and declare her innocence and confirm the lies her siblings had told. But Dusta threatened that if Dakini did not stay and serve her, then she'd destroy the Lambadi right then and there. The Elders were there, and they saw it all. They watched Dakini kneel to that demon. In choosing Dusta, Dakini saved the Lambadi. But the Lambadi had no clue, and they could not forget or forgive her. This only fueled her hate and darkness," he pauses, and a grim look crosses his face. Something about the way he takes her name tells me his heart remains with Dakini. "Then, Dakini made one final plea to her sisters," he says.

"And it backfired?"

"When the sisters refused to help, Dakini struck Aryana, turning her into the banyan tree to forever stand at the river's edge," he says. I look back down at my charred hands, remembering the moment touched the tree. "Shalini has managed to escape her wrath time and time again. In the meantime, Dakini's truth lay buried and lost through time."

"Are you telling me that Dakini sacrificed herself to lead a dark life so that the Lambadi could live? That is a truth that should be known to all. She saved us from Dusta?" I ask.

Appa nods. "Yes, she did. Dakini has always had a brave heart. Like yours," he adds with the tinge of a slight smile.

"And what happened to you, then?"

"The Lambadi sent me to live in exile for my transgressions, and for aiding Dakini." He stares at me, pulling at his beard before adjusting the strap attached to his tabla. "The Elders stripped me of my selavu. I no longer have those abilities. I can no longer see the evil among us. I am useless. So, this is where I've come to live. Among the giant crocodiles. I don't see what you see anymore. I protect the grounds of the Ātmagala dēvālaya—the Temple of Souls. Those who have ventured in never come out."

My mind is racing with multiple options. There must be some way he'll allow me entry into the temple. I doubt he'll fall for the daughter card in this instance. So, I start building a case for giving me safe passage through the temple.

"I don't have the moonstone anymore. Dakini took it, which means they now have all the gemstones to perform the ritual. It is Dusta who is orchestrating everything. She is the one who is trying to destroy the jungle and these people. I need the Golden Trishula to put an end to all of this."

"You will need to find another way. You are the last Kodaguru warrior so you will figure this out. Without the trishula. You must protect—"

"I know it's all on me! But this is all incredibly daunting," I shout, crumbling to my knees dramatically.

I suffocate in the swampy darkness of the canopy as my world collapses around me. My mind fills with a paralyzing doubt.

Why did I think I could do this?

The power I felt moments ago slips from my grasp and a tidal wave of fear pulls me under. I'm lost in a current I seem unable to control.

"I've lost what I was supposed to protect. The moonstone, the people, the last village, and my friends." I throw up my hands to him. "Just let me pass and let me get the trishula. It's the only way I can make this right!" I plead.

"I cannot let you go there," he repeats, stubbornly.

"I faced Dakini and I barely came out of it in one piece. Dusta is a million times more powerful. The trishula can slay her. I know it can." I continue to make my case. "Please, I'm alone. I am one person, not an army!" I release a long breath exhausted by the multiple trials I am forced to face.

"You are wrong," he says.

The rustling leaves in the jungle canopy above divert our attention. The earth shakes violently moving the trees with it. Appa stands still as if this is an everyday occurrence. I finally see with my own eyes what is causing the ruckus. There's a stampede of elephants, monkeys, and large apes on the other side of the swamp near the gigantic stones of the temple ruins. I'm baffled.

"I've channeled a few friends," Appa says, the tone in his voice changes. He sounds almost proud of himself.

"What on earth?" I gaze around in confusion.

"This is it? She's our only hope?" A smooth, steady voice asks from above. I look up to see a half-woman, half-monkey—a being I've only read about in storybooks—standing atop one of the elephants. She slides down the elephants winding trunk to join us. When she unfolds herself in front of me the length of her stands at a whopping six and a half feet. A luscious mane of long black hair cascades along her large oval-shaped face. Her womanly torso ends with a long winding tail of a monkey. She has long arms that almost touch the ground. A golden chest plate adds to her armor along with the thick leggings, and tall boots that look like they're made from large green leaves dipped in gold. A hatchet is strapped to her left thigh and a machete on the other.

She glares at me with brilliant, jade-green eyes, and long lashes that go on forever. I can tell that she's unenthused with what she sees.

My eyes shut tight, willing away everything in my line of sight. When I open them again everything remains the same like I've stepped into an alternate universe.

"I am General Haauna, a descendent of the monkey General Hanuman who fought alongside the great Lords Rama and Lakshmana," she speaks confidently and shoots me another stone-cold glare. Of course, she has ties to one of the greatest Hindu epics.

"I'm..."

"A mess," she says, flatly. "You can't possibly be what our very existence hinges on?" Her eyes move to meet Appa's. She turns to him and directs her question to him. "I guess she's coming with us?"

"Actually, no. I have business here," I interject. I turn on my heels to march in the direction of the temple. Haauna snaps her fingers and a second larger elephant marches forward. The creature gracefully dips down and wraps its trunk around my waist, gently lifting me to his back.

"That's Ibha and this is Ganjandera," Haauna says, climbing up the first elephant and taking her place on its back. "Sit still, Ibha's young and a bit temperamental—sort of like you," she calls over her shoulder.

Sitting atop Ibha makes it easier for me to survey the canopy, which I can almost reach out and touch.

Haauna's companions are a mix of monkeys and larger apes that swiftly move atop the canopy of trees. Several medium-sized baboons drop down onto Ibha and skillfully bind my hands tightly behind my back with twine. Without my hands to help me balance myself, I struggle to stay in place as Ibha trudges after the rest of the herd. "Is this really necessary?" I ask, motioning to my bound hands.

"We can't have you running off in search of the Golden Trishula," Haauna responds, curtly.

Between the gentle flapping of Ibha's giant ears and his rhythmic stride, I nod off but wake every time its ear twitches. Admittedly, the wafting breeze it creates is welcoming.

I am not sure how much time passes, but when I wake next, I find myself under a lush tree surrounded by elephants. It appears this part of the jungle is not affected by the rakshasi plague of death and destruction. I see a dozen sets of eyes staring down at me from treetops. The monkeys begin a persistent, annoying yowl, no doubt sounding an alarm to their leader. My hands fly up over my ears. It is the least pleasant sound I have heard in a while.

"Ah, the Great One awakens," Haauna sarcastically purrs at me. I cannot figure out why she's choosing to be hostile toward me. "Rise, we've got something to show you."

Haauna does not give me a chance to come out of the fog of sleep. She hoists me up roughly, grabbing my arm. She grabs a short knife from her belt and cuts me free of the twine.

"This way!" She commands, forcing me to walk alongside her through a cluster of huts. The trees in this village seem to touch the sky. A complex system of bamboo bridges hangs high above us where I see others who share the same appearance as Haauna—half-monkey and half-human—curiously staring down at me. We walk down the clay path leading into a system of caves and tunnels.

"What is this place?" I ask.

"We call it *Shambala*. It is our home, hidden from the humans, Lambadi, rakshasis, and Dusta. We don't like to deal with their dramas," she says with a scowl. "Gowramma has helped us find our way, kept us protected. But our loyalty to her cost us greatly. We now find ourselves embroiled in this fight to keep the river flowing and saving lives."

We move to an area where there are several, circular inground fire pits approximately half the size of a football field. Heat rushes through my body as I stand over a large, metal vat containing what must be hundreds of gallons of swirling liquid gold. I watch it churn in the vat and I'm reminded of the healing ointment Gowramma had used on my wounds.

"Long ago, my ancestors were blacksmiths, makers, and warriors, forging spears, bows, arrows, and armor. We provided armor for soldiers in the Maharaja's court. Our trade earned us the food and materials to sustain our livelihood and remain hidden for so long," she explains. "Few of us know how to do any of that anymore. It's been a good while since we had such a task."

Appa appears from the shadows. "But Gowramma tasked us with an important project for you." He steps forward and takes my hands. I search his eyes and don't feel the need to pull back. His hands move to my forearms. "These gold cuffs are part of the traditional Kodaguru warrior armor. Our friends here have been busy creating the rest of your armor. To protect you when you protect the others."

I'm not sure if it's the heat of the vats or the weight of his words, but a dizzying sensation creeps through me. I *hear* the blood rushing through my veins. I stumble forward toward the vat of bubbling gold liquid, but Haauna acts fast and reflexively grabs me around my midsection and pulls back. I scramble away from her once I regain feeling in my legs. This may perhaps be the first pleasant thing she has done for me since we met.

"This thing I'm expected to do—to face Dakini and Dusta—you can build us all the armor we need, but we need the Golden Trishula. That is the weapon that will strike down both. If they retrieve it before us, this dance is over!" My voice stays surprisingly steady.

"She's right, Guru Ravi. Not only does she not have the Golden Trishula, but it's also obvious her little human heart is too soft for this task. That is far too great a weakness. She's not ready to save humanity. Not like this," Haauna warns, turning to Appa.

"I agree her heart is too soft, but the rest of her can be fairly explosive." A familiar voice comes from behind us, and I turn to see who it could be.

Raya.

My stomach flutters and I rush toward her. Close behind her are Aarav, Varsha, and Tarun.

My outstretched arms wrap around her, and she squeezes me tightly. "That was certainly unexpected to hear coming from you," I whisper to her.

"Now, now, don't get mushy on me," Raya says, but she still does not let go of me. "I've had time to think and reconsider my approach...to us."

"You're all okay? I thought I'd lost all of you," I say, releasing my hold on Raya. I reach for the others, embracing each of them. I stop in front of Tarun and stare up at him awkwardly, unsure if I should embrace him considering we haven't seen each other since that kiss in the jungle. My stomach turns. Maybe he wants nothing to do with me. I bite my lower lip, contemplating how to best proceed.

"Nah, we're too good at what we do," Tarun says, pulling me into an embrace. His eyes are tender and his lips curve into an effortless smile. His easy manner makes me wonder if that kiss didn't mean as much to him as it did to me, but I don't say anything. "Sorry, I had to tell Thaye what I saw in the vision we shared so we could be prepared. Thaye hatched a plan and got herself taken hostage. I wish I could've told you, but we had to act fast," he explains with an apologetic look on his face.

I pull him to the side as the others continue chatting. I don't want the rest of the group to know how we shared the vision. "So, are you a Watcher or something else? Seeing you can channel other people's visions?" I ask.

"Thaye thinks I may be something called a Seeker. I can absorb the visions of others. But that's a story for another time." He stands uncomfortably in front of me, shifting his stance and fidgeting with the elastic band for his hair that's around his wrist. "Just know you have nothing to be embarrassed about."

Seeker?

The word echoes in my head.

My face heats and I blush remembering the stolen moments in the jungle when our lips met. A thousand thoughts bombard my mind all at once, overwhelming me.

Don't be humiliated? Had he only kissed me for his purpose as a Seeker? He only wanted to see what I could?

It hits me like a ton of bricks and my heart sinks into my stomach. I don't want Tarun to notice the hurt look in my eyes, so I quickly bring the conversation back to the plan. "Did you know to come to Shambala because of Gowramma?"

If he noticed the abrupt change of topic, he doesn't show it.

"Aye, it was all part of her plan," he says. Sadness creeps into his face and I understand his worry for her safety.

"We are going to bring her home," I tell him meaning every word.

As we walk back to the others, Tarun gently squeezes my hand. "I'm sorry if I hurt you. Back there, in the jungle after the vision. There's more I have to say, but it's not the right time. Maybe we can talk more later," he says, almost whispering to himself.

Before he can say another word, I move off toward Varsha and Raya. I don't want to talk about it. Not now or ever. When I reach Raya, I collapse into her outstretched arms, and she holds me tight. "I'm glad we're back together," she whispers.

Haauna searches all our faces with a confused look in her eyes. I think watching us hug it out is getting to her. Without another word, Haauna, Appa, and the monkey troupe step away into the background, continuing with their duties while I reunite with my friends.

"Where were you?" Varsha asks. Her gaze falls to the black goo still caked on my hands. "What happened to your hands."

"Dakini. She took the moonstone and obliterated the lines in my hands. The map is gone," I say, trying to scrape away at the black, gel-like substance. "But even without the map, I reached Shadoulyand recalling Varsha's directions. I know where it is!" I tell them excitedly as Varsha lets out a gleeful sound, clearly pleased with herself.

I pause for a long moment, debating whether to drop the biggest bombshell of my existence—the truth about Dakini. What if they abandon me here? What if they think I'll become like her? After all, I am her daughter and maybe share her lust for power and darkness? What if they want nothing to do with me anymore?

I know I can't keep the secret from these people who have allowed me to enter their lives. I don't want to carry the burden of knowledge around for a second longer.

All eyes are on me when I speak. "There's something you should know..." I say in a low hushed tone but pause unsure of the right words to use. Then, I force it out. "Dakini is my mother."

There's complete silence and a tangible discomfort in the air around us. My fear is becoming all too real as my friends don't how to react. Tarun avoids looking at me and stares at the firepit. Varsha covers her mouth as if she's watching a horror movie, and Aarav shifts uncomfortably in his seat. Raya's eyes remain on me, and I fear she's going to strike me hard.

They're going to abandon me here and I'll lose them forever!

After what feels like hours there's a break in the silence.

"That's horrible. But you're nothing like her," Raya says, confidently. Aarav and Varsha nod, agreeing with her.

Tarun breaks his fixation on the fire. "Now it makes sense why she's always followed you. She may be a demon, but she's a mother first."

For the next while, they each bombard me with questions. I tell them everything I learned. About my confrontation with Dakini, her revelations, and how she robbed me of the map. I tell them about Dusta and the importance of retrieving the trishula to kill her before she can use it in the ritual.

"Oh, Gods!" Varsha explodes. "I can't believe the Tale of Three Sisters is *real*!"

"I always had a feeling there was plenty of truth to that story," Aarav adds, excitedly.

I look at Raya and pull her close to me. "I can't take back what Dakini did to your mother Aryana, but please know I mean it when I say I'm sorry."

"The void between our mothers is not our doing, Chandra. I recently became aware of the things my mother supposedly had done. She turned her back on her little sister. We need to close the void between us. I know I have been fighting to keep you at arm's length, but I think we need to make things right somehow. For the greater good, I will try," she says, looking away quickly.

Raya stares off into the distance for a while before she speaks again. "What did you think of Guru Ravi?"

"Appa? Sorry, I'm not even sure what to call him. It's weird to see him again after all these years. Things seem overly complicated with him. He's nothing like I remember," I say, sadly trying not to dwell on it.

"Tell me about what happened in the village," I say, wanting to switch the topic.

Aarav and Varsha quickly fill in the blanks on the details of the attack on the village. They confirmed seeing a strange figure who they believed to be Dusta.

"Your evil twin did not have the marks I gave you on your arms nor did she have the warrior cuffs. She also didn't seem as annoying and all-knowing as you,"

Raya adds, this time with a laugh. The smile on her face dazzles, making her even more beautiful if that is even possible.

We talk for what seems like hours before each of us grows weary. We rise and walk toward a small hut assigned to them when they had arrived from the destroyed Vaidya tribe village. We crowd together inside and before long, everyone is fast asleep.

Everyone, except for me. I make my move.

CHAPTER TWENTY-FOUR

TEMPLE OF LOST SOULS

I know my decision to leave the safety of Shambala is not going to be a popular one, but I must take this chance. The flickering light of the torches guides my way. I dart toward the far back corner of the compound to the elephant stables and a soft twinkle of a mirror catches my eye.

"Raya?" I whisper.

"Off on a hot date, are we?" She hops over a large bale of hay and stands by my side.

"There are a billion reasons why I need to go," I say, looking her straight in the eye.

"You're *my* blood. I'm going with you," she says, moving in front of me and blocking my path forward.

"You mean, *half*-blood," I say, shooting her a smile.

She grabs my hand and pulls me back in the opposite direction, toward the caves where Haauna and her ape army were churning the gold liquid. Raya leads me into a dimly lit chamber where a headless mannequin stands.

"You need to put that on," she says, pointing up to the gold armor on display. The chest plate is more extravagant than the one Haauna had been wearing. "Haauna said the gold used for your armor has been blessed by the Lambadi Elders. It's supposed to be indestructible!"

"We're going to get caught," I whisper, remembering how the monkeys had watched over me as I slept.

"The armor was forged for us. It's fine!"

I run my fingers along an exquisite, sleek, gold bodice etched with a serial pattern of moon phases, suns, and stars. It closely resembles the images embedded into my cuffs. The breathtaking work of art on the bodice deserves to be shown off at the MET Gala. I pull it down and over my cropped lehenga blouse, and almost capsize under its weight. Raya quickly fastens the straps. I untie the strings of my lehenga, trading it out for a pair of dark loose leggings made of an airy fabric that reminds me of my dancer's pantaloons. Gold thread is embroidered into it, much like the lehenga, with a floral design spiraling down the outer surface of the leggings.

Raya hustles over to a second headless mannequin, one of several that stand around the perimeter of the room, and pulls down a copper metal bodice etched with snakes and lotus flowers. I return the favor and fasten her straps on either side. She releases the ties on her mirror work lehenga and lets it fall into a pile on the floor. She wriggles into a pair of leggings with a coppery-colored thread embroidered throughout. Raya then grabs a matching utility belt from the rack, buckles it, and pulls down the conch shell that sits on the shelf next to it.

We stand across from each other, taking a momentary deep sigh, absorbing the vision in front of us. Raya's eyes fall to the center of my chest where there is a disc-sized hole in the armor. I close my eyes and evoke the chakra, which swiftly moves from my hand and hovers over the spot in the center of my chest before attaching itself to the armor.

"It's a perfect fit," Raya exclaims.

And just like that, we're out the door and into the night. We head toward the river.

Somewhere between the darkest night and earliest light of dawn, we come upon large, stone boulders. This time, instead of traveling through the Shadoulyand—the area guarded by our father—Raya ushers us on an alternative route to avoid unnecessary family drama, not to mention the swamp leeches and monsters.

Eventually, we pass the crumbling walls of the temple flanked by stone statues of the celestial dancers called *apsaras*, posing provocatively with seductive grins, created to greet those who enter.

"This is the river entrance Varsha had been telling us about before we found you," she whispers her eyes searching a landslide of boulders to a small opening halfway up the towering, stone temple. "If was with you the first time, I would've recommended avoiding Guru Ravi's monster pack."

"So, are you close to him?" I ask.

"Hardly," she lets out a deep throaty laugh. "When he came back to this side of the world years ago, he was a raving lunatic. I never knew about him and Dakini. I knew him as a man who had lost his marbles. By that point, my mother had written him off. I guess the only thing he didn't mess up was keeping you safe."

"I beg to differ," I respond, glumly.

"So what? You were a weird girl, bullied for all the right reasons when you think about it. I'll bet those prissy, posh girls from your school I had scared away with my snakes would beg to know you now. Not every little girl grows up to become a chakra-wielding, badass warrior with armor made of gold!"

I smile weakly. It was a lot to take in, but I suppose she was right. "I have yet to earn my armor. I have to still prove myself."

"Right now, the *balegalu* is all you need," she says nodding toward my cuffs.

We hear a flurry of voices not too far off in the distance and turn on the rocks to find three figures fast approaching.

"*Old King Cole was a merry old soul, and a merry old soul was he!*"

"Is someone singing?" I ask, looking at Raya.

"Strange! That's one of those old English rhymes taught by the teachers at the British convent school. It must be Aarav," she says.

You have got to be kidding me.

"Well, well, well! Fancy meeting you two troublemakers here," Tarun's eyes shine in the light. He has come prepared, wearing the armor crafted in Shambala. On his back are straps created for the javelin and mace. He has a rope coiled around his shoulder.

"We didn't think the two of you could handle what's in there without us," Varsha, says, plucking her sword from the sheath strapped to the back of her armor plate that covers her torso. A flicker of light shines from the metal pocket of the front right side of her armor. The thunderbolt! "Plus, I know more about this place than any of you. This is Nala's tomb,"

346

"Her tomb?" I stutter, surprised.

"Long story, I'll tell you more later. Now, let's get a move on." Varsha jumps into the compulsive planner mode.

"You've all come prepared," I say, awed by their armor and weapons. "Look at how far we've come."

By the time we make the climb to the opening at the side of the temple, it's mid-morning. With every step we take, the sun is scorching us with her radiant energy. Tarun secures the rope and one by one, we belay into the unknown of the dark cavern below. As we descend into the temple, we move past massive columns that feel as tall as sky-scrappers. Each of the columns are riddled with ancient carvings that tell a story from another time. Figures of men and women dancing in what I assume is the river Kaveri with their hands thrown up above their heads. Scene upon scene, they appear to be making offerings in the form of apples, mangos, and bananas. Several jungle animals like tigers, elephants, monkeys, and wolves gather around a fire pit with human figures. There is a sense of harmony. With entangled bodies and elated faces, they look exhilarated as they worship the elements—earth, water, and fire. These elements give them life. It's fascinating.

I must remind myself several times to breathe and move onward, but there is too much to see.

We survey the stone temple chambers, hanging above it. It must have been a throne room in ancient times. Every inch of the room drips in gold, silver, and bronze. There are mountains of golden chains, vases, and gemstones. Real treasure! It is the stuff of storybooks. This is what Varsha had come for.

I get closer to the temple floor and see something gracefully gliding across the surface.

We land on the stone rubble and treasure. I try to maintain my balance, attempting to walk. Raya closes her eyes and snaps her finger, igniting a small dancing flame on the tip of her fingers. Tarun grabs a large gold-plated lantern and Raya opens the doors and lights it. She places it on the ground, but it illuminates only one part of the room.

Aarav squints at the ground, shuddering. "Nagas," he screams. Hissing erupts and echoes throughout the chamber of the stone temple.

"Calm down farm boy. These snakes want nothing to do with you," Raya says, calmly. "They represent death, mortality, and rebirth. Who better to guard over the treasures of the Lambadi?" She squats down, allowing a large, reticulated python to slither its way up her arm and around her torso, resting on her shoulders. The snake tattoos upon her arms shift in unison with its movement. We all take a cautious step in the opposite direction.

"Raya, that thing will crush you to death," Aarav squeals, jumping from one foot to the other as panic spreads through him.

"No, it won't." Raya stays put. She puckers her lips, letting out a low whistle. The tone is similar to the wooden flute she's played before. The snakes listen to her call and slither up her lean body and then back down. It almost looks as if it's bidding her farewell.

"How on earth did you do that?" Aarav stumbles forward in awe. He falls flat upon his chest, and he is face to face with a giant cobra, its grand hood on display. Its tongue flickers in and out as it remains hooked on Aarav.

They stay in this position without incident for a long time, until Aarav tries to whistle. It's a disjointed sound and the cobra seems confused.

"Shhhhhh!" Raya says in frustration, and he abruptly stops. Raya begins to whistle again and calls the snake away. It chooses a path around Aarav and slithers onward, minding its own business.

"Clearly the serpent is your spirit animal," Aarav says with a shudder, disturbed by his encounter.

My eyes scan the far wall to a set of giant floor-to-ceiling doors. "Varsha, where do you think that leads?" I ask, mesmerized by the carved reddish-brown wooden doors. The intricate battle scene on the doors depicts a woman riding a tiger brandishing a trishula above her head. She's taking aim at what appears to be a demon with the head and horn of a bull and the body of a muscular man. The demon is falling at the warrior's feet.

A script in the Kodaguru language is carved below the battle scene. "*Hindina yōdhara.*"

"The ghosts of warriors past," Varsha whispers, translating the script for my benefit. Her expression tells me she can't believe she's here. A place she'd wanted to reach for so long.

"The trishula must be behind those doors?" I say, rushing for the doors that tower over us.

"Wait," Tarun reaches out and grabs my arm, yanking me back against him. He points up at the stone carvings at the top of the door. A demonic stone face with angry bulging eyes glares down. It's incredibly realistic and I get the sense that it's meant to spook anyone that happens upon it—deflect wrongdoers from entering—just like the rakshasi mask at Amma's yoga studio back home in Virginia and Uma Aunty's in the entry of her home.

I look back up and a chill moves up my spine. I feel *this* rakshasi has been intently watching us the entire time since we reached the chamber. If provoked, it could awaken and swallow us whole.

"No wonder this is called the Temple of Lost Souls," I whisper, keeping my eyes on the carved rakshasi above. The gaping mouth with razor-sharp teeth is menacing, and so is the sight of its mile-long tongue that hangs out waiting to lasso those passing by. The stone figures around it are fleeing in the opposite direction.

"You had asked me about what it's like to have selavu. What I see when I look at a rakshasi or look at Dakini?" I say to Tarun, keeping my eyes fixed on the carving. "Well, you're looking at the gray-washed version of a rakshasi."

We all take several steps back.

"There, between its eyes, in the middle of its forehead is an empty space. Looks like it's missing its third eye—the eye of intuition," Raya shouts, pointing up at the stone mural.

Varsha runs for the doors and pulls at the large, curved handles. Tarun and Aarav run to help her.

"These doors won't budge," Tarun shouts.

Varsha backs up to where Raya stands and looks up. She makes the clicking noise in the back of her throat. A puzzled look smears her face as she thinks long and hard.

"There's got to be a key!"

"Well, we didn't come equipped with that," Tarun says, reaching for the mace and the javelin before taking a running leap for the door.

"Stop," I yell. My hands clench into fists as a familiar burning sensation rips through them. A feeling I had almost forgotten, but in a sadistic way, have missed. It's the first time I've felt this since Dakini destroyed my map.

"Chandra, I can hammer through this door in seconds," Tarun shouts, competing with the chakra for my attention.

"Don't destroy the door," I say, calmly. I bite my lip and open my hands flat, palms up. There's a vibration in my chest plate and the chakra releases itself, taking flight. It hovers above my open, blackened palms. Instead of glowing the iridescent pale moon color, it glows an incandescent green.

I look up at the monster's savage face and the empty spot between its eyes in the middle of its forehead. The chakra begins to spin counterclockwise in my hands, lifting the blackened gel-like substance left by Dakini. Little by little, the black sludge falls away to reveal a brilliant moon-glow surface in my cupped palms. I want to stop and look at what's become of my hands more closely, but I need to finish the task at hand. I shut my eyes as the chakra begins to spin and moves upward like a tiny, unmanned drone.

"I think I have the answer," I whisper.

CHAPTER TWENTY-FIVE

RISE

With sharp focus, I guide the chakra high above the towering teak doors toward the wall until it's hovering near the empty groove between the rakshasha's protruding eyes. For a moment it spins in concentric circles, trying to find a sweet spot in the empty hole.

The temple chamber we are in goes dark before a starburst of green light illuminates the room from above. A thundering boom explodes through the chamber before the double doors separate from each other as they open.

"The chakra was the key," Varsha exclaims, stating the obvious, but nonetheless jumps up and down in celebration. But it's short-lived, and she darts for the doors. "Move quickly! They will only stay open for a few seconds."

We run for the open doorway and as I cross the threshold, I summon the chakra. It releases itself from the spot in the wall and floats back with ease. A moment later the teak doors slam shut with a great force that creates a strong, howling wind through the next room.

Inside, we stand huddled together. It is not a chamber like the room before it. It is a narrow hall made of shimmering pale-gold marble flanked by a dozen solid gold pillars. It resembles the Lambadi armory where Gowramma had teleported us to retrieve the warrior's weapons.

At the far end of the hall, high atop a marble pedestal statue of a woman stands holding a long, golden staff with three prongs above her head. The trishula. My heartbeat quickens. It is much more magnificent than I could have ever imagined.

"This is the Hall of the Warrior," Varsha says, standing in awe as she observes the solid marble walls with beautiful gold inlay. "This is where the Lambadi once memorialized their fallen warriors."

Tarun and Aarav charge for the Golden Trishula, but Varsha grabs them by their wrists.

"What? It's right there," Tarun says as he turns to her impatiently.

"Haven't you learned anything?" Varsha shoots an incredulous glance at the boys. "There were hundreds of snakes in the room before this, there was a secret key to unlock this tomb. Don't you think that there's something here guarding that thing?"

"You guys, seriously!" I smack my forehead with the palms of my hands.

"Chandra, your hands! The lines—they're glowing!" Raya exclaims, coming toward me.

I look at my hands in shock. "Dakini had extracted the moonstone. I don't understand what's happening."

"It's old Lambadi earth magic or maybe you've just had that moonstone embedded in you so long that it's become part of you?" Raya says, trying to make sense of it all. "Do you feel okay?" She asks, looking at my face. She raises a hand to my cheeks. I flinch and pull away from her ice-cold hands.

"Why do you feel like you live in a freezer?" I ask, shocked by the temperature of her hands.

An eerie chill creeps into the air and Raya backs away from me. Then Aarav begins to shiver uncontrollably. Moments later, Varsha drops to her knees in pain. Her lips are quickly losing their usual cherry color. She cries out in agony, collapses to the marble floor, and cradles her head in her arms.

"Nala?" Varsha whispers repeatedly. "You're here?" Her hands flail out in front of her and reach out to something above her that only she can see.

Tarun kneels by her side and scoops Varsha up into his arms. "Shhhhh. Nala is gone. C'mon Varsha, stay with us." He rubs her bare arms trying to create friction to warm her up.

"Tarun, do you feel the chill?" I ask, stepping closer to where the trishula stands.

"Slightly. Can you?"

"Not at all! It must have something to do with my hands." I take a few more steps toward the pedestal. "Stay with them! Huddle together and keep warm."

As I get closer, I can now decipher the details of the marble sculpture. The woman is wearing heavy armor, remarkably like mine. Her face bears a serene yet determined look as if she is at peace with whatever her fate may be. Her arms raised above her head holds the trishula. My eyes travel the length of the majestic weapon in her hands and back at the sculpture. Her forearms show Lambadi cuffs exactly like my own. She has the same amaryllis tattoos etched into her biceps with the golden inlay decorated upon the marble walls.

I stare into her marble eyes. They are eerily familiar even for a marble statue, and I feel as if I am staring into a mirror. My heavy gaze drops to the gaping hole in her chest plate, reminding me of the vacant third eye of the rakshasi's forehead above the teak doors.

Without any hesitation, I grip the chakra from my chest plate and twist. But before I can try anything, Varsha begins to shriek, "Nala! Nala! Don't go there! Don't listen to *it*!" Her body springs free from Tarun's robust grip as she shakes in a convulsive fit on the cold floor. I run to them and crouch down by her side.

I sense something I could not feel earlier. I follow Varsha's gaze and immediately wish I could unsee what she has been seeing all along. Hovering above us are dozens of ghostly figures—all women warriors, each adorned in long, flowing hooded cloaks, embellished with embroidered handiwork. Beneath their open robes, they sport similar armor to ours. Shadows cast across their faces, which appear youthful and lively in one instant but become shockingly hollowed and skeletal in the next.

We are under attack as they soar up and down the hall at warp speed before they torpedo down, barely touching us, yet inflicting lacerations that sting and bite on our exposed skin.

Varsha reaches for the ghostly figure of her long-dead sister. "Nala?" Tarun and Raya cry in unison, now seeing the ghosts.

"How dare you come to this place?" The ghostly warrior, presumably Nala, rumbles. Her voice fills the hall, shaking the marble walls.

"We're the warriors that time has forgotten." Another screeches as she dives through us, tearing at our exposed flesh.

"You will stay here with us for all eternity," a third one roars. She barrels down the hall, stirring a mighty dust cloud that blurs our vision.

Through trembling lips, I attempt to use my voice, "We mean no harm, but we need the trishula."

"You need it, do you?" Nala scowls. "You must be the next in line?"

Her eyes narrow as she watches me closely. She's sizing me up, from top to bottom. "You? A little girl. Barely even a woman?" She mocks me.

"I have these," I raise the Lambadi cuffs above my head.

She studies them closely but does not speak for a long moment. "Moon? Sun? Stars? You must be what was prophesized. The Ārisalpatta. If you're not, you'll end up just like the rest of us," she screeches wildly. "Some of us were able to drive away the foul creature Dusta, but she always comes back. And what did the Lambadi give us in return for our service? Nothing! We were cast aside like damaged goods by the very people we protected.

Left to be tormented by the dreams that Dusta locked us in."

"Wait, what about Dakini?" I ask.

"Dakini is just one of many rakshasi Dusta has conjured in her lifetime. The rakshasis are at Dusta's bidding. Dakini is merely a pawn. But the creature the warriors are truly meant to destroy is Dusta. She is one part sorceress, but ten parts demon. Don't be fooled! She is the evil thing that needs to be destroyed. She abused our minds, made us weak, and drove us mad," another ghost warrior says. Half her face is missing. The skeletal jawline protrudes from beneath her hood.

"We were never honored for what we did. We were locked away in this tomb and forgotten."

"Each one of us was driven to a dark, unrelenting madness. We were simply locked in this tomb until we starved to death, or the madness took us."

"We are the ancestors time has forgotten," another growls, waving a skeletal finger at us.

"We sacrificed everything. Our youth, our wonder only to live an eternity in this darkness. Look at what ghastly ghouls we've all become!"

"These things you say, it's not how your people remember you," I say as flashes of the stories Amma had filled my head as a kid begin to churn through my mind. "Your people believed in you, and they still believe in you. Tales of your fight have been passed on from generation to generation," I say boldly, and with great fervor, wanting them to understand that we're all on the same side.

"Who brought you here? To this tomb," Tarun asks, trying to understand why the warriors think nobody cares for them.

"The beautiful Lambadi sister who dances in the light and floats on clouds. Her name is Shalini," Nala says.

"Shalini has always had her own agenda," I say. Anger surges through me as I realize all the things that Shalini has gotten away with. In my book, she's no better than Dusta. "She will be stopped!"

"Nala, please! You have to release the trishula to us," Raya pleads.

"You want us to give the mighty celestial weapon to this child—this outsider? Never!" Her eyes are wild with rage.

"Nala," Varsha struggles to speak. "She's almost the same age you were when you went up against Dusta. I've waited a long time to find you. I miss you so much. I told you I would make it back to you."

Nala's ghostly eyes go soft as she gazes tenderly at Varsha—the little sister she was torn from years ago. She flits around the air before settling near Varsha. Her ghostly hand reaches out to touch her sister's face, but she is unable to make contact as it passes through Varsha's cheeks.

"I watched as those nightmares ravaged you for an entire year after you fought Dusta. When they came and took you from the house, there was nothing Uma Aunty or I could do for you. We thought Shalini was taking you someplace in the mountains to heal your mind and your soul. I never knew you were *locked* away in this place. I'm so sorry," Varsha cries. Tears wash over her cheeks. The color is slowly returning to her face.

"You didn't know?" Nala asks, confused.

"She made it her life's work to get to this tomb and find you," I say, realizing how extraordinary Varsha's journey back to Nala has been.

"None of us could imagine what you—all of you—have experienced," Tarun adds, looking up at the other warriors soaring above us.

"Each warrior here failed to defeat the evil one," Nala says, nodding at her sister warriors. "What makes you any different?" She stares me squarely in the eye.

There is a long pause before I speak. I stare at Nala and the warriors and down into my glowing hands. My hands are still miraculously glowing an incandescent golden light. Finally, I look up and speak. "It's what is in my hands," I say confidently as I stare up at the ghostly figures. I close my eyes, focus on the chakra, and snap my wrists up to the ceiling palms up. The chakra releases itself from my armor and hovers above my glowing palms. It spins a hundred times faster than ever before brewing a miniature windstorm of its own accord.

The earth shakes and the air moves violently around us. The others stay on the floor, crouched together, arms protectively around each other.

I reach my palms up toward the sculpture standing at the end of the long hall—my marble essence—and I set my target on the vacant groove in her chest armor. The ghostly warriors stand down in silence as the chakra connects to the sculpture. I bolt toward the opposite end of the hall to the trishula. With my right arm stretched out, I evoke the chakra and send it spiraling into the statue. I sprint down the long, ornate hall toward the statue with my palm out, until I collide with the statue. My palms press flat against the statue. The chakra fits in the empty groove of its chest armor, and I turn it in place, releasing the trishula from the sculpture. I reach up and pull it down from the pedestal. It's lighter than I imagined but razor sharp as I spin it around vertically several times, it slices through my leggings, creating a jagged opening, before catching the ankle strap on my leafy boots on the second pass. Ignoring the warm trickle of blood from the wound, I release the chakra from the statue and place it back on my chest plate.

"Where did you learn to do that?" Tarun's voice echoes down the long hall. My shoulders reach my ears as I shrug. None of this feels like it could be real.

"The chakra? No warrior has had the ability to wield that before," Nala says, hesitantly. She looks at me curiously, her eyes bright with revelation. "Then, go forward, young warrior. Do what none of us could do before. Destroy them!" Nala and the other warriors float toward me, wrapping their ghostly hands upon the trishula. Nala places a hand on the crown of my head.

I instinctively kneel before them, preparing myself to receive their blessings. "Wait!" I say, turning to my friends, motioning for them to come in close to me. "Kneel with me."

And they do. Raya is on my right, Varsha to my left. I reach out for their hands and clasp them tightly, and they reach for Aarav and Tarun.

I look up at Nala and nod. "I am nothing without them."

The fallen warriors chant in unison, the Blessing of the Kodaguru Warrior.

Oh, Mighty Kodaguru Warrior, Protector of humanity

May River Kaveri give you safe passage on your journey.

May the Sun show you your truths.

May the Moon deliver you from your darkness.

May the Stars guide your heart.

We give you our eternal blessing.

As you find your way.

Chapter Twenty-six

Heads Will Roll

L eaving the darkness of the tomb and stepping into the light of day, we bask in the warmth of the sun, silently celebrating our good fortune. I feel lucky to have survived the wrath of the warriors and am thankful for their eternal blessings as we make our next move against Dusta. We follow the river's edge, beginning our trek back to Shambala. Raya and Varsha stay close to me, both clutching my hands tightly.

"What you did back there—for all of us—you didn't have to do that," Raya whispers as we step down into the shallows of the soft, muddy riverbank to cool off.

"Sure, I did. I can't do any of this without all of you," I say. "I may be forever seen as an outsider, but for the first time in my life, I feel as if I belong. And I feel as if I finally have a purpose."

We continue for an hour, mostly in silence. Raya plucks jasmine, hydrangea, and marigold, and weaves them together into a masterful garland as we continue on our way.

We come upon a clearing to find a magnificent banyan tree with limbs full and green, waving in the breeze. All around, there are signs of life that were not there before we had entered the temple. Even the water level in the river has risen as if the blessings of the warriors were heard deep into the jungle.

"Maybe what we are doing is starting to work? We're slowly lifting the dark and bringing the light back to the jungle." I wonder out loud.

Raya ascends the bank, humming something under her breath, as she approaches the banyan tree. She kneels at the trunk and folds her body before the tree, her hands clasped together in prayer.

There's a slight vibration beneath my feet, but it quickly erupts into a violent rumble, shaking everything on the earth. The next moment a familiar inky black mist swarms me.

My heart sinks.

I whirl around to find dozens of Dakini's body-contorting undead destroyers slinking toward us. On the opposite side of the riverbank, there's a deafening explosion and Dakini materializes from the ether.

"Hand it to me and I'll give you all that you ever wanted," Dakini demands, taking down her grey hooded robe. Her long skeletal fingers move rhythmically like she is orchestrating a deadly symphony of chaos. She reaches for me, but my eyes are fixated on the center of her chest from where the black mist pours out around her. I stand frozen in terror as the scorpion tattoos on her grey leathery arms bubble out becoming three-dimensional beings that drop to her feet. They multiply one after the other and within seconds there is an army of hundreds of tiny scorpions, creating a bridge to our side of the bank. *Small scorpions—the killing kind.*

But I know I'm the only one who can see what's happening. I must warn the others. "The rakshasi is here. There are hundreds of tiny scorpions with stingers headed straight for us," I shout to the others. "Climb the trees"

"Where is she?" Raya releases her hand from mine and rushes for Aarav and Varsha. They all follow my instructions and run to the banyan tree, leaping to the downward vines and frantically beginning their ascent.

Tarun's eyes are on me, unsure but hopeful as ever. He draws the javelin and mace as he runs to my side.

"Leena and Gowramma! Bring them to me," I demand as my eyes flit across the far bank, scanning for Dakini's captives. But I can only see her henchmen lurch forward into the river. Dakini towers above them in her giant, demon-scorpion form.

"Hand me the trishula, *daughter*, and take your rightful place by my side," Dakini roars. She flicks her long serpent-like tongue at me. From behind her, several more henchmen appear with a struggling Leena and Gowramma in tow.

The trees above shake violently, a sign that Haauna and her apes have found us. My eyes dart to the branches where hundreds of armored apes grasp large solid maces and pound the earth. Haauna stands above, her eyes hard on me. She gives me a firm nod, letting me know she is ready when I am.

"Chandra, what's Dakini talking about? You're not going to actually give her that thing?" Raya screams. She leaps from the tree and drops to the ground and rushes at me. She shoves me and I hit the ground hard. I scurry back to standing, turning the trishula to keep her at bay.

"Stay back!" I warn her, my heart pounding fiercely. The tiny scorpions are click-clacking closer to us. "Haauna, warn your troops. There are hundreds of scorpions emerging from Dakini!" She signals for her ape army to stay in the trees.

"Whatever you're going to do, it's OK," Tarun says, quietly having inched closer to my side.

I nod in response, straighten my stance, and prepare myself for the next blow. My knuckles turn white as I grip the trishula.

"Hand me the trishula, or Leena's head will roll," Dakini threatens. One of her creatures holds a dagger to Leena's neck, as it waits for me to make my move. I don't waste another second and summon the chakra and send it spinning for Leena's captors. Dozens of śavagala guarding Leena, holding her hostage, crumble to the ground, releasing their hold on her. The chakra takes out many more of Dakini's undead ghouls as it revolves back toward me.

I turn to face Dakini. A low whistle sounds in the air and a cool breeze sweeps over my shoulder. I see Aarav rushing forward blindly without realizing the danger ahead. He forges his bow and nocks an arrow, but when he releases it, the power of the gods who had originally forged the celestial weapons takes hold and the single arrow becomes hundreds.

The arrows plunge into dozens of śavagala on the opposite bank, penetrating their armor and slowing their progress. Unfortunately, the celestial arrows do not penetrate Dakini's armor. She scowls as she whirls around and thrashes her tail firmly upon the earth, sending tremors that makes the earth quake. The others can only feel the ground shake, but I can *see* the chaos we are truly dealing with. She immediately fires her venomous stingers, focusing on the origin of the arrows. Her eyes focus on Aarav.

In a sudden frenzy, the apes descend, clubbing the earth, blindly crushing the murderous scorpions, and attacking the undead enemy. Blood spurts in every direction as weapons clash and death screams fill the air.

I whip around but I've lost focus of Aarav. I catch a glimpse of him and dart in his direction, deflecting Dakini's poisonous stingers with my cuffs. "Move," I shout at him. "She's firing at you. Go to high ground, the scorpions are everywhere!"

Aarav looks at me like he can't hear me, running toward me instead of in the opposite direction. I deflect dozens of stingers as he keeps firing the arrows toward Dakini and her hoard.

"For Leena," he shouts, preparing his bow once again to fire off another round of arrows. "Release her!"

On the far bank, Leena has managed to break away from her captors and is rushing across the river. Dakini comes undone, swinging her tail up high into the air before she starts shooting giant fiery stingers, not only from her tail but from her clawed hands and eyes. She hurls them toward us again. With each impact, I am pushed back several feet despite using my cuffs to deflect the stingers and flames pouring down around us. I turn in search of Aarav, but he is nowhere in sight. I see him on the other side of the bank dangerously close to the invisible rakshasi. He is too far for my reach.

Dakini contorts her body as she seeks the origin of the arrows coming at her. She becomes still, and I realize her eyes are on him. She takes a wild swing and bashes him with her tail, sending Aarav hurling several feet into the air. He lands with a thud several yards away. He appears disoriented when he rises, blood caked on his face and arms. His armor is dented, but he gets up and keeps firing the arrows. Once again, Dakini hammers him with her tail and this time flattens him to the earth. As he pulls another round of arrows, Dakini impales him with a stinger through his neck. A bloodcurdling scream rips out over the crowd. Tarun turns toward Aarav but is unable to break through the crowd of Dakini's undead army. He watches with sad eyes as his friend slumps to the earth. Varsha and Raya call out to Aarav, but he lays motionless on the earth.

Tarun continues to fight, blindly thrashing his mace at the ground just as the apes do to pulverize the scorpions. He fights gallantly alongside Haauna and her army, as do Varsha and Raya. Varsha swings the sword skillfully, cutting through the śavagala while using her free hand to punch out thunderbolts into the air, dispersing a massive wall of the undead army. On the other side of her, Raya blindly blasts the scorpions—invisible to all of them—with flames she generates and throws from the palms while releasing hordes of snakes in the same stroke. She blows through the conch shell, sending a message to the snakes in the same manner she had done with her wooden flute. The snakes strike and bite at the ground where the scorpions scurry, melting them away as if the snake venom is made of acid.

My eyes lower back to our fallen friend.

Aarav. Sweet, gentle, dreamer. He is just lying there. My mind flashes to Amma in the yoga studio.

Savasana. The corpse pose.

Tarun reaches Aarav's lifeless body and gently throws him over his shoulder before making a mad dash for a nearby tree.

Heat rises from my core as anger sears through me. And I can't breathe. I crouch down for a moment and try to inhale and exhale through the anguish, but the pain runs deep. Rage fills me until I am drowning in it. I flick my wrists and close my eyes to direct the chakra toward Dakini intent on wounding the rampaging rakshasi. I send the chakra spiraling toward her exposed skin where there is a noticeable break in her armor where her scorpion midsection begins.

But something tugs at my hand holding the trishula. I am unable to turn my attention from the chakra directed at Dakini.

"I'll take that for you for safe keeping." Leena, now free from the śavagaḷa, gently slides the trishula from my hands. At first, I resist, but then I ease my grip, knowing it'll be safe with her.

I stagger forward, wielding the chakra deep into Dakini's gut, and watch as she collapses to the ground. Black tar-like blood gushes from her wound as she lays rolling on her side. Now that I've disarmed her, I hope to talk some sense into her.

But I don't get a chance. A sickening sound rises out from Leena as she raises the trishula high above her head. I watch in horror as she moves at a superhuman speed toward the patch of earth filling with Dakini's black tarry blood. Leena's eyes are focused on an area where the grass and debris are moving violently—where Dakini's unnatural blood is staining the earth. I make the disturbing realization that although Leena cannot see Dakini, she *can* see Dakini's blood and the crushed land beneath her.

"Stop!" I scream out loud as I run after Leena. She takes a running leap and flips through the air and comes down upon Dakini with unbreakable force. Dakini realizes what is happening and she grabs for Leena with her twisted claws.

Her eyes glow red as she raises Leena skyward. Leena does not waste another moment and she plunges the trishula deep into Dakini's chest, crushing her heart on impact. Dakini roars in agony and hurls Leena to the ground. In the same instant, like a snap, Dakini's śavagala army turns to dust and vanishes.

"No!" I roar, rushing to Dakini's side. I glare at Leena, confused by her action and wondering how she was able to use the trishula on the rakshasi. "I had her where I wanted her!" I yell at Leena, before rushing toward Dakini.

Dakini crumbles. The giant rakshasi before me shrinks and shrivels, contorting and thrashing upon the earth. Her beastly form withers away to reveal the beautiful woman with gentle brown eyes that remind me of my own. And she transforms into her true form.

I fall to my knees. My heart is throbbing as my head explodes with hundreds of images from a past that a few months ago I never knew existed. Now, I know each and every memory is real. I see Dakini the human, as she was before, playfully chasing me around the hut by the river, braiding my hair, drying my tears.

Dakini doing everything she was meant to do with me as *my mother*.

"No, no, no," I cry, throwing my body over Dakini's human form. "What have you done?" I ask Leena through sobs.

"Here it is, as promised, your future of death and destruction," Leena roars as she towers over me, clutching the trishula that drips with Dakini's black blood.

"Give it back!" I yell, rising to grab the sacred weapon from her. But Leena pulls away with a great force, her brown eyes unfamiliar to me—filled with a dark, wretched ugly jealousy. "Dusta has compelled you? They forced you to drink her blood!" I say, rising and moving toward Leena, my hands in fists.

"Maybe I wanted it! A taste of the power. To be something feared even by an Ārisalpatta! Dusta has promised me so many things." Leena waves her arms and the trishula dramatically like she has gone completely mad. "You've now fulfilled the destiny that was always written upon your horrid ugly palms, Ārisalpatta! *Their* blood is on your hands," she says, pointing at Dakini's body in front of me, and then, toward Aarav's lifeless body cradled in Tarun's arms. She holds the trishula to the sky as lightning rips through the dark storm brewing above. "You're no hero. You're just a weak powerless girl."

"How long have you known that I'm the Ārisalpatta?" I ask, my heart pounding in my chest.

"Ever since the night that monster broke into our kitchen and changed our lives forever! For years, I stood by and watched as Amma doted and invested time trying to protect you. Teaching you how to dance," she screeches at me. "And then you led Amma to her death. She was my mother! It's only fitting I get the chance to kill your monster of a mother."

A strange mist pours out of Leena as her selavu emits grotesque shades of greens and browns.

"I didn't kill Amma. That wasn't me!" I whimper.

"Amma's duty was to protect you. Her death is on your hands," Leena spits back.

"It was Dusta! Why are you saying these things? This is not you. Where is my sister? Leena, you have such a pure heart. You are everything good in this world!" I pour my heart out to her.

My eyes are distracted by her rapidly degrading selavu. "Why are you staring at me?" Leena shrieks. Her eyes narrow in on me, studying me, watching my reaction. "Selavu? What a joke! Your love for me—your pathetic sisterly love for me is your weakness—it has made you blind. You can't see me for what I really am."

But she is wrong. The colors are swirling again, uncontrollably.

"No, I can see you now...I see you clearly," I say, a quiver touches my lips. My head is spinning. I cannot keep up with the tarnished words that drip from her mouth.

And then, before my eyes, Leena's selavu turns completely black.

"Dakini was weak. You made her weak. She was weak because she loved you. I answer to Dusta. She helped me see the light and has promised me great fortunes." A ghastly smirk rips across Leena's face. Leena's human form begins to morph into something otherworldly. She staggers back and forth as a pair of buffalo-like horns protrude from her skull. Her hands draw into claws as razor-sharp blades erupt down her spine, and a long whip-like tail spontaneously grows.

"Leena! No...stop!" I shout through trembling lips.

"Dusta has promised me many things," she continues to spurt her brainwashed nonsense. "All I had to do was remove that monster—*my mother's* murderer." She points the sharp blades of the trishula at Dakini.

"I didn't kill Amma and Dakini didn't kill Amma. It was Dusta from the start," I repeat, wondering why I can't get through to her.

"I'm part of the prophecy, Chandra," Leena says.

When the stars turn upon the moon and the sun, darkness will prevail.

"Did you forget Akashleena, *means* star! I am the star that turned on the moon and the sun and I will not be stopped. I have the trishula and the gemstones. The power is mine," she roars.

I don't know what to say or do. I'm dumbfounded. How did I miss the translation of the prophecy? I can't believe that the woman who had been raised as my sister has become this beast.

Gowramma stumbles forward, reaching out to Raya to steady her, but Leena takes the staff end of the trishula and knocks the weakened, older woman to the ground.

"Not so fast. You're coming with me. I've got a dark ritual to complete," Leena says as she grabs Gowramma's wrists and pulls her into her rakshasi body. They step onto the surface of the river and appear to stand on an invisible plank. "Don't follow us, or I will kill her right now."

Leena watches cunningly as I try to lunge at her, but Tarun puts a heavy hand on my shoulder, forcing me to stop. "We can't see you, but we hear every word," Tarun says, angrily to the invisible entity. He then turns to me. "Please don't follow her...not yet," he whispers. I look up into his face, confused, and begrudgingly back down, knowing that he wouldn't want me to take any chances with his grandmother in harm's way.

Within seconds, the river sweeps Leena and Gowramma swiftly downstream and out of my sight.

CHAPTER TWENTY-SEVEN

COSMIC LOVE

B ack at Shambhala, nobody speaks as we lay the dead to rest and mourn our fallen brothers and sisters.

Within hours of our retreat from our face-off with Dakini and her army, we bid farewell to our sweet beloved Aarav. Tarun, Raya, Varsha, and I sit in silence for a long period of time as we drown in tears. His demise is more than I can handle. I fully expect to be blamed for his death at the hands of Dakini. After all, she was my mother.

"Dakini was never yours to tame. You're not at fault," Tarun reminds me. The empath in him probably feels the guilt I'm feeling inside. I wish I could change everything. I wish this had gone differently for so many reasons. Although it's merely been hours, he urges me to keep my head on for what's to come next—rescuing his grandmother. Tarun drapes his arms around me and holds me close. I lay my head against his chest and want to forget everything as if it's all just a bad dream. But my heart wallows in the intense feeling of broken sadness for Aarav, for our people, for Dakini, and for Leena. I'm in denial of her betrayal.

Before Aarav's pyre is set ablaze, I lean over his body and kiss his forehead. I whisper in his ear, "Until the next life, brother." As I pull away from him, a beautiful white-yellow light twinkles at his heart's center and sweeps up into the air above his body. It is the same as the light I had seen when Amma died. The small orb floats up into the air, dancing in the breeze, and moves on to freedom.

Shalini and a few others I've never met from the Elder Council descend upon Shambhala shortly after our return. With Gowramma held hostage, Shalini has come to help moderate the discussions between the groups, but I cannot bear to look her in the eye knowing the role she's played in Dakini's life and demise. She and the other Elders listen intently to Haauna and me explain at length about what had transpired. Haauna is told several times over to watch her temper. Deep down, I am grateful that she has come equipped with all her fight and fire still intact despite being gravely wounded by Dakini's forces. Haauna had suffered a near-fatal blow and was nearly decapitated by Dakini's bloodthirsty creatures on the battlefield.

"Chandra, we can't allow you or your friends to stay here any longer. You've brought danger to Shambhala and we can't risk any further bloodshed," Shalini says. Her voice is calm yet stern, reminding me of the way Amma had led her yoga classes back home.

My head hangs, and my eyes focus on a spot on the ground.

"I was going to bring Dakini back, so you, the Elders, and everyone could hear Dakini's side of the story. You know, so she could be handled fairly for once," I say, slowly and surely as I look into Shalini's eyes unafraid and knowing. The other Elders share concerned glances with each other.

"You thought you'd rehabilitate that monster?" Haauna glares at me, almost busting the stitches across her neck in the process. "You fought valiantly, but your emotion is getting the best of you!"

"That monster was *my mother,* and she was a monster created by *all of you,*" I throw back. My eyes pass over the Elders, and I glare at Shalini. "You and Aryana accused her of something so horrible. That voodoo doll was *yours*! Not hers. Dakini's choices after that were not right, but she felt she had no other way. You *turned* on your youngest sister! And it was you and Aryana who made sure the Elders decided to have me sent away because you thought Dakini was unfit to raise her daughter. You robbed the both of us of a lifetime of happiness," I bark at her.

Shalini sits silently at first, shifting her weight in her chair. The Elders look from me to Shalini.

The Elder wearing a large ruby red amulet like Raya's shakes her head and looks alarmed. "I had heard rumors about this sibling squabble, but that's all I thought it could ever be."

"This is most disturbing!" The Elder wearing the sapphire amulet representing the Mēkar tribe says shifting in her seat.

Haauna grunts. "Shut this down, Shalini! This can't be true?"

Shalini's lips tremble ever so slightly. "I can't. Chandra is right," she says slowly, raising her hands to her cheeks. "I can't rectify what I—we—did in the past. We accused Dakini of the unthinkable, we told the Elder Council that she practiced dark magic when we found her with that doll. We were scared and we did not believe her. It was a horrible misunderstanding. We were so young and just so stupid. But I assure you that I've spent all these years trying to make her come back to the Light, but she was too far gone..."

"No! There was no misunderstanding. You blatantly lied to protect yourself," I spit. All eyes are on me once again. I rise to my feet. "You changed nothing. You never did anything to help Dakini. And now we must face a far worse foe—Dusta."

Before I leave the room, I add, "And, just so we're clear, my father had tried to explain all of this before, but the short of it is that Dakini sacrificed herself so that the Lambadi and this jungle could live on. Dusta had wanted to destroy it all from the start. Go talk to Guru Ravi and this time, please listen to what he has to say!"

As I angrily leave the room, I hear the tinkle of tiny bells of Shalini following me. She walks out in front of me and blocks my passage. She reaches for my hands. "I believed with all my heart that when you came home, Dakini finally found what small shred of humanity she still had left."

"She *never* stopped looking for me. And now she's dead and there's a new monster fighting for immortality," I say. I drop her hands and storm away. "Gowramma and the trishula are still in dangerous hands. If you're not going to help me rescue them, I will just do it myself."

Once all the fallen are cremated, I walk to the river's edge in the back corner of Shambhala. I search the jungle. The vegetation is struggling, but it appears to be growing. I reach into the thicket trying to find the hiding spot Appa and I had agreed on hours earlier. There, shrouded beneath the brush is a pyre where Dakini's body lays alone. Just as she was in life—always alone. As I have always felt myself. I guess that's the connection we shared.

I fetch jasmine, marigolds, and wildflowers from the riverside and weave a garland to place upon Dakini's pyre. I couldn't leave her where she had fallen dead, and I figured the others would be livid if they know I pleaded with Appa to help bring her back for a proper burial.

I sit among the willowy jungle grass and sob for the loss of the many who fought by my side today, the innocent and the malevolent. But most of all, I weep over the woman lying still before me, for she was misunderstood in so many ways.

I gaze down at her face. Peaceful and serene at last. Her hair is an ocean of black waves. I see it now, how much I look like her. I sweep at a fallen marigold petal upon her brow when I see something shimmering in the void between her eyes. Her bindi is a large teardrop-shaped yellow crystal. I sweep my index finger over it, and it rolls under my fingertips. I lift it to my eyes and watch in awe as it twinkles in my hands under the darkened sky.

The moonstone.

It moves into my hands where it swells and grows to the size of a tennis ball, becoming the orb I'd seen in my childhood. It shimmers as I turn it in my hands. Inside, the scenes of the past play out. There are shadowy figures swirling in the mist of the ball before becoming clear. Three little girls play in a circle, holding hands, singing, and dancing together in the shallows of the river. It looks to be a reunion. I recognize them as the three sisters who once were. Shalini, Aryana, and Dakini. The light emitting from the orb grows so bright before breaking apart into a million little pieces. Flecks of the white-yellow gemstone lay across my palms before they dissolve back into my hands.

Many lines form across my palms like tiny snakes, twisting and turning, and flaring out in every direction. I place the chakra upon my palm and focus on Gowramma. On her smiling eyes, charming manner, and courageous essence.

I'm coming for you.

When I open my eyes, I see the tiny tributaries upon my palm have turned a radiant gold in color and they highlight the path I must take to reach Gowramma. I eagerly view it through the lens of the chakra.

I'm coming.

A rustling in the nearby bush distracts me, and I close my hands tight. Appa emerges. "I had a feeling I'd find you here, Moon Child."

I look down at the ground, at a peaceful Dakini. "I couldn't leave her in the jungle. I had to..." I stammer.

"Send her onward," he says, kneeling beside me. "In her youth, before her darkness, she was a force of nature, much in the way you are."

"I'm not five years old anymore. You don't have to sugarcoat this," I say as he silently recoils and lets out a sigh.

"I'm just trying..."

"I know, Appa, I know," I whisper to him. "None of us are who we were before."

I rise to my feet and attempt to push the pyre into the river, but it doesn't budge. I don't want to say goodbye. Appa stands on the bank, his hands folded in a prayer position at his chest as he chants a fire prayer to light the torches.

"You don't need to do this all alone," Raya comes through the jungle grass and places her hand in mine.

"We're right beside you." Tarun wraps his strong arms around me as Varsha joins us.

"I thought you'd revolt. She's terrorized and slaughtered so many for so long," I whisper. "She took our Aarav." The tears pour down my cheeks.

"She did but she also brought you to us," Raya says.

We spread out to guide the pyre into the river. Appa hands me the torch, and I set the pyre ablaze. We watch in silence as the river moves it along setting Dakini's once trapped soul free.

As we prepare to leave Shambhala, Haauna approaches me and I brace myself for impact because I'm ninety-nine percent sure the giant general is going to deck me.

"I may have been too hard on you, but you've proven to be more than any of us bargained for," Haauna says.

"There are many sides to every story. I didn't know Dakini long, or even really at all, but I know what she did share with me in our little time together was the truth. I needed her truth told," I say. "I know I brought a heavy burden to Shambhala, it was never my intent."

"I know. It is the hard truth about conflict. We wanted to be there, to fight alongside the Ārisalpatta! I must admit, you make a fine warrior. You make your Kodaguru ancestors proud," she puts her hand out to me very formally and I reach out and shake her hand. She flips my hand over and there is a sudden sparkle in her eyes as they fall on the golden lines of my hands. "I see the moonstone is back where it belongs."

As we walk toward our path, Appa makes his way out from the crowd and moves toward me, awkwardly.

"For what it's worth, I wish I could've been half as brave as you, Moon Child. Maybe Dakini would have had a different fate. You're doing good by our people," he folds his hands in prayer before placing his right hand upon my head with a silent prayer. Raya waltzes over and stands by my side.

A smile, the old smile I remember from my childhood, spreads across his face. A smile so genuine it touches his eyes. "Chandra and Surya. My Moon and Sun." He places his right hand upon Raya's head and whispers a blessing for her.

We kneel before him and touch his feet in respect before turning to leave.

CHAPTER TWENTY-EIGHT

SOMETHING TO FEAR

We use what little daylight we have left to trek through the jungle away from Shambhala and on to our next destination. Since reuniting with the moonstone, I've been blindly following the new set of lines on my hands, without any idea where that destination will be.

After a couple of hours, we stop to make camp. I notice that the script on the map is finally clear.

"*Bhayada kōte.* That's where Gowramma is," I remark, excitedly staring into my palms through the illuminated chakra. The scrolled letters come and go like a flickering neon street sign about to fizzle out. "I swear it says *Bhayada kōte,*" I say, crouching closer to Varsha. "What does it mean?"

"The literal translation is fear fort." Varsha looks at us in disbelief as the rest of us blankly stare at her. "You've got to be kidding. No way!"

"Varsha, we get it. It's not ideal," Tarun grumbles under his breath as he swats at a swarm of gnats buzzing at the side of his head. "But it's the only way."

"Not ideal? It's literally a place that feeds on human fears," she whimpers, shaking where she sits.

"It can't be any worse than what we've already lost," I say, gently.

I lay my palm out and have each of them take another look at the lines in my hands through the chakra.

"Nooru varshagala amavasye is tomorrow night," Raya says, using large rocks and coconut husk to create a makeshift mortar and pestle. She crushes the leaves of a nearby banyan tree, jasmine buds, and a ton of other herbs she's been gathering in the darkness as we huddle together around our campfire. She adds several drops of river water.

"Wait! How is it that we see the map?" Tarun asks. "I thought you lost that ability."

"I got the moonstone back," I whisper. "It was Dakini's third eye. It was her bindi."

"If you have the moonstone, then Leena doesn't have everything she needs for the ritual. Right?" Raya asks, handing me a coconut husk full of her strange concoction. I take a whiff and lurch.

"Right. I'm going to bait her with it," I say, gagging as I put the bowl of the elixir to my lips. "Do we really need to drink this stuff?"

"If you want to go undetected for as long as we possibly can, yeah, you should drink it," Raya says, handing me a second bowl.

"Like make us invisible?" I ask, once again attempting to sip. The cool bitter liquid swirls in my mouth, but its pungent odor makes it hard to swallow. Instead, I spit it out, spraying it all over Tarun, sitting beside me.

"Drink it," Raya says, taking hers to the head. "To answer your question, yes, it's a cloaking potion. Hopefully, we can get through most of the fort ruins quickly and undetected, which means, it will be hard for the fort to read our fears."

Tarun, Varsha, and I look at each other. "Let's do this!" We gulp hard and down the rest, gagging all the while. We sit up a few moments longer before the dizzying spell of the potion sets in.

"You didn't warn us about how fast this works." Varsha's speech slurs slightly as if she's drunk.

"Well, I may have added a special ingredient. Triple X rum. It's a favorite of the shopkeepers in the village when they bet on the mongoose versus cobra fights.

You'll sleep super well," Raya responds, seemingly unaffected by her concoction.

"Why...why's this not affecting you as much?" I look at Raya through bleary eyes. Tarun is on his back stretched out on the ground, smiling at me.

"Because, I've got a higher tolerance than you wimps," she says with a smile.

As the dark night breaks into an early dawn, a large black bird perched in the tree overhead caws an off-pitch melody. It swoops down upon our camp and lands on a large rock, inches from my head. There it continues to squawk at the top of its lungs.

"Are Ravens typically songbirds?" I ask Varsha, who is stirring and attempting to wipe the sleep that is still heavy in her eyes.

"I don't think they are at all," she responds confused, and covers her ears with her hands.

"If it could sing a nursery rhyme, I bet it would," Tarun says, gleefully smiling at the bird, luring it toward him with a couple of red berries he yanked from a nearby bush. The raven glides down from the rock and hops over to Tarun and onto his arm before hopping up to his shoulder. "I have a feeling this is our dear friend." I flash a concerned look at Tarun, wondering if Raya's potion has messed with his head in a bad way.

"I'm not following. You think the bird is Aarav?" I ask.

"Most definitely. We have this belief that the souls of our loved ones are carried up and away in the body of ravens. They have a way of returning when we need them the most," he explains as he gently fluffs the bird's feathers. "This is the first time I've heard one try to be a songbird, though."

We look at the bird in awe.

It pecks at the broad leaf of a neighboring plant and flutters back to the rock, twitching its head from side to side, as if he's following our conversation. And I smile at the thought that the bird is Aarav. Soul free somewhere between worlds, watching over us on this final leg of our journey.

We nibble on a few more of the red berries before we hoist the rudimentary bamboo raft we've been lugging around since we left Shambala. Up it goes, above our heads, as we march on toward the river. We walk unsteadily down the bank into the water, and the four of us get on board. As we push away from the bank the river knowingly takes us on our course.

The lone black bird follows along and circles above us when we approach the abandoned ruins of Bhayada kōte. It's not long before we see it in the near distance, a vast mountain of reddish-colored stones.

Varsha starts spouting out reminders of the things we had discussed before we all fell victim to Raya's fortune teller bartending skills. "First, we'll see the overgrown mangled creeper maze when we enter the fort. Creepers are basically thick thorny vines. If we make it past the possessed walls and creepers, we'll find a series of ramps that will take us upward towards the summit of the fort." She stops talking to examine our perplexed expressions.

"Sorry, I think Raya's elixir has messed with my memory," Tarun says, sounding almost serious.

Varsha rolls her eyes and continues. "The fort is said to be an enchanted labyrinth that came together with dark Lambadi magic from centuries ago. Back then, Dusta, sacrificed humans, sometimes without ritual, simply for pleasure. The fort will play tricks on the mind. Be alert! It is said that the magic within the walls of creepers can read you like a book, figure out your worst fears, and kill you!"

Raya elbows me in the gut. "Pay attention!"

"At the summit, there's an ancient altar, where Dusta or possibly Leena, will perform the ritual that will plummet our world into an eternal darkness," Varsha explains, and we listen to her intently. "But we must be careful. The bricks on the summit where the altar stands are booby trapped. There are inscriptions on them—numbers and directions, I think."

I gulp hard. "Are you sure that's it? Is that *all* we should worry about?" My words are drenched in sarcasm, but I wonder just how we are going to make this work. We float further down the river in silence.

We yank the raft out of the water and tread toward the main entrance of the fort. The creepers hanging from the fort walls appear remarkably like the ones circled on the petrified trees we had encountered not too long ago. They eerily resemble the human form. It looks like bodies were pulled in by the wall with their arms and legs stretched out in opposite directions. I'm convinced now more than ever that each creeper was likely a human before.

"The Elders have said that going into a labyrinth is death," Varsha says, nervously. Her eyes grow wide as she takes in the scene before us. I imagine seeing this live is a stark contrast to having only read about it. I wonder if her own stories were beginning to creep her out.

"Yes, but coming out of a labyrinth represents rebirth," Raya says. "And we *are* coming back out!"

"Varsha, remember eyes on the ground. You were the one who told us all the rules." I say surprised that I have to say anything to our resident expert of Lambadi myth and legend.

"I'm trying! But they seem so familiar," Varsha says, stretching her skinny fingertips toward them. "Ahh!" She shrieks, backing away from the wall with a human skull in her hands. More remains—an empty ribcage, part of a pelvis, and a femur—pop out from the wall at her and she blindly turns and barrels me over. Raya marches over to Varsha and forces her head down.

"Eyes on the ground," Raya warns again. "And don't touch *anything*!"

We follow the path of the maze until we come to a fork. The chakra vibrates in my chest plate, and I release it, watching it glide in front of us. It flies down the passageway to the right. We follow it, tunneling deeper into the dark labyrinth until we come to a dead-end where the creepers have overgrown the path.

"Maybe we must go through it?" Tarun asks, releasing the mace and javelin from the back holsters of his armor. Varsha follows suit, drawing her sword back and hacking away at the dried vines. She keeps the thunderbolt withdrawn for fear of setting everything on fire. I channel the chakra. Revealing its sharp blades, I send it ahead of us again. It seamlessly cuts and trims away the decrepit creepers.

Varsha stops in mid-swing and becomes still. "Nala!" She screams. Varsha's eyes are vacant. Her pupils turn white as she stares into the abyss in front of her. She drops the sword making a clattering noise against the stone floor, acting as if on command from an invisible entity. In a zombie-like trance, she reaches into the creeper wall with both arms. "Nala, come back!" The creeping vine forges toward her possessed by something sinister. It binds itself in tight spirals around Varsha's wrists and waist pulling her into the wall. Tarun grabs Varsha's sword from the ground and swiftly slices away at the creepers, cutting her free. But his progress halts when he is captivated by the creepers on the adjoining side.

A shrill echo of what sounds like a bird outside reaches us deep inside the tunnel, forcing us to look upwards.

Aarav, trying to keep us safe.

"I thought you said that crap you made us ingest last night would prevent us from seeing things," Tarun barks at Raya.

"It wasn't foolproof, and it works differently for each of us. We're taking too long to come through this part of the maze. I didn't anticipate how long it would take us." Raya replies, scowling at him.

"Varsha, stop!" he yells, dropping the sword and running to Varsha who is repeatedly smacking her forehead into the wall. Blood drips down her face in a crimson lace veil. Tarun holds her arms down against her side. Raya and I cover Varsha's eyes to snap her out of the hallucinations.

"You saw her. You made your peace," I whisper in her ears. "Come back to us!"

After several minutes, Varsha breaks away from her trance. She shakes her head, snapping out of her daze.

"Keep your eyes straight ahead," Raya instructs her.

We don't get far before we notice Tarun behaving strangely. His eyes have changed. A vacant sheath of white covers them and he begins to have conversations with an imaginary version of Gowramma.

"*Thaye*, I'm coming," Tarun calls to his invisible grandmother and dives into the wall of creepers. The creepers bend and weave around his massive physique, turning him over and over. It pulls him backwards into the wall. Varsha grabs the sword and Raya zaps them with a flame from the tips of her fingers.

I grab either side of his face and force him to look into my eyes. A new fear is unfolding within him, and his body begins to tremble.

"Aarav, don't go! Come back," Tarun cries. "I shouldn't have let him come. He died because of me!"

"Tarun, look at me," I shout, shaking him hard.

"I led him to his death," Tarun cries. A creeper lurches up around his neck and progressively tightens around him like a noose.

"Nonsense," I tell him, pushing his head back so he looks up above us. I wrap my hands around the thorny vines and pull, releasing the strain around his neck. The thorns rip the flesh of my hands. I bleed gold instead of the crimson red. I watch as the blackened vine in my grasp turns green in my hands.

"Raya," I say, "look at this!"

I touch one more creeper followed by another, and they all turn green.

"It must be the power in your hands. The power of the moonstone regenerating and giving new life to the dead," Raya offers.

Red blooms begin to bud and blossom before our eyes, like the other day in the clearing when I saw the giant tiger. Raya puts her hands on the creepers, and the walls come to life with colorful pink lotus blossoms. The vibrant colors spread over within seconds.

"Chandra, we must get to the summit. Get to the altar! Time is running out," Raya whispers in my ear, trying to convince me to leave him.

"Chandra, I can do this. I will stay with him and get him out," Varsha says. "The creepers are regressing thanks to the both of you!" We look around to see that the once-possessed wall of creepers is no longer a threat.

"Okay. Raya, help her," I instruct, but Raya pulls in front of me.

"No, I'm going with you," She protests, refusing to move out of my way. "Take Raya with you. We'll be fine," Varsha says.

"Fine, let's move," I say as we zip down the hall. We race through the maze up an inclined ramp, brushing against the creeper walls. Green vines replace the dark ones each time we touch the creepers. Pink and red blooms fill the halls, brightening the gloom.

Something Dakini said in our encounter surfaces to mind as we zip through the tunnels.

Even the darkest of souls want to walk in the light of love.

I stare at the life now plastered across the former dark walls for a moment, and my heart smiles. Raya tugs at my arm and we rush away from the beauty in front of us to face the wrath of a fallen star.

CHAPTER TWENTY-NINE

Nooru Varshagala Amavasye

Dusk is upon the jungle when we make our final approach to the summit of the fort. Nooru varshagala amavasye starts her ascent into the sky, showing off a red-orange glow. Radiant light from this cosmic wonder illuminates the environment around us.

Leena stands in front of what must be the beginnings of her own śavagala army. Her hands firmly grip the trishula. Her rakshasi form is a cross between a vampire and a monitor lizard that appears straight out of a nightmare. She struts around with a pair of strange giant bat-like wings that protrude from her spine. Her long wiry reptilian tale swats at the air carelessly, taunting her new recruits—dozens of zombie-like creatures. The śavagala moan and lurch forward, milling around in circles.

"Hurry up, old lady," Leena yells. Her red oval eyes are hooked on a tiny figure hunched over in front of the altar. She smacks the figure with the blunt end of the trishula's staff.

Gowramma.

Leena's splayed claws reach for the tiny packets on the altar Gowramma is making. Gowramma uses a large brick to crush and grind samples from each of the larger Lambadi gemstones into a fine powder before folding it into the betel leaf. She lifts her crooked pointer finger to her lips, spits on it, and uses her index finger to seal the tiny leaf envelope, tying it with twine. Gowramma's walking stick lays at the side of the altar snapped in two.

"You get Gowramma out of here and I'll get the trishula," I whisper to Raya, who nods in agreement.

"Wait! What is that?" Raya asks, pointing to the ground where Leena stands. "There's a bunch of inscriptions on the bricks. It could be rigged with traps. Leena will likely throw the sacrifice and the gemstones into the river from that bridge over there," she says, pointing toward a narrow, jagged lookout point. "Make sure you do the steps in the right order!"

I nod as I look at the bricks. There are numbers and directions on each of them and they look vaguely familiar. I rack my mind, trying to figure out what they could mean. I close my eyes and summon the energies of the chakra before setting it free upon the crowd. The śavagala scatter in different directions, creating enough chaos to allow Raya the opportunity to rush to the altar and reach for Gowramma.

Heads roll and bodies crumble as I direct the chakra through the crowd. Raya and Gowramma move together with the broken Ūrugōlu in tow back down the ramp from which we ascended to the fort's summit where I hope they'll reunite with Varsha and Tarun who should be free of the creeper walls.

I continue to use the chakra to destroy the remaining zombies, using it like a boomerang that comes and goes as I command it.

Leena attempts to come at me across the brick floor, but as she rushes toward me, her scaley flesh begins to burn, and layers of skin peel back revealing her tissue and bones. She roars in agony and steps back. Again and again, she attempts to cross the enchanted barrier in an effort to attack me. Each time, she catches fire and her skin peels back, just as it had happened with Dakini when she had tried to cross the Valley of Souls. Dakini could not cross the poisoned earth. It occurs to me that these stones may have some of that same deflective power against the rakshasi without being poisonous to me.

I'm about to find out.

I stand nervously at the edge of the decoy floors that likely hide a series of dangerous traps, snares, or mines. I look out at the inscriptions as far as I can see, and it finally occurs to me what they mean. They are symbols representing the five jaatis or beats from the folk dance Amma had taught me last summer. Amma had called my winning dance the "*Dance of the Cosmic Moon.*"

I bite my lower lip and start with the first steps. But I'm rusty and unsure. I blink, apply pressure to the stone step, and ten bolts of star fire burst through the air narrowly missing my head, singeing my hair. Wrong move. My memory is failing me. The smell of my fried hair fills my nostrils.

Breathe. I remind myself.

Focus! I hear Amma's voice in my head. I look forward to the darkness beyond Leena. I see the glowing eyes of a giant tiger like the pair tattooed on my arms. The tiger stands in the shadows. Then I hear her voice.

Always anticipate the next step. Know what you're going to do before you do it. That is how you float through a room!

Determined to get it right, I do just that.

Ta Ki Ta Tishra jathi. I move forward three beats.

Ta Ka Dhi Mi Chatushra jathi. I move to the right four beats.

After the first two steps, the beats flow through me easily. The dance steps come back to me as if I had never stopped dancing. I stop looking at the inscriptions on the bricks and spin and stomp gracefully moving my arms around my body.

Ta Ka Ta Ki Ta Khanda jathi. I move forward five beats.

Ta Ki Ta Ta Ka Dhi Mi Misra jathi. I move left seven beats.

And lastly, *Ta Ka Dhi Mi Ta Ka Ta Ki Ta* Sankeerna jathi.

I move forward another nine beats ending about twelve feet away from where I want to be. The sound of the tabla plays in my head, locked in my memory. I sway and move, without caring what could happen to me if I make another wrong step. I move my body to the beat, twirling to my heart's content, moving across the summit of the fort, making my way closer to the demonic Leena and the bridge where she'll make her sacrifice. I multi-task each step of the way as I continue to command the chakra to keep the undead at bay, but steer clear of harming Leena, who doesn't seem to give up on crossing the boundary of the enchanted brick floor.

Leena growls when she finds me a few feet from her. "Glad you came," she says, scooping up the packets of powdered crystals from the altar and turning the sharp end of the trishula upon me. "I'm not an idiot. I know I need the moonstone for this ritual to work." Leena looks down at me from where she stands and opens her hands to reveal the four packets. "I'm going to have to slice it out of you," she says, flickering her reptilian tongue at me.

"Get your hands off me!" A voice erupts from behind me. I whip around and see two henchmen, dragging a furious Raya flinging her body around wildly like a rabid hyena.

"So, the old lady is gone?" Leena spits out angrily as she glares at her mute henchmen. "Fine! She'll do."

"Leena, Dusta will be angered by your insolence and stupidity. I'm Atīndriya—a Lambadi mystic. My magic is rare. I'd serve you better if you kept me alive," Raya snarls, trying to intimidate her, but I'm not sure if it's working.

Raya breaks free sending flickers of flames at her captors. As she moves away, she stumbles to the ground and hits her forehead hard. She rises, and blots at her open wound as a dazed look crosses her face. She wipes the blood trickling down the side of her face, wobbling uncertainly toward me.

I look at Raya, but something past her left shoulder catches my eye. A flash of yellow metal flies toward the center of Raya's back. The gleaming object is moving at warp speed.

Leena is going to slice Raya in half with the trishula!

I duck and pounce upon Raya, knocking her to the ground away to safety. She rolls away from the slope and back toward the altar where she takes a moment to steady herself before she conjures a mass of snakes from her hands. The snake tattoos on her arms swell, become three-dimensional and drop to the ground one by one. As hundreds of small snakes slither across the ground, Raya commands several of them with an incantation. She gracefully rotates her hands in circles through the air and pours her energy into them. The snakes begin to swell in width and length, becoming giant serpents, nearly twenty feet in length. With the massive serpents under her control, Raya drives Leena's henchmen and undead army over the side walls of the fort and down to the jungle and river below. As the serpents twist and glide across the brick surface at warp speed, they devour the undead. Raya appears unstoppable as she mounts a massive cobra and disappears over the side of the fort, following any stragglers down to the jungle floor. I have a feeling she won't stop until she's got them all.

I turn my attention back to Leena, whose eyes are upon me. Fierce and full of loathing.

There's a sharp shooting pain coming from my left bicep and a sudden gush of blood. The pain is excruciating. I scream out in anguish and cover the gaping wound with my other hand with the moonstone. When I remove my hand, a swatch of gold is seen in place of the wound. It looks like a splash of thick, gold paint on my arm. The bleeding stops—at least for now.

A flicker of gold shimmering beneath the glowing cosmic moon catches my eye. It's the trishula. I dive for the trishula and rip it from Leena's hands. But in the struggle, it is sent flying through the air and smashes to the ground with a thunderclap.

Two sets of eyes linger on the fallen trishula. We race to it from opposite directions, each determined to be the first to the weapon. My hands grip it first. I'm moving with such momentum that I collide violently with Leena, and we tumble toward the narrow pathway leading to a gushing waterfall. The impact throws the trishula from my reach, sliding further down the narrow bridge near the cliff and the water's edge.

I look back down at the misty cliff and realize it is familiar from the vision of Dakini with her sisters when she was pleading with them, to tell the truth. It is a crumbling bridge.

A fog sets in and it begins to rain, but the moon hangs in the sky, right where she needs to be for the ritual to commence. I need to shut this down. We each struggle to reach the trishula first, but the mist makes for hazardous conditions. We are sent spinning together toward the far end of the busted down bridge of slippery rocks. The trishula is teetering on the edge of the bridge but is almost within Leena's reach. Her eyes are wide as she struggles to reach for it, worming her way out to it on her stomach.

"This is your fault," she yells. "You ruined everything!"

"Leena, come on. You're going to get hurt," I call out. "Come back this way!"

But she ignores my pleas and continues to inch her way toward the trishula. She accidentally knocks it with one of her wings and we watch in dismay as the trishula falls to the bank below.

She swiftly rises to her feet but slips on the rocks backward in slow motion unable to use her bat-like wings. I slide myself to the edge and find her dangling by one arm. Her wings slowly retract, and the tail disappears. The horns on her head vanish into the air.

"Chandra, help me!" A very human Leena screams in terror. "I have failed. Dusta is taking everything back!"

"Give me your hand. Give it to me now," I shout.

"Your arm is turning gold," she says frantically scrambling to climb. "What's wrong with you?"

"It doesn't matter. Give me your hand or you're going to fall," I scream over the sound of the waterfall that is unexpectedly gushing with water.

Leena looks at me and then down. Her eyes fixate on the weapon of her desire.

"If I retrieve it, she'll reward me," Leena says, controlled by the invisible source. I watch as reddish-black smog whips around us, and I know exactly what's compelling her.

"Stop, Leena. Dusta is here. She doesn't care about you," I scream.

"Take these so I can reach the trishula," she says. With her free hand, she flings the pouches of powdered Lambadi gemstones up to me and I take them and carefully secure them to my armor.

"I almost have it. Just a bit further," she shrieks. "Leena, just stop. Let's go, you don't need it!" "Don't tell me what I need...I've got it ..."

"Your hand is slipping...Leena, give me your other hand. Now!" I plead. But she releases her hold on my hand and tumbles several feet down to the perch to the trishula. Leena scrambles for the weapon, but something else reaches it first.

A noticeable chill fills the air and the sky above us opens on command. Giant drops of water begin to fall from the sky. The reddish-black smog floats around Leena. It takes the shape of a dark faceless figure with long tentacles for fingers.

Dusta is ready to reap havoc.

The earth around us shakes, snapping mighty trees in half. Boulders the size of elephants take flight, and I dodge everything thrown my way.

"Leena, behind you," I point, but she's too lost in her greed to hear me. She motions with her free hand, yelling back at me, but her words never reach me.

"You have failed me," a deep inhuman voice booms, shaking the earth beneath. "You've lost the gemstones. This was the one chance!"

The reddish-black smog comes up and traps her in a funnel cloud and shakes Leena back and forth violently until she goes limp, before dumping her lifeless body from the cliff. The current sweeps her downstream. The broken pieces of my heart shatter again and all I feel is rage. My breathing is ragged, and I release a primal scream.

The smog funnel stops spinning and slows down. Finally, a faceless giant dark figure cloaked in a blood-red robe emerges.

"The Ārisalpatta?" It slinks toward where I stand. "So, we finally meet."

CHAPTER THIRTY

OF MONSTERS AND WOMEN

I leap from the bridge down to the bank, not far from Dusta. She moves with a strange morbid grace. Cocking her head to the side she looks at me from a different angle.

"It comes down to you now," she says. "Help awaken the dead. Together we can raise the darkness."

"Never!" I scream at her, reaching for the chakra from my chest plate.

"That doesn't work on me, child." She raises her hand from her stance and like a magnet, my body lurches straight into her.

"You've taken everything from me. You killed Amma and Leena. You bestowed the Curse of Death on me. But I won't let you harm my people or this jungle anymore," I spew with ferocious rage.

"Hmm. A brave little girl. But you're a useless warrior. You're no different from the others locked away in that temple," she cackles. Her long tentacle-like fingers move up from around my waist toward my head and she closes them over my throat. I sputter and gasp for air. Her touch is ice cold. She dangles me out over the edge of the cliff from where she had thrown Leena's body. Her grip tightens around my throat, baring down forcefully on my windpipe, and I struggle to get away from her.

She holds me up in front of her. I shudder as I stare into the ghastly void.

"I see the fury in your eyes. The hatred you carry for me. That's right, child—use your hate. Use all of it." She's toying with me, doing everything she can to trigger me and I'm ready to give in. I'm so tired of fighting.

But I hear Gowramma's voice in my head, reminding me never to strike out in hate or let my ego get the best of me. I focus on my newfound purpose and attempt to simmer down.

Be in control, Chandra, she's egging you on.

Dusta roars, "Release the gemstones. Give them to me!"

"No," I sputter my voice hoarse, refusing to give in. I reach my hands up to my throat, trying to tear away from her death grip. Dusta releases an unexpected shriek. Bright red scorched holes appear on her wrists, at the spot where my hands met hers. My hands glow, the moonstone within emitting a powerful wondrous light. I put my hands back on her and clamp down until she releases her hold on me. I drop to the ground, summoning the chakra. I channel the energy, focusing on Amma, my jungle home, and my new tribe, and send the chakra spinning into the air. It weaves in and out through Dusta's shadowy figure, punching dozens of large holes through her body, wounding her. But it does not dent her power. She raises her tentacles and directs a streak of electric current at me, hurling me several feet in the air.

I land with a thud on the riverbank. A sharp pain shoots up my back causing my head to spin. I lay stunned from the agony of pain, gasping for air, and painfully roll to my side and see the giant tigress, hovering above me. The feel of metal in my hand grabs my attention as I slowly prop myself up. It's the trishula.

Taking the celestial weapon in my hands through the excruciating pain, I lunge forward. The tiger retreats to the perimeter having served its purpose. I glance down at my stance and suddenly it feels like I'm back at Amma's yoga studio practicing my last dance.

Dusta has moved to the shallows of the great river for relief from wounds that cannot be fixed with sorcery. I weave between the towering blades of jungle grass in stealth. My heartbeat is steady and strong.

A voice in my head prompts me.

Be the mighty warrior.

I stomp my feet over and over upon the earth until my wrath can be felt by Dusta, challenging her.

I feel the power of my rapid footsteps.

Taa Ki Ta... Taa Ki Ta... Taa Ki Ta

The trishula is firm in my hands. Dusta's flaming red eyes are ripe with hate. Before she has a chance to react, I strike hard and fast with the staff, knocking her off her feet, and swiftly turn the weapon to reveal the trishula's three razor-sharp prongs. She does not have the strength to deflect my advances. I impale her deep in her chest. Dusta snarls before she stumbles forward in agony breathless, falling dead at my feet. I spiral around swiftly, lift the trishula high above my head, and land firmly on both my feet. There is not one trace of Dusta on the riverbank.

The giant tiger watches from the tree line and flicks her head back as she paws at the air. I raise my hands to the beast acknowledging her support.

You did it.

I reach out to a nearby tree and place my hands upon it and watch in wonder as the jungle fills with life.

Everything around me turns green. The trees become ripe with fruit, and the river swells and flows with renewed energy.

A burning sensation originating from my wounded arm overwhelms me. It then spreads to my shoulder and chest. I glance down to see that the trishula has punctured my armor—probably when I shoved Raya to safety. Deep pounding pain in my chest takes over my conscience, crushing my heart. I can barely breathe.

My head is heavy as I fall back into the grass as the weight of my body sinks into the earth. There I lay, smiling up at the cosmic new moon.

CHAPTER THIRTY-ONE

IN MY HANDS

The sweet familiar aroma of curried spices bubbling in a pot awakens my senses. I sit straight up in a plush cot of hay. I'm in a small hut with a skylight to the lush jungle canopy. I scan my surroundings but recognize nothing. The soft rhythmic whoosh of the river moving swiftly tells me I'm home.

"Hello?" I call out, but my voice is hoarse and my throat sore.

From the corner of the room, Gowramma rises and approaches my bedside. "Moon Child, you have to take it slow," she says gently, placing a hand on my cheek. "You've endured so much."

White fabric bandages are wrapped tightly around my shoulder and across my chest where the trishula punctured my armor. My movement is restricted by intense pain. I look at my palms. My right hand is tightly bound, and the shape beneath appears deformed. It feels heavy. I can barely flex my fingers. A sense of panic takes hold of me, and my body becomes stiff from the physical pain and all the emotional scars. Snippets of the events leading up to my current state become real. The steps of the cosmic moon dance, the powerful trishula slicing through my armor as I came between my sisters, witnessing Leena's demise. And then there was Dusta.

Tears pour down my cheeks. "You have been here a month. In and out of a dream-like trance caught between the pain of loss and suffering," Gowramma says, caressing my face. "It will hurt for a long time, Moon Child," she says wiping my tears, "but you will come out on the other side."

"Where am I? The Lambadi villages were all destroyed," I croak, searching the tiny, one-room hut. My eyes scan for my sister, my friend, for Tarun.

"When there is nothing, we rebuild," Gowramma says. "This was an abandoned hut by the river where you once lived with Dakini. Not everything she created was done with ill intent. She created this place with a good heart for her one true love."

I look around the simple surroundings. At the door, several garlands of jasmine and wildflowers hang. I smile. No doubt that is Raya's handiwork.

"The others?" I make a feeble attempt to rise to my feet and Gowramma comes to my side with a new and improved Ūrugōlu in her grasp. It has the same beautiful etchings of elephants and flowers, but now also has a series of moons, suns, and stars.

"*Sahāya banni*," she shouts toward the open doors, before laughing. "I cannot carry you alone, Moon Child!"

Raya is the first one through the wooden door and she comes at me with such speed I am worried she may not stop in time. She throws her arms around me and wraps me in an embrace.

"Finally awake sleeping beauty?" she whispers into my ear, gently touching my hair. "I was worried you were never coming back." She holds my face between her hands and doesn't let go. "We're all here. Tarun, Varsha, and Aarav our spirit raven. It is beautiful what we've created in just a month."

She gently leads me toward the door. Just outside, are a series of at least fifty other small huts and canvas tents.

"The Elders have decided that all the Lambadi tribes shall grow together, here," she explains.

Tarun makes his way up to where we stand and takes a few steps into the hut. Without a word, Raya swiftly passes through the door and out into the daylight. Distracted by the disarming smile on his face, I clumsily stumble forward. Tarun catches me before I fall. He pulls me into his chest, kisses my forehead, and hugs me tight. He takes a step back and looks deep into my eyes. "I have to tell you something..." He says as his hands uncharacteristically tremble. There's a long awkward silence as he takes a moment to collect his thoughts.

A million thoughts swarm through my head all at once, and before he has the chance to say a word, I fill the void before he can shatter me. "I know you had to do it because you're a Seeker. You *had* to kiss me to see the vision. I know that now! And that's just...that's jus..." I begin to stutter, but he doesn't let me finish. Instead, he gently places his pointer finger on my lips.

"Shhhhh," he says, softly. "You're completely wrong about that kiss. I didn't do it because I'm a Seeker. There was *never* any intent to betray you." He pauses, gulps hard, and continues whispering into my ear. "I kissed you that day because you *amaze* me in every way. I can't believe what you've done for all of us. You're a force of nature, Chandra. You're fearless! All this time, I've been drawn to you, but I was so scared that I wouldn't ever get to tell you that. Thankfully, here you are." He exhales a long sigh of relief and squeezes me again.

My heartbeat quickens and relief sweeps through me. The dread and doubt of my feelings for Tarun fade away.

"You don't know how long I've wanted to hear that!" I say to him smiling brightly from ear to ear. I reach up and wrap my arms around his neck. I pull him in close and kiss him sweetly on the mouth. This time when our lips meet, there are no visions to interrupt us, and we get lost in a moment of tangled tongues and lips. I don't want to let him go. Ever.

Giggles erupt from the hut's entrance. "Move over you two, we're here!" Raya says coming through the door with Varsha. We gently pull apart and they rush toward us with their arms wide open. We huddle together in a group hug—arms wrapped around one another—for a long while.

I will be eternally grateful that we all made it back to each other.

Raktada halli
Six months later

We call this place *Raktada halli*, Bloodstone Village. We created a place where all the Lambadi tribes and villagers alike can grow together in harmony. A place for us all to call home. I don't know how much longer I will stay. There is nobody back in the US who would miss me, anyway. However, here in this place, the connection runs deep. Here I have Raya and Varsha, and a blossoming relationship with Tarun. A future here with the people I love makes the most sense.

Today, we bless the Lambadi gemstones. Soon after my healing had begun, the betel leaf pouches of powdered gemstones that had been created for use in Dusta's dark ritual were submerged in a wooden box in the river Kaveri. During these past months, the Lambadi Elders have performed rituals to revitalize the tribes and the land. Appa took the opportunity to go before the Elder Council and tell Dakini's true story in its entirety. Shortly after, Shalini was stripped of her high-ranking position with the Elder Council and exiled from living in Raktada halli. She is permitted to participate in the life around the village. We see her from time to time during some of the Lambadi festivals. Rumor has it that she spends a lot of time on the other side of the river, near a banyan tree she holds dear. The Elders have allowed her to be here today, to witness the blessing of the recovered gemstones.

As the people gather in and around the riverbank, Gowramma instructs me to wade into the water with my bandages still on. I'm scared to see what is beneath the bandages. I don't know what happened to me because the Vaidya tribe healers have been caring for me and dressing the wounds without allowing me to see them. Each day my physical pain dissipates, but my heart remains heavy and hollow.

I wade into the water gingerly, taking carefully measured steps. Soon I'm nearly neck-deep in the water, and I move my feet back and forth to find the wooden box holding the gemstones that the Elders placed in the river. I use my left hand to draw circles upon the surface and chant to awaken the ancient river as Gowramma had instructed.

"*Nānu nadige kare māduttēne. Nānu nadige kare māduttēne. Nānu nadige kare māduttēne,*" I say the words softly at first, becoming louder and more forceful with each iteration. The river begins to stir with a forceful current, washing over and clinging to my bandages. One layer at a time, the river Kaveri pulls and pushes, setting me free of the dressings that have been a part of me for many months.

I use my feet to locate the wooden box holding the gemstones. I fork the box between my feet and pull it up towards me. Everything feels much heavier than I had anticipated. The box and my broken body.

I emerge from the river with the box. The sun above kisses me with warmth and shines with extraordinary brightness. The villagers and Lambadi drop to their knees when I walk past them. I notice they've clasped their hands into a prayer position.

I reach Gowramma, still holding the box in my hands, and whisper, "Should I be kneeling, too?" Knowing that I should be honoring the gemstones.

"No dear, they are kneeling to honor you," she replies with a smile. "What do you mean?" I glance around and realize their eyes look at me in wonder. I realize the remarkable brightness is not solely from the sun but is emitting from me. I place the wooden box at my feet and my eyes drop to my wounds. There are patches of gold over each of my wounds. Same with the palms of my hands, the ugly scars are still there, but they are cloaked with gold.

"Why am I covered in gold?" I ask, unsure whether I need to be horrified or excited that my new body is worth a billion bucks.

"You are being honored and celebrated. You have earned it," Gowramma says. "You saved these people. They will likely worship you as a deity for the rest of your days. Now open the box."

My mouth hangs open at her words. I cannot tell if she is joking or being serious. I do as she instructs, and unwrap the betel leaves to find four full-sized, oblong gemstones—ruby, amber, sapphire, and jade—each representing a Lambadi tribe. Gowramma directs the Elder representing each tribe to place them together at the altars in front of a banyan tree, by the river's edge, and at the center of the sprawling village.

Once the last gem is placed upon the altar, I whisper to Gowramma, "What about the moonstone?"

"Moon Child, you *are* the moonstone," she says with a smile that makes her eyes sparkle.

We step back from the altar and rise to a standing position. As I look out at the smiling faces of the people in front of me, I am reminded of the images we had seen when we entered the Temple of Lost Souls. There on the walls of those sacred ruins, we had seen the people and animals of this jungle standing together near the river raising their hands up to the light above. "They can't *worship* me!" I whisper uncomfortably, wanting to bury my head in the red muddy earth.

"Being the moonstone has its perks," Tarun says. He gently reaches for my hand and squeezes it tight.

"You're a legend now. It's not a bad thing! You know how much I love a good legend," Varsha remarks.

"Yup. You're the moonstone, Chandra. And you've now been dipped in gold, so get used to it," Raya says, jumping up to my side. "Don't worry, you're no goddess to me. You're *just* my *sister*."

"So, not half anymore? I like the sound of that!" I say with a laugh as Raya links her arm to mine. The four of us stroll out to the riverbank to an area of large trees, where the amaryllis blooms prominently, and a large black raven spies upon our every move from its perch above. The curtain of vines hanging from the trees dances in the warm breeze.

And I have an idea.

Leaping from the riverbank, I grab a hold of a vine and rock back and forth, the warm breeze whips around me and moves through my hair before I let go and drop into the water below. When I surface, my friends are following my lead. They all land around me and laughter echoes through the river.

Submerging my cupped hands to gather water, I become distracted by the gold lines in my palms shimmering under the light of the mid-afternoon sun. My eyes lift to where my friends splash in the water. A flash of color in the distance hovers in the air, first near Tarun, and then surrounding Varsha and Raya. I brace myself fully expecting a stabbing pain to spread across my hands or the scent of jasmine to fill my nostrils.

But that doesn't happen.

There's no black inky mist. Instead, the colors are vibrant, and my eyes follow the bursts of violet, orange, and bright green as they cling to the silhouettes of my loved ones. The swarm of colors hugs each of them before swiftly moving skyward, where they dissipate into the lush jungle canopy above. At that moment, peaceful energy moves through me, as if a weight has been lifted off my heart for the first time in forever. I release a long sigh, hold my palms against my chest to feel the rhythm of my heartbeat, and free-fall back into the river. At last, I've finally found where I belong.

IN MY HANDS: GLOSSARY

1. **Amma** [*am-ma*]: mother
2. **Appa** [*ap-pa*]: father
3. **Apsaras** [*ap-saa-ras*]: celestial dancers of the heavenly courts
4. **Ārisalpatta** [*aree-sal-pat-ta*]: The Chosen One
5. **Ātmagala dēvālaya** [*att-ma-gla day-va-laya*]: The Temple of Souls
6. **Atīndriya** [*ad-din-dri-ya*] **tribe**: The tribe of Lambadi mystics who wear red ruby amulets
7. **Balegalu** [*bee-ga*]: Chandra's magic Lambadi cuffs
8. **Bhayada kōte** [*by-yah ko-tee*]: Fear Fort
9. **Bindi** [*bin-di*]: a colored dot or design worn on the center of the forehead
10. **Chakra** [*chak-ra*]: the celestial discus that is Chandra's primary weapon and reveals the map that is inlaid on her scarred palms

11. **Dupatta:** [*dup-at-ta*]: a long scarf

12. **Dārk myājik gombe** [*dark magic gom-bey*]: dark magic doll

13. **Dārk māntrika** [*dark mon-tri-ka*]: dark sorceress

14. **Diya** [*di-ya*]: an oil lamp that is made of clay

15. **Dosa** [*tho-sa*]: Indian pancake-crepe, a popular south Indian breakfast food

16. **Duhkhagala kanive** [*duke-kai-vala can-knee-vey*]: Valley of Sorrows

17. **Dusta** [*dush-ta*]: the evil one

18. **Golden Trishula:** a celestial three-pronged weapon that looks very much like a trident. Each prong represents the past, present, and future

19. **Hiriya parisattu** [*here-y-a pari-sat-tu*]: Elder Council

20. **Idli sambar** [*id-ly som-bar*]: South Indian rice balls served with lentil curry, a popular south Indian breakfast food

21. **Jaati** [*ja-tii*]: beats

22. **Jipsi jānapada nritya** [*jeep-sea gen-a-padth-a noor-three-ya*]: a fictitious form of South Indian folk dance that borrows from the more classical forms of Indian dance including Bharatnatyam

23. **Kodaguru** [*code-a-guru*] **tribe:** The Lambadi tribe of warriors who worship the moonstone

24. **Lambadi** [*lamb-ba-dee*]: travelers, nomads, the original gypsy people. Tribes include: Atīndriya tribe: mystics, Vaidya tribe: healers, Kodaguru tribe: warriors; Mēkar tribe: Lambadi makers and craftspeople; Vidvānsa tribe: scholars

25. **Lehenga choli** [*lay-heng-a cho-lee*]: a long skirt with a blouse

26. **Mēkar** [*meek-er*] **tribe:** The Lambadi makers and craftspeople who worship the sapphire gemstone

27. **Moella** [*mo-wella*]: endearing term of endearment meaning 'dear'

28. **Mosale rakshas** [moe-sa-lay rak-shas]: river monsters that are a humanoid-crocodile mashup that live in Shadoulyand guarding the perimeter of the Lambadi Temple of Souls

29. **Nooru varshagala amavasye** [*noor-rue vars-hag-ala ama-vash-he*]: the hundred-year cosmic moon under which Lambadi magic can be most powerful

30. **Nagas** [*naa-gas*]: snakes

31. **Pandi curry** [*pun-the curry*]: pork curry

32. **Raktada halli** [*rak-ta-da hal-lee*]: Bloodstone Village

33. **Rakshasa** [*rak-sha-sha*]: male form/humanoid blood-thirsty, power-hungry demon

34. **Rakshasi** [*rak-sha-she*]: female form/humanoid blood-thirsty, power-hungry she-demon

35. **Rani** [*Ra-knee*]: Queen

36. **Shadoulyand** [*shad-ou-land*]: Shadow Lands is a mythical place where the hidden temple of the Kodaguru warrior stands, protected by creatures that are half-man, half-crocodile

37. **Śavagala** [av-ag-al]: the undead

38. **Shakti** [*shuck-tee*]: a universal force

39. **Shambala** [*shum-ba-la*]: A Sanskrit word meaning "place of peace, tranquility, and happiness" and home of General Haauna, a descendant of Lord Hanuman, and apes.

40. **Tabla** [*tub-la*]: small hand drum

41. **Thatha** [*tha-tha*]: grandfather

42. **Thaye** [*thuh*]: grandmother

43. **Unnath Purohitharu** [*un-nath puru-hith-aroo*]: Lambadi high priestess

44. **Ūrugōlu** [*you-ru-galu*]: walking stick

45. **Vaidya** [*Vaa-ya-di-ya*] **tribe**: The Lambadi tribe of healers who worship the amber gemstone

46. **Videshi** [*Vy-desh-he*]: foreign

47. **Vidvānsa** [*vid-vin-sa*] **tribe**: The Lambadi tribe of scholars who worship the green jade gemstone

48. **Vīksaka** [*vee-k-ca*]: the watcher

49. **Yodhana sastrasthragalu** [*yo-yan-who sas-tra-ga-loo*]: The Warrior's Weapons

ACKNOWLEDGMENTS

Creating this story—envisioning it, molding it, and loving it—into this finished book in your hands, has truly been a labor of love. My wildest dreams have become a reality. While IN MY HANDS is the story of my heart, it would not have been possible without the love, support, and encouragement of many individuals through many the seasons of my life: my family, friends, mentors, critique partners, beta readers, writing circles, and many more.

A huge thank you to the Ravens & Roses Publishing team, for seeing the potential in my creative work and Chandra's story and for helping to bring my vision for IN MY HANDS to life. Thank you to Rashmi P. Menon, my editor, for the insightful feedback, enthusiasm, and intuitively understanding my characters. Thank you to Emily, who wholeheartedly shared in the excitement of bringing Chandra, her vibe, and her world into existence and created the stunning cover.

Thanks to my incredible writing family and all the amazing and talented creatives I've had the honor of meeting through the 22Debuts, the WriterFriendsChallenge, the Desi KidLit community, the Middle-Grade Writer's Hub (#MGBees), the YA Writer's Hub (#YAgothis), and the Desi Author Chat crew. Your words of wisdom, feedback, and support have been invaluable.

My deepest adoration and gratitude to my extended family of dear friends who have been by my side, supporting, loving, and celebrating with me every step of the way. Whether it be those couch chats or the video chats or the texts—I could not imagine any of this without you by my side.

A heartfelt thanks to my Abraham/Varkey tribe for your love and support as I navigated through this adventure. My father-in-law was one of the first readers of my novel and I appreciated the excited phone calls telling me where he was on Chandra's journey and how he was in awe of my big imagination.

A special thank you to my nieces, Annika, Aysha, Mila, and Priya, for your endearing video messages and excitement along the way. I hope this story is one you will treasure, and that it fills you with hope, strength, and courage to live large and reminds you to be your own hero.

Huge love and appreciation to my brother, Sunil, and his family. My wise brother told me to never stop chasing THE dream. To think it all started at that fold-out table when we were small where we would sit side by side, drawing and writing to our heart's content. And neither of us have stopped creating since.

A heartfelt thanks to my grandparents for filling my head and heart with culture, tradition, myth, and legend. How I wish you were here to see this book on the shelf and revel in it with me. May your love for the art of storytelling live on in these pages.

Love and deep appreciation to my parents, Umesh and Daisy, who handed me my very first notebook and a rainbow of markers and encouraged me to journal every adventure. Well, it stuck because I haven't stopped creating since. This passion of mine started with the two of you, who nurtured my love for word and story, reading to me every day before I could read myself. My mother has read every page of every version of this story countless times, while day after day, my father eagerly asked about characters and plot and wondered when it would all finally be ready. Well, Pops, here it is! All my life, you both have given me the license to let my imagination run wild and free—you let me be me—and for that, I will always be grateful.

Lots of love and gratitude to my partner in life, Vikram, who has always been willing to read what I've written. You've been there from the first page, until the last one, and have always been eager for more. You, with your eternal optimism, never let me back down from following my heart and my passion to create.

Finally, much love to my children, Eashan and Naveen—my heart and soul. You have transformed my life in the most magical of ways and I am forever changed. Your endearing love and support through the years pushed me through the long days and nights as I worked to finish this book. May you know that dreams do come true and don't ever stop chasing yours!

ABOUT AUTHOR

Sathya Achia was born and raised in a small town in Southwestern Ontario in Canada, where she grew up devouring books, playing along the pebbly shores of Lake Huron, and dreaming about writing her own stories of adventure and folklore.

Sathya's creative work is influenced by her South Indian Kodava culture. She spent many summers in the remote hills and enchanting jungles of the Western Ghats in India, where she learned the art of storytelling from her grandparents. As a young reader, she missed seeing heroes like herself—of two worlds and cultures—so she enjoys writing stories inspired by her East meets West roots, mythology and folklore, and the natural world. She believes in the importance of diversity and representation in children's literature and creates stories of adventure and discovery for picture books, middle-grade, and young adult readers.

By day, Sathya is an award-winning communications professional who currently serves as a senior editor at one of the world's largest global advertising agencies. Previously, she has worked in public relations and as a health/medical writer and editor for both consumer and trade publications, pairing her curiosity for understanding what makes the world tick with a love for communicating across print and digital formats.

When not spinning stories, Sathya can be found trying a new yoga pose, exploring the great outdoors, traveling the world, or wrapped up in her greatest adventure of all: Motherhood.

For more about Sathya, visit www.sathyaachia.com

ALSO BY

In My Hands is Sathya Achia's debut novel.
Watch out for her short story *The Crane in the Mist* in
<u>Tales Untold – Mythos from Around the World</u>.
Coming soon - October 2022.
The Crane in the Mist is also based on South Asian
Folklore.
Sign up for her newsletters on www.sathyaachia.com
for the latest updates on Sathya's books
Sign up for the newsletters from Ravens & Roses
Publishing at www.ravensandrosespublishing.com for
the updates on the Tales Untold anthology.

CPSIA information can be obtained
at www.ICGtesting.com
Printed in the USA
LVHW101915220722
723997LV00003B/79